NO PLACE THAT FAR

Praise for *Death in the Black Patch*

"*Death in the Black Patch* blends chronicle with creativity to present a piece of the past." Forward Reviews

"Bruce Wilson's story has a long reach..." Silver City Independent

"...a compelling sense of place" Ron Hamm, author of *Ross Calvin: Interpreter of the American Southwest*

"*Death in the Black Patch* is a must read." Louisville Courier Journal

"...gives us a brutally frank look at agrarian life in the South shortly after the end of the 19th Century" John L. Work, author of *A Well-Regulated Vengeance* and *Murder for Comfort*

"Wilson's *Death in the Black Patch* is historical fiction at its best..." Barbara Bamberger Scott, Chanticleer Book Reviews

ISBN: 978-1-951122-05-8 (Paperback)
ISBN: 978-1-951122-07-2 (ebook)

LCCN: 2019953260

Cover Design: Ian Bristow (facebook.com/bristowdesign/)
Back Cover Photo: Julie Enos (julieenosimages.wixsite.com/mysite)

Printed in the United States of America.

Artemesia Publishing
9 Mockingbird Hill Rd
Tijeras, New Mexico 87059
www.apbooks.net
info@artemesiapublishing.com

Follow Bruce at: facebook.com/bruce.wilson.writes/

NO PLACE THAT FAR

By

Bruce Wilson

Artemesia Publishing
Albuquerque, New Mexico

No Place That Far is dedicated to Joel Wilson (1947-1970)
The first of us a writer.

"You can't run away from trouble.
There ain't no place that far."

Joel Chandler Harris

Chapter 1

Before the echo of the gunshot had disappeared into the moonlit sky, J.D. Hooper was already going through the bleeding man's pockets. He pulled a heavy leather wallet from inside the blood-soaked coat and yanked the gold watch from its chain on the checkered vest. Hooper's heart pounded as he dragged the limp body into the shack and propped it against a wall. He rushed outside, searching in the moon-lit yard for his own pistol and the man's derby. Dropping to his knees, J.D. crawled around the lumpy ground, sweeping his hands through the long, wet grass until he felt the gun. He picked it up and looked around the cluttered yard, finally spotting the hat next to a broken whiskey jug. Eagerly, he crawled through the dirt and clutched it in his fist, then rose, turned back toward the open door of the shack and knelt in front of the dead man, wondering if there was anything else of value he'd missed in the tobacco buyer's pockets. He pulled the man's shoes off, threw them out the door then placed his own worn out hat on the bleeding man's head. Heading outside again, he picked up a can of coal oil and splashed the contents on the shed walls. With the dregs, he doused the body and threw the container onto the straw-filled mattress against the wall. Hooper looked around the yard, making sure no one was watching, then struck a match with his thumbnail and flipped the burning stick through the open door.

A great whoosh of oily flame and smoke roared from the building, forcing Hooper to fall back onto the hard-packed dirt of the yard. He coughed once, and then smiled through smoky tears. *Earned that gold piece and got a fat wad of money too.*

Excited by the growing flames, J.D. sat back and watched the fire, but when a jar of moonshine exploded inside the shack, he stood and scanned the surrounding woods. Fearing the explosion might draw attention, J.D.'s heart raced as he bolted away from the flames and smoke and ran down the dirt road into the darkness. Stumbling in the wagon ruts, he kept going until his lungs burned and his legs gave out. On his knees, J.D. noticed a silhouette of an old barn just off the road. Moving into the weeds, he was exhausted and collapsed in a pile of hay on the back side of the barn.

He tried to calm himself. The fear of being seen, of getting caught, crept into every part of his body. Looking back in the direction from which he'd run, he saw a large plume of smoke climbing out of the woods. He tried to convince himself that it was just a job. *I had to kill him. The Night Riders paid me to do it. That tobacco buyer deserved to die for what he was doin' to them poor farmers.*

Even though his body found rest, his thoughts kept repeating. *Can't stay here, gotta keep movin'.*

A soft whinny from inside the barn drew his attention. Peering into the dark shadows, J.D. spotted an old sway-back horse. A leather bridle and a worn blanket hung by the door. As quietly as he could move, J.D. fit the leather over the horse's head, the blanket on its back, and led the animal out of the barn. Glancing around once more, he grabbed the horse's mane and pulled himself up onto its back. J.D. knew he had to get away from the trouble. Glad that it was still dark, he rode the horse away from the barn.

With the stolen wallet and watch, and the gold piece he'd been paid to rough up the tobacco buyer, he was richer than he'd ever been. Kicking the horse with his heels, J.D.

rode south toward the state line without stopping, and in less than half an hour he crossed into Tennessee. Kentucky was now behind him.

☆ ☆ ☆

J.D. was more than twenty miles south of the state line, having made good time in the dark. But now that the sun was coming up and the local farmers would be working their fields, he needed to find a place to hole-up, a place off the road and away from people. He was tired, sleepy, and needed to rest his troubled mind. Spotting a dense growth of trees near a running creek, he steered the horse across the fallow field. Once inside the copse he hobbled the horse, got himself a drink of the water and swallowed it heartily. Collapsing on the leaf-strewn ground, J.D. threw the horse blanket over his body and immediately fell asleep.

That night, and the one after that, J.D. continued making his way south. He passed scores of darkened farmhouses and fields filled with young tobacco as he rode along the dusty roads on the ancient sorrel. Before the sun peeked over the trees on the third day, he found a deadfall twenty yards off the road and crawled in under the limbs and branches. It was still dark, and J.D. was so tired that sleep overcame him quickly.

But his rest was interrupted just as the sun's rays leaked through the boughs over his head. He heard a voice just a few feet from where he lay hidden. J.D. cringed and his heart pounded in his chest. Instinctively he froze, not wanting to move and give away his hiding place. The brush and branches poked at him as if they wanted to tell someone where he was hiding. Pulling short gasps of air into his lungs, Hooper peered through the branches and dried leaves of the deadfall and saw an old man gazing across a recently destroyed tobacco field. What caught his attention was what stood next to the man—the swayback. The farmer looked broken, as destroyed as his crop, and J.D. heard him mumble as he trudged across the now worthless field to the barn across the road.

J.D. couldn't understand the man's words, but he knew what had happened. He remembered riding with the Night Riders to farms in Kentucky and recalled the times he'd threatened and beaten reluctant farmers who'd sold out to the tobacco company, how he'd ridden his horse through fields of tobacco in order to destroy the young plants, and how he'd even burned barns.

Hooper waited an hour after the man left with his horse and, when no one else ventured across the road to the trampled and salted field, he rested without sleep until sundown. Then, no longer able to ride, he walked all night.

The loss of the horse didn't change J.D.'s objective—getting as far away from Kentucky as he could—but it definitely slowed him down. Walking along the edge of the southbound road, he thought again about the dead man and what he'd done to him. But with a lot of money in his pocket and dozens of miles of road behind him, J.D. felt good about his future. He had been paid to make the tobacco buyer disappear, but the only way he could accomplish the task was to kill him, and he was good at killing.

His mind could not forget the burning memories of growing up on his pa's small farm and the beatings that he and his brother got for working too slow or doing a job wrong. His ma's nagging and pestering about his lack of effort in school and his swearing only increased the fiery memories. J.D. thought about the girl he married and how he'd expected things would be different with her. But they weren't. He might as well have married his mother. When J.D. told his family that his wife was divorcing him and leaving the county, his pa threatened to beat him. J.D. said he was willing to take the chance if his pa was. The threats in his tone of voice kept his pa at bay, but J.D. knew that he couldn't stay around any longer. Grabbing what few things he could call his own, and putting them in a flour sack, Hooper left in the middle of the night. Leaving that part of his life behind, he walked away in the darkness.

After a few months, he'd ended up in Henry County and bought a small farm on credit. The farmers in Kentucky planted wheat, corn, and tobacco. Surprisingly J.D. became good at farming, especially when it came to tobacco. But he never reinvested his earnings in growing and improving his property. He'd save enough for seed for the next year's crops and spend the rest of his profits on moonshine. When other farmers used the cold winter days for fixing and repairing their tools and buildings, J.D. would sit around his broken-down house drinking jug after jug of poorly made whiskey. Hardly sober for those cold months, he'd drink and grumble his days away; blaming others for his situation and thinking of ways to make more money by doing less. After spending some time in the Henry County jail, he burned down his farmhouse and fled west. Hooper's life had become one bad choice after another, always taking the easy way out, discovering that it was easier to be bad, easier to be hated, easier to hate.

After a week on the road, when he finally arrived at the east-west pike, J.D. still wasn't sure which way to go. Pondering the choices, he gazed in both directions, his hands deep in the pockets of the overalls. He fingered the gold piece he'd gotten for handling the tobacco buyer then pulled it out and held it in his open hand. "If it's heads it's Nashville, tails it's Memphis." He flipped the heavy disc into the air. It landed in the dusty road. As J.D. kneeled to pick it up, the standing eagle on the reverse of the coin seemed to point west—to Memphis.

Walking along the dirt roads of western Tennessee that late spring in 1907, Hooper made his way toward the Mississippi River, the frontier he hoped to cross in order to escape and to leave his old life as a farmer and a Night Rider behind.

Chapter 2

J.D. stopped at the top of a rise and saw how the turnpike curved its way into the city. He walked off the road and found a quiet spot on a hill under a tree. He'd never been in a city and was a bit anxious about what he might find. Hooper knew he would have to be careful, cautious even, once he walked down the hill. At the same time, he believed that staying in the countryside was not an option. So, with his fear hidden behind his growing boldness, he walked down the pike to Memphis.

When he reached the city limits, he saw the buildings in the distance, the smoke rising from the steamboats on the river, and the great numbers of people moving about. He stopped walking and stood in awe of the spectacle. There were more people and homes, more wagons and horses, and buildings five and six stories high. Memphis had paved and lighted roads and streetcar tracks down the center of the main avenues. Gazing at the signs on the top of a very tall building, J.D. stepped into a busy street. Only the roaring blare of a horn kept him from being crushed by a speeding automobile. Not until he heard the laughter of the witnesses to his near demise did he step back up on the boardwalk. Although he'd heard about automobiles, his first experience with one left him stunned.

While walking along the riverfront, the cacophony of steel wagon wheels grinding on pavement, screeching bearings on the cranes loading cotton on the riverboats lined up along the quay, braying mules and shouting workers, made it hard for him to think. Yet, in the midst of all the noise and the headache it gave him, J.D. realized that it would be easy to blend in. Not even close to six feet tall, his body lean from all of the farm work he'd done, Hooper wouldn't stand out in a crowd. His only remarkable features, ones he was totally unaware of, were his piercing, deep blue eyes.

☆ ☆ ☆

The next morning, J.D. stumbled out of the foul-smelling alley next to a saloon and peered around the corner of the tall building. Just like every night since he'd burned the shack, he hadn't slept well. Thinking about the need to blend in with the city people and realizing that he didn't look like anyone in the city, he mumbled, "I need to change and do it soon." It would not be that simple. He'd have to become different. Long greasy hair and filthy clothes made him look like a beggar, and changing his appearance meant not only getting some new clothes, but bathing and shaving and finding a place to live. He had plenty of money but knew it couldn't last forever. He'd have to find a job too but didn't know where to start.

Walking into an alley between a bank and the post office, he pulled out his wallet and quickly counted his money. Not sure how much it would cost to get himself clean and then to get at least one set of city clothes, he reached for the gold double eagle, but he knew this was not the time to use it, not yet. Whether it reminded him of the horrific murder or the excitement of the fire, it was a thing he needed to hang on to. Instead, Hooper decided to use some of the dead man's paper money.

"This better be enough," he growled.

While moving with the crowds of people on the street, he looked for a barber shop, and spo*tted one on the next block.* Might as well start with a shave, he thought. The sign in the window advertised hot baths for twenty-five cents—

towels were extra—and a shave and hair cut would still be less than a dollar. *First time in a barber shop*, he thought. Taking a shallow breath of the smoky city air he cautiously pushed the door open and stepped into the shop. The other men who sat waiting for the barber were chatting with each other. J.D. picked up a copy of the day's paper and flipped through the pages, trying to look like he belonged, not wanting to draw attention to himself. When the barber called to him, he jumped a little.

"Sir, it's your turn."

J.D. moved to the chair and waited while the barber drew a sheet across his lap and clipped it around his neck.

"I wanna look just like the fella in that picture on the wall," he said, pointing to the one above the cash register.

"Oh, yes sir, the Business Man's cut. Shall I leave your mustachio, sir?"

"Huh?"

"The whiskers on your lip, sir, should I leave them?"

"Yeah."

"Long or short?"

"Just like the picture. And I wanna hot bath, too."

"Very well sir," the barber replied and began to cut and trim. The gnarly look of a hired farm worker, a man who'd lost his home, spent time in jail, and beaten and killed others for money fell away like the hair and whiskers drifting to the floor. But the barber's efforts couldn't cut away who J.D. was on the inside.

An hour or so later, Hooper walked out of the barber shop a dollar poorer but feeling cleaner than he could remember. The barber had given him directions to a clothing store and assured him that they sold good suits. J.D. looked at his reflection in the shop window and hoped that the new clothes would help him hide in plain sight. Right now, he thought he looked like a clean person in dirty overalls.

Feeling conspicuous in his ratty clothes J.D. worked

his way through the crowded street. He found the building only a few blocks away, just as the barber had directed. Walking into the store, J.D. was immediately accosted by a skinny, bald clerk in a brown plaid suit.

"Good morning, sir. How might I be of service?"

"I need some new clothes."

"I see. It appears you've been on the road for some time, perhaps even waylaid by scoundrels."

J.D. scowled at the clerk but saw the man's comment as an opportunity.

"That's exactly what happened. I was ridin' to Memphis from Lynn ... from Atlanta and ran into some trouble. Three men with guns stole my horse and even took my clothes. They tied me up to a fence post and rode off."

"I'm sorry to hear of your difficulties, sir. The ruffians are still at large I presume?" The man scanned J.D.'s appearance then added, "I hope they didn't steal all your money."

"I can pay for the clothes if that's what you're wonderin'."

"Oh no sir, that would be quite rude of me to assume that a gentleman such as yourself was a scoundrel. I only hoped that you were able to..."

"Never mind," J.D. interrupted, "let's get on with this. I need everythin', shirts, shoes, collars, ties, and a suit. I'd like 'em to go with my derby hat, too."

"We can definitely accommodate you, sir. Please step over here by the mirror and stand on this platform. I'll take a few measurements and we'll have you ready and out of here in no time. We can even clean that dirty hat to match your new suit."

Nearly two hours later, J.D. stepped out onto the street. The noise from the wagons and the occasional automobile clashed with the buzzing conversations of the people on the sidewalks and the frequent street vendors pitching their products. Looking more like a businessman, Hooper's next challenge was to find a place to live. As he stood on the sidewalk in front of a bank, wondering what to do, he was interrupted by a boy.

"Paper, mister?"

Startled a bit, J.D. said, "What?"

"Do you want to buy a newspaper, mister? It's only a nickel."

J.D. dug out a nickel from his new pants and tossed it to the paperboy. Hooper folded the newspaper in half and carried it down the street to a small park and found a bench under a tree where he could be out of the sun. Brushing off the seat with the paper, clearing it of dust and the few leaves that had landed there, J.D. sat down and opened the paper, turning to the advertisements he figured would be in the back pages.

"Oughta be somethin' in here about cheap places to stay." A short time later he stood in front of the three-story brick building at 290 South Main and gazed up at the small balconies on the second floor and at the third-floor window. Looking again at the advertisement, he made sure that he'd not misread the price. Hooper opened the wrought iron gate, walked up the short flight of steps to the door, reached for the brass knob and then decided to knock instead. Waiting for a response, he turned around and looked at the river, thinking that he'd made a mistake and didn't belong in a place such as this. Turning back to the door, he was surprised to find it was being held open by a woman about his age, her long brown hair wound tightly into a bun.

"Yes, how may I help you?"

J.D. fumbled with the newspaper, looking for the advertisement. When he found it, he turned to the woman and asked, "Is this the Austin House? Do you rent rooms?"

"We currently have one room open. It's very nice and the rate includes two meals daily and a shared washroom.

Laundry services are available for a small fee." She paused, trying to gauge J.D.'s response. "It's on the top floor. Would you like to take a look at the accommodations?"

Half an hour later as he walked up the street, J.D. glanced over his shoulder at his new home. *Ain't nobody gonna ever find me now,* he thought, a crooked grin appearing on his face. *I'm gonna stay right here and get rich.*

Chapter 3

By the fall Hooper's money had shrunk by half. He'd begun to hang out on the streets of the business district, watching the workers, seeing what they did and where they went, hoping that an opportunity might drop in his lap, but that theory never panned out. Sometimes J.D. would spend his mornings looking through the want ads in the newspaper. By mid-day he would give up on the job hunt and wander down by the riverfront and stop in one of the saloons for a beer. The Tennessee whiskey was good, but it wasn't the moonshine he was used to. Beer was cheaper, and he couldn't afford to buy bottles of whiskey.

J.D. leaned against the bar at the Big River Saloon nursing his beer when two well-dressed men walked in. They wore suits like the rich fellas he'd often watched, but they didn't look like bankers or lawyers. The taller one looked strong, and had an old, deep scar on his cheek. His hands, though clean, looked rough, as if he'd frequently used them. The other man was smaller, thinner and could even have passed for a banker if it wasn't for the steely look on his face. They walked up to the bar, ordered whiskeys and turned around to face the room. It seemed to J.D. that they were looking for someone in particular.

J.D. was curious. For some reason, he sensed these fellas were trouble. He considered finishing his beer quickly, but before he could take the next swallow a well-dressed, portly man at one of the tables in the back of the saloon signaled to the men. They finished their drinks and walked over to him.

J.D. turned toward the mirror in order to watch the three of them. It was clear that they were doing some sort of business. He couldn't hear the conversation but guessed that the seated man was questioning the other two. The scar-faced man nodded once, said something, nodded again and then handed over a large stack of money. The three chatted for a few more minutes before the big man peeled some of the money off the stack, handed it back to the man and waved them away like he was swatting at a fly. They tipped their hats to him and left the saloon. Hooper took a good look at the man seated in the back of the room, wanting to remember his face. A large amount of money had changed hands and he wanted to know more. Finishing his beer, he left casually, not wanting to draw attention. Stepping outside, he looked up and down the street for the two men, hoping to follow them, but they were gone.

J.D. returned to the saloon the next afternoon and the one after that, but the two men never showed up. What he'd seen might have been a one-time transaction, but his curiosity wasn't satisfied. He wanted to know more about the money. On the third day, he walked in and ordered a beer. The bartender nodded in recognition but didn't try to engage him in a conversation. As J.D. sipped his beer, the large man entered the saloon from a back room and took a seat at the same table as before. Moments later the two fellas came into the saloon. J.D. waited until they walked to the back table, then finished his beer and left. He headed across the street and watched the saloon's entrance. Maybe ten or fifteen minutes passed before the door opened and the men walked out. They turned right and strode up the boardwalk as if on a mission. Not wanting to be seen, J.D. followed, keeping pace with them from across the street.

They walked quickly for a few blocks and then stepped into a building. J.D. couldn't tell what kind of business it was; the sign on the door was too small. Across the street and two doors down from where they'd entered was a small restaurant with large front windows. Finding a seat by one of them, he ordered a cup of coffee, glanced out the window, and waited to see what would happen.

The young woman returned quickly and said, "Here's your coffee, sir. Would you like a slice of our pie? It's very good."

Lifting the cup to his lips, Hooper grunted and declined the pie, then looked through the glass again.

"What's that store across the street," he asked as she walked away, "the one with no windows?"

She stepped back to the table and pulled the sheer curtain aside.

"Oh, that's the entrance to the business on the second floor. Look up there. You can see their sign on the window."

Glancing up at the prominent gilded lettering which read, "Railroad Express Agency," J.D. still couldn't imagine what the connection was between the agency, the big fella at the saloon, and the large amount of money that had been exchanged. He continued to sip at the coffee, wondering about the money, the various transactions involved, and what it all meant.

☆ ☆ ☆

Over the next few weeks, J.D. continued to shadow the men as they made their rounds in the city. At night, in his room at the Austin House, he'd scratch out notes with a pencil stub onto the paper the landlady had given him. He'd even drawn a crude map of the city streets and noted the names of the places the two men had stopped, how long they'd been inside, and how frequently they returned to the saloon and the large man at the back table. Hooper had even successfully anticipated one of their stops. While he waited across the street from a three-story building on

First Street the two men walked around the corner and entered the building.

They have a regular routine, he thought. *But what are they doin' and how can I find out without gettin' caught?*

Despite his caution, though, he did get caught. The next day, sitting in his usual spot at the café, waiting for the two men to enter the Railroad Express Agency, a noise from behind made him turn around just as one of the men jammed the barrel of a revolver into his ribs. J.D. grunted and tried to move away, but the tall man with the scar grabbed his arm and asked, "Seen enough?" Then he slammed J.D.'s head against the table and J.D. lost consciousness.

☆ ☆ ☆

"Wake him up," said the big man, his voice gravelly, like he'd swallowed sand. "Let's find out who he is and what he's up to."

The tall man who had knocked J.D. out picked up a pail full of soapy water. He looked down at the unconscious body on the floor and splashed the contents of the bucket on J.D.'s face.

Startled, Hooper sat up quickly, his coughing and sputtering joined by groans as he held his head, trying to determine where he was.

"Wake up, sleepy head," laughed the man with the pail, his ragged scar just touching the edge of his lips.

"Shut up, Axel. You two get him over to the table," said Chester Lowell. He was upset that the wet man on the floor was following his two enforcers, and even angrier at his employees for letting themselves be tailed. "Come on, Mort, get him up on his feet."

Each of the men grabbed J.D. under an arm and dragged him across the floor, shoving him into a chair. The jarring made his head hurt even more. Confused, Hooper turned, trying to see where the men were, but the pain was intense. The seated man signaled the others and they pulled his head up, holding it so that he could only look straight ahead.

J.D. saw his own small pistol on the man's desk.

"Who the hell are you?" Lowell stared into J.D.'s eyes.

J.D. groaned and tried to say something, but his pain was now joined with fear, and he wasn't sure what to do or what to say.

Axel raised his hand and slapped the back of Hooper's head.

"Come on, Mystery Man, answer Mr. Lowell."

"What's your damn name and what're you doing following my boys around *my* city?"

Barely above a whisper, J.D. said, "My name's Hooper."

"Well, Mr. Hooper, answering my question is the first smart thing you've done today. Now I want to know why you're tailing my men."

In an instant, J.D. realized that if he was going to get out of the room alive, he needed to be tough and show that he could handle trouble.

"Do you wanna know the truth?" He paused and looked directly at the big man, his eyes looking at the other men without fear. "I watched you and your men pass money in the back of the saloon. I was curious about the business."

"You were curious?" the big man grumbled and turned to the others. "Getta load of him, he's curious about *my* business."

The scar-faced man grabbed J.D. by the hair and said, "Are you a cop?"

"I ain't no cop. I just need a job and saw an opportunity. So, I followed 'em to see where they got the money and who gave it to 'em."

The big man stared silently at J.D. for several minutes, waiting to see what else he might say. "How long have you been following them?"

"Three weeks," J.D. said, grinning. He knew this would get Lowell's attention.

Lowell looked at his two enforcers with a disappointed sneer. "And you two just figured it out yesterday," he grunted. The others paled a little but didn't respond. Lowell looked at J.D. and said, "So, what is it that you *think* they're doing?"

"The best I can figure is that they're carryin' messages or makin' payments or collectin' money from lawyers, warehouses, steamboats, and such. I've done work like this before up in Kentucky, and I'm good at it."

"You have my attention Mr. Hooper, enlighten me a bit about your experience." The portly man sat back in his chair and waited for J.D. to continue.

"I got arrested for hittin' a Sheriff 'cause he was gonna take away my farm and I spent three months in jail."

"That's not much experience, Mr. Hooper."

"Maybe not, but when I got out, I burned my farm down so the bank wouldn't get it and then I took off."

"Go on."

"You ever heard of the tobacco war up in the Black Patch?"

"Perhaps."

"I was workin' on a fella's farm and the Night Riders, well, they paid me to scare people. We burned barns, tore up tobacco fields, and beat up farmers when they wouldn't listen to reason."

J.D. sucked in a big gulp of air before going on, knowing that he was taking a big risk by telling Lowell about Lynnville.

"A while back the Night Rider boss paid me a bonus to rough up a buyer from the Tobacco Trust." He paused and glanced at the others. "Well, I found the buyer and dragged him into the woods." He hesitated once more, then the rest of the story rushed out of him like a flash flood. "I beat him up pretty bad, then I shot him in the chest. I threw his body into an old shack and burned the whole thing down so there'd be no evidence."

Lowell finally broke the silence that followed J.D.'s revelation. "What part of Kentucky?"

"Huh?"

"I said what part of Kentucky? Where did this murder take place?"

"Why do you wanna know that?"

"I've got contacts in the state who can confirm your claim. If you're telling me the truth, then maybe I can use your skills. It seems that my other employees are a bit remiss in using the proper cautions required in the performance of their duties." He looked at each of the two standing men. "But, if you're not telling the truth, I'll find that out and I'll use these two to help you disappear. Do you understand what I'm saying to you? Do you still want me to pursue my efforts to verify your claim?"

J.D. looked directly at Lowell and said, "I ain't lyin'. I did it and I can do it again if there's money in it." He gave Lowell the information he wanted and told him more about his time in jail for assaulting the sheriff of Henry County. Then Lowell told his men to back off from J.D.

"Well, then Mr. Hooper. I'm going to have my boys keep an eye on you for a few days while I check into your claims. You be sure to show them where you're staying in Memphis and you stay there. Don't go out, don't follow them around, don't do anything but stay put until I send for you." Lowell watched as J.D. nodded and then he told the others to make sure J.D. got home.

Chapter 4

For two days J.D. stayed in his room at the boarding house, telling the landlady he was tired and not feeling well. Yet most of his time was spent standing by the window watching the traffic and noticing that Lowell's men took turns keeping an eye on the house. On the morning of the third day, Axel showed up and asked the landlady if Mr. Hooper was available. After checking with J.D., she led the visitor up to his room.

"Mr. Lowell is ready to talk with you Hooper, but he ain't gonna sit around all day waitin'. Get your hat and coat and let's get goin'." They joined Mort in front of the house and took a streetcar to the saloon.

☆ ☆ ☆

J.D. and Chester sat alone at a table in the back of the saloon. The bartender had just delivered a beer to Chester, but not one for J.D.

"Alright, Hooper, I checked out your story and I'm gonna give you a chance to prove yourself." The big man leaned forward, taking care not to get his sleeve wet in the ring of moisture from the beer mug. "You do this job right, and then I'll decide if you can work for me."

J.D. listened, waiting for Lowell to continue.

"I'm going to give you an easy job just to see how you perform. But know that in the future I'll demand much more from you. I can't afford to send a new fella on anything important." He paused again, staring intently at J.D.

"You and Axel are going to pay a visit to a lawyer who's not paying his bill. But it'll be up to you to put the squeeze on this shyster." He sat back in his chair and took a long pull on his beer.

"Who's the lawyer," J.D. asked, "and what's he owe you?" J.D. kept his eyes on Chester.

"I'll tell you later. But if you mess up this job, I'll have Axel knock you cold and dump you in the river."

Chester turned toward the bar and gestured to the bartender.

"Will, get over here."

Throwing a towel over his arm, the bartender approached the table. "Yes sir?"

"Go outside and tell Axel to get in here. Tell him I got a job for him.

"Okay, Mr. Lowell. I'll find him right away."

"Why don't you take off," Chester said to J.D. "Be here tomorrow night at eight sharp."

J.D. rose from the table and said, "I'll be here." Then he tipped his derby, turned and walked past the bar and out the door.

☆ ☆ ☆

Hooper walked into the saloon at eight o'clock and glanced at the bartender who called him over.

"Mr. Lowell is still in the back with Axel. He said he wants you to stay here and have a beer."

J.D. threw a nickel on the bar. Will took a clean mug off the shelf and filled it from the tap, leaving a good two inches of foam on top. He slid the glass toward J.D. and then leaned in close.

"Mr. Lowell ain't hired any help for a long time." The bartender leaned toward J.D. and lowered his voice. "He's 'specially careful when he does."

"Why's that?"

"Just before he hired Axel and Mort, there was a fella who worked here for a while. But he wasn't, uh, respectful."

"What happened to him?"

"All I know is that he went into Mr. Lowell's office one evenin' and he must've left by the back door 'cause I never saw him again." Will looked around the saloon and then whispered to J.D. "I heard the cops found him all beat up and lyin' down by the river."

J.D. slipped Will a silver dollar as he thanked him for the information. The dark-haired bartender smiled and refilled J.D.'s beer, then turned toward the door as a group of men from the rail yard entered and took seats at one of the tables.

A short time later, Axel and Mort walked out of Lowell's office and glanced at J.D. as they sat at a table in the saloon. J.D. looked toward Will. The bartender tilted his head toward the back and nodded. J.D. walked to the office and thought about the information Will had given him.

"Evenin' Mr. Lowell."

"Good evening, Hooper. Are you ready to go to work?"

J.D. removed his derby and said, "I am sir. What do you want me to do?"

"I want you and Axel to pay a visit to Mr. Alvin Davison, Esquire at his home. Counselor Davison is in debt to me and he's missed two of his hundred-dollar payments. These payments constitute only a small portion of the total debt of two thousand dollars, and his reluctance in paying is causing me great distress. Do you understand the details, Hooper?"

"I do."

"Then, I want you to, how should I say this, *convince* the good counselor to bring himself current in his obligation to me this very night. You need to be aware that his beautiful wife and lovely children may be present while you're there, but you needn't worry about offending them by using whatever methods you choose. In fact, I believe Mr. Davison might be properly moved if he thinks either his wife or his progeny are placed in a frightening situation. Do I make myself clear?"

"Yes, sir, perfectly clear. We'll be back in a while with your money and with Mr. Davison's promise to stay current." He looked at Lowell and said, "I'll need my gun."

Lowell handed J.D. a slip of paper on which he'd written the lawyer's address, then opened his desk drawer and lifted out the gun. "Don't be afraid to use it."

J.D. took the weapon from Lowell, nodded and left the office. In the saloon he stepped up to the table where Axel and Mort were sitting and said to Axel, "Let's go."

The two men caught a late east-bound streetcar and rode without speaking. When the car got to the street where the lawyer lived, Axel and J.D. stepped to the curb and walked another block or so to the address Lowell had provided.

"You can come up to the house if you want," J.D. said. "But don't interrupt, got it?"

"You do what Mr. Lowell told you. I'm just along to see how you work."

"Good, then stay out of my way."

They walked up the steps and J.D. knocked on the door. Axel stepped behind J.D. just as the door opened.

A round-shouldered, older man stood in the doorway, the dim electric lights from the room beyond silhouetting him. He held his suit coat in his hand as if he was about to hang it up.

"Can I help you gentlemen? It's awfully late for a social call."

J.D. stepped forward, his shoulders tight. Looking down on the man the scowl on his face must have said more than his words. "I'm here at the request of Mr. Chester Lowell, sir. It seems that you've chosen to disregard your obligation to him and he's very upset."

"This is preposterous. You can tell Mr. Lowell that I will discuss this with him at my convenience and that he needn't send any of his thugs to my home. Good night gentlemen."

Before he could close the door, J.D. pushed it back hard enough that Davison lost his balance and nearly tumbled onto his backside. Then J.D. pulled the door shut behind him leaving Axel on the stoop. Hooper leaned in close to the lawyer's face, his voice icy cold, repeating the request.

"Mr. Davison," he said, "I don't think you understand the situation. Mr. Lowell wants his money tonight. He'd prefer the entire two thousand dollars, but is aware that you may not have that much in your house. Besides, he'd prefer not to disturb your wife and children however necessary that may be." J.D. started to walk down the hall toward the room at the back of the house. The lawyer backpedaled in front of him, his hands held up toward J.D.'s chest.

"Sir, I protest. This is truly unnecessary." He looked over his shoulder and saw that his wife had appeared at the end of the hallway to see what the commotion was about. "Belle, please take the children upstairs. I'll only be a moment. I must discuss some business with this gentleman. Go on, now, please."

The woman moved slowly out of sight and Davison turned to face J.D.

"So, what's it gonna be, mister lawyer?" J.D. pulled the sleeves of his coat up toward his elbows and clenched his hands into tight fists. "Are you ready to pay the two thousand or can you only afford the two one hundred-dollar payments you owe today? Which means I'll have to come back again." The look on his face was not civil, hardly even human. Davison understood the message behind J.D.'s cold eyes.

"If you'll wait just a moment I'll go upstairs and get the money for you."

"No, you won't. I'll go with you and maybe see if your wife wants to know what's goin' on. Let's go, Mr. Davison, I ain't got all night." J.D. moved toward the end of the hall.

"Wait. Perhaps I have enough in my coat here. You needn't bother my family." He reached into the inside coat pocket and pulled out a stack of bills. He started to count out two hundred dollars but was interrupted when J.D. grabbed the entire bundle.

"I think Mr. Lowell will be satisfied with your payment, mister lawyer. But I suggest that you keep the payments comin' on time. If you don't, I'll be back to visit you and your missus again." With that, J.D. shoved the wad of money into his coat pocket, opened the door and walked onto the porch. He turned to look at Davison and smiled. "See you soon, shyster."

☆ ☆ ☆

When J.D. and Axel walked into Lowell's office an hour later, Chester was sitting behind his desk. J.D. took the money out of his pocket and set it in front of Lowell.

"Did he pay up?"

"Yes, sir, he sure did."

"How much did you get?"

"I don't know, but it's more than the two payments he owed."

Chester lifted the stack and began to count the money. It took him a few moments to count and recount, but when he finished, he said, "There's fifteen hundred dollars here. What did you say to him, any blood spilled?"

"I told him that you were very disappointed in him for missin' the payments. I guess that he wanted you to know that he was sorry and that you could count on him to never fall behind again—ever."

Lowell looked over at Axel, who shrugged his shoulders. "I missed the whole thing, sir. J.D. left me on the porch."

Lowell returned his eyes to J.D. "I'd planned to test you further before giving you a job, Mr. Hooper. But it appears that I might have underestimated your skills. You've done quite well for a beginner." Lowell looked at the stack of money briefly and then took one of the fifties and handed it to J.D. "Here's your first week's pay and a little extra for showing initiative. Now go on home and I'll see you here tomorrow morning."

J.D. tipped his derby to Lowell and walked out of the office. Axel followed him and caught up with J.D. before he left the saloon.

"I never seen him smile like that. He never gave me a tip, either."

J.D. looked into Axel's eyes and said, "Let me buy you a beer. Then we can talk about how to make Mr. Lowell happier."

Chapter 5

Over the next two weeks, Lowell gave J.D. plenty to do. For a while he insisted that Axel or Mort tag along, but soon discovered that J.D. did well enough on his own. He'd easily managed to collect some barely late payments from a few wharf workers, convincing them that keeping Mr. Lowell happy would ensure their continued employment. Without having to resort to rough handling, J.D. was also successful in escorting a wagon driver to the saloon for a meeting with Lowell. J.D.'s presence in the office seemed to be enough for the driver to come to an understanding about his obligations. It annoyed Mr. Lowell that he had to work Axel and Mort as a team and that they were far less effective than Hooper, but he needed the coverage and with all of them collecting, his revenues were growing.

But Lowell had another problem, a big one and he was anxious to get it resolved. He told Will to send Hooper into the office as soon as he showed up.

When J.D. arrived, he went straight to the office, tapped on the door and walked in. He was surprised to see Axel and Mort standing in front of the Lowell's desk.

"You wanted to see me Mr. Lowell?"

Axel and Mort turned toward J.D. Their bruised and swollen faces still showed traces of blood.

"Come in, Hooper," said Lowell, "and you two stay put and keep your mouths shut."

J.D. walked around to the side of the desk and waited for Lowell to speak.

"I've got a job for you, Hooper. Since these two morons have tried to resolve it a number of times without success."

J.D.'s co-workers remained silent, but their faces screamed embarrassment.

Lowell turned from them and said to J.D., "Karl Vogler owns a string of wagons and a warehouse. He's a bully and seems to enjoy slapping these two around. He's in business because I allow him to be, but his reluctance to stay current with his payments to me is disrespectful and I won't stand for that."

J.D. listened, sensing that a reply was unnecessary.

"So, I want you to go to Vogler's and make him understand his situation. He's violent, he's tough, and he's mean, and I won't stand for his disrespect."

J.D. looked at Axel and Mort again then spoke to Lowell. "I'll handle this today, Mr. Lowell."

"Don't leave his warehouse without the money," Lowell said. "He's got to believe that he can never be late again. So do whatever you have to do and bring my money back by tomorrow morning."

"Where do I find him?"

"His place is on the waterfront on the south end of the levee. He's there most days, but he spends a lot of time at Tony's Saloon on Beale."

J.D. nodded again and rose from the chair. "How much does he owe you, sir?"

"Twenty-two hundred."

"Alright, I'll see you early and I'll have your money." J.D. paused and added, "Mr. Vogler won't be late no more."

☆ ☆ ☆

J.D. found Vogler's warehouse on the riverfront that afternoon and spent nearly an hour watching the wagons entering and leaving the massive brick building. The freight they hauled was mixed: crates of machine parts, bags of flour and grain, and a lot of paper cartons filled with cans of food.

J.D. crossed the wide avenue, looking both ways for speeding automobiles, and walked through the door marked "Office." A counter stood in front of shelves stacked with ledgers and a closed door was on the far wall. The man behind the counter glanced up as J.D. approached him.

"Help you?" the clerk asked, clearly not interested in Hooper.

"I'd like to see Mr. Vogler."

"Ain't in," the man said without looking at J.D.

"When will he be in?" Hooper asked.

The clerk looked up, a frown wrinkling his forehead. "Who's asking?"

"Mr. Smith," J.D. lied, "Mr. John Smith, from St. Louis. I'll come back another time."

"Suit yourself," the clerk said, turning back to his paperwork.

☆ ☆ ☆

Twenty minutes later, J.D. stood on Beale Street across from Tony's Saloon. Even late on a mid-week afternoon the place was busy. He could hear the buzz of chatter, clinking glasses, and the occasional outbursts of laughter. Hitching up his pants and adjusting the derby on his head, J.D. walked into the saloon.

In the enclosed space, the noise was louder and the smoke from dozens of cigars rose like a cloud above the tables and the bar. The smell of beer dominated the various aromas—sweat, vomit, tobacco—but J.D. noticed none of these things. He was looking for Vogler.

He scanned the crowded room and spotted a narrow space at the bar. He squeezed in between two fellas wearing overalls and signaled to the busy bartender. He ordered and paid for a beer then turned around, sipping and looking for Vogler. Lowell had described him as a short, stocky, bull of a man with a bushy mustache. J.D. saw a number of short men and many of them could be described as stocky. But when his gaze reached the far corner of the saloon, he saw a man who fit the description. Chester hadn't lied about the mustache. The wiry brush of it covered the man's lips and drooped down the sides of his mouth.

Stepping away from the bar, Hooper wandered toward the table where the man sat talking with two younger men. Positioning himself in the crowd so he could listen to the conversation without being observed, J.D. took another sip of his beer.

"But Mr. Vogler, you said we'd have our goods by yesterday."

"I did say that, but that was before I found out what was in those crates," he said, smirking at the well-dressed gentlemen. "How much do you think I'd have to pay the cops if they found out I was carryin' illegal liquor on my wagons?"

The men looked at one another but remained silent.

"Look, I know you're gonna make a lot of money when you sell your...merchandise, so I just want my fair share of the profit."

"But we already paid you for the delivery."

"Let's just say you made a down payment. Give me another hundred right now and you'll see my wagon at your place in two hours. Or, just walk out and wait for the police to drop by." He smiled broadly.

The men considered Vogler's offer and one of them reached into his vest pocket, pulled out five gold coins and slid them across the table.

"Glad to be of service to you gentlemen. You should probably leave now so you can be ready to unload my wagon when it arrives." Vogler pocketed the heavy coins and rose from his chair, then walked out of the saloon tipping his hat to the men as they headed toward the streetcar stop. He turned in the direction of his warehouse and walked away.

Knowing that he couldn't take Vogler for granted and would need to get him alone in order to catch him off-guard, J.D. followed him to his warehouse. When Vogler arrived at the building and entered the office, J.D. found a spot across the street where he could watch the door unobserved.

As the sun dipped toward the river, the street traffic thinned. J.D. saw a wagon loaded with crates leave the warehouse. Thinking that the two men would have their liquor soon, he watched as a dozen men, led by the clerk, left the warehouse, closing and locking the large sliding doors.

In the dim light of near dusk, J.D. crossed the street and stood outside Vogler's door. A faint golden glow seeped around the edges of the shade drawn on the window. Hooper waited until the street was clear and tried the handle on the door. It was unlocked, so he opened it and slipped inside. The only light came from the room behind the counter.

J.D. crept around the counter and peered through the crack between the door and the wall. Vogler sat at his desk looking at some papers and drinking whiskey from a short glass. J.D. pulled his pistol out of his pocket, cocked it, and stepped into the room.

"Vogler!"

Startled, the man dropped his glass, spilling the contents on his papers. He stood quickly and reached to open one of the desk drawers.

"Don't do it, Vogler." J.D. kept the pistol pointed at the man across the desk.

"Who are you? Whatta you want?"

"You owe Chester Lowell twenty-two hundred dollars and he wants it now, tonight."

"What," scoffed Vogler, "didn't he learn anything after I sent his two men back with bloody lips? Get outta here or you'll get the same."

Unaffected by the outburst, J.D. smiled at Vogler. "I'm

not those two fellas. I'm just me and I ain't afraid of you. So, here's how this is gonna go. You'll give me the money now and I won't shoot you."

"Shoot me? You're gonna kill me for two thousand dollars?"

J.D. smiled again. "It's twenty-two hundred and no, I ain't gonna kill you. But I do plan on shooting you if you don't pay up."

Realizing that his bullying wasn't working, Vogler tried a different approach.

"Why is Lowell in such a hurry for the money? I told him I'd pay it."

"Mr. Lowell isn't convinced that you intend to keep your promise."

"Okay, mister, uh..."

"My name isn't important, Mr. Vogler, but you giving me the money is. Now hand it over or I'm gonna put a bullet into some important part of your body."

Vogler started to say something and reached for the drawer handle again. J.D. fired his pistol, hitting Vogler in the elbow. The echo of the shot was joined by the man's scream.

Vogler grabbed his broken, bleeding arm, a howling sound, deep and guttural roared from his mouth.

"I was just..."

"No, I don't think you were." Still aiming his pistol at Vogler's head, J.D. moved to the side of the desk and slid the drawer open. He reached in and pulled out a handgun.

"What's this?" he asked. "You weren't gonna use it to shoot me, were you?

Vogler shook his head.

"But now you'll get the money, won't you?" J.D. smiled, unaffected by the growing puddle of blood. "Where's the money?" J.D. asked.

"It's in the damn safe."

"Then I suggest that you get up and get it for me. If you can't, I guess I'll have to shoot you again."

"No, no, no!" Vogler screamed and stumbled to the safe. Letting go of his wounded arm, he pulled on the handle and opened the heavy door, reaching in for a stack of bills.

"Take the twenty-two hundred and get outta here. Be sure Lowell knows I won't be doin' business with him again."

"I'm sure Mr. Lowell will be disappointed about that, Mr. Vogler." J.D. nudged the man away from the safe and grabbed the money. "Just so you don't have any plans to call the cops and claim you were robbed; you need to know that Lowell's got friends in the police department. Understand?"

Vogler groaned and nodded as he watched J.D. back out of his office.

Once he was outside of the warehouse, J.D. looked around the dark street to see if the gunshot had alerted anyone. Seeing no one, he sucked in a deep draught of the night air, filling his lungs. Hooper walked briskly away from the river, knowing he'd done a good job. A feeling of power and pleasure ran through his body like a huge swallow of moonshine. Hooper wanted to get back to the saloon—not for a drink—but rather to tell Lowell what had happened, but he decided to wait until morning. *Damn, that felt good,* he thought as he walked up the street away from the warehouse.

☆ ☆ ☆

The next morning, J.D. got to the saloon before Lowell and finished a cup of Will's coffee just as Lowell walked into the large room.

Noticing J.D., he said, "Come on back, Hooper, and tell me how the job went."

J.D. stood and followed Lowell into the office. He waited for him to remove his coat and hang it on a coat tree near the window.

"Take a seat, Hooper."

J.D. pulled the chair back, sat down and reached into his coat pocket for Vogler's money.

"Here it is, Mr. Lowell. Twenty-two hundred." He handed the bundle to the Lowell and added, "Don't mind the blood, sir. It ain't mine."

"Hmm," Lowell mused for a moment. "What happened?"

"Vogler was just like you described. He tried to be tough and thought he could treat me like Axel and Mort. He even tried to pull a gun on me, so I shot him in the arm."

Lowell smiled and asked, "Do you think there'll be any trouble about that?"

"No, sir. I believe that Vogler won't give you any more trouble."

"Good work, Hooper." Lowell put the money into the desk drawer and pulled out a ledger. "I've got some business to finish up, so tell Will to bring me some coffee. Then try to round up the bloody-faced boys and see if they need any help." J.D. smiled and walked out.

☆ ☆ ☆

Lowell didn't have much for Hooper to do for most of the next week, but when J.D. met with him on Friday, he seemed to be in a bad mood.

"What did you want to see me about, Mr. Lowell?" asked J.D. as he sat in the chair in front of Lowell's desk.

"You've been cleaning up my list of problems so well that I've decided to dig into some old ones. There's a man who owes me more than money. He owes me an apology and it's time he paid me both. I'm not going to give you all the background on this, because it doesn't matter as far as you're concerned. But enough time has gone by that he probably thinks I've forgotten him and his debt to me."

"Okay, Mister Lowell, who is he and what do you want me to do?"

Chester slid a piece of paper across the desk and J.D. picked it up. Recognizing the name of one of the city's politicians, J.D. glanced up at Lowell.

"You've heard of him, J.D.?"

"Yes, sir, I read about him in the paper."

"Here's what I want you to do, and I want you to do it exactly as I describe without deviation." Chester watched Hooper, looking for a reaction of some kind. When he simply nodded, Lowell spent the next twenty minutes laying out a plan that required J.D. to go to the man's mansion during the workday and leave a message with the wife. The message, Lowell said, would be ugly and verbal and the woman must be frightened and feel greatly threatened.

J.D. didn't feel good about threatening a woman but decided to go along with Lowell's plan. He left the office, had a shot of whiskey at the bar, and walked out of the saloon. He caught a streetcar heading up town. Half an hour later, J.D. arrived at the address and banged loudly on the door. It opened slowly and the person standing before him was not what he expected. A young pregnant woman with a toddler at her feet softly asked, "Can I help you?" The presence of the child and the woman's innocence numbed him. J.D. took a couple of steps back, turned and walked away. *I can't do this, it ain't right.*

Needing time to think, instead of taking the streetcar back, he walked.

The boss will fire me for sure, but I just can't threaten a woman. Especially a woman who is pregnant and with a child clinging to her skirts. Every step he took drew him closer to the saloon and a confrontation with Lowell. *Maybe I think too much. Maybe I should just do it like he says.* But each step, each breath dug away at his gut, nagged at him to face Lowell and the consequences rather than to frighten a woman, her baby, and a child.

When he walked into the saloon and back toward the office, he was sure that his employment with Lowell was nearing the end.

"How'd it go, Hooper?" asked Lowell as he worked in his ledger.

"It didn't sir."

"What do you mean?" he growled, looking up at J.D.

"I mean I didn't do it." J.D. paused, knowing that the next few moments could be the end of his job. "I gotta be able to do these jobs my own way, sir. When you give me something to get done, it will get done, but you hafta let me figure out how to do it."

Lowell didn't much like what J.D. was telling him, but he paused just long enough to remember how Hooper had handled Vogler and Davison. He also considered that his collections were much better since he'd hired J.D.

"Why can't you do it like I told you?" asked Lowell, his voice calm, soft even.

J.D. knew why he couldn't do the job, but it wasn't something he'd ever talked about with anyone.

"I just can't, and I can't tell you why." J.D. looked directly at Lowell. "If you want me to threaten, or beat, or kill this fella, I will. But I can't do this job the way you want."

Chester said, "Okay, Hooper. Do it your way, but get it done."

☆ ☆ ☆

Two days later, J.D. walked into Lowell's office and handed him an envelope.

"What's this?"

"It's an apology and the money. I made the politician write it out himself so you'd know it was from him."

When Lowell slit open the envelope and unfolded the

sheet, he said, "This is a mess and hard to read. I'd have thought a man in his position would write a better hand."

J.D.'s voice was flat, emotionless. "Maybe he could before his accident."

"Accident?"

"Yeah. Seems he got his fingers caught between the floor and the heel of my shoe."

J.D. stood and left the office, satisfied that Lowell would let him do things his own way.

☆ ☆ ☆

One Friday, J.D. showed up at the saloon early. He wanted to talk to Mr. Lowell without Axel and Mort present. He walked in as Will was wiping down the bar and a young boy was mopping the floor. J.D. stepped around the bucket and the long, wet streaks on the floor as he approached the bar.

"Is Mr. Lowell in, Will?"

"Yeah, he is but he told me he doesn't want to be interrupted."

"Do you think he'll be mad if I knock on the door? I got somethin' important to talk about."

Will thought about it for a moment. "Tell you what, I just made some fresh coffee and he don't usually mind if I bring it in." He poured the hot dark liquid into a clean mug and headed to the back of the room. "Fix some for yourself. I'll be right back."

J.D. poured some coffee into a mug and watched the boy as he swung the mop back and forth across the floor. The kid knew he was being watched but understood in a way that all of the people who looked like him in Memphis did, that he couldn't say or do anything about it.

"Hey, kid."

"Yessir?"

"You know anybody who can shine shoes? Shine 'em so they look like a mirror?"

"Yessir, I can do 'em pretty good, but my brother, he's real good."

"You tell him that I'll give him ten cents every mornin' that he shows up here to shine my shoes. If he's as good as you say, I'll give you a dime too. All you need to do is keep your ears and eyes open. Sometimes I might need to ask you what goes on around here. Can you do that?"

"Yessir, mister, I can. But the big boss, he..." The boy was clearly being cautious, perhaps even frightened.

"Don't you worry about Will, or Mr. Lowell. You keep it to yourself and I'll make sure they don't know you're helpin' me." J.D. walked over to the boy and handed him two dimes. "One of these is for you and the other is for your brother. Do we have a deal?"

"Yessir, boss."

"What's your name, kid?"

"Samuel, boss."

J.D. watched Samuel until the boy turned back to his work. He poured himself another cup of coffee just as Will came out of Lowell's office.

"Mr. Lowell says you can go in, but you gotta talk quick 'cause he's busy."

"Thanks, Will," said J.D., setting the cup on the bar and walking briskly toward the rear of the room.

Chester Lowell was bent over his desk, scratching his bald head as he looked at a ledger when J.D. came into the room.

"What is it, Hooper? I'm pretty busy here."

"I've been thinkin' about how we can improve our collectin' and I wanted your permission to try somethin'."

"I tell you what, J.D., you don't need to improve your methods."

"I ain't talkin' about my work, Mr. Lowell. I'm thinkin' I could teach Axel and Mort how to do things the way I do 'em. But I sure would need you to talk to 'em first. They might not take too kindly to me tellin' 'em, me bein' new and all."

"So, you think that you can teach those bums how to do things your way if I tell them they have to?"

"Yessir, if you tell 'em to listen, they'll do it. Plus, I got an idea that they been watchin' me anyway, so why not give it a try?"

Lowell looked up from his ledger and stared at J.D., perhaps wondering if he was telling him everything he had in mind. Deciding that it likely didn't make any difference as long as collections were up, he said, "I'll make sure they hear it today. But you keep me informed. I want to know what you tell them to do and if they are actually improving."

"You'll be the first to know, Mr. Lowell."

"Alright, get on out of here and make me rich."

☆ ☆ ☆

Later that afternoon, Lowell's three enforcers sat in the café where J.D. had first been caught snooping. Even though he knew that Lowell had instructed them to follow his lead, he could tell they were reluctant, even angry that he was now in charge.

"Look, fellas, I ain't really interested in bein' in charge of collectin' Mr. Lowell's debts. I just thought you might want to learn how you can make more money. Mr. Lowell pays us good, but as long as he's gettin' his money, he don't seem to care what we do." J.D. looked at each of them. "You would like to have more money, wouldn't you?"

Axel looked over at Mort, then turned back to J.D. He lifted his cup and took a sip of coffee. Axel wasn't very good at reading people, but he knew how to frighten them, to manhandle them, and even use his fists if necessary. Lacking J.D.'s skills, he couldn't tell if the new fella across the table was being honest or was just pulling some scheme. He and Mort had talked a lot about J.D. and had even discussed getting rid of him.

"Why do you want to help us?" Axel asked.

"Why not? You've both been straight with me. You helped me understand Mr. Lowell and what he wants done. You showed me how to get around this big city, how to talk to people to find out information." J.D. looked into Mort's steely eyes. "You fellas are the only friends I have." He looked down at his cup, hoping they thought he looked embarrassed.

"We know you been makin' extra money somehow. You've only been workin' a month or so and you already got a new suit. That ain't easy to do even with what he pays us," said Axel. Mort just nodded. His eyes were like slits and his lips were pressed into a tight, thin line as he glared at J.D.

"Let me just say this, fellas. We've got a job to do and I just figured that you'd want to know how you can do everythin' Mr. Lowell asks and pick up a little extra money while you're doin' it. I got some ideas, but if you ain't interested, then at least I tried to share it with you."

J.D. knew they'd go along. Lowell was already looking around for more help and J.D. really didn't want to share any of his new-found wealth with fellas he didn't know. His two friends were pliable and with a little extra money in their pockets could be molded into working for him even as they were being paid by Lowell.

"Look, Axel, you were with me the first night I did a job for Mr. Lowell."

"Yeah?"

"When I threw that big wad of cash on his desk, did you see the look on his face?"

"Yeah, I did. So what?"

"You saw him count it, didn't you? You saw how happy he was that the lawyer had given up fifteen hundred dollars, right?"

"I did, yeah, but what're you gettin' at?"

"That stack of money I grabbed from the scared little man was nearly seventeen hundred dollars. Where do you think the extra cash ended up?" He waited, watching to see if they were smart enough to figure things out.

Mort looked confused, not seeming to understand what Hooper was saying. But Axel understood. A smile began to spread across his angular face as he looked at J.D.

"Why you sneakin' son of a bitch. You stole money from him and he didn't even know it."

J.D.'s face turned red, his eyes grew dark. "I didn't *steal* from him, Axel. He got more than he expected. I took the money from the lawyer." Axel sat back in his chair, frightened by what he saw on J.D.'s face. "I'm tellin' you about this because I think you'd like to have more money, but if you go blabbin' to Lowell about what's goin' on you'll truly wish you hadn't."

Mort started to say something, but Axel elbowed him in the ribs.

"Wait a minute, J.D. We ain't gonna tell Mr. Lowell nothin', are we Mort? We know he likes you. Hell, we like you too," he lied, "and if you're gonna be in charge and help us make some cash why should we care how it's done."

Even seeing through Axel's lie, Hooper's face softened a bit, his eyes cooled. He lifted his cup and sipped the cold coffee. "So, do you wanna hear how this all works?"

Chapter 6

Hooper liked the money he was accumulating. The new-found wealth fed his need for recognition and the power it brought him in his small world. With money he bought the loyalty of Axel and Mort. His generosity ensured that information continued to flow from Will and the young janitor, Samuel. He liked the sense of control that money gave him and was willing to do anything that kept his wallet full. J.D. was now simply a cleaned and polished version of himself—a greedy man who liked to hurt people, to frighten them, to see them cringe, cry, and grovel. If he gained power and wealth in the process, so be it. He had, it seemed, found a home in Memphis.

Sipping on his beer, J.D. asked Will, "Do you know what he wants?"

Will shrugged his shoulders and ran his fingers through his black hair. "Nope, but he's been in a good mood lately. Maybe he's gonna give you a bonus." He smiled and began wiping the already spotless bar.

Flipping Will a silver dollar, J.D. headed to Lowell's office. As had become his practice, he tapped twice on the office door, opened it, and walked up to the desk.

"Take a seat, J.D." Lowell closed his ledger, pushed it to the side of the desk, and leaned forward on his elbows. He watched J.D. remove his derby and sit in the padded leather chair.

"I'm very pleased with how things have been going since you started working for me, J.D. You clearly have a knack for this line of work and your enthusiasm has profited me a great deal." He paused, watching J.D.'s expressionless face. "I wonder if you would be interested in doing something else for me, something related to another part of my business."

"I know I'm still new around here," J.D. said, "and I'm tryin' to get used to Memphis. It's a lot bigger and busier than where I came from. But, if you think I can help, I'm willin' to try."

Lowell opened the humidor on his desk and offered J.D. a cigar, then took one for himself. The two men went through the ritual of lighting the cigars and exhaled clouds of smoke toward the ceiling. J.D. appeared confident and relaxed, but he was anxious to hear what Mr. Lowell had to say.

"As you've probably guessed, I'm in the business of arranging commercial transactions." J.D. nodded and Lowell continued. "I make it my business to..." he paused, searching for the right word, "to *coordinate* the flow of goods into and out of Memphis. Whether it's cotton transferred from the steamboats to the warehouses, or contracts for labor to load freight cars, or even drivers and wagons to haul canned goods to markets, I have a part in the process. Do you understand?"

"I think so. I mean, I know that the people I've had to visit are involved in those businesses, but I never asked them why they owed you money. It was none of my business. I just did what you wanted me to do."

"Yes, yes of course you did. I like that you follow instructions and that you get results. That's why I want you to take on some more responsibility, to do something a bit different than collecting payments. Of course, I'll increase your wages, substantially in fact, but I'll need to know that I can trust you, and that you'll do as I ask without question or complaint. Can I count on you, J.D.?"

Hooper wondered if Lowell was changing the rules or didn't trust him. "I'll get the results you want, Mr. Lowell," he said confidently, "but I still need to do it my own way."

Lowell looked across the desk at J.D., taking a slow puff on his cigar. "Of course, J.D., as long as you *do* get results."

Hooper looked at Lowell, nodded and said, "What is it you want me to do?"

"What I need to know, Hooper, is who's doing work in my part of this town without making a deal with me first. I don't care if it's lawyers writing contracts, wagons hauling goods, or laborers emptying or filling boats or boxcars. If they're not on my list, they're stealing from me." He paused and looked at J.D.'s eyes. "I don't want you to take any action against them, at least not yet. But before we do anything, I want to find out who's behind them, who's really making the decisions to take what's mine."

No one had ever given J.D. this much responsibility. But Chester Lowell had just shown that he trusted him. J.D. could barely get the words to slip across his tongue. "I'll find out who they are, sir. Trust me, I'll find out."

Lowell smiled, blew a cloud of smoke across the desk and reached for the whiskey bottle on the table by the window. He filled two glasses with bourbon and handed one to J.D. He lifted his glass toward Hooper. "Here's to *more* business."

☆ ☆ ☆

J.D. stood in the shade of a brick warehouse near the rail yard. Looking over the top of a long line of boxcars, he could see the half dozen side-wheeler steamboats moored along the river front. Teams of mule-drawn freight wagons moved between the river and the rails like ants at a picnic. Over the past few days, he'd watched as dozens of laborers had moved bales of compressed cotton off the boats and stacked them in piles along the cobble-stoned wharf. Today he expected that other workers would begin loading the scores of box cars lined up on the tracks and by the end of the week the cotton would be on its way to the textile mills in the east.

"Do ye see anything interesting?"

J.D. turned quickly at the sound of the man's accent and the first thing he saw was a badge. Caught off guard, he said, "No, not really, I'm just takin' some time before gettin' back to work. He looked up from the badge and into the man's blue-green eyes.

The blue-coated policeman chuckled. "This is my office," he said, making a wide sweep with his billy club. "This is where I work every damned day and as all good Irish men do, this is where I find a drink at the end of my shift."

"Hunh," J.D. mumbled, his heart slowing a bit. "It's a pretty busy office, ain't it?"

The cop looked at him and then smiled. "It sure is. It's big and busy and I know everything that goes on here." He paused, his eyes gazing past the trains and boats to the river and the trees along the bank of the far side. "Everything," he whispered, his accent softened.

J.D. sensed an opportunity but decided to move cautiously.

"Then I bet you could use a cup of coffee, officer." J.D. offered his hand. "I'm J.D. Hooper."

Surprised by the offer, the cop shook Hooper's hand and said, "Frank Kelly."

Over the next hour, J.D. let Frank talk about the riverfront, and he discovered the cop knew a lot. Hooper learned more from the policeman's stories than he could have by watching the activity on the dock for a month.

"I'd better get back to the office," Frank said with a lop-sided grin. "There's likely some criminal activity going on."

"You're probably right," J.D. forced a smile. "We certainly can't have that sort of thing in our little town, can we?"

They laughed and walked out of the café. Hooper and Kelly shook hands and headed off in opposite directions, one of them seemingly happy for the brief respite, the other amazed at the amount and type of information he'd gathered. Frank hadn't given J.D. any names, but from the description of the activities, J.D. knew who the men were. Hooper knew he'd still have to confirm a lot of the information, but unknowingly Frank had given him a huge head start on helping Lowell.

As he went back to wandering around the riverfront, J.D. chuckled as he recalled Frank's story about how a certain freight hauler had been shot in the arm but wouldn't tell the police how it happened. Frank knew the man was crooked, but it wasn't his job to investigate the illegal activity. He'd told J.D. that he didn't get paid enough for that kind of work, he was going to leave it for the detectives.

☆ ☆ ☆

A few days later, J.D. walked out of Chester's office and up to the bar. Even though it wasn't yet noon, he asked Will to pour him a beer.

"Everything okay, J.D.?"

"Yeah. Just tired. It was a long night."

Will nodded and turned back to the newspaper he'd been reading. J.D. watched the bartender for a moment then lifted the foaming glass to his lips. *This ain't moonshine*, he thought, *but it's good enough for now*. He'd just set his hat on the bar when Mort came into the saloon, shoving Samuel ahead of him, yelling at the boy about some inconsequential infraction, and grabbed him by the neck.

Hooper set his beer mug down and turned toward Mort and the boy.

"What the hell are you doin'?"

Mort let go of Samuel.

"The lazy rotten kid won't do what I tell him." He lifted his hand as if to strike the boy, but J.D. stopped Mort, grabbed his arm and twisted it behind his back. "Besides, he's a nig..."

"That don't make no difference. Don't hit him, he's just a kid and he ain't as stupid as you. What if I cuffed you for all the dumb things you do? What if I just tell Mr. Lowell about yesterday's mistake? Ain't that what you said it was?" J.D. waited for Mort to reply, loosening his hold on him.

"It was a mistake, but that don't have anythin' to do with this little bastard."

"Get it through your head, Mort, we don't hit kids. You keep pickin' on him and I'll make sure you won't hit anyone again. You understand?"

Mort glared at J.D. but grew afraid by the fire in Hooper's eyes. He turned away from J.D. and the boy and stormed back out of the saloon.

"You okay?" J.D. asked.

"Yessir, boss."

"Then get back to work and don't worry about that fella."

Samuel walked to the back of the room, grabbed his broom, and started sweeping the floor.

Will started to say something but instead he turned away and began arranging the bottles of whiskey on the shelves below the long mirror.

☆ ☆ ☆

As J.D. began to learn the flow of commerce along the Memphis riverfront, he made regular reports to Lowell. He'd discovered that some new fellas in the city were interested in controlling business like Lowell did, but, for some reason, none of Lowell's regular clients were interested. They had a good laugh about that. J.D. had also gotten wind of a planned hijacking of Vogler's wagons. When he told

Lowell about this, they agreed that warning Vogler would, perhaps, ease some of the pain in his arm.

Most of what he shared with Lowell was minor activity. J.D. met frequently with Frank and kept their conversations casual, allowing a sort of friendship to grow. J.D. hadn't had many friends in his life primarily because he hadn't wanted any. He convinced himself that staying close to Frank was part of his job. Then one afternoon while they were sitting in the café drinking coffee, Frank talked about something he'd heard at the police station.

"I was walking past the Sergeant's desk on my way home when I heard one of the detectives say something to him about the riverfront."

"But this is your beat, ain't it?"

"Yeah that's why it caught my attention." He sipped his coffee and continued. "Anyway, what I heard was that some of the independent wagon freight haulers—you know, the fellas with a wagon and a couple mules who'll haul a load here and a load there—well, some of them are trying to work together to take business away from the freight companies."

"That's what the detective said?" asked J.D.

"Yeah. I didn't stick around 'cause it's supposed to be none of my business, but I've been looking around for something like that going on, just in case."

J.D. was interested. "Have you seen anything?"

"No. Things seem pretty normal. I mostly deal with drunks and pickpockets. Oh, and the occasional uptown businessman with his pants down in an alley."

They laughed, finished their coffee and left the café.

As J.D. watched Frank walk away, he decided to spend the afternoon watching independent haulers to discover what he could, and then come up with some ideas to share with Lowell at the end of the day.

A few weeks later, Lowell told J.D. that he'd considered his ideas and decided to advise the freight companies about the independents' plans.

"That way," Lowell said, "we don't disrupt the flow of all of my other business ventures and we retain the profitable loyalty of the freight companies."

Lowell opened the drawer of his desk, pulled out an envelope, and handed it to J.D.

"I hope this modest bonus is sufficient."

Without looking at the packet, J.D. said, "I'm sure it is, Mr. Lowell. Thanks." He stood and walked to the door. "Better get out on the street," he said as he tipped his derby and left the office, shutting the door behind him.

He opened the envelope and counted the five twenty-dollar bills. J.D. smiled and went to work.

Chapter 7

Edward H. Harriman, the president of the Southern Pacific Railroad, stared out the window of the twelfth-floor office which belonged to his west coast manager. His gaze took in the vast panorama of the city. The devastating earthquake of 1906 had created extensive damage, but American industry—people and companies just like his—were remaking the city and he felt a great deal of pride in that. His reverie was interrupted when he heard the door open and the secretary speak.

"Mr. Jensen is here, sir."

Harriman turned and said, "That will be all." He looked at Noah Jensen as the secretary closed the door.

Jensen was rooted to the floor, and familiar with the protocol, he knew enough to wait until he was addressed by Mr. Harriman. He'd been busy wrapping up his investigation of some major pilferage from company warehouses when he was ordered by his boss, Sam Decker, to "get his ass up to the twelfth floor and make it quick." Decker told him that the company president had arrived from New York and was waiting in the manager's office. Following orders, Noah grabbed his casebook and hurried upstairs.

"Thank you for being so prompt, Mr. Jensen. Have a seat please." Harriman, a slight, balding man with a very heavy mustache, pointed to the chair in front of his desk.

Tall and broad-shouldered, Jensen sat on the plush seat and looked across the very large, very cluttered desk that was Harriman's temporary working space.

"Of course, Mr. Harriman, how can I be of service?"

"Before I get to the real purpose of my trip here, I wanted to talk to you about your recent work." He looked directly at Noah, not expecting a response, but giving the detective an opportunity to do so. Noah obliged him by remaining quiet.

"Do you mind if I call you by your Christian name, Noah?" Noah shook his head and Harriman smiled. "Your work here in San Francisco and especially the resolution of the fiasco in Kansas City was fine, fine work. You have saved my company tens of thousands of dollars, allowed us to retain customers, and put criminals and devious employees in jail." Harriman paused, letting the praise settle on Noah. "This brings me to the real reason I am here. I need you to go to Memphis. We have a new man running the detective office there—Allenby's his name—and I want you to teach him how to do what you do."

"I've heard of Allenby, sir. He's a good detective, perhaps a bit young, but he knows how to solve problems."

"Of course, Noah, but I want you to take him under your wing for a while and see if you can cultivate in him the kind of drive and persistence that makes you so effective."

"I'll try, sir."

"Noah, you amaze me. You, a man who never gives up, who works more hours in a day than most of our employees do in a week, who's persistence is nearly legendary says he will 'try'." Harriman smiled at Jensen and added, "I believe you will succeed if Allenby is willing to work with you."

"Thank you for the compliments, sir. I like working for the Southern Pacific. If you believe that my presence in Memphis will help you and the railroad, then I'll settle things here and get back there as soon as I can."

"That is what I wanted to hear, Noah. You will report directly to me in New York." He stood and walked Noah to the door, shook his hand and said, "Keep up the good work, young man."

Noah stepped into the outer office, turned and thanked Harriman, then headed back to his small office five floors below.

☆ ☆ ☆

The next morning, Noah caught the Southern Pacific's express train to Memphis. He'd checked with Decker and others in Accounting and Routing to gather as much detailed information about the Memphis operation as he could on short notice. During the several days the trip took, he made extensive notes in his leather covered journal about his own routines and practices—things he'd pass on to Allenby.

On the second day out of San Francisco, Noah set aside his notebook for a while and stared out the window of the Pullman. It was night and the light of the moon reflected off a thin mist as the train crossed some unnamed river. The moonlit night drew his thoughts back to when he'd been a beat cop in San Francisco, before he'd become a detective for the railroad.

One foggy night in 1895, Noah had been walking his beat in the Mission district. He was twenty-two at the time and had been on the force almost two years. He wanted to be a good cop and worked hard at even the most mundane tasks—checking storefront doors to insure they were locked, rousting drunks and bums, and hauling pickpockets to the precinct house.

That night a chilling air blew off the bay and found its way into the city. An occasional gust ruffled the handbills attached to the windows of shops and those that hung on every lamp post. Noah had studied one of the handbills before his shift, soaking up the detail and memorizing the face of eight-year-old Laurie Ann Walls. The young girl had been kidnapped from her backyard by an unknown person two days before. The handbills had been printed by Laurie's parents, desperate to find their daughter. They covered the city like an eerie blanket of snow.

Since the kidnapping had taken place in another part of the city, Noah didn't expect to see her on his beat, especially after midnight, but he kept his eyes open just the same. He turned off the commercial avenue and entered a residential area. The houses were tall and narrow in the well-kept neighborhood. The street was empty, and the only light came from the few glowing gaslights that filtered past the lace curtains hanging in the windows.

Noah had worked his way nearly three blocks up the street when he spotted something unusual. A large man in a long coat and slouch hat was walking away from him toward a carriage on the corner. That wasn't necessarily unusual in itself, except that the man held tightly onto the hand of a small, coatless girl whose whimpers floated on the breeze.

Noah wasn't sure, but he sensed that the child was Laurie Ann, so he drew his revolver and raced as quietly as he could toward them. But even so, his shoes pounded against the cobblestones. Just as the man reached the carriage, Noah called out her name and she turned her head, trying to pull away from the man, sobs escaping from her mouth. The man also turned, dragging the tiny figure roughly in an arc, to face Noah, his gun drawn as well.

Noah and the giant were just a few paces apart, each pointed his gun at the other. Laurie's tiny hand clamped in the kidnapper's great fist, the girl's whimpers became sobs even as she tried to escape. Noah was afraid he might hit the girl if he fired his pistol at the kidnapper, so he tried to coax her to move away. She shrieked and pulled at the man's hand, breaking free just as he fired his gun at Noah. The bullet grazed the cop's left arm. At the same time, Noah aimed at the man's head and pulled the trigger. The rest happened quickly as the kidnapper fell to the street, blood streaming from his already dead face. Noah went down on his knees, looked around for the girl and saw her hiding behind a bush a yard away. He stood and calmly walked toward her, then sat down, pulled her into his lap and said, "You're safe now, Laurie Ann."

It turned out that Laurie Ann's grandfather was a vice president of the railroad, and because Noah had saved the girl's life, he wanted to reward Noah. He couldn't accept a reward and wouldn't have anyway, but when an invitation to meet with the family in the office of the chief detective of the Southern Pacific Railroad arrived at the precinct, Noah decided to accept. Within a few weeks, Noah resigned from the police force, became a railroad detective and never again picked up a gun.

Looking out at the vast moonlit landscape that spread away from the tracks, Noah shook his head in wonder. Even a dozen or so years after the event, Noah knew that had little Laurie not jerked on the hand that held her captive, the bullet that hit his arm might have killed him instead.

☆ ☆ ☆

The next day, when the conductor told him that they would be in Memphis within the hour, Noah thanked him.

"Please make sure that my bags are ready. I want to get to the company offices and start working immediately."

When Noah stepped onto the platform at the Union Depot, the bitterly cold wind stole his breath and made him glad he'd packed his overcoat. *This is not San Francisco,* he thought, glad that he lived in the coastal California city.

"Shall we take your luggage to the Peabody hotel, Mr. Jensen, or do you want me to carry it to Mr. Allenby's office?"

Word travels fast, Noah mused. "Take it to the hotel and tell them I'll check in later." He gave the porter a silver dollar and added, "Make sure they give me a warm room." *If there is such a thing here.*

Noah headed across the train yard and walked into the Illinois Central building. Allenby was waiting for him in his private office.

"I need to send a telegram to Harriman," Jensen said to the younger man. "Then we can talk."

While Noah filled out the form, Allenby paced behind his desk, convinced that Jensen was in Memphis to fire him. He'd followed all of the rules and procedures, and spent nearly all of his time on solving the various cases he faced.

Noah handed the paper to the clerk and turned to Allenby.

"Sit down, Ben, please." Noah took off his hat and coat, ran his fingers through his straw-colored hair, and sat in the straight back wooden chair across from Allenby. "I know you think I'm here to fire you, but that's not why I'm in Memphis."

Ben was only slightly relieved. "Can you tell me then why you had to come here, Mr. Jensen?"

"It's Noah, and the reason I came is that Mr. Harriman asked me to come. Mr. Harriman's concern has always been about our customers and his railroad and making sure that they continue to make money. Now Mr. Harriman knows that you have been doing good work here in Memphis, and he wants me to spend some time with you. He thinks I have some skills and methods that could work for you here in Tennessee. I believe that he wants to give you the opportunity to learn from an old man like me." Noah smiled and watched the confusion and relief wash across the young detective's face.

"What I plan to do, Ben, is look at your city and your operation, and try to understand the things you face on a daily basis. You are an experienced detective and know what goes on in your town. Together we'll look at your challenges, your procedures, your strengths and weaknesses, if there are any, and work on the process of detecting." Noah thought briefly about what to say next. "For some reason, Mr. Harriman thinks I have some magical ability to solve cases, and with respect I'll tell you that he's wrong. Nothing I do is special or magical. What I do is work hard and I never quit. Maybe that's what he wants me to pass along to you."

"That's a lot to take in all at once, Noah, but if Mr. Harriman thinks I'm worth keeping then I guess I can go back to school and learn from you." He didn't actually smile, but his face took on a youthful warmth.

"So, Ben, let's go find something to eat. You can tell me about your city and how it works. Then later we'll come back here and start at the beginning." Noah looked at the younger man and added, "Maybe I can show you a few things that'll help in your next investigation." He smiled and watched Allenby relax, then asked, "Is it always so cold here?"

☆ ☆ ☆

While the waiter cleared the table of their plates, Noah reflected on what he'd learned about Memphis: the riverfront corruption, the reluctant cooperation from the police, and the fact that Memphis was not unlike every other large city in America. This was a new century and America was growing. People were working, getting rich, and looking at ways to get richer. He'd never been in Tennessee and hadn't expected Memphis to be as urban and as modern as San Francisco, yet it was.

Allenby asked the waiter to bring a bottle of sipping whiskey to the table.

"I don't usually do this," he said, "but if I'm going to learn anything from you, Noah, I might as well be relaxed."

"I've got no problem with relaxing," Jensen said, "but

these will likely be our last drinks for a while since school starts in the morning."

Chapter 8

Winter in Memphis was miserable. The icy wind blowing off the river kept most people in their homes, offices, and factories. On the frozen riverfront and along the icy rail yards, traffic had dwindled to only that which was necessary. The few steamboats tied up along the levee were quickly unloaded by the laborers and the crates and boxes hauled even faster into the waiting warehouses and trains.

Even in these coldest weeks of the year, Lowell's business carried on. He continued to make arrangements between freight haulers and the steamboats, using contracts written by lawyers under his thumb. The same held true for essentially all of the warehouses, railroads, and factories in Memphis. Yet, because Lowell's demands—the fees, charges, and payments—were modest and his service was quick and effective, most of his clients, both buyers and sellers, continued to work with him.

One cold afternoon in early March, J.D. hurried along Main Street toward the saloon. He'd spent the day with Axel and Mort at a small barrel making factory at the far south end of the levee. For several weeks they had been trying to convince the owner, James Williams, to work with Lowell and, thus, improve his sales. But, despite their efforts and promises of new customers and quicker service—all for a small fee—the man was reluctant. On this day, needing his help, Axel and Mort brought J.D. along to see if he could change the man's mind. J.D. sent them off on a bogus errand then asked the potential client if he'd like to join him for lunch.

"It'll only take an hour, Mr. Williams. If we can't come to a mutually beneficial arrangement, we won't bother you again."

During their meal at a nearby café, J.D. reviewed the process with James and pointed out that there were a number of risks faced by merchants and contractors who chose not to cooperate. He shared a few examples with Williams and didn't hold back on the details.

"Perhaps my friends weren't specific enough Mr. Williams. They are often reluctant to provide all of the necessary information to businessmen such as yourself. Mr. Wheeler, down the wharf, didn't accept Mr. Lowell's business arrangement, and a week later he suffered a terrible fall that broke both of his legs. Mr. Craig, perhaps you know him, decided he could do better on his own, but then there was that tragic fire at his business that destroyed everything. But I think you are smart enough to see that turning down this offer from Mr. Lowell would not be wise for you or your family."

Williams wiped the sweat from his forehead with a red kerchief, cleared his throat and said, "I understand, Mr. Hooper. I sure wouldn't want anything to happen to my business and I definitely don't want my family bothered with any of this."

"I think you've made a wise choice, James. I need to head back up town, so I'll let you return to your office. We'll be in touch to finalize our deal."

When J.D. stepped out onto the street, he buttoned his coat against the cold wind. Axel and Mort were standing at the corner, trying to stay warm.

"What happened with Williams?" a usually quiet Mort asked.

"He has decided to cooperate and looks forward to

your meeting to finalize the arrangement."

"Are you gonna tell Mr. Lowell?" Axel asked.

"Nope. I'm gonna let you two tell him. This was your assignment and you two were able to convince the barrel-maker to do the right thing."

"But..."

"Let's get back to the saloon and have a beer."

Axel and Mort followed along behind J.D. like kids hanging around an older brother.

☆ ☆ ☆

The next night, J.D. went to Beale Street and stepped into Tony's for dinner. A beer and some good food was all J.D. wanted at the end of his day. But on this night his attention was drawn to one of Lowell's wealthier clients sitting by himself at a table. While J.D. drank his beer at the bar, two men came into the saloon and sat down with the client. Thinking he might gather some interesting information from their conversation, J.D. sat at a nearby table. He seated himself with his back to the client. This technique, hiding in plain sight in order to overhear people, had become his normal practice. He ordered one of Tony's suppers and began to listen.

"Here's my problem, gentlemen," said the client. "Doing business in Memphis today is very costly. I am not always free to make choices about who I work with. Despite being a respectable businessman, I am ordered by one man who tells me which company will unload my goods from the boxcars and which freight companies will deliver them to my factory. In the past this arrangement worked well for me because the work happened quickly and efficiently. But now," he said, scanning the crowded room and lowering his voice, "now, working together, I believe we can find laborers and freight haulers that won't cost as much. I've got a huge load of goods, probably a dozen boxcars ready to ship next week. I want to use your company to move them, but this one powerful man has existing arrangements with your competitors."

Over the next quarter hour, the client and the railroad men made plans for a late-night transfer of the product to the railcars a few days before the scheduled shipment.

J.D. waited until the three men left the saloon. He finished his meal and his beer then began formulating a plan of his own. He walked up to the bartender, paid his bill, and left Tony's. On his way to the Big River Saloon, J.D. decided to keep the new information to himself for now, knowing it would have more value if he could present a plan to Lowell at the same time he told him about the client's planned betrayal.

Hooper checked in with Lowell as soon as he got to the saloon then had a beer with Will before heading to his boarding house. He had some things to think about and his quiet room was the best place to do that. J.D. sat at the small table he used as a desk. Despite his poor skills in writing, he often managed to scratch out his thoughts in a fashion that served him. The issue he addressed on this cold night was one that he believed would make him indispensable to Lowell, but he knew that the details of his plan had to be perfect if his boss was to buy into it.

☆ ☆ ☆

The next morning, when J.D. filled Lowell in on what he'd discovered, Lowell was angry.

"I want you to make an example of these people J.D. Let them load the boxcars, but don't let the product out of Memphis." Lowell's gravelly voice was even harsher, scratchier when he was angry. "Make sure the railroad and my client don't ever want to by-pass me again. I don't care how you do it or what it costs, but this should be something that makes everyone afraid of turning against me."

"Okay, Mr. Lowell, I'll do it. Just so you don't get caught in the middle, I'll keep the details to myself."

"That's good," Lowell said. "But these people in particular need to know that crossing me is a mistake."

"They'll know, sir."

☆ ☆ ☆

With little more than a week to keep the freight from leaving Memphis, J.D. couldn't waste time. In the hours after he left the saloon, he wandered into the train yard, thinking of and then casting aside a number of ideas—track damage, explosives, even stealing the goods from the boxcars.

Until he got to Memphis, J.D. hadn't thought much about trains and rail yards. As a hired hand, his focus had always been on doing farm work, getting paid, and getting drunk. But as he walked between the boxcars lined up on the sidetracks, he noticed a number of things. The cars were large, bigger than the shack where he'd lived in Kentucky. They were made of iron, steel, and wood. As J.D. stood staring at the train, a past memory reminded him of an idea—boxcar, shack, wood...and fire. He reached up and placed his hand on one of the cars, touching the wood, feeling the splinters and the deep grain. Then an image, a vision of the dozen cars burning in the night, just like the shack, flashed in his mind. *Fire*, he thought, *a huge, roaring fire would keep the cars in Memphis and would send a clear message to Lowell's enemies.*

Money wasn't an issue, but burning a dozen freight cars wouldn't be a one-man job. He'd need help, perhaps a dozen men and he had to find them quickly.

Hooper walked away from the rail yard and down to the river. Even in the icy weather, there were plenty of people moving freight from the steamboats and loading wagons. The entire river front was a place of movement and energy. There were all kinds of men wherever he looked. *But how can I find just the right men, the ones willing to break the law and keep their mouths shut*? He couldn't just walk up to a crowd of men and ask if they were interested in getting paid to burn a train, he had to find them another way. *But where do I look*?

As he headed back toward the saloon, J.D. noticed his friend the cop, Frank Kelly, talking to a few rough looking men near the streetcar track. J.D. couldn't hear what was being said, but he could tell that Frank was being a cop. He grabbed one of the fellas by his coat, spun him around and pushed him away from the others. The tough guy jerked his coat from Frank's grasp and came right back at him. Words were exchanged. Frank tapped the man's chest with his billy club and pushed him again.

The other two men crowded in behind Frank, as if to trap him, but the cop turned quickly, his billy club ready, rapping it in the palm of his hand. He yelled at them and pointed his stick up the wharf. Looking back only once to say something to Frank, the men slowly walked away from the corner. The cop had made his point with them, but it wasn't easy. To J.D., they looked like they were from the rough part of town, the kind of men he'd need for his job.

J.D. followed them at a distance for several blocks along the river. When they turned into an alley, he lost sight of them. Reaching the corner, J.D. gazed down the narrow passage, but they were nowhere in sight. He walked to the end and stepped out onto a busy street. Looking both ways, he could see no one who resembled the men. *Must've slipped into one of the doors*, he thought, and walked back into the alley.

A barely legible, hand-painted sign on one door convinced J.D. that the men had entered Paddy's Irish Pub—Members Only. He stared at the sign, anxious to enter the bar and put his plan in motion. But a thought flitted across his mind. *I probably ought to think about this before I go barging in. Maybe I can find some other fellas.*

J.D. walked out of the alley and found a nearby café. He sat at a table, ordered a cup of coffee from the waiter, and considered his options. He didn't like how his caution made him feel. The past few months he'd done a lot of things and done them well. He'd become stronger and more confident. He had trusted his judgment and hadn't failed at anything. J.D. finished his coffee, paid the waiter, and walked back to the alley.

Full of confidence, Hooper walked to the pub, opened the door, and stepped in. The place was small, dark, and it smelled like boiled cabbage. Hooper blinked, his eyes not yet adjusted to the darkness. A man moved quickly in his direction and J.D. knew he'd made a bad decision. He turned, reached for the door handle and found the exit blocked by the fella Frank had pushed with his night stick.

"Keep him right there, Michael me lad."

J.D. looked over his shoulder and watched as a beefy young man with ginger-colored hair pushed his way through the crowd.

"This is my place. Whatta you want?" he asked, his face inches from J.D.'s.

"Are ya wantin' me to hit him, Paddy," said Michael.

"Not yet, boy."

J.D. knew he was in trouble. This time he was not only outnumbered but he was trapped too. His eyes darted from Paddy's face to the others in the room. They were hard men, he could tell, and would probably enjoy beating the life out of him. Not wanting to panic or show his growing fear, his only recourse was to answer the question.

"My name's Hooper," he blurted out. "I'm lookin' for some men to help me do a job."

"Well, Hooper," said Paddy, his accent strong. "Ye're either very brave or very stupid to come into me own pub without bein' asked."

The other men moved in closer and sounded their agreement with Paddy.

"Is it that ye're a dumb copper, or just new to our part of town?"

J.D. tried again to pull out of Michael's grasp, but the boy slammed him against the wall.

"I ain't no cop." His voice was bold, but the ember of panic was ready to ignite. "But I do need some tough men who ain't afraid to do a job and keep quiet about it."

Paddy looked around the room, the smile still on his face but his eyes said something different.

"And yourself thought to find such men here? Why, Mr. Hooper, we are simple, law-abidin' citizens and wouldn't think of breakin' the law."

Michael tightened his grip as Paddy moved closer and sniffed J.D.'s cheeks.

"I think, Hooper, that ye're growin' very afraid. Smell it I can in your sweat."

"Paddy is it?" J.D. stared into his eyes. "Paddy, I need ten men for a one-night job. They need to do what I ask, keep their mouths shut about it, and enjoy spending the money I'll pay them. That's it. It looks like you and your friends are the kind of men who can do that. If you ain't, then I guess I can make my offer to the wops. Those Italians would probably want my money." J.D. didn't move, didn't blink, and didn't breathe. Paddy stared back, also unmoving, but J.D. thought he could see a spark in his eyes.

"Interested?" He added a smile, confident that if Paddy hadn't told his friends to attack him by now, that he'd gotten his attention.

The room was quiet, and then Paddy asked, "How much money are ye thinkin'?"

"Ten men, fifty dollars each, and a hundred dollars for you to make sure they don't talk about the job."

"Paid in advance?"

"Now that would be stupid, wouldn't it Paddy." Knowing he had the man's attention he said, "I'll pay *you* in advance, if you agree to the deal, and pay the others when the job's done."

"How do I know ye won't tell the coppers about this job?"

"If I'm payin' you to keep this quiet, why would I tell anyone, especially the police?"

Satisfied, at least for the moment, Paddy nodded, signaled Michael to release J.D. and walked him to the tiny bar.

"I'll do this for ye Hooper, but if you cross me, you're a dead man. Understand?" J.D. looked into Paddy's eyes, convinced that the Irishman meant what he said. Hooper also couldn't overlook the crowd of tough men who stood around them.

J.D. nodded.

"Aye, then let's drink to our deal. I'm buyin'."

For the next half hour, J.D. and Paddy discussed the plan—at least the part Hooper wanted him to know—and agreed that he would give Paddy twenty-four hours' notice. They had several more drinks of Irish whiskey then J.D. walked out of Paddy's Pub into the alley.

Heading back to the corner, he got on a streetcar and rode toward the boarding house. Halfway home, he let out a long, deep breath. *That was too close and not very smart.* But he allowed himself a small smile at having twisted the lion's tail and survived. Then he began to work on the rest of the plan.

After J.D. left his pub, Paddy told Jimmy to follow him. "Stay with him and see where he goes. I want to know everyone he talks to."

☆ ☆ ☆

After breakfast the next morning, J.D. rode the streetcar back to the train yard. He spent an hour or so walking by workshops and warehouses, searching for a vacant building. At one point he ran into Frank Kelly and took him to a café for some coffee. They found a quiet spot on the cop's beat and sat at a table. After their coffee was served, J.D. asked Frank, "What's new my friend?"

"It's been pretty quiet. All the criminals are behavin', most of 'em anyway."

"Must be because they're afraid of you, Officer Kelly." J.D. smiled.

"What else could it be? It's just me and my billy club," he said.

Frank put sugar in his coffee and stirred it for a moment. "There are still some bad boys around, though, but mostly they are no more than a bother."

"You keep 'em honest, do ya?"

"These boys don't know 'honest,' but they know they can't mess with me."

J.D. heard Frank's determination, but it didn't bother him. *The job will get done and with Paddy's help it'll be quick and quiet.*

Two men walked by the window and nodded at Frank. He acknowledged them and asked J.D. if he knew who they were.

"Don't think so. Who are they?"

"The younger one is a detective for the Illinois Central. I don't know the other one."

"How'd you meet him?" he paused, caught off guard. "The detective?"

"Oh, he's been here a couple of years. We caught a fella tryin' to break into one of his boxcars and found a home for the thief in the state prison."

Not wanting to discuss the subject, J.D. said he had to get back to work. He left some money on the table and they went outside, shook hands, and walked away.

By early afternoon, J.D. had located a shop that sold coal oil and arranged with Paddy—for an extra payment—to have some of his boys steal a barrel and a dozen pails. Paddy agreed to store them at the bar until J.D. needed them.

Before dusk, J.D. found a storage building several blocks from the rail yard. A sign on the street-side wall indicated it was for rent, but the padlock hung open on the hasp and the building was empty and dirty; perfect for J.D.'s needs.

With a newly purchased padlock in hand, J.D. met Michael and another of Paddy's men at the vacant warehouse at midnight two days before the cars were scheduled to leave the yard. They moved the barrel and pails inside and then the three of them went to Paddy's.

"Have your men meet me tomorrow night at 11:30," he told Paddy. "Michael can show 'em where it is." J.D. wanted to ensure Paddy's compliance with their deal, so he bought beers for everyone in the bar and gave Paddy an extra fifty dollars.

"You must be Irish, Hooper," Paddy laughed, pocketed the money and went down the bar to talk to his boys.

J.D. looked around the room, finished his beer, and went home.

☆ ☆ ☆

J.D. arrived at the railyard just after dusk. He spent a little time in the warehouse, setting up the pails and the coal oil. At one point he looked out the small window by the door and saw the railroad detective and the man he'd been with a few days earlier outside the café. They walked through the yard, deep in conversation. J.D. waited, giving them enough time to be well past the warehouse, then he stepped out and followed them at a distance. When he got to the end of the long line of cars, he spotted them going into the Illinois Central office. Shortly thereafter, a light glowed from the office window. J.D. wondered how long they might be in there and if they would still be in the building when he burned the railcars. But after just a few minutes, the light went out and the two men left the building and headed away from the railyard.

That's good, Hooper thought as he headed back to his warehouse. *Certainly don't need cops sittin' around when I got things to do.* He left the warehouse and found a good hiding place between some cars just down the line from the ones designated to hold the client's goods. Later Hooper observed the late-night loading of the client's product onto the Illinois Central boxcars and got back to the borrowed warehouse just after eleven o'clock.

The wind had picked up by midnight when J.D. and his helpers, each carrying a pail of coal oil, snuck into the dark freight yard. They crossed three or four loaded side-tracks before arriving at the targeted box cars. J.D. watched the men as they splashed the liquid on the dozen cars which held the client's goods. Then, working their way back across the side-tracks, they carried the pails to the empty warehouse to wait for him.

After all of the men left, J.D. lit a torch and ran along the side of the train. Each car began to burn, and by the time he reached the far end of the line of cars, all of them were ablaze. The raging flames reflected in J.D.'s eyes, highlighting a deeper glow; a darker, blood-red, hell-deep fire. Intoxicated by the scene, J.D. felt a powerful surge in his gut. The odor of coal oil was quickly consumed by the smoke churning from the boxcars. It created a new smell—a mixture of burning sacks of grain, barrels of salt pork, and crates of equipment. The fire was so hot that the wooden walls of the cars roared and crackled, sending firebrands into the night air, spreading the flames over the entire area. He was surprised when the fire jumped to the other cars on the adjoining tracks. J.D. wanted to stay and watch the destruction generated by the inferno. He needed to feel the heat, but knew, also, that the fire would draw people to the rail yard. Reluctantly, but quickly, he ran back toward the warehouse. When he arrived, he paid each of the men fifty dollars and they dispersed, heading off in different directions according to his instructions. He neatly stacked the empty pails along the wall and left the warehouse.

Chapter 9

The heavy pounding on the door woke Noah from a deep sleep.

"Hold on," he yelled and sat up in the bed. "I'm coming." The chill in the room made him shiver. Through squinted eyes he saw a red glow through the curtains and was surprised that it was already dawn.

Noah stood and rubbed his face, trying to clear his head. He walked to the door and opened it to see Ben Allenby standing with a clerk.

"Ben, what's going on?" Noah yawned loudly.

"We've got a big fire in the yard, Noah."

"A fire? Whatta you mean?"

Jensen looked out the east-facing window in the direction of the railyard and realized that the red light was coming from a fire and not from the rising sun.

"There's got to be a hundred cars on fire," Ben said. "All the tracks are blocked and there isn't much the Fire Department can do."

"Get some of our workers up and over to the yard now!" he told Ben as he pulled on the clothes he'd worn yesterday. "I'll meet you at the railyard." When Ben hesitated for a second, Noah said, "Go, now."

☆ ☆ ☆

Five minutes later, Noah and Ben stood among throngs of shocked and curious onlookers—night workers, drunks from the saloons and bars, and the firemen and police officers—watching the inferno. The detectives were stunned, their minds filled with questions.

"Was there any lightning?"

"No," said Ben. "It's the wrong time of year for that kind of thing. "These fellas were working in the shop getting ready for the day crew when they heard a commotion coming from the railyard." Ben gestured to the three men standing off to the side.

Frustrated, but still in control, Noah quickly turned toward them and asked what they'd seen.

"We didn't see nothin'," one of them said.

"Nothing?" he asked.

"No, sir," said a second man. "We just heard a lot of noise, cracklin' and such, and ran over here."

Noah turned back to Ben. "There's not much we can do now. It's too hot and too dangerous to get close to the fire. Let's see if any of the other railroad folks are around now. Not all of those cars are ours, so maybe they have an idea how something like this happened."

Ben sent the workers back to the shop and joined Noah as they walked the perimeter of the destruction, staying back from the intense heat. They spent another three hours talking with people in the crowd, most of whom knew nothing. The few officials they spoke to seemed as ignorant of a cause as were Ben and Noah.

"The firemen are busy, the police are trying to keep the crowd back, and we don't have a clue what caused this." Noah wiped the oily soot from his face and stared at the flames. "We won't be able to get close until later today. When we can get close, we're going to be busy, so let's go back to the office and figure out what we're going to do next."

☆ ☆ ☆

J.D. was too excited to sleep, but undressed and lay

down on the bed just the same. He had done a good job for Lowell, he'd paid his Irish workers well, and set a fire that filled his body with a strange energy. He was too awake, too alive to close his eyes. Much later, the effects of a single beer and the waning alertness allowed him to drift into a dream of satisfaction.

Chapter 10

The next evening, wrapped in his long coat, J.D. sat in a chair on the wide veranda at the Austin House, his legs stretched out across the porch rail, a recently lit cigar clamped in his teeth. As he flipped through the pages of his newspaper a familiar combination of letters caught his attention. He moved his feet off the rail and sat up straight in the cane back chair. Slowly and with a growing anxiety he read the short article.

KENTUCKY KILLER STILL AT LARGE LYNNVILLE KENTUCKY AUTHORITIES CONTINUE SEARCH

Legal authorities in this small western Kentucky village continue their efforts to find the person or persons responsible for the fiery death of a local hired man. Last May, a shack that had been inhabited by two itinerant farm workers was destroyed by a fire which, according to the local constable, had been deliberately set. Among the soot and ash were discovered the charred remains of one of the workers believed to be Charles (Charley) Randall, recently of Henry County. It is believed that Randall's associate, who disappeared from the community at about the time of the fire, might have been involved. The constable was unwilling to provide a name for the associate, a known trouble-maker, claiming he didn't have sufficient evidence to consider him a suspect. He did add, however, that the unnamed man was certainly capable of committing such a heinous act.

☆ ☆ ☆

J.D. crumpled the paper in his fists and rose from the chair. A flood of emotions rushed through him. His thoughts raced from anxiety to panic. J.D.'s stomach was knotting up as he stepped off the veranda and paced back and forth across the small, fenced-in yard. His shadow marched with him, lengthened by the light from the lantern on the steps. The evening frost on the patches of grass wet his shoes and the cuffs of his pants.

"Mr. Hooper is everything alright?"

"What?" J.D. stopped and turned toward the house. His landlady stood in the doorway, a dish towel in her hand.

"I asked if everything was alright, Mr. Hooper."

"Oh, yes...yes ma'am, everything's fine. I was just, um, thinking about something, that's all."

"Is there anything I can do? Would you like some tea?" She paused, wiping her hands with the towel. "Supper will be ready soon."

"No tea, thanks. I'll be right in."

J.D. watched as she closed the door. He stared for a moment at the lantern and then looked around the yard at the fence, the lawn, and the leafless tree hanging over the small dead garden. The quiet made him feel safe. *What am I doin',* he thought. *This ain't Lynnville and they ain't lookin' for me here. So calm down.*

As he sat at the table, sharing supper with his landlady and the other boarders, the feeling of panic had disappeared, replaced by one of resolve. He needed to leave Memphis, but not in the middle of the night this time. He didn't want to draw attention to himself since the whole city was talking about the fire. *I'll just move on.*

Despite his sense of relaxed confidence, J.D. didn't sleep much that night; instead he did a lot of thinking. As often happens in sleepless nights, ideas and plans become jumbled and confused. But in the morning, as J.D. sat at his window table, drinking a cup of coffee, his plan started to come together. He began to craft a story, one that would be believable and that would cover his tracks. There would be some problems and pulling off the plan would be difficult. But J.D. had learned a lot about handling hard tasks. *There's no hurry and I got plenty of money to slip out of town quietly.*

☆ ☆ ☆

Hooper walked into the saloon and headed straight for Lowell's office. He tapped twice on the door, ready to begin the toughest part of his plan.

"Come in."

J.D. opened the door and approached Lowell's desk. Covering his anxiety with bravado, he said, "Good mornin' sir. We need to talk."

"Indeed we do, J.D. We need to talk about a number of developments."

As J.D. had expected, Lowell had read the newspaper article He'd already heard J.D.'s story about the killing in Kentucky, so lying about that would be futile.

"You've read the newspaper, then?"

"I have, and we'll talk about that in a bit. But first I want to tell you that our friends who so recently suffered tragic losses in the rail yard have contacted me."

J.D. asked what they wanted.

"They dropped by, separately of course, to inquire about arranging new agreements with me, agreements which will increase my revenue." A warm smile spread across his face. "Of course, they asked if I had any losses, but I told them not to worry about that. In any case, your efforts have paid off remarkably well."

"Thanks, Mr. Lowell."

"But, before we move onto the article in the paper, I

want you to know that over the past half-year I've seen a remarkable change in you. You are no longer the rough-edged farmer trying to look like a gentleman I met last fall." He watched J.D. closely, waiting for a response. When he didn't get one, he said, "You, Mr. Hooper, are my most trusted associate. You learn quickly, act resolutely—always in my best interest—and are extremely loyal."

"Well, Mr. Lowell, you've taught me a lot and trusted me with so much more than anyone else ever did. You pay me well, too."

"Nevertheless, based on what I read this morning, I expect you've come to ask for a leave of absence."

"Huh?"

"You want to leave Memphis. Am I right?"

"You are, Mr. Lowell. I don't *want* to leave here. I like Memphis and my job. But what happened back in Kentucky is too fresh and too close," J.D. lied to Lowell. "I don't wanna quit the job, though. I just thought I'd leave town for a while, maybe go to Atlanta for a month or so until things settle down around here."

"I suppose a short vacation would help. So, you don't plan to disappear entirely?"

"No sir, just 'til summer and then I'll be back."

"Well, J.D. that sounds like a good plan. Will you need any additional funds?"

"I've got plenty. You've paid me more than I'd have earned in my whole life. I'll be fine with what I have."

"Then I'll make up some excuse to tell Axel and Mort about your disappearance, so they don't get curious."

The two men talked for a while, then J.D. said he was off to buy some luggage and a train ticket. Lowell stood, and they shook hands. J.D. left the office, said good-bye to Will and Samuel, and walked out onto the busy Memphis street.

☆ ☆ ☆

Hooper spent the rest of the morning running a few errands. He bought two inexpensive suitcases at a general store then returned to his room at the boarding house. Taking the nearly three thousand dollars he'd accumulated working for Lowell from a box in his wardrobe, J.D. put the money in his coat pockets and his clothes into the suitcases, looked around the room, and walked downstairs.

"Good morning, Mr. Hooper."

"Good morning, ma'am. I'm sorry, but I've been called away on business. I may be gone for several months. My company needs me in Chicago."

"Oh, I am sorry. You've been such a nice boarder. Would you like me to hold your room for you?"

"No thanks, ma'am, that won't be necessary. But I would like to give you an extra month's rent to cover any additional expenses. Would that be okay?"

"Yes, thank you. If you ever come back to Memphis, please consider staying in my home. I hope your business in Chicago is successful."

☆ ☆ ☆

J.D.'s next stop was the train depot. The massive stone and brick building with its arched doorways had, in time, become invisible to him. Now, however, it was a vital link in his plan.

Inside the vast open space of the passenger waiting area, J.D. asked a porter where he might find the ticket office. The man directed him to the left side of the cavernous room and tipped his hat when J.D. gave him a silver coin.

"May I help you sir?" asked the clerk at the counter.

"You may. When is the next westbound train leaving?"

"There are several. There will be some delays because of the fire, but several lines are still running. What is your destination?"

J.D. knew that if he said anything specific, someone

might remember him and his destination. The opposite was likely true as well. Instead, he responded, "I'd like to see California, but I may stop along the way. Do you have any suggestions?"

The man gave J.D. a printed schedule for the Southern Pacific Railroad and pointed out the various stops on the two thousand miles of track.

"I think, then, I'll take a ticket for Dallas. If I should decide to stop in Little Rock for a few days, will my ticket for Dallas still be good?"

"Yes sir, it will." Looking at Hooper's clothes and luggage, he said, "So, one first-class ticket to Dallas?"

J.D. nodded and handed over the fare.

"Your train leaves in forty-two minutes on track two." The man rang a bell and the same porter J.D. had met earlier picked up his luggage and led Hooper to the train.

The long wooden platform that ran along the track was crowded with people—families, porters, and men pushing carts filled with freight headed west. When J.D. spotted a familiar face at the far end of the platform, he nearly called out. He quickly decided that his policeman friend Frank was the last person who should see him leaving town.

Wending his way through the scores of busy travelers, J.D. followed the porter. Strangely, the man who could threaten lawyers, wound stubborn businessmen, and kill for money was a bit afraid of what lay ahead. He'd never ridden a train. He stepped from the platform into the passenger car, tipped the porter again, and sat down in the plush first-class seat next to the window.

Soon the passenger car filled and, as J.D. handed his ticket to the conductor, the train lurched forward. As the station slid past, J.D. saw the long line of burned-out boxcars.

"That sure is a mess isn't it," said the old woman sitting next to him.

"It sure is." *It sure is.*

Lurching and straining, the train moved slowly through the rail yard and approached the long bridge across the Mississippi River. J.D. was afraid of being on a train for the first time and even more so about crossing the biggest river he'd ever seen. Great clouds of smoke from the steam engine drifted by the window of the Pullman car as the train crawled across the bridge. J.D. didn't want to look down, but he couldn't stop himself from doing it. Thrilled and frightened at the same time, he shuddered as the sweat crept out from under the brim of his derby and coursed down his cheeks. He clenched his hands into tight fists and sat up straight in the seat as his heart pounded in his chest. When the last car cleared the end of the mile-long span and entered Arkansas, Hooper finally took a deep breath, sat back in his seat, relaxed, and watched the dry, solid land slide past his window.

☆ ☆ ☆

J.D. stood on the platform of the depot in Little Rock and watched as the train pulled out of the station heading west. The trip had taken only a few hours, and all the while, J.D. had stared out of the window taking in the scenery.

The platform was busy. Porters were hauling luggage and freight away, working their way between debarking passengers. J.D. followed a crowd of people to the end of the platform and walked down a short flight of stairs to the street. He was tired and needed to find a place to stay. The Marion Hotel stood tall opposite the depot. Crossing the street, he entered the lobby and took a cheap room on the top floor. Tipping the young boy who carried his bags up the stairs, J.D. closed and locked the door to the sparsely appointed room.

Finally alone, J.D. enjoyed the silence. He took off his hat and coat and sat on the end of the bed. Leaning down, he untied his shoes, slipped them off, lay down, and fell asleep. But he didn't rest. What dreams he had were scattered, messy, filled with racing trains and fire. Lots of fire. The screeching sound of a passing freight train woke him before dawn. He rose from the crumpled bed and looked out the window, watching the eastbound freight until it disappeared into the rising sun.

J.D. turned from the window and glanced around the room. He reached into the breast pocket of his coat and took out a half-pint bottle of whiskey and drained it in one large gulp. Tossing the empty bottle onto the bed, he put on his shoes and coat, grabbed his hat, and left the room. In the lobby of the hotel, he asked the clerk where he might get some breakfast, but what he really wanted was more whiskey—it was the only thing that would calm his nerves.

"Our café will be open in an hour, sir. But if you can't wait there's a place close by that's usually open."

"How do I get there?" Hooper asked.

"Just turn left outside. It's in the middle of the next block right next to the general store."

"Can I get a paper anywhere?"

"We get the morning paper out of Memphis on the noon train, sir. Can I hold one for you?"

"Yeah, thanks," J.D. said. He walked out onto the boardwalk, looked up and down the block, and then walked toward the café.

J.D. was surprised when he discovered that the café was really a saloon that, according to the man behind the bar, was always open.

"You serve breakfast?" J.D. asked.

"We sure do. We got eggs and ham and coffee."

"Do you sell whiskey?"

"Yep."

J.D. picked a table by the window and waited for his food. He rubbed his scratchy cheeks and stared out at the depot and the boxcars stored along the sidetracks, thinking about how things had changed in the last several months, how he had changed. He was convinced that no one back in Lynnville would recognize him. *I look different,* he thought, *maybe even sound different.* J.D. had money and he'd discovered that the skills he had made him valuable to some people, like the Night Riders in Kentucky and Chester Lowell in Memphis. *Could be I can get the same kind of job here in Little Rock or maybe even in Dallas. All I gotta do is look around, keep my eyes open, and see what's goin' on.*

His contemplative mood was interrupted when the barkeeper delivered his food.

"That'll be seventy-five cents," the man said.

J.D. looked at the full plate and then up at the man. He slipped two silver dollars from his vest pocket and set them on the table. "Keep the cup filled with hot coffee and when I leave you can keep the change. Oh, don't forget to leave me a pint of whiskey."

The barkeeper went back behind the bar as J.D. finished his meal.

Hooper's next stop was a barber shop. *Gotta keep my clean image,* he thought. The barber leaned the fancy chair back and spread the warm lather on J.D.'s face. He paused to hone the razor on a leather strap and then carefully removed the day-old stubble. J.D. listened to the muted chatter coming from the men waiting for their turn. The traffic had picked up on the street and the growing clamor of a city going to work reminded him of how quiet things had been in the country. But he'd gotten used to the noise of industry and didn't remember when that change had come about.

His belly full and his face smooth, Hooper walked down the street and crossed over to the depot. He walked up the stairs and into the ticket office and asked the clerk when the next west-bound passenger train was leaving.

"It'll be in at noon. Do you need a ticket sir?"

"I've already got a ticket," he said. "I need to check on a few things first. I may stay around for a few days. I'm not sure." J.D. thanked the man and headed to the door. He noticed a large route map on the wall next to the counter and stopped to look. What surprised him was how close Little Rock was to Memphis. *Hell, Dallas is too close*. He began to wonder how far would be far enough away from his past. It didn't take long for him to conclude that wherever he ended up would need to be a long way from Tennessee.

When he got back to the hotel, he picked up a day-old Memphis newspaper and went up to his room. Looking at the newspaper had become a habit and it was one that sometimes paid off. Spotting the article in the Memphis newspaper about the fire in Kentucky had led him to Little Rock. When he got to page five, he knew he needed to get out of Arkansas today. He read the short article about the fire in Memphis, noting that nearly eighty cars had been destroyed and that the police, although they couldn't confirm the story, believed that the fire may have been an accident. There was no mention of suspects or reasons. J.D. hoped that he had covered his tracks well enough, but any one of the men he'd hired to help with the coal oil might talk and eventually the trail could lead to him.

Hooper picked up his two suitcases and left the room. When he checked out at the reception desk, he told the clerk that he needed to head west to conclude some business. At the depot, he showed his ticket to the man behind the counter and said he'd be leaving for Dallas on the noon train. He went back to the map on the wall and measured the distance from Little Rock to Dallas and then from there to El Paso.

He turned to the clerk. "Does the train go as far as El Paso?"

"Yes sir, it does, but it'll take a few days and you'll have to make changes in Dallas and again in San Antonio."

"Thanks," J.D. mumbled, already thinking about that distant city, wondering what it was going to look like and if there would be work for him to do in far west Texas.

Chapter 11

Two days later, after the fire department had put out the flames, and soaked the remaining coals, the detectives watched as the men in bibbed overalls pulled charred pieces of wood from between the rails. They tossed the boards onto the pile growing next to the track. Jensen bent down and inspected the wood, lifting one piece and sniffing it.

"It's faint," he said, "but I can smell kerosene." He handed the board to Ben and pawed through the other pieces. "Can you smell it?"

"Barely, but it sure smells like kerosene."

"Last night the police weren't convinced the fire was intentionally set."

"That's what they told us," Ben agreed. "They seemed pretty sure that this was an accident."

"We'll go talk to them later, but I want to see what else we find out here. If we don't find any melted pails or cans, it might mean that whoever set the fire took them away." Noah rose and looked at Ben. "Have you heard anything about an explosion?"

"No, just that there was a big fire."

"Then it was set by more than one person. That many cars wouldn't burn as quickly as they must have if one person started only a few cars on fire. They would have to douse the whole line, or most of it, for the fire to grow as quickly as it did."

"Seems right to me," said Ben.

"Alright, send these fellas back to their jobs and let's go talk to the police."

☆ ☆ ☆

The railroad detectives walked the few blocks to the police station. Noah said that he'd do the talking, that he wanted Ben to watch the faces of the men they met.

"One thing I've learned is that sometimes you can tell if a person is lying by what their eyes say. What they say with their mouth doesn't always match."

They checked in with the desk sergeant and were quickly escorted upstairs to meet with the precinct captain. Noah thought about all the other cops he'd met with, and how, most often they resented his questioning of their procedures and results. He didn't expect that today's meeting would be any different.

The captain was a tall, rangy man, older than both of the detectives. He stood up from his desk as they entered his office.

"Good morning, gentlemen. How can I help you?"

Noah spoke up first. "We wanted to talk to you about last night's fire and see if you or your investigators had any new information for us."

"It seems pretty clear to us that it was some sort of accident." He paused and looked at Noah, then at Ben. "Things like this do happen occasionally."

"When we were at the scene this morning, Captain, we noticed that the site smelled like kerosene."

"My officers found nothing like that," he said, folding his arms across his brass-buttoned chest.

"That's odd," said Noah. But not wanting to totally alienate him he added, "We'll be carrying out our own investigation and will be happy to share anything we discover."

The captain spoke briefly about how his detectives

follow rigid procedures and have a fine record of closing cases. Throughout the man's monologue, Ben watched and listened.

☆ ☆ ☆

Once the two railroad detectives were back on the street, Noah asked Ben to tell him what the cop's eyes had said.

"You were right. Every time he said something about procedures, or what his men did, his eyes didn't seem to match what his lips were saying." Ben shook his head. "If he wasn't exactly lying to us, he sure wasn't telling the whole truth."

"You're right," said Noah. "but we won't need to do anything about that now. Pointing it out to him later when we do solve the crime will be a lot more fun. By the way, let's get some wanted posters made. We don't have a picture or description of a suspect or suspects, but we do have a crime and a time-frame."

Ben said he'd get on that when they got back to the office. "I'll send them out on all of the outgoing trains. They'll get dropped off at each stop going in all directions."

Back in Ben's office, Noah laid out the rest of his plan. He told Allenby that he'd want to meet with each of the customers who'd lost product. "Since we held the manifests, they will want to file claims against the company and against their insurance companies as well. Maybe we'll find out if one of them wanted or needed their product destroyed."

"Alright, Noah, I'll try to get them in here tomorrow. If they won't come here, we'll meet at their offices here in town."

"Good." Noah looked at his notes and said, "Then, I'm going to spend a few days snooping around Memphis. I want to find out where the union offices are so I can pay them an official visit and ask them if they have any concerns I could share with Harriman. After that, I'll need to hang out in some of the city's nicer areas to see if I get a sense of any anarchist involvement."

"How are you going to do that?"

"Most anarchists aren't Americans, so I'll go where the Italians or Greeks or Serbs drink in town. Their organizations are very secretive, but the individuals usually like to brag about what they do. I'm thinking that a few nights of listening should give me an answer to my questions." Noah stood. "After I send an update to Harriman, I'm going back to the hotel and take a nap. I'll need the rest if I'm going to spend my nights drinking *Chianti* and *Ouzo*."

Chapter 12

Hooper watched the conductor make his way from the front of the car, stopping at each row of seats, checking for tickets and chatting with the passengers. Little Rock was already twenty miles behind him and Memphis farther still, yet J.D. could feel the piercing eyes of the police as they searched across the miles for the Kentucky killer and Tennessee arsonist. Part of him knew that he was being foolish, but he couldn't shake the feeling of being followed.

The scenery out the window hadn't changed much since leaving Little Rock. The trees and fields, farms and towns, mules, cows, and sharecroppers always seemed to be there. The swaying of the railcar had nearly rocked him to sleep when the conductor tapped him on the shoulder. Startled, J.D. stared up at the uniformed man.

"May I see your ticket please, sir?"

J.D. blinked his eyes and then pulled the ticket out of his coat pocket, looked at it, and placed it in the conductor's hand.

"Looks like you can go as far as the end of the tracks, sir." He punched a hole in the ticket and returned it to J.D. "We'll be in Dallas late this evening unless we're delayed."

"Does that happen much?" asked J.D.

"More than we'd like it to. Sometimes we have to stop for coal and water, other times we have to pull off onto a siding so the express train can pass us." He smiled at J.D. and added, "We don't get attacked by Indians much any-more and the last group of mounted train robbers has been in prison for a long time." The conductor chuckled at his own humor, but J.D. just looked away and put the ticket back in his coat.

"When's the next stop?"

"About two hours. We'll give the passengers a chance to get out and catch some fresh Arkansas air. In any case, I hope you enjoy your trip." He stepped out of J.D.'s sight and continued punching holes and telling his tired joke to the other passengers. J.D. glanced over his shoulder, wondering if he'd been recognized by anyone on board. He had started to wonder how far he'd have to go to get rid of the feeling of pursuit. He believed that putting hundreds of miles between him and what he'd done would be enough. But something else was poking at his thoughts, something he couldn't pin down. Whatever it was, it unsettled him and made him edgy. *Only one way to fix that*, he thought as he pulled the whiskey bottle from his pocket and sipped the pungent liquid. By the time the train stopped for water and coal, J.D. had relaxed.

He'd exited the train along with most of the passengers and wandered from the tracks to a small saloon across the dirt road. The place was crowded with thirsty passengers. Reaching the front of the line, he bought two pints of whiskey and walked back outside. The conductor had been right about the Arkansas air. The surrounding fields of cotton and corn smelled a lot like home. The breeze pushed the foul smoke away as it carried the aroma of plants and dirt from the rolling fields. J.D. wasn't often nostalgic, but being in the country did remind him of where he'd come from and that he'd likely never go back. J.D. took a swallow of his new whiskey and walked to the train.

☆ ☆ ☆

When the train arrived in Dallas, Hooper wanted a few days away from the constant motion of the passenger car so he rented a room in a hotel a few blocks from the station. This city didn't appeal to him. Like Memphis, Dallas was built on a river, but the Trinity River wasn't nearly as majestic as the Mississippi and seeing the rail yard and warehouses reminded him too much of the mess he'd left in Tennessee.

He wandered around the growing city and found it interesting that commerce in Dallas wasn't much different than he'd seen in Memphis. Freight moved from the boxcars to warehouses and then from storage to the stores on the streets. He supposed that there were people like Chester Lowell doing business as well, but he wasn't ready to get back to work yet.

Later that evening, when he stepped out of the hotel lobby onto the crowded sidewalk a man bumped into him. J.D. grabbed onto the man's arm to keep from losing his balance then noticed that the man was holding J.D.'s leather wallet.

"What the hell are you doin'?"

J.D. grabbed the fella's wrist with his free hand and snapped it over his knee. The man screamed as the bones broke. Dropping the wallet onto the sidewalk, he tried to pull away from Hooper, but J.D. wouldn't release his limp arm.

"Let me go," screeched the man. "You broke my arm."

"How'd you like me to just rip it off and beat you over the head with it?"

The thief's cries of pain had drawn a crowd that was soon joined by a police officer. He blew on his whistle and muscled his way through the mob until he got close to J.D. and the pickpocket. Hooper was instantly on alert, uncomfortable being so close to the officer.

"What's going on here?"

"He broke my arm an' I didn't do nothin'," croaked the pickpocket.

"Did you break his arm?" the cop asked J.D.

"I did when I found it was holdin' my wallet." J.D. bent down and picked up the leather pouch from the sidewalk. He showed it to the policeman. "This crook was tryin' to steal it from me."

"What's your name?" the cop asked.

J.D. just ignored him and started counting his money. "It's all here."

The cop looked around at the crowd and said, "Alright, folks, the excitement's over. Let's move along." He pushed a few boys out of the way and then asked J.D. if he was hurt.

"No, I ain't. But this fella is."

"As long as you aren't hurt, Mister, you can go about your business and move along. However, violence isn't acceptable in our city, no matter what the reason. As for you," he said, looking at the crook, "you are going to spend the night in my jail and maybe tomorrow or the next day we'll look at getting your arm wrapped." He grabbed the pickpocket by the collar and held onto the damaged arm as he dragged him down the sidewalk through the remainder of the crowd. J.D. could still hear the screaming pickpocket as the cop turned the corner, and it felt good. J.D. smiled happily. *Got what he deserved.*

Hooper slipped the wallet back into his pocket and settled his hat firmly on his head. A few of the men in the crowd patted him on the back as he walked away. While he headed to the restaurant he'd been at earlier, J.D. decided that maybe he'd get a chain put on the wallet to keep from losing it again. *I guess there's crooks in Dallas too,* he thought. As he walked down the street, he thought he might even stay in the city longer than he'd planned. *Maybe this town will grow on me.*

☆ ☆ ☆

But two days in Dallas convinced J.D. that the city just

didn't feel right. The activity in the city wasn't like Memphis. There were no steamboats, no bales of cotton, no crates filled with tools. He'd looked around, watched the activity on the streets and decided that it was time to head west. He went to the depot and confirmed that he could still ride the train. As he was leaving, he passed a wall that was covered with advertisements, notices, and the occasional wanted poster. He'd taken a few steps beyond the wall before he realized that he'd seen a poster that mentioned a fire in Memphis. J.D. returned to the wall and pulled the sheet of paper from the board.

WANTED
Person or Persons Unknown
For Arson
A SUBSTANTIAL REWARD
will be offered for information leading to the arrest
and conviction of suspects wanted for the
Wanton Destruction of One Hundred Railcars
Contact Southern Pacific Railroad or Illinois Central
Railroad Office, Memphis, Tenn.

Crumpling the paper in his fists, J.D. rushed back to the hotel to pack his bags. *Ain't nothin' to worry about yet,* he thought. But the knowledge that information about what he'd done had already reached Dallas nipped at his mind. He checked out of the hotel and returned to the depot.

The train took J.D. south and west into the Hill Country of Texas. The landscape was a little different than he was used to. There were lots of trees and limestone bluffs, but Texas was different than Kentucky and Tennessee. He finally arrived in San Antonio but decided to stay on the train until he reached El Paso. *It's gotta be better there, don't it? I mean, there is the Rio Grande River and Mexico.*

Chapter 13

The next week was a busy one for Noah. During the days, he and Allenby met with a half dozen customers who had lots of questions. Most of them had legitimate concerns about their own customers and wanted assurances from Jensen that the railroad would make them whole. For these individuals, Noah made commitments he felt would be honored by Harriman. There were two of them, however, who were less forthcoming with information and even seemed unconcerned about their losses. Although he had plans to look deeper into this situation, he decided to let the issue rest for a few days. During the nights, however, he hung out in a handful of bars and saloons to try and gather intelligence on the fire.

On this night, Noah was wearing worn out overalls and a dirty shirt, and he sat slumped over a glass of *chianti* in the back of a place frequented by Italians. Two fellas, one old and the other much younger, sat down at his table.

"Hey," said the old man, "you gonna drink all of that vino by yourself?"

Noah looked up at the wrinkly face and put his hand over his mouth and covered his ear then shook his head.

"What? You a dummy?"

Noah frowned and nodded, then looked down at his half-filled glass.

"Tha's too bad."

Noah forced a confused look onto his face, then shoved the basket-wrapped bottle toward the men. He watched the man's mouth hoping he'd think he was reading his lips. Playing the mute, he thought, would keep him from revealing his American accent.

"You wanna share?" asked the young man.

Noah shrugged his shoulders and took a drink. The others filled their own glasses, lifted them toward Noah and smiled. Then they began to talk to each other and Noah listened.

For the rest of the week, he used the same cover in other bars but heard nothing that suggested any subversive group had a role in the fire. He was surprised to learn that a lot of the laborers seemed to hold a grudge against some of the anarchists. Noah was certainly going to let Harriman know about this discovery.

His meetings with the union had provided no surprises. The leadership was cordial but continued to press the company for changes in hours and pay and benefits. They made no threats, at least no specific ones, but left the option open. When he questioned them about the fire, they stressed how concerned they were that now many of their members would be out of work until the tracks were cleared and trains were running again. They suggested that he might try to get the company working harder to accomplish their long-standing requests for better pay. In short, they pushed him and he, as a member of company headquarters, pushed back.

"What this means," Noah said to Ben as they sat at lunch, "is that unless I can get some clarity from the two customers who seem disinterested, the fire was an accident—which I don't accept—or it was intentionally started by another party to either assist these customers or to influence them. It has to be one of these last two options."

"How will you find out which one it is?" asked Ben.

"This is where your knowledge of riverfront operations comes in, Ben. I want you to walk me around the wharf area, tell me about the movement of freight from the river to the yards to the warehouses. Then tell me who's involved in each of the movements. If we can find out who controls this activity, the man who holds the power, we might be able to discover if he had a role in the fire. Maybe he was trying to make a statement."

"Even if we do find out, do you think that whoever this person is he'll even talk to us, let alone tell us why he started the fire?"

"Good thinking, Ben. I don't believe anyone is going to openly confess that they burned our boxcars to influence their customers to be loyal, but loyalty is important, and we shouldn't overlook it. I also think no one will tell us what really happened because of their fear of the man in power." He smiled at Ben and said, "But if I sense that either of these things led to the fire, I have one more trick up my sleeve."

Allenby nodded slowly. He knew that Noah would tell him about his plan when it was necessary for him to know. "Then I guess we'd better get out to the wharf and start nosing around. I'll tell you what I know, and we can ask the people who work down here. Lots of the wharf workers will talk if you hand them a little money. But you still can't entirely trust what they say. The foreigners will take the money and maybe give some truth in what they tell us. In any case we can probably put a story together and might even get the name of who's in charge around here."

For the next few days Noah and Ben snooped around the wharf and the rail yard. They walked along the riverfront where the warehouses stood and where wagon traffic flowed seemingly without end. They talked to local and immigrant workers, warehouse and wagon owners. Ben even introduced Noah to the cop whose beat was the wharf.

"Good morning, Frank."

"Hi, Ben. How's your investigation goin'?"

"We're still trying to find out information." He paused

to introduce Noah. "This is Noah Jensen, a detective with the Southern Pacific."

"I've seen you around the area," Frank said.

"Nice to meet you, officer." The two men shook hands. "I've been here a while, but right now we're trying to find out who decided to burn up our railyard. Maybe you can help."

Frank knew Ben, but not Jensen. Cautiously, he said, "I might."

"Who in the city would stand to gain if the yard or a hundred cars were destroyed? Who runs things down here?"

"Well, Mr. Jensen, most people would agree that Chester Lowell runs a lot of different businesses in the area."

"Would he have benefited from the fire at the rail yard?" asked Noah.

"Not that I've heard."

"Would he have used a fire to convince his...associates that it would be in their interests to work with him?"

"Now, see here," said Frank. "Mr. Lowell is an upstanding member of the community. I don't know what rumors you've heard but Chester Lowell has never been in trouble with the Memphis Police Department. We keep things under control down here."

"I'm sure that's the case, Frank." Noah said, realizing he'd touched a nerve. He had no reason to believe that this officer was on the take, but it was all too common in police departments. He'd seen it in San Francisco.

"I hope we can call on you for your assistance when we have any suspects." The detectives shook hands again with Frank and walked away. Footsore and dry-mouthed, they went back to Ben's office.

"We discovered two things," Noah said. "We know that the man with the power down here is Chester Lowell, and that using violence, including fire, to influence his customers or potential customers is entirely possible. We also found out nothing about any specific individual who may have carried out an assignment for Lowell. But I know that someone like Chester Lowell would have trusted employees."

Noah sat quietly for a moment then leaned across the desk. "Ben, it's time to spring the trap. If Lowell ordered the fire and he hired an individual to set it, then that man had to have some help to spread the kerosene. His helpers might be able to give us a name."

"How do we find out who helped?"

"That's the trick up my sleeve. I'll offer a reward for any information that leads to a name or description. Some underpaid laborer who picked up a few dollars to splash kerosene on a boxcar will probably be willing to come forward for a large reward as long as he knows we'll keep his name out of it."

☆ ☆ ☆

Ben sent Noah's reward notice to a printer and by the next afternoon most of the two hundred copies could be seen all over the wharf. A half dozen boys earned a dollar apiece to stick them on the sides of buildings, lamp posts, and the back of freight wagons. Noah was confident that one or more of the arsonist's helpers would see the notice and be interested in having the two-hundred-dollar reward in his pocket.

While they waited for the bait to catch the fish, Noah and Ben watched the activity at the saloon where Lowell carried out his business. They wanted to see if he had any regular visitors.

"Lowell is pretty smart running his business out of a saloon," Noah said to Ben.

"I was thinking the same thing. With all the fellas going in and out of the place it's hard to tell the drinkers from his freight customers or the ones who work for him."

"That's why I think we need to try something else. We're going to stop watching this place. Let's get something to eat and head back to your office."

They left the alley and walked back toward the train yard, spotting several of the reward notices along the way. "We should've heard from someone by now, don't you think?"

"Maybe someone has stopped at the office, Ben. But think about this. If you helped burn up eighty railcars and only got paid a few dollars, would you walk into the office of the fella who owned the cars and hope that he was going to give you a lot of money and not turn you in to the police?"

"It would take some consideration, I suppose." Ben was lost in thought as they walked along the street. "But maybe he'd just come in and say he *heard* about someone who *might* have been involved and then give us a name or a description?"

"If I was an arsonist's helper that's how I would do it," said a smiling Noah. "You must be a detective."

They laughed as they entered a small café near the wharf. It was an hour after lunchtime, so they had no trouble finding a table. A waiter took their order, poured them some coffee, and rushed away to the kitchen. While they waited, Ben asked Noah about his other cases. He was interested in some of the techniques Noah used, especially when it came to investigating the often mundane problems that railroad detectives encountered. Noah gave him some ideas, and, like a good detective, Ben began taking notes.

After the waiter dropped the check on the table, a man in baggy overalls leaned over Ben's shoulder and spoke quietly.

"If ye're the railroad men and want to hear somethin' about the fire, meet me in the alley." The man turned away and walked quickly out the door.

"What'd he say?" Noah asked.

"He said to meet him in the alley if we want to hear about the fire," Ben said.

The two detectives rose from their chairs, left some money on the table, and walked out the door. They saw an alley just to the right of the café, so they walked to it and looked into the shadows. Ben spotted the man standing behind a broken crate.

"Let's go find out if he knows anything," said Noah.

When they drew closer, the man walked another few paces into the alley and stopped at the back corner of the building. He turned to face the detectives and asked, "Would ye be the fellas givin' the reward?"

"Yes we are. Why don't we go over to our office where we can talk in private?"

"No!" the man said louder than he intended. "I can't be seen with ye. They'd beat me or worse if they saw me talkin' to ye." The man's eyes shifted around.

"Then why are you talking to us?"

"Do you wanna hear about the fire or not?"

"Hold on, calm down and tell us what you know about the fire. We won't let anyone beat you up."

"Maybe I might just be knowin' someone who coulda been around when that fire was set," he said, his voice barely audible.

"Well, sir, 'might' and 'coulda' aren't the kinds of words that earn rewards of two hundred dollars." Noah paused and watched the man's face. He could tell that the fella wanted the money but also didn't want anyone to know he was talking to the detectives.

"But," Noah continued, "If you had a name or description of someone you *know* was involved in setting the fire, and if it turned out that you were right, the reward money would probably be enough for you to travel a long way from Memphis."

Noah was certain that getting out of the city was on the man's mind. He'd questioned suspects before and was fairly sure that this fella had probably splashed kerosene on a railcar or knew who did. But he was more interested in who wanted the cars destroyed than in some broken down worker who needed a few dollars.

"This is how the reward offer is going to work. You tell me what you know, and we'll check out your story. While we do that, you go about your business. There isn't any reason for you or us to let others know what's going on. If we discover that you've given us what we want, we'll give you the money in cash."

The man looked at each of the detectives, clearly wishing he was someplace else. "The fella I know who was at the fire said he was hired by a man who worked for some important people in town." He swallowed hard and kept talking. "He said the man who paid him usually hung out at the Big River Saloon."

"Did your friend know this man's name?"

"He didn't say the man's name but he told me that this fella wore a derby hat and when he was done with the job he went to an old warehouse and paid him good money to keep quiet."

"So, all I need to do is walk into the Big River, look for a man with a derby hat—half of the men in the country wear one—and then ask him if he paid a bunch of men to burn my railcars?"

The man looked nervous and he started to walk out of the alley.

"Hold on, fella," said Noah. "I just need more information than the kind of hat this man wears. Did your friend say anything else about the man with the hat, like how tall he was, what kind of clothes he wore, did he have a mustache? Anything like that?"

It appeared to Noah that the man knew more than he

had told them. When he spoke again, the words had authority and truth in them. "The man had a mustache and wore good clothes, like he was in business and didn't just work on the wharf. He had scary blue eyes, like he could look into your head and know what you were thinkin'."

"Go on. Did your friend say anything else?"

"He said that the fella didn't have a real name, that he used letters."

"You mean that instead of a name he used initials?"

The man nodded.

"Did your friend say which letters?"

Shaking his head, the man whispered, "No, that's all he said and that's all he knows."

Noah leaned toward the man and looked into his eyes. "Stay here for a minute while my partner and I talk and we'll be right back." The detectives walked away up the alley and spoke quietly. Ben was convinced that the fella had helped with the fire and Noah nodded. The two men agreed on a plan and returned to the back of the alley.

"If you can get your friend to go back to the Big River Saloon and find out what initials the other fella used, I'll be ready to give you the two hundred dollars."

"He can't."

"He can't what?" asked Noah.

"I...my friend can't go there and even if he could he wouldn't find the man."

"And why is that?"

"The man with the derby hat don't come around anymore. Maybe he left town."

"So, you...I mean your friend...knows that the man who paid him, the one with the strange first name, doesn't live in Memphis anymore?"

"That's right. He did say that the fella worked for someone at the saloon, someone who was a big shot. That's all I know." He looked at Noah. "When can I get the money?"

"My partner and I need to find out if your story makes sense. We have to pay a visit to the Big River and confirm some of the things you've told us. If it turns out that your friend told you the truth, you will get the reward. I want you to keep all of this...all of this to yourself and come back here first thing tomorrow morning, alright?"

The man nodded and scurried out of the alley.

"What do you think?" asked Ben.

"I think we need to go get a drink. What do you say we drop in at the Big River Saloon? There won't be any reason to talk to Chester Lowell because he wouldn't tell us anything anyway. But I imagine that the bartender would know if someone with initials for a first name used to work for Lowell."

Ten minutes later they walked into the saloon, stepped up to the bar, and ordered beers. Noah placed a twenty-dollar gold piece in front of the bartender. They chatted with the man a few minutes, but got nothing from him but their beers and change. Then Will walked out from behind the bar and headed back to Lowell's office.

"He certainly wasn't any help," Noah said, glancing around the room. Spotting a young boy sweeping in the back of the room, Noah walked away from the bar and approached the boy.

"Excuse me, young man, can I ask you something?"

The boy stood stiffly in front of Noah, both hands clutched tightly around the broom handle.

"I'm looking for a man who may have worked around here."

"Yes, sir."

"I've forgotten his name, but I know he uses his initials and not a regular name." Noah's voice was gentle. "Do you remember a man who used his initials and wore a derby hat?"

"I gotta get back to sweepin', sir. The boss don't like

me talkin' to the customers an' not doin' my work," he said, looking toward the office door.

Noah sensed that the boy knew something, so he took a silver dollar out of his pocket and offered it to him.

"I have another one of these for you if you tell me this man's name."

Samuel looked toward the office door again and licked his lips. Turning to Noah, he quickly said, "The man's name is Mr. J.D. Hooper, sir."

"You're sure?"

Samuel nodded, took the second coin from Noah, quickly moved away from the detective, and went back to work.

When Lowell and Will came out of the office, the detectives were gone.

"Samuel, get over here."

The boy walked up to Lowell.

"Did you see where the two men who were at the bar went?"

"No sir, Mr. Lowell, I didn't see nobody."

"You sure?

"Yes, sir. I didn't see no one."

"Okay, get back to work." Lowell told Will to get Axel and Mort and to make it quick.

☆ ☆ ☆

Once they were on the street and walking away from the saloon, Ben asked, "Did that kid have anything to say?"

"J.D. Hooper," Noah said. "The boy said his name was J.D. Hooper. It sounds like we have ourselves a suspect."

Back in the office, Noah sent a telegram to Harriman telling the president that he had a named suspect who may have left Memphis. The description of the man was vague—medium height, medium build, always wears a derby—but he also added that he'd keep looking for him. Noah told Ben that they needed to find out where Hooper lived and if he truly had left Memphis. For now, though, they were going to keep this information to themselves.

"Let's get another wanted poster made and be sure to add the description, maybe even get a sketch drawn. Put some up here in Memphis in case he's still here, but do like you did earlier and put them on all of the outbounds. It may take a week or so for them to catch up with him, but they will catch up."

Chapter 14

Noah had a suspect, a name, a description, but no one in custody. The morning after hearing J.D. Hooper's name for the first time, he expected to be the first one in the office. But when he tried the door, it was open and Ben was making a pot of coffee.

"Morning, Noah. Coffee will be ready in a few minutes."

"What are you doing here so early?"

"I never went home. It didn't seem to make sense 'cause I probably wouldn't have slept anyway."

"If you don't sleep, you won't be much help when the days start getting long."

Ben took the coffee pot off the coal stove and filled two cups. Noah held his cup to his lips and blew the steam away.

"Did you come up with any ideas during your long night?" asked Noah.

"Not exactly, but I made a lot of notes, mostly on two lists."

"What do you mean?"

"I figured there were two parts to our case—what we know and what we don't know."

"Okay, good start. Did you write these things down or did you lose them in your sleep-deprived brain?"

"Drink your coffee, Noah, and I'll share them after you wake up."

They laughed, but not heartily, and grew serious. Ben had dragged a long wooden table into his office and spread his notes across the flat, smooth surface. Noah noticed that each side of the table held several different stacks of paper.

"Might as well start with what we know," Ben said. "That way we can start with the little good news we have."

"So," Noah said, "what do we know?"

Ben went through the various short stacks of notes, giving Noah a summary.

"We know that the fire was not an accident, it was arson caused by coal oil. We know that it was probably set by a team of men, led by a man called J.D. Hooper. We know that he likely worked for Chester Lowell, a seemingly successful businessman who is suspected of controlling the labor and movement of goods and services on the waterfront."

"We know, or are at least fairly certain, that our chief suspect, Hooper, has *probably* left Memphis for parts unknown. We also know that Hooper paid his arson team with cash, and that at least one of these men is an Irish immigrant. This suggests, but can't be confirmed, that likely the rest were Irish."

Ben stopped for a moment and sipped his cooling coffee.

"Hooper seems to have lived somewhere relatively close to the Big River Saloon, Lowell's center of operations, but we haven't been able to find a specific location."

Noah rose from his chair, went to the stove, and refilled his cup.

"We know that the damage to the cars was extensive, but the yard, the buildings, and the rails sustained little damage. The losses in money are unknown at this time, but eighty or more totally destroyed boxcars filled with customers' goods will cost us and the insurers several hundred thousand dollars."

Ben stopped, shuffled through his notes, and looked up at Noah. "That's it, as much as I can remember anyway."

"Good work Ben. But what *don't* we know?"

"That list is longer, but to put it short and sweet, we

don't know *who* authorized, and likely paid for, the arson. We don't know *why* the cars were burned. We don't know *where* Hooper is, where the arson crew came from, or where they stored the coal oil and the means to carry it to the tracks."

Noah set his cup on Ben's desk, stood, and paced across the floor. He was silent. Ben simply watched him.

"I guess that means we go to work. We have to find Hooper. He's the one who can lead us to the others. He's the one with coal oil on his hands and dirty money in his pockets. He is the key." Noah paused and pulled his necktie tight in his collar. "Let's go find him."

The detectives spent the rest of the day laying out plans, discussing possibilities, and dividing up the work. Ben would meet with the reward-seeker, and before paying him would try to get more information. His objective was to identify the crew and, as a result, get a dozen new pieces of information.

Noah would find out where Hooper lived, ate, and drank. Somewhere in all of that would, or at least might, be a clue to where Hooper went.

"Ready to go to work, Ben?"

"I am. How about you?"

"Yep. Let's go solve a case."

☆ ☆ ☆

The detectives split up to work the investigation. Ben went alone to the alley as they had planned. The Irishman may not show, although Ben believed he would. So, he carried two-hundred dollars in his coat pocket and a revolver in a shoulder holster under his left arm. He walked from the office to the alley near the café and arrived before the Irishman.

A pile of rubbish had been tossed in the alley which gave the dark, narrow space a foul odor.

Ben knew that anyone coming into the dark alley from the bright daylight of the street would need a few seconds before their eyes could attain a reasonable level of sight. But those first ten to twenty seconds were critical and would give him an advantage he might need, especially if the Irishman had changed his mind and had plans to not play fair.

But his concern was unfounded. About fifteen minutes after he'd come into the alley, Ben heard footsteps on the walk and then a silhouette of a man filled the space at the mouth of the alley. The visitor stopped, unable to see, and shuffled slowly into the narrow space.

"Are ye there?" said the Irishman, his voice low. He moved a few more paces into the alley.

"I'm back here," said Ben. "Do you still want to talk in here or go into the café?

"There ye are. I see ye now." He moved to within a yard of Ben and stopped.

"Do ye have the money, the reward?"

"I do, but I want to talk a bit first. Stay here or get out of this stinking alley, it's your choice."

"If they see me with ye, I'll be a dead man."

Before he spoke again, Ben made sure he had room to maneuver if it became necessary. "We checked out what you told us and it's mostly true," he fibbed. "But before I can give you any money, I have a few more questions."

"That ain't what we agreed to yesterday," the Irishman said, his voice taking on an edge.

"As I said, most everything you told us checked out. But I need to know one more thing. You give me an honest answer and you'll get your reward."

"I ain't gonna answer any more questions."

"Then I'll be leaving," said Ben as he walked toward the street.

"Wait then," said the Irishman, "don't be hasty. Whatta

ye wanna know?"

Ben stared at the man's face in the alley's shadows and could tell that he'd be willing to answer the questions—at least one of them.

"I've got the money in my pocket and it'll be in yours when I get an honest answer to one of the two questions I'm going to ask."

"I only gotta answer one?"

"Right, but the answer has to be true. Don't try to lie to me, 'cause I'll know."

The Irishman wiped his face with his gnarly hand, considered his options, and afraid that he'd not get the money, said, "Go ahead and ask."

"The first question is where did the fella with the derby find you and the rest of the crew."

"He didn't find me. I didn't..."

"You're lying."

"No..."

"You are lying, and if you still want the reward, you gotta tell the truth."

"What's the other question?"

Ben watched the man's eyes as they shifted in their sockets, and his nostrils flared as he took in a deep breath.

"Where did you store the coal oil and fill the buckets?"

The Irishman considered his choices—give up his friends or point out a building. He'd be leaving Memphis soon anyway, but his loyalty ran too deep to tell the detective about Paddy's Pub.

"We filled the pails in a warehouse."

"Which warehouse? Where?"

Ben opened his coat, letting the distant daylight reflect off the steel of his pistol, then repeated the question. "Where?"

"It's close to the railyard," gulped the man. "Not more than a block away."

"Before I give you the money, you'll either show me the building or draw a map." Ben waited for a response. "What's it gonna be?"

"I'll show ye, but we can't be seen together."

"That's fine," Ben said. "You walk out of this alley and go directly to the warehouse. I'll follow you a half-block behind. When you're in front of the warehouse, you take off your hat and put it back on, then keep walking."

"Then I get the money?"

"Keep walking at least a block and step into the first alley you come to. I'll follow in a few minutes and you'll have your reward."

The man walked out of the alley and headed toward the railyard. Ben walked to the street and waited a minute then followed him. Five minutes later, just a block past the tracks, the man slipped his hat from his head and quickly replaced it. Without stopping he continued away from the building and turned in to an alley.

Ben noted the building's address and walked quickly into the narrow alley. He pulled the small stack of twenty-dollar bills from his pocket and handed them to the Irishman. After quickly counting them, the man looked at Ben then walked briskly away.

Ben waited for a few minutes, then walked back to the warehouse. The only remarkable thing he noted about the building was the new lock on the hasp of the door. Ben looked through the spider web-covered window into the dim open space and saw an oil drum and a dozen or so stacked pails against a wall.

Better get to Noah and fill him in, then bring some lights so we can search for clues, he thought. *Then maybe we can find out who owns this place.*

Chapter 15

The first thing J.D. saw when he woke up and looked out the window of the train was that there was nothing but brown dirt and scattered, dull-green cactus plants. As far as he could see the land was flat and sandy. The sky was still blue, but it was a blue he'd never seen before. There were no clouds and the few visible birds were large, black ravens floating high above the desert. J.D. was looking at a strange new world. Keeping his eyes focused on the distant mountains, he imagined that the train was standing still, and the ground was coming toward him. The tall, dark, rocky crags grew larger as the earth moved beneath him.

Even though it was still spring and early in the morning, the heat from the relentless sun was intense inside the passenger car. J.D. removed his coat, loosened his tie and slid the window down as far as it could go. But even his sweat didn't last long in the oven-like heat. He thought about taking a drink of whiskey but couldn't seem to make the effort. *First thing I'm gonna do when we get there is go jump in the river. Clothes and all, it won't make no difference. I gotta cool off.*

The quiet in the passenger car was interrupted by the yelling conductor. "Good mornin' folks! We'll be in El Paso in forty minutes." He strode up the aisle, his voice booming. "We'll be in El Paso in forty minutes, so start gathering your things together."

Church is over, J.D. thought as people began scurrying

around and talking with the folks they'd been quietly sitting next to for the past few days. Most of them seemed to have forgotten about the heat as they slipped on their coats and knotted up their ties. J.D. remained seated and continued to stare out the window. He saw the city and its tall buildings, the rising smoke from factories and smelters, and the spread of shacks among the hills on the far side of the valley. J.D. finally noticed a long, green band of trees running from the northwest right into the middle of the town. *Must be the river, the Rio Grande. Sure hope the water's cold.*

The train screeched to a stop in front of the Union Depot, a large brick building with a tower. J.D. stepped from the car and, as relieved as he was to be outside, he discovered that the noon sun was bright and hot. He didn't wait for a porter, but picked up his bags and hurried into the cavernous interior hoping to find relief. The crowd from the train began to blend into the throng inside the building and J.D. got shuffled off to one side of the massive doors. Hungry and thirsty, he spotted a Harvey House Restaurant. Dodging luggage carts hauled by young porters, he trudged across the tiled floor toward the eatery. Fortunate enough to find a seat at the counter, he ordered the first thing on the menu and told the waitress to bring him a glass of cold water.

"We're kinda busy right now, so your lunch'll take a while. But I'll get the water right away."

"Thank you," he croaked. "Is it always this hot?"

"Yes sir, most of the time, except maybe at Christmas."

J.D. sat on a stool much softer than the hard, wooden seat of the passenger car. The freshly delivered glass of cold water soothed his dry throat. The large room was filled with the sound of people talking, laughing, and yelling in Spanish. In his whole life he'd heard nothing but English and even though the foreign tongue made no sense to him it sounded different, even musical. *If I end up stayin' here,*

I'm gonna need to learn some of them words.

The waitress delivered his steak and potatoes, gave him a napkin, fork, and knife, and asked him if he needed anything else. Hooper asked for more water and began to devour the meal. With a full stomach and a moistened throat, J.D. handed her enough money to cover the check and the added tip. He pulled on his dusty derby, picked up the two suitcases and walked to the ticket counter.

"Are there any hotels nearby?"

"Yes sir," said the clerk. "There are several, all within walking distance. The Hotel Bristol is just across the street."

He crossed the street to the Bristol and took a room with a view that did not look out onto the rail yard. The bell boy carried his bags up to the third floor, opened the door to the room, and handed the key to J.D.

"Will there be anything else, *señor*?"

"Uh, no, thanks," he said, handing the boy a quarter.

"*Muchas gracias, señor.*" The young man smiled, doffed his straw hat and hurried back down the stairs.

J.D. closed the door, walked across the room, and opened the window. Pulling the curtains to the side, he slipped off his coat, placed his hat on the small desk, and stared out at the busy street. He could tell El Paso was smaller than the other cities he'd been in lately, but it certainly was just as busy. The noise from the rail yard hadn't disappeared, but it was muffled by the sounds of steel-rimmed wheels on the cobbled street and the whining of the streetcars. Most of the taller buildings were brick or stone, but beyond the busy main street, the smaller buildings were a soft brown colored plaster. He'd not yet learned about *adobe*, but in the days ahead he'd see more of it than any other type of building material.

J.D. reclined on the soft bed and quickly fell asleep.

It was just after six o'clock when the sun went down, and J.D. stepped out onto the avenue in front of the hotel.

Remembering the incident in Dallas, he checked to see that his wallet was secure in his coat then headed toward a saloon the hotel clerk had recommended. He found a seat at a small table not far from the bar that would give him a view of the patrons coming and going as well as an opportunity to overhear the conversations at the nearby tables. J.D. ordered a beer for himself and even bought one for the bartender.

"Thanks, mister. Let me know when you need a fresh one."

J.D. nodded and touched the brim of his derby. He swallowed the cold liquid and wiped the foam from his mustache, all the while scanning the room. A hazy cloud of blue smoke hung high over the tables and the buzz of conversations floated in waves. Despite the noise and the energy, Hooper was able to consider his current options now that he was a thousand miles and more than a week away from his troubles. *Nobody here's gonna recognize me. There ain't gonna be any news about a fire in Memphis or a dead body in a Kentucky farm town. I should be able to stay here for a while if I want to.* J.D. looked around the room again, *but I better have another plan just in case.*

J.D. raised his empty glass toward the bartender who quickly returned with a fresh beer. *I wager I could hear about opportunities in commerce,* he laughed to himself about his choice of words, *or maybe even look into investing in some business venture.* Once just a scraggly farmhand and more recently an enforcer for a riverfront tyrant, J.D. was surprised that he was sitting in a saloon in west Texas drinking cold beer and wondering how to handle his money. Laughing out loud and nearly spilling the fresh beer, he sat taller in the chair.

When a policeman stepped into the saloon swinging his nightstick, however, a dark cloud seemed to form behind J.D.'s sharp eyes. During the long ride across the desert he'd tried to put his concerns about pursuers into the back of his mind. He actually felt less vulnerable than he had the week before, but that nagging feeling that there was something else to fear, climbed back into his thoughts. Hooper drank the rest of his beer, thought about ordering another one, and then changed his mind. *All I gotta do is keep sober and stay out of trouble.* He rose from his chair, dropped a silver dollar on the bar and, avoiding the cop, walked out into the cool night air.

For the next few days, J.D. walked the streets of El Paso. Because of the relentless mid-day heat, he'd get up early, come back to the hotel or the saloon at midmorning, and then start out again as the sun was going down. Most of what he discovered was that El Paso was a busy town, especially in the area surrounding the rail yard and the commercial district. Just like the other cities he'd been in, freight moved in and out, money changed hands, and it seemed like everyone was buying or selling something. J.D. was certain that his recently acquired skills would work here. Opportunity awaited him; he was sure of it.

J.D. had overheard a number of conversations about the Mexican city of Juarez across the bridge. He'd learned that there were plenty of saloons and the food was spicy, but good. So, one afternoon he took a streetcar down to the river to see what the town looked like. Sitting in a front seat, he asked the streetcar driver if the people spoke American there and if they took dollars.

"They do," the driver said.

"Do what?"

"They all speak a little English and they *always* take American dollars." He stopped the car at a corner to pick up some harried passengers. Once the car was moving again, he smiled at J.D. and told him that Juarez could be a fun town but recommended keeping his money out of sight. "You might think about getting back across the bridge before dark."

Twenty minutes later, the driver pulled on the brake handle and said, "End of the line."

J.D. looked toward the man and paused at the door for a moment before he stepped onto the street and walked toward the bridge. The sun was beginning to set off to his right and cast its bright orange glow against the sparse clouds and the azure sky. The driver's words were fresh in his mind as he walked toward the bridge. Better not stay too long, he thought, still uncertain about crossing into Mexico. Approaching the structure, a strange feeling persisted, and J.D. stopped and gazed across the surprisingly narrow river to the foreign city on the other side. What he saw didn't seem fearsome—tall old buildings, dirty streets, people walking, and mules pulling wagons—but something in his gut resisted his advance. Hating his response to the feeling and angry at himself for giving in to it, J.D. turned around and walked back toward the hotel. *I can still go tomorrow*, he thought.

☆ ☆ ☆

The next morning the sun was high in the sky and its intense heat beat down on Hooper as he walked onto the bridge that crossed the Rio Grande. Stopping for a moment, he cautiously looked over the rail, and thought, *ain't as far down to the water as the one in Tennessee*. Still angry at himself for turning back the night before, he strode toward the other side. When he placed his foot down on the Mexican street he had another thought, *same dirt as on the other side. I'll just act like I belong, maybe like I have important business to do*.

A young voice interrupted his thoughts.

"Welcome to Mexico, *señor*."

J.D. looked down at the kid, frowned at him, and started to cross the street.

The boy followed J.D., pulling on the cuff of his coat. "I know the city. I can show you around. You need a hotel or a saloon or a girl, I can take you."

J.D. pulled his arm out of the boy's grasp, said no, and kept walking.

"But *señor*, I'm a good guide. For only one peso I will work for you all day."

"Listen, kid, I ain't gonna be here all day. I'm goin' to find a saloon somewhere in this town and drink some Mexican beer, so I don't need a guide."

"But, *señor*..."

"I said I don't need a guide." J.D. turned away and walked across the broad street.

The heat was merciless. Hooper took off his dark coat and slung it over his shoulder, feeling some relief, and walked into the first saloon he saw. The large room was dark and crowded, but not near as cool as he'd hoped. *Don't care how cold the beer is, this ain't gonna work*. Hoping to spot another saloon, he started walking down a side-street away from the river. The boy followed J.D., staying a few paces behind him and watched J.D. enter and leave several more places before he approached him again.

"Excuse me, *señor*, I know a place where you can get out of the sun and where the air is cool."

"I told you I don't need a guide."

"I know, *señor*, but if you follow me, I can show you a very nice, very cool place to sit." He walked closer to J.D. and looked up at him. "Please, you don't have to give me any money. Just follow me one more street. I promise that you'll like this place."

J.D. squinted in the bright sunshine, wondering if he should trust the kid.

"How far is it?"

"It's just down the street," he said, pointing toward a low adobe wall perhaps a block away.

"Okay, kid, show me."

The boy crossed the street and led J.D. to a spot next to a tall building. The adobe wall joined the taller structure and was shaded by it. In the middle of the wall was an arched gateway, and on the top of the arch was a small sign which read *Felipé's Cantina.*

J.D. looked through the arch and saw a large, pleasant courtyard with a bar and a dozen or so tables. There were several trees along the walls and, as the boy had promised, it was a lot cooler than the other saloons.

"It is cooler, *señor. Verdad*?"

"Yeah, kid, it is. Here's a nickel," said J.D., reaching into his pocket for the coin. "Thanks." He watched the boy walk away.

In the far corner, J.D. saw a group of four men in sombreros, each playing a different sized guitar, singing a song whose words he couldn't understand. Many of the Mexican patrons were singing along, especially those in the large group along one side of the courtyard. *I don't belong here. I don't understand the language and I don't know anyone,* J.D. thought. A new fear began to take over and he turned back, facing the gate. *Nope, I ain't gonna run away again*. He turned around and approached the long wooden bar.

"What would you like to drink, *señor*?" said the bartender, a fidgety man with a long drooping mustache.

"Gimme a beer."

"*Si, señor*, one *cerveza* coming up."

As soon as the foaming drink was placed in front of him, J.D. lifted it to his lips and drank nearly half of it in one draught. The cold liquid felt good in his mouth and the tingle of anxiety he'd had a moment ago disappeared quickly. He drank the other half of the beer and signaled to the bartender for another.

"Would you like something to eat, *señor*?"

"No," J.D. said, thinking about what he had heard in El

Paso. He'd been warned that sometimes the food in Juarez would make a person sick. He decided to wait and eat when he got back across the river—if he could find his way. "Thanks."

"As you wish, *señor*," said the bartender. "On this side of the river, when a man wants to thank someone he would say '*gracias*.' It means the same thing." He smiled at J.D., hoping he hadn't offended the American.

"Then *gracias* for the *cerveza*," J.D. said, remembering the word for beer the man had used before.

"Very good, *señor*, that is correct. '*Gracias por la cerveza*.' You are welcome. *De nada*."

J.D. nodded and relaxed, sipping the beer slowly. *I wonder what's the best Mexican whiskey*, he thought as his anxiety drifted away like the dust in the air.

For the next hour J.D. drank more beer and tried to not think about his problems. He focused his attention on the large group of Mexicans seated at the corner table. A heavy, round-faced fella in the middle, the one with the large sombrero and huge mustache, seemed to be an important man. When any of the Mexicans approached him, they would remove their hat and give him a little bow. J.D. clenched his jaws at the display, his ever-present loathing of authority pushing itself to the front of his thoughts. He noticed, though, that the man seemed never to lose his smile and those who came to him, despite their awe, never left afraid. *Wonder who this fella is? He kinda reminds me of Mr. Lowell.*

J.D.'s musing was interrupted when two well-dressed, extremely noisy Americans came into the saloon. They walked directly to a table in the middle of the courtyard, sat down, and yelled at the bartender.

"Felipé, bring us a bottle and make it quick."

The bartender looked at the two and reached for a bottle of clear liquor. J.D. noticed that Felipé first glanced across the cantina at the round-faced Mexican, as if looking for approval, and when the man nodded, he delivered the bottle and two glasses to the Americans' table.

"Took you long enough," one of them said. "You Mexicans are too damned slow."

"Ain't that the truth," said the other as he filled each of the glasses. He lifted one of them and handed the other across the table.

They touched their glasses together and then quickly swallowed the contents. Each of them gasped at the power of the liquor, but quickly refilled the glasses.

It must be moonshine, J.D. thought. *I might have to try it sometime.*

The two Americans continued to drink the liquor while their conversation grew louder, seeming to smother the calm atmosphere of the shady courtyard. Two children, the boy who had led J.D. to the cantina and a smaller girl, entered through the arched gateway. The girl followed the boy as he approached the Americans and asked, haltingly, if they wanted to buy a souvenir of their trip to Old Mexico.

"These are true relics of the Aztecs," he said. "Only five pesos."

"How about I give you five centavos for your hat," one of the men said, snatching the sombrero from the boy's head. He tossed it across the table to the other man and turned back to the now frightened youngster. "You want to sell me your shirt? I'll give you another centavo for it."

"No, *señor*, I need my shirt and my hat. They are not for sale."

The boy started to move away from the table but stopped when the second man said, "Ask him how much he wants for his sister." The two men roared with laughter as the boy backed away.

J.D. had heard enough. He reached into his coat pocket, pulled out his small pistol and approached the table. Keeping the gun clutched in his fist, he swung it at the man holding the boy's hat, hitting him squarely on the side of the head. When the other man began to rise from his seat, J.D. pointed the gun at him; his blazing eyes forcing the man back down. Without speaking, J.D. cocked the gun and walked around the table. He shoved the short barrel under the man's nose and pushed hard, causing blood to cover the noisy American's trimmed mustache. Hooper kept pushing until the chair tipped over backward and the man slammed into the ground.

Turning toward the first American, J.D. saw that he was already rushing for the door, dark red blood streaming from his temple, covering his ear. The man on the hard-packed ground didn't try to stand, but crabbed his way across the dirt, following his friend out of the cantina.

J.D. looked around for the kids and saw them hiding under a nearby table. He gestured to the boy to approach him. The kid was reluctant, but when J.D. slipped the pistol back into his pocket, the boy crawled out from under the table, took his sister by the hand, and walked up to J.D.

"Here's a dollar, kid. I'll buy your little statue." He handed the coin to the boy and said, "Now you and your sister get outta here and go home."

"*Gracias, señor.*"

J.D. watched them leave, finished his beer, put some money on the bar, and walked outside.

Before he reached the road, J.D. felt a hand on his shoulder.

"*Por favor*, please, *señor*, come back inside. *Es bueno*, it's okay, please," said a young man. He let go of J.D.'s coat and gestured toward the archway. "*El Jefe* would like to talk to you."

"Who's L. Heffee?" J.D. asked.

"He is a very important man, *señor*. He wants to meet you. Please, it will only take a short time."

Reluctantly J.D. followed the young man back into the

cantina, who led him to the table with the round-faced man. As he approached, he noticed that most of the people who'd been gathered around him had disappeared.

"Please, sit down," the man said in heavily accented English. "*Señor*, please relax. All is well."

J.D. turned to look for a chair and was surprised that the young man who'd escorted him to the table had placed one directly behind him. He sat down and looked warily at the big Mexican.

"*Como se llama*?"

"What?" blurted J.D., clearly not understanding the man.

"I'm sorry, *señor*," he said, a smile spreading across his face, his teeth large and smoke-stained. "I mean what is your name?"

"Hooper."

"*Señor* Hooper, let me introduce myself. I am Francisco Villa. My friends call me Pancho. My enemies call me Pancho Villa." Still smiling, he reached across the table to shake hands with J.D.

Cautiously, J.D. took his hand and waited until the Mexican finished pumping it up and down a half-dozen times.

"Well, Mr. Hooper, you are a very brave man, perhaps a little foolish, but very brave."

"What do you mean?"

"Those two *pendejos* you chased out of here are very bad men. They are well known for their evil deeds." He waited for J.D. to say something. "Tell me, *Señor* Hooper, why did you challenge them? Why did you, a *gringo*, prevent them from harming the *niños*, the boy and the girl? Most *americanos* would not care."

"It just ain't right to pick on kids."

"*Verdad*," said Villa, "that is true. Real men will always protect *los niños*. I, myself, have done this often."

J.D. watched as Villa seemed lost in a memory.

"*Señor* Hooper, you shall be my guest today here in Ciudad Juarez. Please join me and my friends. I want to hear about how a brave American such as you ended up in our beautiful country."

"I don't know," he struggled to find the words that would allow him a safe exit.

"Have no fear, *señor*, you are in the company of *El Jefe*, the greatest hero in all of Mexico," whispered an old man seated behind him.

"Tomas, don't lie to Mr. Hooper. I am a simple man, a farmer—that is all."

"As you say, *Jefe*, but you are not a simple anything," said the old man through his smile.

The two men continued to talk about other matters for a few minutes. J.D. watched them, listening to the mixed Spanish and American words. He could tell that they liked each other, but it was clear that the larger man was in charge.

"*Señor* Hooper, please join me for a drink."

J.D. Hooper and Pancho Villa spent the next several hours talking about themselves. Although J.D. confessed to having been a farmer, he didn't reveal that he'd also killed a man and destroyed the property of some very powerful men. The two men told sanitized versions of their histories while they ate Mexican food and drank more *cerveza* and some of the Mexican moonshine.

"It's called *tequila*," said Villa. "It's made from agave."

"It tastes a lot like the moonshine I used to drink in Kentucky, *Señor* Villa."

"Please, J.D., call me Pancho. You are my friend, are you not?"

"Yes sir, I guess I am." He looked out over the courtyard wall and noticed that the sky was dark. Feeling drunk, he said, "I think I'd better head back to El Paso, Pancho."

"Mr. Hooper—J.D.—please allow me to send a few of

my men with you to the bridge. I wouldn't like to hear that those cowards decided to get back at you for your valiant effort."

"I can take care of myself."

"I believe you can, *señor*, but I would be very sad if your unfamiliarity with Juarez or El Paso should result in harm to you."

"I'm going across the bridge," said J.D., "if your men want to walk with me, I can't stop 'em."

Villa and Hooper shook hands. J.D. tried to leave some money for the food and drinks, but the Mexican stopped him. "It has been *my* pleasure, J.D."

Accompanied by two of Villa's men, J.D. walked away from the cantina. They led him back through the narrow streets all the way to the river. J.D. wouldn't say so, but he was glad they'd helped him. Before he walked across the street and onto the bridge, one of the men told him about the gringos he'd confronted earlier in the day and advised J.D. to keep his eyes open for them.

"They are truly bad men," he said. "*El Jefe* is a much-loved man in *Chihuahua* and all of Mexico. Like you, he stands up for *los niños* and all of the poor people of our country. Any time you come to Juarez, you will be treated well. All of *El Jefe's* friends are treated well."

J.D. thanked them and staggered up the street, stepped slowly onto a streetcar and headed toward the hotel. Full of good food and tequila, he fell back onto his bed and thought about his new friend Pancho and passed out.

☆ ☆ ☆

After J.D. left the cantina, Villa sat with Tomas. The old man was attentive as always, ready to meet his *patrón's* needs. Villa puffed on his cigar and leaned back against the adobe wall.

"Tomas, I have been thinking how valuable it would

be to have a *gringo* I can trust, one who will be loyal." He turned to Tomas. "Perhaps *Señor* Hooper is that man."

"May I say something, *Jefe*?"

"Of course, amigo." Villa watched as his old and trusted friend struggled with his thought.

"*Señor* Hooper, is," said Tomas, "a different kind of *gringo*, of course. But *Jefe*, you have never really liked Americans."

"That is true, Tomas. But I have been thinking how useful a *gringo* would be—a *gringo* who would work for me, fight for me, trust me. I think I will give *Señor* Hooper an opportunity to prove himself to me. If he is successful, he might truly become my friend."

Tomas was old, his skin furrowed with soft wrinkles, his bushy gray brows shaded intense, youthful eyes. He'd been Villa's friend for most of the younger man's life and had learned when to talk and when to listen. This was a time for listening. If Villa wanted to test the American, Tomas would watch J.D. as well.

Chapter 16

Noah's day didn't go well at all. Although he couldn't be absolutely sure, all of his available evidence told him that Hooper had left Memphis. Even with a name and a basic description, his canvass of the saloons within ten blocks of the Big River yielded no results. He concluded that Hooper drank only at Lowell's place.

But the man had to eat and sleep, he thought, so he planned a search of cafés in a much wider area around the Big River Saloon. Thinking that Hooper likely spent much of his time at the saloon, he probably ate at least one meal somewhere close by. The few cafés in the area catered to a clientele that included bosses and office workers and Jensen couldn't picture Hooper fitting in with that crowd. But since the regular visitors he observed going into the Big River included a number of men in suits and derbies, he decided to not skip any local eateries.

He stopped at the nearest café after the morning rush was over and sat at a back table.

A tired looking waitress walked up to the table and, in a weary, yet faintly cheerful voice asked what he wanted.

"Just coffee for now," Noah said. "But I would like to ask you some questions."

She glanced back across the empty room toward the kitchen, then turned back to Noah.

"Lemme get your coffee first." She disappeared for a moment and returned with two cups and a pot of coffee.

"Here you go," she said, filling Jensen's cup and one for

herself. "You said you had some questions?"

"Yes, I do. I know your time is valuable, but I'm investigating the fire in the railyard." He slid one of his cards toward her. "I'm a detective with the Southern Pacific Railroad and I'm trying to find a man who worked in the area and may have eaten at your café."

"We get lots of men in here, lots of 'em, and they mostly all eat."

"I realize that," he said politely, hoping to relax the woman. "The man I'm looking for is of average height and weight, has a mustache, and wears a derby hat. I know all of that sounds very common, but this man's name is J.D. Hooper." He reached in his coat pocket and pulled out a folded copy of the latest wanted poster and spread it in front of her.

"Could be I've seen this fella, but it looks like a lot of the men that come in. She picked up the poster, looked at the sketch for a moment, then handed it back to Noah.

"Do you know what color eyes he has?" she asked Noah.

"We think his eyes are blue, dark blue, and piercing, like he could look into your head and know what you're thinking."

The waitress closed her eyes for a moment and then looked at Noah. "Blue, you said, and piercing?"

"Yes, ma'am, that's right."

"There's a fella who comes in here at least once a week who might be your man. But if you think he burned a train you're mistaken. I don't know his name, but the man I'm thinking about is soft-spoken, always courteous, and tips well."

"This man, your courteous customer, do you know where he lives? Have you seen him in the last week?"

"No sir, I don't know where he lives, and I haven't seen him for over a week."

"You're sure?"

"Of course. Most of the men who come in here are certainly not courteous and none of them had eyes like his."

Noah considered what she said, folded the poster, and returned it to his coat pocket. "If you see him, could you send a note to the Illinois Central office at the railyard? There's a reward for anyone who helps us find him."

"Of course, sir. I'll help if I can," she said as she rose from the chair, picked up the cups and pot, and walked to the kitchen.

Noah paid for the coffee and walked out the door.

☆ ☆ ☆

Over the next three days, Noah drank a lot of coffee, asked his questions of waiters and waitresses, cooks, and dishwashers, but got no solid leads. He sensed that most people in the café business see their customers as mouths ready to be filled with food or drink and then pushed out the door to make room for others.

"That's how it is sometimes," he mentioned to Ben when the young detective brought him up to date on his search for the fire crew. Ben had found the owner of the warehouse who was surprised that his vacant building had been used to perpetrate a crime. But he had no idea who might have done it.

"Since our snitch was Irish, I'm going to talk to my Irish cop friend, Frank, and see if he knows of any Irish gangs in town. Maybe there's a place they frequent."

"Good idea Ben. I might want to talk to Frank as well, once I finish my search of possible living quarters."

They talked about hotels, rentals, boarding houses, and such for a while, then each went back to work.

☆ ☆ ☆

Over the next two days, Noah visited all of the hotels within a mile of the saloon but discovered only that Hooper hadn't stayed in any of them. Retracing his steps, in the same neighborhoods, he found a number of boarding houses and canvassed them as well.

On the morning of the third day, he walked down South Main Street and climbed the steps of the Austin House. He knocked on the door with the brass knob and waited.

The door opened and a woman asked, "May I help you?"

Noah smiled and introduced himself. "My name is Noah Jensen. I'm looking for an associate of mine who lives here in Memphis. He never gave me his address, but I know he liked to stay in fine homes. Perhaps he stayed here at the Austin House."

"Thank you for the compliment, sir. I do have a number of gentleman residents. What is your friend's name?"

"His name is J.D. Hooper."

Noah noticed the woman's eyes sparkle.

"Mr. Hooper did stay here for a number of months, but he is no longer in Memphis."

Noah was stunned. He'd actually found where Hooper had lived.

"You say he's gone?"

"That's correct." She paused, a quizzical look on her face. "If Mr. Hooper is an associate of yours, how is it that you don't know where he lives?"

Noah quickly contrived a story. "Mr. Hooper and I worked for the same company in Baltimore a few years ago. He'd told me he might go to Memphis someday. I was in town on business and thought I'd look him up."

"I see," she said, still a little suspicious. "I'm reluctant to give out any information, since Mr. Hooper may return, and I wouldn't want to violate his privacy."

Thinking quickly and taking a chance, Noah said, "Ma'am, Mr. Hooper is my friend. Perhaps if I told you that he was a bit taller than you, had a trimmed mustache, and always wore his favorite derby hat, I could convince you to discuss him."

The woman visibly relaxed. When she spoke, her face softened. "That's certainly Mr. Hooper. I'm sorry to tell you that you've missed him. He left only a week or so ago. He said he had business elsewhere."

"Did Mr. Hooper say where he was going?"

"Hmmm," she said. "I believe he mentioned Chicago." She paused again. "Yes, I'm certain he said he had business in Chicago."

"Did he give you a forwarding address?" Noah hoped he had.

"No, just Chicago."

Noah spent a few more minutes digging gently for information, but the landlady knew nothing more that would help him find Hooper. He thanked her and headed back to the office. He planned to wire Harriman and get a train ticket to Chicago.

☆ ☆ ☆

When Noah arrived in Chicago, he didn't check into a hotel, go to the police station, or search bars for J.D. Hooper. He walked out of Union Station and headed straight to the Illinois Central office. Since the Southern Pacific owned the IC, it made it easy for the detectives to work together.

Noah wasn't sure who was in charge of the Chicago office, and he didn't have an appointment, but these things didn't matter. His badge was a free pass, an entrance card to the office of the chief detective. Noah dropped his bags behind the counter in the lobby and was led to Weldon Brackett's office.

"Mr. Jensen," he said, "please have a seat. I'm Weldon."

"It's Noah, sir. Thanks for taking the time to meet with me."

"You're welcome. How can I help you?"

"I'm looking for a suspected arsonist."

"And you think he may have headed here to Chicago?"

"Yes. I realize it's vague and inconclusive, Weldon, but we're talking close to a million dollars in losses."

"That's a significant loss whatever the cause. So, how can I help you, Noah?"

"We are convinced that this man, J.D. Hooper, planned and implemented the destruction of nearly a hundred railcars. We think he was getting paid by a Memphis criminal, but we cannot prove it yet. We believe that he might be in Chicago."

"Of course, I will make any of our free assets available to you, but Chicago is a large and complicated city. Its neighborhoods are crowded, the immigrants are typically close-mouthed, and the criminal elements, although they battle each other, stand together against the authorities."

"Not unlike many large cities," said Noah.

"Of course, but Chicago is also very, very large. The last I heard, our town is second only to New York City in population, crime, and corruption."

"Which makes my task even more difficult." Noah had thought about possible ways to find Hooper in Chicago, but what he was hearing from Weldon wasn't encouraging.

"Is there any reasonable way I could search for an individual in the city when all I have is a sketch of his quite normal face and a description that would fit half of the adult males in America?"

"Seriously, Noah, I think you'd waste time and money, drive yourself crazy, and after months, perhaps years of desperate hunting, still come up empty-handed."

"I hear you, Weldon, but I think you and I were cut from the same cloth." He paused for only a moment before he said, "You don't give up either, do you?"

Brackett's laugh was more like a howl, a joyous, belly-shaking burst of sound.

"You were a city cop before the railroad, weren't you

Noah?" His eyes dripped tears and his face turned rosy.

"I was," said Noah, and Bracket roared again.

After Weldon caught his breath and wiped his eyes, he looked out his window for a moment. When he turned back to Noah, the look on his face was serious, his voice calm and measured.

"If we were searching for a criminal in Chicago, we'd pretty much know which gang he was associated with. Like I said, they won't give us any help. They wouldn't even help for a crook they don't know. But the bigger problem is you'd be looking in an unfamiliar city, for an essentially unknown man...unknown to anyone in Chicago. Not being from here, you couldn't tell if something looked out of place or sounded odd."

He looked at Noah and saw his growing disappointment.

"I suppose you're right," Noah said. "But as much as my trip up here appears to be a lost cause, I've got to at least see the police and stop in the hotels around the immediate area. I've got plenty of copies of the wanted poster."

Weldon asked Noah if he'd checked into a hotel.

"Not yet. I came right over here."

"Tell you what, let me take you to lunch and point you in the direction of the local precinct. I know the lieutenant there and he'll actually listen to you. Then you can find a hotel, check in, and stay as long as you want."

Weldon and Noah walked out of the office a few minutes later. Then, after a brief lunch they walked to the police station. After checking in with the desk sergeant, he sent them upstairs to the lieutenant's office. Brackett introduced Noah to the officer and before heading back to his own office, said, "Good luck with you case, Noah. I hope you find your man."

They shook hands and Noah watched as he left. He spent nearly an hour with the police lieutenant describing the case and got essentially the same message from him as he had from Brackett.

Disappointed and tired, yet not discouraged, Noah set about canvassing the hotels near the railyard and depot. In the few short hours he searched for a trace of Hooper in Chicago, he realized that both Weldon and the policeman were telling him the truth. It would be futile to keep searching. He would truly be looking for a needle in a haystack. He went back to the depot, got a ticket on the next morning's train to Memphis and checked into a hotel.

☆ ☆ ☆

When he got back to Memphis, Noah met with Ben and filled him in on the wild-goose chase. They decided to re-visit the Big River Saloon.

"We can push the bartender a little harder this time," said Noah. "Maybe even talk to Lowell."

"It can't hurt to try, Noah." Ben thought about something for a bit, then said, "I've been wondering about something, but I want to make sure you agree with my idea. It's something you'll have to approve anyway."

"Tell me what you're thinking."

"It seems to me that we could approach Lowell, but not accuse him of complicity. We say we're pretty sure Hooper spent a lot of time in his saloon and was maybe even known to Lowell. But we suggest that Hooper likely acted on his own, out of anger or vengeance or something. It might get Lowell to think he's in the clear. Then we can say any help, any little bit of help he can give might lead us in the right direction. If Lowell doesn't cooperate, we will have lost nothing but time. But he just might give us a lead."

Noah was pensive a moment, then he looked at Ben. "That's brilliant, Ben. Let's go see Lowell."

☆ ☆ ☆

In his office in the back of the saloon, Lowell said, "The man had become a regular in the last several months, but he didn't work for me."

"Did you ever meet him, speak with him?" asked Ben.

"Actually, no. He was pointed out to me by Will, the bartender, but I never spoke to the man."

Noah spoke next. "Mr. Lowell, since Hooper never worked for you, yet he was a regular patron, do you think you could encourage your bartender to speak with us?"

Lowell looked at the detectives, clearly considering his situation and his options. "Let me speak with Will in private. Perhaps he'll tell me something he'd rather not tell you."

The detectives nodded, so Lowell stepped out of his office and left the door ajar.

When he returned a few minutes later, he sat in his chair and faced Ben and Noah. With a smile on his face, he said, "It seems your suspect left Memphis shortly after the fire. He told Will he was moving to New Orleans, that he didn't like the weather in Memphis."

The detectives stood, shook hands with Lowell and walked out of the saloon. Once they were a block away from the Big River, Ben asked Noah if he believed Lowell.

"Maybe," he said, "but as weak a clue as it is, it's still a lead. Lowell may think he's in the clear, but we made him no promises. So, when we do catch Hooper we can still go back on Lowell. We'll squeeze Hooper until he gives us the name of his money source."

Noah patted Ben on the shoulder when they arrived at the office.

"Good job, Ben."

The more Noah and Ben considered Lowell's clue, the more they disbelieved it.

"If Hooper went to New Orleans," Noah said, "why would Lowell send us there with the chance we might find him? And if we did, it's likely that Hooper would hand us Lowell on a silver platter."

"Right, so Lowell's lying." Ben slumped in his chair. "What do we do now?"

"On the train from Chicago I thought about our next steps. I never considered New Orleans and heading south, but that's turned into nothing anyway. That is if we've read Lowell right."

"I think Lowell lied," said Ben.

"I do too, which means Hooper didn't go north like his landlady said or south like Lowell said."

Ben asked Noah if he thought Hooper would have gone east, to maybe Atlanta or Baltimore.

"Heading east wouldn't take him far enough away from here." Noah paused, and Ben noticed a strange look on his face.

"What?" said Ben.

"That slippery bastard," Noah muttered.

"Huh?"

"Hooper told the landlady he was going to Chicago. I think he did tell Lowell he was going to New Orleans. But I believe that J.D. Hooper is a smart, conniving, slippery-as-a-catfish liar." He looked at his partner and said, "Hooper is heading west. He's running to the wide-open half of the country—from Mexico to Canada and the Mississippi River to the Pacific—and pretty much the only way to run is on a train." Noah laughed out loud. "And we know trains."

That night, Noah packed his bags, told Ben to keep looking for the coal oil crew, and made sure he would have a seat on the west-bound train the next day.

☆ ☆ ☆

Ben met him at the track and shook his hand while steam billowed from the warmed-up engine.

"Good luck, Noah. Find Hooper and bring him back."

"I will, Ben. I'm not going to give up until I catch him. There's no way he's going to get away with this."

The conductor started yelling, late-comers ran along the line of passenger cars, and Noah climbed the steps into his car. He looked back at Ben, tipped his hat, and found his seat. He took a deep breath and said, "I'm coming, Hooper."

Chapter 17

When he woke up, J.D. had a hangover and a sharp pain behind his right eye. The strange food he'd shared with Pancho Villa had smelled great and tasted good, but this morning his belly was rumbling, and his head didn't just ache, it was sore. The tequila had hit him like a hammer. Rolling over in the bed, J.D. fell out onto the floor with a resounding thud and realized he was still fully dressed—shoes, suit, and derby. He struggled to his knees and pulled himself over to the night jar just in time to throw up nearly everything he'd eaten in Mexico.

"What happened?," he croaked. Even trying to remember the events of the day before made his brain pulse and his eyes feel like they'd been rubbed with sand. He crawled back to the bed and pulled himself up onto the mattress. Afraid to lie down, he rested his elbows on his knees and buried his face in his hands. "What the hell happened?"

J.D. quickly felt in his side pocket and was relieved to find that he still had his pistol and his money. Sighing with relief when his hand clutched the stack of cash, he rapidly counted the bills and discovered that none of the money was missing. He also checked for and found that his gold double eagle and watch were still in his vest.

The midmorning sun seemed to burn its way through the brick walls of the hotel. Whether it was from the oven-like heat of the day or the internal fire of the tequila, J.D.'s body was sticky with sweat and his damp, smelly clothes clung tightly to him.

Little by little, he became aware of the street noises outside the curtained window. The rumbling sound of freight wagons and the streetcar mixed with the buzzing chatter of the drivers and street vendors screeched like a saw in his tequila-damaged head. J.D.'s eyes felt swollen and his tongue gummy. Pulling off his shoes and tossing his hat onto the floor, J.D. flopped onto his side and struggled to find a comfortable position; but nothing seemed to work. In time, his head got used to the noise, his brain gave up the fight, and J.D. fell back asleep.

☆ ☆ ☆

The next morning, after a hot bath and a shave, J.D. walked slowly down the stairs to the hotel lobby. He spoke to the desk clerk for a moment and then headed out the door to the street. He raised his hand to his brow as the early morning sunlight pierced his still aching eyeballs, but the soft breeze felt good on his face. He crossed the street to a café and sat at a table with his back to the window.

"Just coffee," he said to the woman who appeared next to him. She brought him a cup, set it on the table, and disappeared.

Quietly groaning, he tried to recall what he'd seen and heard and done in Juarez. The dominant memory was that of the round-faced Mexican, Pancho Villa. Despite the man's obvious authority, J.D. felt strange *not* hating him. *He ain't like the bankers and the law. It seems like he hates them fellas as much as I do.* He sipped the hot coffee, feeling its warmth flow across his raw throat. *Pancho called me his friend, his* amigo, *all because I chased them two fellas out of the cantina.*

He signaled to the woman for some more coffee and when she brought it, he asked her to bring a couple of fried eggs.

"You want some chiles on them, *señor*?"

"No," he gagged, "just the eggs and some bread."

She walked away, and Hooper returned to his thoughts. *Why me? Why would Villa want me as a friend*? He stared into the cup, the light from the window behind him reflected on the dark surface of the steaming coffee. *There's somethin' else goin' on*.

An hour later, feeling better with food in his belly, J.D. left the café and stood on the sidewalk. The sun's heat was already intense and the noise in the street grew as the city seemed to come to life. J.D. headed back across to the hotel and walked into the lobby. When he got to the foot of the staircase, the clerk called out to him.

"Mr. Hooper," he said, "there's a message for you sir."

"A message for me?"

"Yes, sir, a boy dropped it off a while ago. He said it was *muy importanté*."

"Huh?"

"He said it was very important."

J.D. wondered who would have sent him a message. Reluctantly, and a little afraid, he took the folded paper from the clerk and slowly read the note.

My dear friend, J.D., I will be in Juarez only one more day, but I would like to meet with you to discuss a business opportunity. From our discussion yesterday, I know you may have some reservations about seeing me again. But I assure you that my intentions are honorable and that, if you choose to help me, you'll discover that our objectives will be similar and that I am very generous.

J.D. struggled a bit with the tiny script but continued on.

At two o'clock this afternoon, Tomas, the man who shared our table, will meet you in front of the hotel. He will take you to the hacienda of a friend of mine. There I will share my plans with you. I understand that you may not want to come, but I assure you it will be worth your time. Your amigo, Francisco Pancho Villa.

Wondering what kind of help Villa needed, he folded the note away and headed upstairs.

✯ ✯ ✯

A few miles south of J.D.'s hotel, across the narrow, drifting waters of the Rio Grande, *El Jefe* was busy holding court in a barn close to Felipé's. This time, however, the atmosphere in the room wasn't relaxed like it had been at the cantina. Villa sat at a large, hand-carved table; unruly stacks of paper held in place by smooth rocks standing like sentinels in front of him. To his left sat a young man, his secretary and scribe. The young man's eyes focused on the papers and, his ears missing none of the words of his boss, he scratched a few notes with a pencil.

The trembling man standing across the table was attentive as well. He, too, heard everything Villa said, and he felt the venom in each word.

"Do you remember the last time you came to see me, the same day you had promised me for the second time that you would pay back the money I loaned you?"

Staring at the tile floor in front of him rather than looking into *El Jefe's* eyes, the man nodded, afraid to speak up.

"Do you also remember the morning, the day you had promised to have the money? You stood in that very same spot, tears coursing down your cheeks, wailing about a bad harvest and telling me that your wife was spending too much on your children." Villa paused, using the silence as an ally. "Did I hesitate at all when I agreed to give you some time to gather the money? No, I did not. I trusted you that day and let you walk out of here with all of the fingers on your hands."

A shudder coursed through the man as he nodded. The air in the hot room was still and the sweat crawling from his hair did little to cool him.

Looking past the cowering man, Villa said, "Grab him

and put his hand on the table."

One of *El Jefe's* troopers clutched the man's arm and held it down between two of the paper stacks. Gripping the man's wrist, he splayed the fingers like a fan.

With his free hand, the trooper gave his broad-bladed knife to Villa.

The bitter smell of urine drifted around the room and the frightened man began to wail.

"Listen to me," Villa thundered. "You sorry excuse for a man, you have no honor. You are a liar and a thief. I listened to your sad story the day you first came to me. I listened again when you couldn't pay me like you promised. Now you come once again to beg for more time." He paused, lifting the knife from the table checking the edge of the blade with his thumb. "You owe me two hundred pesos, Garcia. How much is your thumb worth?"

The man's cries grew louder as he tried to pull away from the table. The trooper held him tightly while another grabbed him around the chest. Villa stood and leaned across the clutter in front of him and placed the sharp edge of the knife on the first joint of Garcia's right thumb.

"Do you have my two hundred pesos?"

Between sobs the man said, "I can get it, *Jefe,* I can. Please don't cut me."

Villa grabbed the man's sweaty hair and lifted his head in order to see his eyes. With a sigh he let go of Garcia's hair and said, "I don't believe you. You leave me no choice." Then, with the heel of his hand he pushed down hard on the back edge of the knife.

Two of Villa's men grabbed the screaming Garcia under the arms and dragged him out of the building. Blood poured from the stub of his thumb and ran down the front of his shirt.

Villa stepped out of the large doorway and sat on a bench under the shade tree at the corner of the barn, the faint smell of blood still present in the vast space. Tomas followed him and waited for Villa to speak.

"When you come back with the gringo, bring him to me here."

"Si, *El Jefe*."

"And don't let anyone remove the blood or the thumb from the table over there. I want Hooper to see the mess, so I can find out what kind of man he truly is."

"I will do as you wish *Jefe*."

Shaded by the tree, Villa pondered his next move. In order to accomplish his plans, he had to have an American on his side, one who could be trusted, and who could be ruthless. He had a strong feeling that J.D. was the right man for the job but needed to be absolutely sure. *But what will it take to convince him*, he thought, *what does he want*? *What does he need*? Villa crafted a mental list that included money, women, and a number of other things that he thought might convince J.D. to come to work for him.

☆ ☆ ☆

J.D.'s hangover lingered in the form of a slight headache. Still not sure what Villa wanted, he looked again at the note. "Generous and honorable." Knowing that he himself was neither generous nor honorable, he wondered what the Mexican meant and why he thought J.D. would fit into whatever plans he had.

J.D. wanted to be on the walk in front of the hotel before Villa's man arrived. He walked downstairs and out the door at 1:30 and was surprised that Tomas was already there.

"*Buenos tardes, Señor Hooper*," Tomas said. "Are you ready to leave? *El Jefe* is anxious to see you again."

J.D. nodded, and Tomas led them to the corner. The old man knew when to talk and when to keep silent, so he said nothing as they boarded the southbound streetcar and headed toward the border. Despite the numerous stops, the trip took only fifteen minutes. The two men got off the streetcar, crossed the bridge, and walked to Felipé's Cantina. J.D. stared at the adobe building, remembering the events of the previous day.

J.D. was surprised when Tomas didn't go into the cantina but led him across the road.

"Ah, here you are," said Villa as he walked out of the barn. "J.D., my friend, it is good to see you. Would you like something to drink, some Tequila perhaps?"

"No. No Tequila."

"Perhaps you would like some water or a *cerveza* instead?"

"I'll take a *cerveza*," he said. "*Gracias*."

Tomas hurried across the road to the cantina to get the drink while Villa took J.D.'s arm by the elbow and led him into the wooden building. When Tomas arrived with J.D.'s beer and a bottle of Tequila for Villa, he gave a slight bow and turned away.

Villa lifted the bottle to J.D. and touched it to the beer-filled glass the American held.

"*Siempre*," he said, tilting the bottle to his lips.

J.D. responded with a nod.

Villa took two quick swallows of the liquor and sighed loudly.

"J.D., I think that soon there will be much trouble in Mexico, especially here in the north. Chihuahua is my home and the thought of poverty and violence plaguing us here concerns me deeply."

He looked at Hooper again and added, "In our talk the other day, you told me of your work in Memphis; how you had taken care of certain difficult situations in America."

J.D. held the glass at his lips and looked at Villa. He took a sip of the beer and said, "Yes I did." *I wonder what else I told him*, he thought.

"I would like for you to do the same things for me, here

in Mexico and in *los Estados Unidos*, the United States." He took another shot of liquor and continued. "I need an American who despises greedy men, who believes that children should be protected, who is willing to do anything necessary to do his duty."

"Go on," said Hooper.

"In Mexico today, almost all of the money, all of the wealth, is held in the hands of a few rich men: politicians, bankers, and the men who own the railroads and the mines."

"That sounds just like every place I ever lived," J.D. responded.

"You mentioned that you were part of a group of men whose job was to prevent weak-willed farmers from giving in to the greed of a tobacco company. You said that, on occasion, you had to use force or violence to convince these farmers to be loyal to their neighbors."

"I did say that. I was a Night Rider."

"Did you ever have to stand up against the company or the leaders of the vigilantes?"

"Sometimes I had to. I went to jail once just because I hit a sheriff who was trying to kick me off my farm."

Villa nodded, as if this was exactly what he wanted to hear. "Then you said that when you were in Memphis you collected debts."

"I worked for a man in the freight business, at least that's what he called it. But really, he wanted power and control of all of the activities—the rail cars, the wagons, the warehouses and all of the people involved in the business."

"And you helped him achieve his goals?"

J.D. hesitated for a moment, then said, "I did until I left town."

"If you two were successful, why did you leave? You had to be making lots of *dinero* in the process."

"I'd had some trouble up in Kentucky and the cops were looking for me."

"What kind of trouble, J.D.?"

Wondering if he'd said too much, Hooper stopped. When he was in Memphis, he'd told Chester that he might have killed someone, but he'd never actually been specific. What if Villa was interested in turning him over to the police? What if ...

But his thoughts were cut short when Villa spoke again.

"J.D., I'm just trying to find out if you have the *cojones* to work for me. You see, there are some very powerful men who do not love the people as I do. They use their power to steal the land that the people have owned and then they sell it, sometimes to Americans and other foreigners. And I, Pancho Villa, want to stop these men. I don't care if they are Americans or Mexicans. I hate their greed and their power. I think that sometime soon there will be a revolution in Mexico. I intend that whoever ends up winning will find a way to take care of the common people rather than line his own pockets with the land and the riches and the gold that belong to all Mexicans."

"Do you think you can win, that you can defeat the crooks in Mexico?" asked J.D.

"I can, and I will if you will help me." He paused then added, "It is the poor who pay for the greed of others. You witnessed some of this before. Those two gringos you dealt with are such men. They promise many things to poor people, but only pay them with grief and abuse, just as they did with *los niños*."

J.D. drank the rest of his now warm beer. He'd never thought of himself as a soldier or a revolutionary, but if there was money to be made doing the things he'd done before, then maybe the two of them could come to an agreement. He sat a little taller in the chair and looked directly at the round face of the Mexican. Staring deeply into his obsidian eyes, J.D. said, "If I agree to come to work for you, what will I have to do and how much will you pay?"

"You will be well paid, amigo," he said. Villa stood and led J.D. to the large table at the back of the barn and shuffled with some papers.

J.D. noticed the shriveled thumb on the table. Unfazed by the bloody mess, he looked at Villa.

Villa looked up at J.D. "A man who made me a promise, a man I thought I could trust, broke his word and lost his thumb. In the future the man will have only one hand to hold himself *cuando tiene que mear*...when he has to piss."

"Likely he'll have trouble undoin' his pants at the same time," J.D. said with a chuckle. Villa turned to look at J.D. and then laughed as well.

Having made his point, Villa led them across the road to the cantina and they sat at a small table that was placed to catch the breeze that drifted over the wall and through the arched gate. Tomas must have anticipated his *Jefe's* needs because he arrived at the table carrying a pitcher of beer and a plate piled with yellow cheese and sliced peaches. While they ate, Villa and J.D. talked about their pasts. J.D. learned that the Mexican had shot a man who tried to rape his sister. Hooper asked him how old he was at the time and learned he'd only been sixteen.

"Did you kill him?"

"No, but I wanted to. I had to run away. I was afraid that I would go to prison." Villa pondered that thought for a moment then he said, "But that was the last time I ever ran. I did not get back home for a long time and I learned to live on my own for a while. I finally joined a gang of *banditos* in Durango."

When Villa asked him about Memphis, J.D. told him about the lawyer and the fella in the warehouse. However, he held back the story of the railyard fire.

When Tomas returned to clear the plates off the table, he brought a box of cigars, a pitcher of beer, and some glasses. Villa took a cigar for himself and offered another to Hooper. Soon a cloud of pungent smoke hovered among the leaves above the two men. Villa took off his sombrero and rubbed his forehead. He poured beer into their glasses.

"You asked me what I wanted you to do for me and also how much I would pay you." Villa took a deep swallow of the beer before he continued. "I want you to visit some people in El Paso and here in Juarez. Some of them owe me money which I would like you to collect."

J.D. watched Villa closely, nodding his head as he listened.

"Another man owes me a great favor, and I want to be sure he hasn't forgotten this. Do you think you can do these things for me?" He slid a small stack of American money across the table toward J.D.

"I can," J.D. said. He picked up the money and then finished his beer.

Villa stood up and put on his sombrero. He led J.D. into the room behind the courtyard and asked Tomas to get him some paper and a pencil. Villa stood directly in front of Hooper and spoke softly.

"J.D. you may be an American, but you have the heart and the soul of a Mexican. You shall always be *mi hermano y mi compadre*."

When Tomas returned, Villa wrote the names and addresses on the paper, folded it in half, and handed it to J.D., who slipped it into his coat pocket.

"Now," said Villa, "I must prepare for my journey. We will go to the hacienda."

Villa mounted his horse and rode away. J.D. and Tomas followed in the wagon.

J.D. took off his coat to get some relief from the heat. "How far are we goin'?"

"The hacienda is a short ride south of the city. The owner, *Don* Hernando, is a patron of *El Jefe* and lets him use it whenever he is in Juarez."

Hooper had expected the hacienda to be small, like the buildings on either side of the road, but when they came over a short incline, he saw, instead, a big white-coated adobe home. There were numerous trees along the walls and in the courtyard. He saw a barn and a long, low building divided into stalls. Beyond the barn was a large fenced-in area and J.D. counted at least a dozen horses.

"I believe that *El Jefe* has planned on having dinner in a few hours, but he will want to see you before we return to El Paso," said Tomas.

While waiting for Villa, J.D. wandered around the hacienda grounds. When he asked Tomas how much of the land Don Hernando owned, the old man said, "All of it," and smiled at him. Tomas led him into a tree-shaded courtyard and gave him a cup of water.

When Villa walked into the courtyard, J.D. looked into the man's eyes and saw that whatever was on his mind, he wasn't quite ready to talk about it. Instead, the Mexican told him about his friend, Don Hernando and his rancho. Villa told J.D. about his own history with the Don and how their friendship had come about; how they'd been in the cattle business together for a long time.

"I would steal the cattle from the ranchos in the south or from those in your country. Then I'd bring them here to Juarez where Don Hernando would fatten them up and sell them to the Americans. He got rich and built this wonderful home. I got rich and gave most of my money to the poor families here in the north."

J.D. said nothing, but was curious. *What? Give your money to the poor*? He couldn't understand why someone would do such a thing.

As if reading his mind, Villa continued. "I don't need a big hacienda; my home is Chihuahua and Durango. I don't need all of these buildings and corrals. I have my friends and those loyal to me. I have the freedom to go anywhere at any time and do whatever I want. I am a free man and I intend to always be free."

Villa stopped talking for a moment and said, "I will see you here at the hacienda in one week. Tomas will leave a note for you at your hotel telling you the exact day of my arrival. In the meantime, *vaya con dios*—go with God."

J.D. watched as Villa headed into the house. Almost instantly, Tomas appeared at J.D.'s side.

"It is time for us to go, *Señor*."

Sitting next to Tomas in the wagon, J.D. thought about the task ahead and was confident he could get the money, just as he'd done in Memphis. The other job—the favor—would take some planning but didn't seem too difficult. Tomas agreed to meet him in Juarez at Felipé's before noon two days later. He would help J.D. find the two Mexicans on the list and translate for him.

"Here we are *Señor*. I will see you in two days."

"Gracias, Tomas. Thanks for the ride."

With a new-found confidence, J.D. walked over the bridge and nodded at the border guard as he stepped into the United States. He'd noticed that the guards never stopped Americans coming back into the country and infrequently stopped Mexicans.

Chapter 18

J.D. sat in the lobby of his hotel. He'd rested well, bathed, gotten a shave and a haircut, and felt ready to go to work for his new and powerful friend. He perused the list of four names and their addresses supplied by Villa. For three of the names, Villa had written the amount owed.

Villa's note was very specific about the fourth person. More than a decade ago, the man, now an American politician, had bought stolen cattle from Villa for several years. He'd never revealed Villa's role in the transactions and had always been prompt in his payments. Villa had given him prices much lower than the illegal market rate, which allowed the man to profit handsomely, but, in return, had received a promise from the man that he, Villa, would be granted a favor in the future.

Villa's note clearly specified that J.D. was to first communicate the information to the Texas congressman that it was time to collect on the favor, and second to receive confirmation that the man would deliver as promised. J.D. read the final note to himself. "If this man does not comply, or you are not convinced by his words or tone of voice that he is being honest, I want you to threaten him. You can tell him that I won't merely reveal his involvement in buying stolen cattle, but that I will visit him in his home where his wife and children live."

Hooper felt confident he could carry out Villa's wishes, but this task was probably the most difficult to accomplish. *Might as well get it done first.*

Once he'd asked the hotel desk clerk how to get to the Congressman's El Paso office, J.D. set off to find the office and arrange a meeting with the official. *Ain't never talked to no Congressman, but they probably cry and bleed just the same as any man.*

J.D. took a streetcar to downtown El Paso, an area of taller buildings, cleaner streets, and larger crowds of people. When he found the correct address, he pushed open the tall windowed doors and walked toward what looked like the ticket counter at a train depot.

"I need to speak to Congressman Connett," he said to the young man across the counter.

"The Congressman's office is on the fifth floor, sir, room 501. The stairs are to your right." J.D. nodded, walked toward the stairwell, and started the long climb. Finding the room, he pushed the door open, walked up to the lone desk, and eyed the man who sat behind it.

"My name is J.D. Hooper, and I need to speak to Mr. Connett."

"*Congressman* Connett is busy," the man said, checking J.D.'s appearance, "and he only sees people by appointment."

"Yeah? Well he'll want to see me now. Tell him Mr. Hooper has a message for him from his friend Francisco about a debt between them."

"I'm sorry, sir, but that won't be possible. You see, the Congressman..."

J.D. put his hands on the desk and leaned in close to the man. "I said *tell* him that I have a message from his friend." J.D.'s eyes bored into those of the scrawny little man as he added, "And tell him that it has to be now."

Beads of sweat appeared on the balding man's temples and J.D. noticed that his lips were quivering.

"Let me see if the Congressman can make an exception," he croaked rising from his chair. The man tapped on the door, opened it, and disappeared quickly.

A moment later, with a baffled look on his face, the secretary came out of the office and looked at J.D. Clearing his throat, he said, "The Congressman will see you now."

J.D. walked into the room and spotted a large, pot-bellied gentleman seated in a high-backed leather chair. "You Congressman Connett?"

"I am, sir, and what do you mean by coming to my office without an appointment?"

"Congressman Connett, Mr. Villa wanted me to give you a message. He says that it's time for you to pay back the favor you promised."

"Tell that greaser that I don't owe him anything."

"Mr. Villa said your memory might be failing you. There is the matter of two thousand head of cattle he sold to you at a very generous discount because they were not acquired in a legal manner. Mr. Villa said I should remind you *that* sale gave you the opportunity to achieve your current office. He also said that you promised him a favor in return. Now do you remember?"

Connett shuffled some papers, then rose from his chair and said, "Well, you see sir, I never actually..."

"Actually, you did, and Mr. Villa hopes that he doesn't have to provide details to the newspapers and the American authorities about the transactions between the two of you."

"And why would the papers care what a thieving greaser like Villa has to say. Nobody will believe him."

"You must realize, sir, that Mr. Villa keeps meticulous records so that he and his...friends always know where they stand with each other. Mr. Villa is certainly willing to share these records with your government."

"But I never said...I...err..."

Cutting him off, J.D. said, "I have been instructed to collect your promise to honor the arrangement with Mr. Villa."

J.D. paused, moved right up to the man, staring directly into his sallow face. "And to make sure that I don't leave this office without your promise, no matter what I have to do."

For a moment, there was no sound in the office. The Congressman paused and J.D. moved in closer, their noses almost touching. He watched the fat man try to swallow whatever liquid remained in his dry mouth and then collapse into the leather chair.

"Please convey to our mutual friend that everything we discussed back then will be arranged within the week. He will receive a note from me when the final details are ready."

"You understand, Mr. Connett," J.D. said softly but firmly, "that if these things don't happen as you've promised, I'll go to your home and introduce myself to your wife and children?"

Recapturing some of his bluster, Connett said, "Yes, I do. Now get out of my office."

J.D. tipped his derby and smiled at the man, turned away, and left the office. As he walked past the secretary, J.D. slapped the man on the back of his bald head, smiled at him, and strolled out.

Job well done, he thought. *Villa will be happy*.

☆ ☆ ☆

The next morning, J.D. crossed the bridge and found Tomas waiting for him at the cantina.

"Buenos dias, *Señor* Hooper," said the kindly man, a bright smile spread across his deeply wrinkled face.

"Good morning, Tomas."

Hooper spent a few minutes reviewing Villa's list. He asked Tomas about the men on the list and the Mexican told J.D. about the debtors' previous dealings with Villa.

"These are old obligations that *El Jefe* has not had time to collect. The amount of money is modest, but because these men have not paid, they are dishonoring my *patrón* and I believe that he wants them to face the consequences of their inaction."

J.D. nodded his understanding and they headed toward the wagon in front of the cantina.

"We will not need the wagon this morning, *señor*. The men live close by and we can walk."

"Tomas, could you call me J.D.? If we're gonna work together, then we should talk as friends."

"I will do as you wish, J.D.," he said awkwardly. "But when we are with *El Jefe*, I will...no, I *must*...be more formal."

"Agreed." J.D. nodded.

The next two hours were an education for Hooper. When he approached the two men—the first at his home and the second at his *bodega*—he expected to be challenged by them. What he discovered was that his presence had certainly put both men on edge. When Tomas started translating his demands, each of them quickly presented the money to him. At first, J.D. wondered if they had seen his pistol or if his words had been so powerful that he'd truly frightened them into compliance. But the more Hooper watched what was happening, he realized that these men feared Tomas. He, not J.D., was Villa's representative.

"Tomas, I'm just a gringo. I don't think that anything I said or did made those fellas pay what they owed. They were afraid of you; they know you are *El Jefe's* man."

"I think, J.D., that your words and presence frightened them. They know who I am, of course, but I have never before been involved in collecting money for *El Jefe*."

"Either way it was good work." J.D. paused before he continued the conversation. "Have you heard from Villa?"

"No, I have not. But I expect him to return before the end of the week. Perhaps he will be here by *sabado*...Saturday."

"Then I need to get back to El Paso and make plans for the last man on the list. I've already located his home and his saloon, but I'm not sure how to approach him. I'll think on it tonight and do the job not later than day after tomorrow."

"If you need my assistance, just find the boy at Felipé's and send him to the hacienda. Otherwise, just wait for my message that *El Jefe* has returned."

J.D. left the money they'd collected with Tomas and walked up the street toward the bridge. After passing the border guard, he stopped for a moment and looked out across the railing toward the west. Surprised to see people walking across the river in both directions at places where the water was shallow, Hooper's first thought was that the American and Mexican guards were clearly not doing their jobs. But then he smiled, realizing that if he ever needed to leave the U.S. in order to get away from the police, he could do it up river and no one would ever know.

☆ ☆ ☆

On Wednesday afternoon, J.D. walked into the saloon owned by the last man on Villa's list. He felt that taking care of business away from the man's house would leave him the option to use his home and family as additional pressure points, if necessary.

The Alamo Saloon was in the seedier part of El Paso, nearly a mile away from his hotel and only a few blocks off the river. Inside the dark room, the floors were covered with sawdust, and even this early in the day the well-placed spittoons were full. A loud song was coming from the player piano in the far corner yet it could barely be heard over the noisy crowd of soldiers from Ft. Bliss.

J.D. stepped up to the bar and signaled to the bartender that he wanted a beer. The white-aproned man sauntered toward J.D., looked him over, and said, "Kinda out of your neighborhood, ain't ya?"

"Whatta you mean?"

"It's just that we usually only get soldiers in here, 'specially on pay day. Besides, you dress like one of them bankers or lawyers, so I figured that you mighta been lost." He filled a mug from the tap under the mirror and set it in front of J.D.

J.D.'s heart slowed a bit and he put on a false smile.

"Sorry, friend, it's just been one of them days—too much work and too little beer." He sipped from the mug and threw a half dollar onto the bar. "So, it's payday and the army comes here to celebrate, huh?"

The bartender picked up a towel and began to wipe off the spill marks from the bar. "What usually happens is the troopers come in to pay off their tabs and drink 'til their money runs out. Then they start all over again."

J.D. looked around the room and quickly counted more than a dozen heads, most of them in khaki uniforms.

"I do need to talk to Mr. Sam Alexander. He and I have some important business to discuss."

"What'd you say your name was?"

"My name's Hooper and we need to discuss a matter that concerns him and Mr. Villa."

The bartender told J.D. to wait while he checked to see if his boss was in, then walked to the end of the bar and went through a door, closing it behind him. When the door opened a few minutes later, a large man crossed behind the bar toward J.D. The room got quiet.

Sam Alexander was tall, far taller than J.D., and clearly outweighed him by forty pounds. To his own surprise, J.D. wasn't afraid, but he was instantly cautious. Feeling trapped, he thought, *Mighta made a mistake comin' in here.* He saw no weapon on Alexander or any of the burly men who'd followed him out of the back room, but the weight of the pistol in J.D.'s pocket didn't feel sufficient.

"You lookin' for me?"

"I am if you're Sam Alexander. My name's Hooper. I'm here about a business arrangement you have with Pancho Villa. I think it might be a good idea if you and I meet privately to discuss it." J.D. was glad that the bar stood between him and the giant, and he never lost sight of the others in the room. Even if the soldiers were simply observers, J.D. realized that he was still outnumbered. If the soldiers came in on the side of the owner, then he had to make sure he could get out in a hurry.

Alexander walked past J.D., lifted up a hinged part of the bar and walked through the opening. He came around to where J.D. was standing, passed by him, and leaned on his bar.

"Well, *mister* Hooper, it appears that you have a very big problem. You're in *my* bar, you want to talk about something that is not *your* business, and you are embarrassing me in front of my friends, my employees, and my customers. That's not very smart if you ask me." He moved in close to J.D. and added, "So I suggest that you get your scrawny little ass out of my saloon, and you tell that fat Mexican Pancho Villa that if he wants to talk to me, he'd better do it himself."

"I'm sorry, Mr. Alexander. You're right."

J.D. turned around quickly and without hesitation left the saloon. As soon as he turned away from the door, he ran as fast as he could for two blocks, cut through an alley, and turned onto a much busier street. Spotting a streetcar moving away from him, he chased it and jumped onto the rear platform. When he spun around to see if he was being followed, Hooper saw a crowd of soldiers spill out of the alley. *I'm gonna have to pay Mr. Alexander a visit at his house tonight,* he thought. *It'll be just me and him and...his family.* Hooper walked through the rear door of the streetcar and found a seat next to a window.

☆ ☆ ☆

Alexander lived in a medium-sized frame house a mile or more from the river in the northwest section of El Paso. The homes on the narrow street had been built close to one another but over time the owners had added fences and rows of shrubs and trees to create privacy. The saloon owner's house sat back ten yards from the street and had a covered porch with a fence-like railing along the front. This far from the center of El Paso there were no streetlights, so the only light came from the windows of the homes and the half-moon that was just rising in the east.

From behind a hedge across the street, J.D. had seen Alexander return home alone just after dark. While he waited, J.D. reviewed his plan. He considered his options, and seethed with anger at himself for getting cornered at the saloon. Still, he'd done well enough to let Alexander know why he'd come, and that Villa wanted his money. J.D. touched the pistol in his coat pocket and then pulled a very sharp, broad-bladed knife from his belt. *It's big enough to cut off a thumb,* he thought, *or even a hand.* His plan was to wait until the light in the upstairs room went out, believing that would be a child's bedroom, and then to bang on the front door.

J.D. stretched his back and rubbed on his legs, trying to work out the cramps. Looking across the street through the hedge, he saw that the only light left on in Alexander's house was in a room to the right of the door. Hooper stood up and walked out onto the street. He glanced both ways, checking to see if anyone was around. He knew that witnesses would be a problem and, although he didn't think that any of Alexander's men would be standing guard, thought it was important to be sure. But he was alone in the dark and ready to finish the job. He walked across the street and up onto the porch, stopping in front of the entrance to the house. Scanning the darkness once again, he pounded heavily on the large wooden door then stepped off to the side away from the lighted window.

J.D. braced himself when he heard heavy footsteps approach the door.

"Who is it?" he heard Alexander growl. "Whatta you want?"

Hooper reached over to the door and pounded on it again. As he expected, Alexander pulled the door open and stepped out onto the porch, his face turned away from Hooper. Seeing nothing in that direction, the saloonkeeper turned around and stared down the barrel of J.D.'s pistol.

"Evenin', Alexander," said J.D., cocking his pistol and shoving it up under the man's chin.

Alexander started to reach for J.D.'s hand but stopped when J.D. pushed the gun deeper into his throat.

"You don't wanna do that," he said. "Havin' your brains splattered all over the porch will make a mess for your wife to clean up."

"Whatta you want?" Alexander repeated, this time through clenched teeth.

J.D. gripped the man's arm and pushed him into the yard. He kept his gun tight against Alexander's throat and backed him up to the porch railing, not allowing him to escape.

"What I want is for you to give me the money you owe Mr. Villa. That's what he wants too." J.D. knew that he had to maintain control of the situation or he could find himself overpowered by the larger man. "He told me to get the money from you. He didn't specify how I was to get it. I tried to do it the polite way at your saloon, but you've decided you want me to do it the hard way. Here, at you home. So here I am again, only this time, there're no soldiers, only your wife and kids.

"I don't have the money here and even if I did, I wouldn't give it to you, you little piss ant."

"Now who's the one not being very smart, Alexander. Now *you* have to decide if I'm gonna pull the trigger and blow your brains out, or if you are going to cooperate. Please tell me *again* you don't have the money. Then I'll get to go into your house, find your wife and have her show me where you keep it." J.D. slipped the knife out of his belt and placed the tip into the soft flesh of the man's belly. "I ain't afraid of killing you or roughing up your wife to get the money." J.D. didn't want to give Alexander any time to think of an escape move, so he pushed the knife into his belly a half-inch. The saloonkeeper flinched; a whining sound crept from between his teeth.

"Now, before you tell me again that you don't have the money here, you better think about how your wife will feel about cleaning up the mess out here with one of *her* hands chopped off." Even in the dark, J.D. could see Alexander's eyes open wider and he could smell the fear in the man's sweat. "So," he whispered, "what's it gonna be?"

"Alright," the man grunted. "I got the money, but it's in the house."

"Here's what we're gonna do then. You're gonna call your wife out here, tell her to get the money and bring it to me." J.D. paused and pushed in the knife a fraction more. "Don't try anything stupid, 'cause I will hurt her if you do. Do you understand?"

Alexander nodded once and then called out to his wife. "Anna, get out here and make it quick." His voice was raspy.

The woman must have been waiting behind the door, because she appeared on the porch in just a few seconds. Standing there in her night clothes, she whimpered when she saw her husband.

"Quit whinin' and go to the wood-box in the kitchen. There's a can in there with some money in it."

"But, Sam..."

"Shut up and do as I say. Open the box and get three

hundred dollars out of the can then bring it here." Alexander still had his back to the porch so he couldn't see his wife. Not hearing any movement, he yelled, "Now, damn it, get the money."

The woman turned and rushed into the house. J.D. kept the pistol tight against Alexander's throat and the knife at his belly. Scarcely a minute passed before she returned.

"Now, Mrs. Alexander, I want you to bring the money down here into the yard," J.D. said. "Come on now, do it quickly or..."

She didn't wait to hear what else J.D. had to say but rushed down the steps and held the wad of bills out for him to see.

"That's good. Now set the money on the ground right next to my foot then get back up on the porch and face the window. You don't wanna see what's happenin' next."

"No, please," she whined as she approached J.D.

As she passed her husband's back, J.D. shoved the knife into Alexander's belly an inch and cracked him on the side of the head with his gun. The instant pain in two different places disoriented the saloonkeeper and he fell to the ground. J.D. leaned over, picked up the money where the wife had dropped it, and walked quickly to the edge of the yard.

Hooper watched Alexander's wife rush to her husband's side. He put the money in his pocket, slipped the knife into his belt and, keeping the pistol in view, said, "I'll be sure to tell Mr. Villa that you sincerely apologize for not payin' your debt on time." Then he ran down the street and out of sight.

☆ ☆ ☆

Back in his room an hour later, J.D. put the money, knife, and gun on top of the dresser and collapsed on the bed. He smiled as he thought about the work of the last few days. *I think I'm gonna like it here. I collected all the money and the promised favor and didn't have to kill anybody. I think Mr. Pancho Villa is gonna be satisfied.* Then he closed his eyes and fell asleep.

Chapter 19

Pancho Villa reined in his horse on the crest of the hill that overlooked Don Hernando's hacienda. Even though everything looked peaceful, he sent a rider into the valley to make sure that it was safe to return. They had been on the road since sunrise and were eager to rest and wash away the trail dust. Although he'd had little time to think about his American friend while dealing with problems in Sonora, he was curious to find out how J.D. had fared.

He watched the rider circle the hacienda and ride through the corral. When the young man stopped in front of the barn and waved his large sombrero, Villa rode his horse down the road. At the corral, he dismounted, stretched his weary back, and turned just as Tomas appeared.

"Tomas, *que paso*," Villa said, removing his hat and wiping the sweat from his forehead with a large bandana.

"Everything is well, *Jefe*. It has been a very quiet week." Tomas handed Villa a cup filled with cool water.

Villa drank and returned the cup to Tomas.

"There is food and drink inside, *Jefe*," Tomas said, watching the stable boy lead Villa's horse into the barn. "I know you are tired, but I have much to tell you about *Señor* Hooper."

"Yes, of course," said Villa, "but let us eat and drink first. We can talk about my American friend once I've washed the dust from my face and rinsed my mouth with something other than water." He smiled at the older man and followed him to the house.

☆ ☆ ☆

After the sun went down, Villa listened to Tomas's report of J.D.'s activities. Tomas shared what he knew without emotion, providing only facts. Over the years, Tomas had learned that his *Jefe* had little patience for elaborate explanations and always preferred brief summaries. Tomas watched Villa's reaction to the report and then asked him, "Should I make arrangements for *Señor* Hooper to come to the *hacienda* tomorrow?"

"Yes. In fact, I would like you to go early and wait until he is ready to go. We have much to discuss and I want to give him plenty of time to prepare for the task I've planned for him."

"As you wish, *Jefe*."

Finally alone, Villa took a cigar from his shirt pocket, bit the end off, and lit it. He leaned back in the chair and blew a series of smoke rings into the night air.

In the very early hours before dawn on Sunday morning, Tomas walked into the hotel and handed a silver dollar to the night clerk in exchange for Hooper's room number. The old Mexican walked quietly up the stairs to the third floor and tapped lightly on the door. Hearing no noise from within, he tapped again a bit louder.

Inside the room, J.D. snorted as his dream-clouded ears reacted to the noise. He shook his head and sucked in a draught of air, then rose and crept to the door. Cautiously picking up his gun from the dresser, he waited.

Tapping again, Tomas whispered, "*Señor* J.D., it is I, Tomas."

J.D. cracked the door open and looked into the faint light of the hallway.

"Tomas, what are you doin' here so early? It's still dark outside. How'd you get up here?"

"I have learned that no door is ever truly locked to those who are generous." He smiled at Hooper. "*Por favor*,

Señor Hooper, *El Jefe* must see you today...this morning."

"This morning? I ain't even dressed yet." J.D. opened the door and motioned Tomas into the room.

"I am so sorry, J.D., but *El Jefe* wants to talk about your work this past week."

"Alright Tomas, give me a bit to get dressed and I'll meet you downstairs."

"Of course, *Señor* Hooper, but do not wear your vest today. It is already warm outside and will be *muy caliente* by mid-day."

Tomas slipped out the door and J.D. reached for his clothes, leaving the vest and stiff shirt collar on the unmade bed. "*Muy caliente*," he said out loud.

Hooper slid the pistol into the pocket of his coat and grabbed his derby. Glancing around the room, checking to see if he had what he'd need for the day, J.D. put the three hundred dollars in his other pocket, then walked into the hallway, locking the door behind him.

Tomas was talking to the night-clerk when Hooper reached the bottom of the stairs. The Mexican came over to J.D. and led him out the door to the street.

"*El Jefe* thought it would be better to cross the bridge while it is still cool. There is no streetcar running this early, but we have a wagon waiting in Juarez."

"When did Villa return, Tomas?"

"It was late yesterday, *Señor*. He asked me how things had gone for you and I told him only what I knew. He seemed pleased about the money and the promise you acquired."

As they walked down the broad street toward the bridge, J.D. was surprised by how quiet it was. There were no street vendors, no wagons, and, other than Tomas and himself, no people. *Might be a real good time of day to get outta town if I have to leave in a hurry.*

The American border guard waved to them as they passed, and the Mexican guard didn't even acknowledge them. *Yep, a real good time of day.*

When the wagon rolled to a stop at Don Hernando's hacienda, J.D. got down from the bench seat and strode through the moon-lit courtyard into the house. Villa had his back to the door and was talking quietly to a well-dressed Mexican. The man's tight pants were tucked into his intricately tooled boots. J.D. noticed his silver spurs and, especially, his large sombrero. The man looked toward J.D. and said something to Villa.

"Ah, J.D. my friend, please come in," said Villa.

"J.D., I'd like you to meet Don Julio Hernando. He is, like you, my very good friend." Glancing at Hernando, he added, "And this is my American amigo, J.D. Hooper."

As the two men shook hands, Villa said, "Like me, Don Hernando has just returned from a long journey. I have told him that my men and I will be departing tomorrow and that I will only need the use of his hacienda this one more day." Villa and Hernando spoke in rapid Spanish for a few minutes. J.D. only caught a few words—those few he'd come to know—and then Don Hernando nodded briefly to J.D. and walked deeper into the house.

"J.D.," said Villa, "come with me to the corral. We will watch the sunrise and drink some coffee."

When they reached the fenced area in front of the stalls, Villa turned to J.D. and placed his hands on his friend's shoulders.

"I have heard from Tomas that you were able to collect the money from my two countrymen."

"We got the money, alright, but I think Tomas should get credit for that. All I did was say a few things. He translated for me and then the fellas gave him the money."

"Tomas says that your words made the difference. The words you spoke, and your fierce expression, is how he put it. Tomas believes that they thought you were *el Diablo*—the devil." Villa laughed at this and clapped down on J.D.'s shoulders. He turned to the east, gazing at the deep blue sky and the striated clouds that looked like molten copper.

Tomas hurried up to them, handed each a cup of steaming coffee, then placed the coffee pot on the ground. They thanked him, and Villa spoke again. "Tell me, J.D., what really happened with the American politician."

"There really ain't much to say. I guess Tomas told you he's gonna keep his promise. I never met a congressman before, but it didn't take long to figure he's just like every one of them rich, power-hungry men I don't like."

"*Es verdad*, J.D., it's true. Did you have to threaten him?"

"He seemed more worried that I might tell his friends in the government about the cattle and the money."

They watched the sky until the sun had cleared the eastern horizon. Then Villa asked J.D. to tell him about his call on Alexander. Villa finished his coffee and set the empty cup in the dust at the foot of the fence post.

"It was excitin' for a while," J.D. said, and then spent the next quarter hour filling Villa in on the details.

"I did get all of the money." He handed the stack of bills to Villa. "But I didn't know that until I got to the hotel. It didn't seem like a good idea to stand in the street countin' money while his wife was cryin' and he was bleedin'."

Villa chuckled and smiled at J.D. "You have done well, amigo."

The two friends walked back up to the hacienda and sat at a table in the courtyard. Tomas brought them more coffee and then returned to the kitchen. Villa took off his sombrero, tossed it onto the table, and looked at J.D. His dark, expressive eyes seemed sad to J.D. This time when the round-faced Mexican spoke, his voice was softer, more intense.

"When I was a young man in Durango, after the *cabron* tried to rape my sister, I was in the army. Although I learned much from that time, I did not like how the officers treated the soldiers. My dislike of men in authority grew in that time and to this day it is still with me."

"I ain't never been in the army," said J.D. "But them fellas with power, whether they're sheriffs or army officers, don't care much about the men they're supposed to protect."

"This is true, and that is why I became a deserter." Villa paused, working over an old memory. "It is hard for men—soldiers—to follow a man they do not respect. When the revolution comes, I want to know that my men will follow me, that they will trust me to look out for them. Do you understand this, J.D.?"

"Sure I do." He considered his next words carefully. "If you treat your soldiers the way you've treated me, I know they'd follow you just about anywhere."

Villa looked at J.D., feeling a strange comradeship with the American. "J.D. have you ever had a close friend?"

"No," said J.D., his brow wrinkled, and a darkness settled on his face. "Closest I ever got to havin' one was last year. There was a fella named Charlie. Me and him were more partners than friends." Hooper was quiet for a moment. "Mighta been friends if I'd treated him like one."

Villa wanted to ask him what had happened, but changed his mind when he saw what the memory did to J.D. Instead, he poured coffee into their cups and said, "Then let us drink to our friendship, *amigo*."

While they drank, Tomas came into the courtyard and asked Villa if he needed anything more. Villa shook his head and told the old man to come see him at noon. When Tomas disappeared through the doorway, *El Jefe* leaned in toward J.D.

"J.D., because you did so well with the tasks I gave you last week, I have another one for you. It is a very important task I want you to do for me, but if you choose not to do it, I will understand. Although it is a simple thing I want done, it may not be easy to accomplish." He paused a moment before continuing. "I want you to get rid of those two Americans who were in the cantina last week. I want you to make them disappear."

"What do you mean by disappear?"

"I mean that I don't want to ever see them again in the cantina, or in Juarez, or El Paso. I mean, J.D., that I want them dead." He sat back in his chair and waited.

When Villa spit out these last words, J.D. looked into the Mexican's obsidian eyes. He saw another Villa, an angry bitter man who was capable of doing dangerous things. J.D. saw a man like himself and didn't hesitate. "How much time do I have to do this?"

"I am leaving in the morning for Parra, in Durango, and I'll be gone for two weeks. I want them gone when I return."

J.D. slowly nodded, sipped from the cup, and wiped his lips. "I can do it."

The smile returned to Villa's face. "I have their names and I know where they are employed."

"One more question, *Jefe*, but you don't have to answer it if you don't want to. Why do you want them dead?"

"There are several reasons, my friend, but only one that matters. They have more than once disrespected my people. You saw how they treated the boy and his sister. You heard what they said to the little girl. Those men have no honor. *Son asquerosos bastardos.* They are filthy bastards."

"That's reason enough. I can do it." J.D. lifted his cup and drank the remainder of his coffee.

"Thank you, my friend. If you can do this for me, we will always be friends."

Villa reached into his pocket, pulled out Alexander's money, and set the bills on the table in front of J.D.

"Here is your advance payment of three hundred dollars. I will give you another two hundred when I return. I know you will succeed."

"No thanks, *Jefe*. Don't give me the money now. I'd rather you paid me after I've done the job."

"J.D. you continue to amaze me." He paused, a strange look on his face. "No, that's the wrong word. You confound me."

☆ ☆ ☆

The next morning, J.D. went to the office building where the two men were employed. He'd spotted a small saloon not far from the entrance and thought that if he could find a table by the window he'd be able to see them either on the way in or when they left. Otherwise, he'd have to stand on the street. *And that ain't a good idea*. The saloon didn't serve any food, but they did keep a hot pot of coffee going so he tipped the bartender and watched through the window. J.D.'s first challenge was to remember what the two looked like. They'd both been average height and weight and one of them had sported a mustache. By half past seven, fellas started to walk into the building, all of them wearing suits and hats not unlike J.D.'s own. Hooper had just finished his coffee when he noticed one man was carrying his hat and had a white bandage wrapped around his head. Beside him strode a man with a trimmed mustache. J.D. smiled and sipped his coffee. "Found 'em," he muttered. "That was easy."

Less than an hour later, J.D. crossed the street and entered the building. Just inside the door was a woman sitting behind a counter. The company name on the wall behind her matched that given to him by Villa. Since there was no one else in the lobby, he pulled the brim of the derby down to cover his eyes and asked for the two men by name.

She glanced up quickly. "I'm sorry, but they can't be disturbed. Would you like to leave a message for either of them?"

"Hmm, no thanks, I'll try to contact them some other

time." J.D. turned and left the building. *Well that didn't take long. Villa's information is good so all I gotta do is wait 'til they leave the office and follow 'em home.*

☆ ☆ ☆

By four o'clock Hooper was back in the saloon gazing out the window. He noticed in the paper that the government had issued a new immigration law that required the border guards to record the names of any Mexicans who entered the country. J.D. wondered if that might be trouble later, especially when Tomas had to get in touch with him. The rest of the article seemed to focus on the Chinese and Japanese trying to cross into the U.S. He hadn't seen any of those people, but that didn't mean they weren't around. J.D. sipped his beer and looked at the people and wagons moving on the street.

A little past six, J.D. saw the men leave their building and turn left onto the sidewalk. He put a small pile of coins on the table and hurried out of the saloon. They were on the opposite side of the street moving away from him. After a few blocks, they turned left and disappeared. J.D. ran across the street, dodged a wagonload of crates, and rushed to the corner of the building. He took a quick look around the wall and saw the two men just ahead, still walking and as yet unaware of him. Ten minutes later they stopped at a busy corner and J.D. waited a half block behind, pretending to gaze into a store window, but keeping watch in the angled reflection. After a moment, they shook hands and walked off in different directions.

A germ of a plan was forming in J.D.'s head. What dominated his conscious thoughts was that by killing them in Texas, he'd have one more group of lawmen looking for him and that was a situation he couldn't afford.

Hooper realized that Villa was right when he had said that the job would not be easy to accomplish. He walked back toward the hotel, his brain stewing on the faint ideas and their various consequences. Entering the lobby, he went straight to the front desk and asked the clerk to set him up with a bath.

"Of course, Mr. Hooper, I can make the arrangement. You will need to wait while I have the staff prepare the bath. Shall I send someone to your room when we are ready?"

"Yeah, that'll be fine." J.D. walked slowly up the stairs, his feet tired and his mind worn out from thinking. Hooper walked into the room, opened the window above the small desk and looked out onto the broad avenue. Seeing so many people on the street and so few of them using the alleys between the buildings, the idea began to take form. He took off his derby and coat, untied and slipped off his shoes, and sat on the bed. J.D. reached into his coat pocket and drew out his pistol. Holding it by the grip, he pointed the gun at the night jar, and said, "Bang."

An hour later, feeling cleaner and more relaxed, Hooper leaned out the window, considering the risks that his newly hatched plan would create. He'd decided that he would need to use the men's greed to accomplish the task.

☆ ☆ ☆

The next morning, J.D. walked around the area surrounding the office where the two men worked. He checked out the various alleys, looking for those that might have hidden corners and possible hiding spots.

By the next day he'd reduced his choices to two possible locations. The first was only three blocks from the office building and met all of the requirements he'd created. The other place, however, was ten blocks away, was much narrower, and had a small alcove at the back with a second entrance off the next street. This made it perfect for hiding. Best of all, it was closer to the river and to the spot where he'd seen people crossing into Mexico.

J.D.'s next step was to create a reason for them to meet him in the alley. Counting on their greed, he worked on a letter that would be too enticing to ignore. He'd have to find someone to help him write it, of course; someone who could be trusted, and that was a problem. *I can't use the desk clerk or any of the fellas at a saloon. Maybe Tomas can help*. He spent the rest of the afternoon struggling with his thoughts and ideas, knowing that his lack of writing skill may end up ruining the whole job. *I might as well just walk into that damn office building and shoot 'em in the head.*

☆ ☆ ☆

Tomas was sitting at the table in the hacienda's courtyard when J.D. walked through the arched gate the next morning. He was clearly pleased to see Hooper and rose to greet him.

"*Señor* J.D., I am surprised to see you. If I had known you were coming, I would have sent someone to pick you up." The glistening sweat on J.D.'s cheeks was hard to ignore. "Can I get you something to drink?"

J.D. nodded. "Some water, *por favor*, Tomas. It's a long walk from the bridge in this heat."

"I see you have chosen to not wear your vest or coat. You are learning what it is like to live in Mexico." He smiled and rushed into the house, returning quickly with a large cup and a full pitcher of water.

J.D. tilted the cup to his lips and didn't remove it until the water was gone. He held the cup out to Tomas who refilled it. J.D. drank the second helping of water more slowly.

"That's better." He looked at the Mexican and said, "Can we sit somewhere and talk? I need your help with somethin' that's important if I'm gonna do this job for *El Jefe*."

"Of course, *Señor* Hooper, how can I help you?"

"Tomas, I think I can trust you. I'm gonna tell you somethin' that I don't want anyone else to know, not even Villa."

"You can trust me, *Señor*, but I must know that what you tell me will not bring trouble to *El Jefe* before I can agree to keep it to myself."

"It ain't anythin' that'll bring him trouble, I promise." J.D. took a deep breath before he continued. "Tomas, I can't write very well. I ain't been in a school since I was eight, and I ain't ever had a reason to learn how to write 'cause it wasn't important when I was farmin'."

"I understand," said Tomas, "please go on."

"I need someone who can write the words I have in mind and then be able to make them look good...sound like they come from a smart, rich man. Do you know anyone who can do that and keep a secret, someone you trust?"

Tomas looked across the table at J.D. The American had removed his hat when he sat down and now the sunlight shining through the tree's leaves cast a shadow on J.D.'s face. The Mexican nodded slowly and then his lips turned into a gentle smile.

"*El Jefe* has a friend, a young lady who was raised by *los mormones*. They taught her to read and write. She has told me that they insisted that her writing must be perfect. *El Jefe* has always been satisfied with the papers she has written for him."

"If Villa trusts her, then I will too. When could she meet with me?"

"*Señor* Hooper, you are in luck. Josefina is one of the finest teachers in our tiny school. I will send a boy to bring her here when she has finished for the day. Will that be soon enough?"

"Tomas." J.D. struggled with his words. "You have saved me from a lot of trouble. Please send the boy and have him tell her that I will pay for her work."

"That won't be necessary, *Señor*. She will do it for nothing. But if you wanted to give her some money so she could buy books for *los niños*, I believe she would be grateful."

"Then send the boy and pour me another glass of water." Hooper smiled, relieved and satisfied that he was closer to getting the job done.

A few hours later, J.D. listened as the beautiful Mexican woman read the letter she'd written on scraps of paper. Her voice was confident yet sweet.

Gentlemen,

I am afraid that I am unable to introduce myself because of the nature of my business. I have seen you in my country many times, and I believe I can trust you. Suffice it to say that I have a Mexican acquaintance that requires a significant amount of American dollars. He is unable to travel across the border and has engaged me to make an exchange—one I believe you will find quite satisfactory should you agree to work with me. I am prepared to deliver one thousand dollars in gold pesos to a place I have selected for its confidentiality and security. In exchange for this gold, I am willing to accept seven hundred dollars in American currency. Sadly, I am pressed for time and can only give you until the day after tomorrow to acquire the cash. However, I believe that in your line of business you should be able to meet the deadline. Should you agree to the deal, you need not reply, simply show up at the time and place I've noted on the enclosed card. I will wait for you for one hour only, so punctuality and secrecy are vital. I look forward to meeting you, if only briefly, and enjoying the profits we shall share.

☆ ☆ ☆

When Josefina finished reading the letter, J.D. said, "That's not what I said, but it sure is what I meant to say."

"*Señor*, when Tomas told me what you needed, he used the Spanish words Don Hernando often uses when talking to *los politicos* in Mexico City. Then I used the English I learned from *los mormones* and, as you requested, I will write it using the penmanship they taught me."

Knowing that the young woman was modest and afraid he might offend her, J.D. had asked Tomas to give her a twenty-dollar gold piece to buy *libros para los niños*.

J.D. tried to give the woman a smile. She smiled in return and spoke softly.

"*Señor* Hooper, your gift is appreciated so much and my students, the future of Mexico, will be eternally grateful." She looked to Tomas then back at J.D. and added, "I will have the finished letter for you in two hours."

As she rose from her chair, J.D. stood awkwardly following Tomas's gesture.

"*Gracias, Señorita* Josefina," he said.

After the young woman departed, J.D. said, "Tomas, you know what kind of man I am and the kinds of things I do."

"*Si*," was the Mexican's brief reply.

"Even knowing these things, you still treat me better than most of the men I've ever met."

"*Amigo*, I *could* say that it is because *El Jefe* likes you and trusts you. That is true, of course, but it is only part of the reason. In all of my years I have met many men, some very bad and some very good. Most men are both good and bad. But despite the struggles you seem to have and the violence that flows from you like heat from a hot stone, you have a heart for important people, not the rich men and haughty women of course, but the children—the little ones who are so often forgotten and hurt. So, to me you *are* good and for that I like you and want always to help you." Tomas stood and touched J.D. gently on the shoulder. Then he turned and walked into the house.

Alone in the courtyard, Hooper sat listening to the doves in the nearby junipers and the distant croaking of the ravens. But, as peaceful as these sounds were, when he reflected on what Tomas had said, the man's words seemed strange, maybe even undeserved.

Later, while sitting on the bed in his hotel room, J.D. thought about the strangeness of the day. He'd gone to the hacienda to get help writing a letter; one that would help him kill two men. The letter had been written in a way he could never have done on his own, written by a young, unsuspecting woman, a teacher. But Hooper had left Juarez with something else, and it was this thing that was bothering him as he sat on the rumpled bed. He should have felt happy that someone liked him because of who he was rather than hate him for what he did, but no happiness came. Instead of feeling pleased, the new knowledge felt like a burden, like a heavy sack of stones slung over his shoulder. *If I'm gonna survive in this world I gotta be willin' to do things other men won't. Stealin', beatin' people up, killin' and burnin' is what I do. There ain't no good in that and it don't leave room for friends.*

☆ ☆ ☆

The morning light that filtered through the curtained window next to the bed fell on his shoulders. Still awake, J.D. was exhausted, his head ached, and his neck and shoulders were knotted from the battle he'd waged in the darkness. But he had a job to do and things to get done in order to finish the task Villa had given him. He shaved and got dressed, walked out of the hotel and down to the corner. There was a Mexican boy trying to sell newspapers on the street and J.D. asked him if he'd like to earn some extra money.

"What would I have to do, *Señor*?"

Pulling the boy into the shadow of an alley, he said, "All you gotta do is take a message to an office building I'll show you. Do it for me in the next half hour and I'll give you a dollar."

"I can do it now," he said.

The boy followed J.D. as he walked the few blocks to the building. Stopping on the corner, J.D. pointed to the door and said, "I want you to go into the building, walk up to the counter and hand this to the woman sitting there. Don't say anything, don't answer any questions, and don't stay in there too long. Got it?"

"Si, *Señor*. Can I have the dollar?"

"You'll get the dollar when you come back to me. Do it now, come right back, and I'll give you the money."

The youngster rushed across the street and reached up for the door handle. He looked back at J.D., then entered the building. Less than a minute later, the boy came running across the street and found J.D. in the alley.

"I gave the paper to the lady. She started asking me who it was for, but I said nothing. When she looked at the paper, she told me to leave, so I did. Can I have the dollar now?"

Hooper handed him the silver coin, then told him to go away. *It's set up now. I hope they're greedy enough to follow the instructions*. He pulled the tobacco buyer's gold watch out of his pocket, noted that it was just after ten and smiled. *Just need to set up one more thing and I'll be ready*.

J.D. jumped on the streetcar and rode to the bridge, crossed over to Juarez, and went into Felipé's. Knowing that the bartender was a friend of Tomas's, Hooper asked the man to find someone who'd take him to the hacienda. Ten minutes later he was in a wagon and fifteen more after that he walked into the courtyard, looking for his friend.

Tomas walked out of the house and said, "You are back, amigo."

"I am, Tomas. I need to know if you can have something made for me while I wait here this afternoon."

After sending Felipé's helper back to the cantina, Tomas asked, "What is it you need?"

"I'm not even sure what to call it, but it's a leather pouch about this long," he held his hands half a foot apart, "with a thong strap and filled with lead shot. I saw one bein' used in Memphis."

Tomas rubbed his chin and asked J.D. to follow him out to the corral. They walked into the barn and Tomas introduced him to the man who made saddles and bridles for Don Hernando. Speaking Spanish, Tomas described what J.D. wanted and the man nodded. They chatted for a few minutes and Tomas said, "It will be ready in one hour. Come back to the house and we will rest in the courtyard."

In less than an hour the *peletero* entered the courtyard. He handed the sap to J.D. Tomas looked at the finished product and then watched Hooper slap it into his hand a few times. Hooper thanked the leatherworker and put two silver pesos on the table.

"This'll work just fine, Tomas. Can I get a ride to the border?"

"I must see Felipé this afternoon, so I will take you. Let me find the things I need, and I'll meet you out front." He called to the woman in the kitchen and she sent a boy to get the wagon.

Chapter 20

Back in his room, J.D. cleaned his pistol and checked to see that each of the chambers was loaded. Then he slid his knife out of the scabbard, ran his thumb gently over the cutting edge and decided it wasn't sharp enough. Using the leather strop hanging on the wall, J.D. worked the blade until the edge was honed like a razor. Finally, holding the sap by its strap, he slammed it hard onto the bed and smiled. *If I can't take care of them two fellas with these, then I ain't good enough for this job.* He looked at the tools arrayed in front of him. *But I am.*

☆ ☆ ☆

By seven o'clock the next night, J.D. stood in the small, dark alcove at the far end of the alley. The only light came from the faint glow of the rising moon. Knowing he'd be leaving El Paso that night, Hooper had purposely left his good suit in the hotel and wore the oldest clothes he owned. The only items he couldn't be without were his derby, the one he'd taken from the dead man in Kentucky, his weapons and his money.

The deadline for the exchange of money was ten o'clock. J.D. expected the two men to arrive early, maybe even an hour early. On the card he'd told them to come halfway into the alley and wait along the east wall, and that at ten he would enter from the main street. The card said that they would recognize him by his tall hat. Hooper wasn't foolish enough to think that everything would go according to the plan. He had set up some obstacles in the alley—an empty crate, a pile of rubbish, and a putrid dead rat—so they would stop short of where he'd be hiding. To his own advantage, he knew exactly where the obstacles were so that they wouldn't get in his way when he rushed them.

"Ain't nothin' to do now but wait," he whispered.

As he settled into the alcove, J.D. began to think about how the men might approach the alley. He'd assumed that they would simply follow his instructions on the card. Yet, if he had found the short alley to the back street, they might find it too. Realizing that one more piece of cover was necessary, he looked around in the alcove and found some long pieces of scrap lumber. Setting them up lengthwise at an angle gave him a narrow hiding place. From his position behind the boards, J.D. had a clear view both up and down the alley.

J.D. couldn't see his watch in the darkness and had no way of knowing what the time was. But given the cramps he was getting in his legs and the cottony dryness of his mouth, he figured that it had to be near the deadline. Several times during the hours he'd stood hidden by the boards, he'd nearly convinced himself that they wouldn't take the bait. Somehow, though, he knew that their greed would overcome any fear that they would be walking into a trap.

"Looks like we got here first."

"Yeah," the second man said nervously. "We don't want him to get the jump on us."

J.D. froze at the sound of the voices and could tell that the first one had come from the back of the alley and the other from just beyond the obstacles.

"Get on up here and watch out for the stuff in the way."

Through the gaps, J.D. watched the two men come together just short of his hiding spot.

"Why'd we agree to meet in an alley, anyway? It stinks in here."

"Because we're gonna get rich. We don't know who this Mexican is, but if he's carrying a thousand dollars in gold we got a good chance of keeping it without giving him the seven hundred."

"You have it, though, the seven hundred? I mean, just in case he's brought along some protection."

"I have it, don't worry."

They stood quietly for a few minutes and then the man with the bandage lit a cigar and blew a cloud of smoke through his lips.

"If he comes alone, we'll try to get all the money. We can put the seven hundred back in the safe and no one will be the wiser. If not, we'll make the trade and get outta here."

They stood quietly by the wall, facing the open end of the alley. J.D. could hardly stand still. Adrenalin rushed through his veins, his hands dripped with sweat, he could hear his heart pounding, and was almost afraid to breathe. Everything in his body said Now! Without stopping to think, Hooper pushed the boards away from the wall and they crashed with a deafening sound.

Startled, the men turned toward the noise. "What's that?" one of them said.

J.D. darted around the crate and swung the sap at the back of the bandaged head. He heard it crush the man's skull and watched as he fell. With an uncontrollable fury, J.D. turned and struck the other man with the sap. Clutching his arm, and groaning in pain, the man cried out, "What the hell," then fumbled as he pulled a gun out of his pocket and tried to cock the hammer. J.D. moved right up on him and plunged the long, flat blade of his knife into the man's gut. He held it there for only a second, and then, with an evil grin on his face, he pulled it out and shoved it in again just to make sure. Driven by his rage, he turned quickly toward the man on the ground, who moaned and reached for the back of his head. J.D. leaned over him and drove the bloody knife into his throat just below the ear. He pulled out the knife and wiped the blade on the dead man's coat, then stood back looking at the mess he'd created.

Even in the darkness, J.D. could see the growing puddles of blood on the ground. He could smell it and feel it on his hands and clothes. His heart thundered and his body trembled with a pleasurable excitement as his brain slowly absorbed the reality of what he'd just done. When his thoughts caught up, the excitement curdled in his stomach. J.D. fell to his knees and vomited on the dead men. He grunted and struggled to his feet, backing away from the bodies. He quickly searched through their coats and found the letter and the card in the envelope. He took the seven hundred dollars from the bleeding man's pants and stuffed the bills into his own coat pocket. Turning around, he ran through the short back alley to the quiet street and sprinted in the direction of the river.

☆ ☆ ☆

The darkness and quiet of El Paso's streets gave J.D. cover as he ran through alleys and across avenues. Chased between the tall buildings by his echoing footfalls he grew weary and short of breath. The lingering smell of blood on his hands and shirt drove him like a red-tinted storm. Wanting to stop to rest, but afraid, J.D. didn't quit until he reached the riverbank.

Near the shallow ford he'd seen the week before, J.D. fell to his knees, and washed the blood from his hands. Even in the dark he could picture the flowing water carrying the red stain away. The image of the carnage he'd created flashed in his head, each plunge of the knife, each swing of the sap, elicited a small spark of pleasure that quickly soured into fear.

Several minutes passed before Hooper raised his head. He glanced down river to the bridge and saw that the sentinels—both Mexican and American—were on duty, highlighted by the single electric lamps hanging on their guard shacks.

Rising clumsily, he thought, *I need to get to the hacienda*. J.D. looked again at the guards and walked quietly through the river, doing his best to find the shallow spots. Catching his foot on a hidden rock, he stumbled and fell. The splashing water roared in his ears, but the noise brought no reaction from those on the bridge.

Reaching the Mexican side of the river, Hooper snuck up the bank and moved quickly between two adobe buildings onto a dirt path. He crossed the narrow dirt streets and wound his way back to the one place he'd recognize—Felipé's Cantina. Hooper rested a few minutes to catch his breath and then walked south down the road toward Don Fernando's.

The same smile-like sliver of moon that had illuminated the alley provided enough light to reveal the occasional obstacles on the dirt road. Other than a few barking dogs and one squalling baby, J.D. heard only the soft moaning of the wind through the junipers. Physically and emotionally exhausted, he stumbled along his way. Finally reaching the hacienda, he found a dark quiet spot behind the barn, lay down in the dirt, covered himself with his old coat and closed his eyes. The desert night was cool. He was safe…for now.

☆ ☆ ☆

"*Señor* Hooper."

A voice echoed through J.D.'s mind. Lost in his dream, numb and uncertain, he reached for his gun and pointed it wildly into the air.

"My friend, please, it is I, Tomas!"

"Tomas?" J.D. cried out, his eyes red and swollen. "I'm sorry," he mumbled, and lowered the pistol.

Tomas blanched when he saw the blood-crusted shirt.

"Are you hurt, *Señor*? Do you need a doctor?" The old man reached toward J.D.'s belly.

"This isn't my blood, Tomas." J.D. fell silent.

Tomas knew not to ask more questions.

"Can you tell me when Villa will return?"

"Oh, J.D., *El Jefe* won't return for at least another week."

"Then I need a place to hide until he does get back. For now all I need is a bath, some clean clothes, and a bed. I've got plenty of money, so I can pay, but I have to stay out of sight."

"Do not fear, my friend. Don Hernando is away from the hacienda, so you may use one of the empty rooms in the casa, and you do not need to pay for his hospitality. I will make sure that you have plenty of food, rest, and a place to wait for *El Jefe's* return." He extended his hand and helped J.D. to his feet. "Now, let us go up to the house. You have arrived in time for breakfast."

As the two friends walked up the path, J.D. thought about telling Tomas what had happened in El Paso but decided that he didn't want to burden the old man with the details. *Better wait for Villa. He'll be glad I did what he asked, and maybe he can help me get out of this part of the country*.

J.D. spent restless days and hellish nights at the hacienda. Whenever he tried to relax in the courtyard or wandered by the corrals, or even while eating with Tomas, J.D. was nervous and agitated. He wasn't concerned that he'd killed the men; that had been done out of loyalty to Villa and because the gringos had deserved to die. What kept him awake was the way he had enjoyed killing them. The rage that tore through him in the dark alley and visions of the crushing sap and the plunging blade, made his heart race with pain and pleasure, a complicated feeling that he didn't understand. Even when he could sleep, his dreams were filled with rivers of blood. Thick churning waves of it followed him as he ran from the faceless men who chased him.

On Friday, while the two friends were sitting in the courtyard, a boy rushed up to Tomas and thrust a newspaper toward him. The old man patted the boy on the head, thanked him, and quickly looked at the front page.

"Perhaps this is the news you've been looking for, J.D."

J.D. slowly worked his way through the column of print. The article was an update on some news of the previous week. The reporter told a tale of two well-known businessmen who had apparently been robbed and then killed in an alley several blocks from their workplace. The writer described in detail the brutality of the crime and speculated that, because of the weapons used, a gang of Mexicans had killed the two men. The police had said that they did not expect assistance from the officials south of the border, but would continue to investigate.

"Some fellas got killed last week in El Paso and the police think Mexicans did it," said J.D.

"They always accuse us when they don't know the truth."

"It says they're gonna keep lookin' and that they don't think the Juarez police will help 'em." J.D. rubbed his face with his hands then stared at his friend. "Tomas…I'm the one who killed 'em. I did it for Villa."

"These men, *El Jefe* asked you to kill them?"

"He did, Tomas, but I can't even describe it to you. It's just," he stopped and took a breath. "It was ugly and it keeps me awake at night. I keep lookin' up the road, thinkin' they're gonna come for me." J.D. didn't tell Tomas that what kept him awake was more than the paranoia—it was the pure excitement he'd got from killing the gringos.

"I am sorry that you are troubled by this thing, J.D. *El Jefe* must have had a good reason for having you do this task, but I believe that when he returns, and you tell him what happened, he will make sure you are safe."

They continued their conversation, but the mood remained somber. J.D. wondered if he'd have to stay in Mexico. *I hope Villa has a plan.*

The gentle breeze from the west kicked up a little dust and caused the junipers to rustle. "Do you think Villa will come back today?" J.D. asked.

"I do not know, *Señor*, but I hope so."

☆ ☆ ☆

An hour past sundown, a rider circled the hacienda and a few minutes later Villa and his riders rode up to the stable. Villa walked to the casa and left his men to take care of the horses. Tomas met his *patrón* as he entered the softly lit courtyard.

"Welcome home, *El Jefe*." Tomas handed Villa a cup of water. "Can I get you something to eat?"

"*Gracias*, Tomas."

Hooper walked into the courtyard from the house. His appearance surprised Villa.

"J.D., my friend, I did not expect to see you here." Noticing how the American was dressed, he smiled broadly and said, "I see that you have decided to rid yourself of the stuffy *gringo* clothes and dress like a true Mexican."

"It's good to see you, too, *Jefe*. I'm glad you're back. There's some things we need to talk about."

"First, I want to eat. Then we will talk." Villa turned toward Tomas, spoke to him in Spanish and watched as the old man headed briskly into the casa. Villa walked to the corner of the courtyard and washed his hands in the basin. Turning to Hooper, he said, "J.D., please sit down. Whatever is on your mind will still be there later. *Por favor*, sit and have a drink with me."

Hooper sat down, his shoulders slumped. He rolled his head, trying to work out the knots in his neck. Tomas came out of the house and brought a bottle of tequila and set it and some glasses on the table. Villa sat next to the American and aware of his discomfort, said, "Relax, *amigo*."

J.D. was anxious to tell Villa what had happened. But he was also concerned that how he'd killed the men and where he'd done it might make Villa unhappy. Trying to stay calm, he gripped the glass of tequila with both hands. Inside, however, his heart raced, and his nerves felt like ants were crawling through his veins. He'd patiently watched Villa eat, and when nearly an hour had passed, and he'd reached the point where he wanted to shout out the story, Villa set his glass on the table and turned to him.

"Tell me what happened with the gringos."

The story rushed out of J.D., his excitement riding the words like tree limbs pushed along by a flood. He told Villa how he'd planned and carried out the murder, how he'd used the letter to draw the men to the alley and his rushed escape across the river. He spent the longest time describing how he used the sap and the knife and how the blood and his own rage had continued to fill his head. All the while, Villa sat peacefully, listening to the words and watching J.D. When Hooper got to the end, he just stopped. His mouth dry, he looked at Villa and said, "That's it, *Jefe*. I don't know what happened to me in that alley, but I'm scared that someone's lookin' for me."

Villa filled J.D.'s glass. "Drink it." Hooper hesitated. "All of it, now." J.D. lifted the glass to his lips, tilted his head back, and swallowed the burning liquid. Calmly setting the glass down, he took a deep breath and let the air out slowly.

"Better?"

J.D. nodded.

"Do you think anyone saw you?"

"No one saw me."

"You are sure of this, J.D.?"

"Yes. It was late and dark, and I stayed in the alleys and

crossed the river upstream of the bridge. Once I was on this side of the river I didn't see anyone, and no one saw me."

"Then why are you worried? You are safe here now, are you not?"

"For now, but what if ...what if someone *did* see me. What if they're lookin' for me?"

"Do not worry about 'what if'. We will rest tonight, and I will think about how to get you out of Chihuahua." He leaned into J.D.'s face, staring at him with his dark eyes. "You have served me well by ridding the world of these men. I will take care of you, my friend."

Chapter 21

The sun rose behind J.D. and Villa's lieutenant, Miguel, on their third day out of Juarez. The air was still night-cool and the mist on the small pond just outside the village disappeared as the golden rays spread across the rocky plain ahead of them. Reluctantly, J.D. mounted his horse while Miguel finished checking the burro's load. Hooper's eyes took in the vast openness of the Chihuahuan desert spotted with clusters of *cholla*—cactus with tiny irritating stickers—and the occasional tall *ocotillo*, whose defenses were inch long needle-like spikes. What amazed J.D. was how little affected were the birds that flitted in and out of these dangerous plants.

J.D. followed Miguel as he led them into the west. Despite the relief he felt leaving the city behind, his butt and thighs were sore, and the back of his neck had been roasted a deep red by the unrelenting Mexican sun. The cerulean sky was cloudless and the soft breeze from the west caressed J.D.'s face.

Their ride led them away from another tiny, nameless settlement of adobe houses whose inhabitants had welcomed them as visiting royalty. They'd recognized Miguel, of course, and once he'd told them of Villa's great love for the American, the people crowded around Hooper, touching his home-spun shirtsleeves with their hands, their smiles genuine and their voices full of laughter. J.D. wasn't sure how to respond, but his weak smile seemed to work. The night before, the villagers had shared the bounty of their labors with the two travelers and they'd feasted on squash and beans and roasted goat. The mescal J.D. shared with the village's men reminded him of the moonshine he'd often swallowed in Kentucky.

By mid-day, the travelers had covered another fifteen or twenty miles. Miguel had spoken only once to let J.D. know that tonight they'd reach the town of Ascension where they would stop for a day to rest the horses. The trek through the flat, sandy country provided little distraction. But J.D.'s mind was full of images he'd left behind in the alley. He may have put miles between himself and the dead men, but the ugliness, the brutality of the murders remained fresh, so fresh that he could still feel the sticky blood on his hands. When he could clear his head of these thoughts, Hooper would remind himself about the money and the friend who'd given him a horse and an opportunity to get away from his troubles. J.D. was grateful for Villa and his aid, but it was Tomas he would miss. The old man had been helpful, kind even, and a willing teacher. J.D. shook his head in wonder at the kinship he'd felt with the ancient Mexican.

☆ ☆ ☆

The day and two nights in the large town of Ascension had been a respite for J.D. He'd worked some of the saddle-weariness from his legs by resting in the plaza and watching the busy morning activities of the Mexicans. J.D. only saw Miguel once during the long day when the young man strolled through the market with a young woman who reminded him of the letter-writing teacher in Juarez. After noon, the plaza cleared out as the locals enjoyed their afternoon siesta. Resting in the shade of a willow, J.D. ate a bean-filled tortilla and thought about how different his life had become in the year since leaving tobacco country. Then he'd been a hired hand living in a broken-down shack. In those days, J.D. had thought of himself as a man with little future. *It ain't like that now. Now I get paid to do things for people. But I'm still runnin' from...* His thought ended suddenly, unable to name the fear. *Even bein' down here in Mexico in this worn-out, dried-up land is better than bein' in jail.*

☆ ☆ ☆

"Only a few more days, *Señor* J.D., and your journey will end."

Hooper groaned. "How close are we and where are we headed?"

"Perhaps we are forty miles, maybe fifty miles away," said Miguel. "*El Jefe* told me to not tell you the name of the village. He said it was better that you not know. But it is in Durango, near *El Jefe's* hometown. He is well known there and you will be safe."

That don't make any sense, J.D. thought. *What difference would it make for me to know the name of a place in a country where I don't even speak the language*? J.D. wiped the sweat from his face and neck and shifted in the saddle. Tired of swallowing the dust kicked up by Miguel's horse and the burro, he angled off the track a bit and rode next to the Mexican. Hooper wanted to ask Miguel more about Villa but changed his mind when the man quickly jerked the reins to his chest.

Miguel pointed off to the northwest and said, "The wind is picking up. Do you see those *diablos de polvo*, the dust devils?" Miguel frowned and added, "We should keep moving. If the wind gets stronger, we will have to find a place to protect the horses and the burro."

They trudged on for what seemed like hours, then just before sundown the wind picked up and started blowing sand and dust into the faces of the two riders. Miguel pulled the neckerchief from around his neck and tied it over the lower half of his face. J.D. did the same and held onto the brim of the derby when a gust nearly pushed it off his head.

He wanted to turn away from the wind, but his squinted eyes were drawn to the monstrous wall of dust that was moving toward them. At a distance, J.D. could see the sun-touched clouds, pink and copper above the eerie, frightening storm. To him it looked like a cloud; muddy brown and curling along the desert floor rather than floating in the sky. It was an endless, rumbling wall of dirt and it was headed directly at them. When he turned to Miguel, he watched as the man became lost, swallowed by the dark storm. Instantly Miguel was no longer in sight. J.D.'s horse reared up and tried to turn away from the wind, but he held the frightened animal in place. When he looked back toward the approaching cloud of dirt J.D. saw that it was nearly upon him.

The horse reared again and spun quickly down wind. The dust and sand blasted the animal's hindquarters and J.D.'s back. Surrounded by the grit, blinded by the dust and sand, J.D. wasn't sure which way his panicked horse was headed. They were enclosed within the cloud and Hooper couldn't see or hear anything except the howling storm-driven wall of dust. He no longer had control and it took all of his strength to stay on the saddle. The howling wind blasted his face above the kerchief. J.D. squeezed his eyes shut yet the grit tore at his battered lids. Charging off blindly, the animal rushed in frenzy, brushing into the scrubby trees and cactus, stumbling over rocks and jerking left and right, blindly seeking shelter. Hooper felt entombed in the thick dust. He couldn't breathe and choked, swallowing more of the flying dirt. The roaring storm was so loud that he barely heard the horse scream as the ground disappeared from beneath its hooves. J.D. was suddenly tossed from the saddle and flew blindly into the cloud. The last thing he heard as his body slammed into the sandy ground was the human-like shriek of his horse. Then mercifully, he blacked out.

Chapter 22

Even as a well-paid employee of the Southern Pacific Railroad, Noah Jensen was tired of riding on trains. After he'd left Memphis, he got off at every scheduled stop on the route west. In Little Rock, he'd learned that Hooper had stayed in the hotel near the depot one night before departing the next morning. Then Hooper had spent at least two nights in Dallas. Encouraged by these quick successes—and angry at himself for going to Chicago—Noah went to San Antonio.

In that city, he lost Hooper. He stayed a few days and canvassed the hotels and saloons, but concluded that Hooper had either passed through or headed to Austin or Houston. Still determined to find Hooper, but frustrated by the lack of information, he wore himself ragged considering the alternatives. Why would the arsonist go south, where would he hide, what place would give him immunity and a chance to avoid getting caught? *El Paso and the Mexican border. That's it,* he thought as a sense of relief filled his head. *He's gone to El Paso.*

☆ ☆ ☆

Noah Jensen arrived at El Paso's Union Depot hot, tired, and travel-sore, and the blazing sun did little to welcome him. The depot was crowded with all sorts of cranky people: beggars, gringos with sour attitudes, porters and vendors, as well as a prevailing odor of sweaty bodies.

Noah picked up his suitcase and headed to a hotel. The

piercing sunlight stabbed its way into his brain and squinting did little to relieve the pain. Pushing his way across the crowded, dusty street, he stepped into the lobby and approached the front desk. The clerk, a neatly dressed young man, greeted him cordially.

"Yes, sir, how may I help you," he said, sliding the registration book forward.

Noah dropped his gaze to the bound ledger and said, "I need a room, a good room on the top floor."

The clerk turned toward the back wall, grabbed a key out of a slot, and slid it toward Noah.

"Room 402 is nice, sir, it faces the street rather than the alley."

"That's fine. I'll take it."

"Can I call a bell boy for your bag?"

"No, I'll carry it," Noah said, signing on the empty line. He grabbed his case and crossed to the stairs, taking a moment to scan the large room before starting his ascent, looking for, but not expecting to see J.D. Hooper.

The small room's northern exposure provided some relief from the bright sun, but the heat was still intense. Noah opened the window, hoping for a little breeze, and was gifted with a gentle flow of fetid air. Choosing a little coolness over avoiding the crowded street smell, he left the window ajar. He tossed his hat on the bed, hung his coat on the back of the chair, and sat on the mattress.

He tried to sleep, but it was too hot and he was anxious. Maybe it's cooler outside, he thought. Noah rose from the bed, grabbed his hat and coat, and walked down to the lobby. He stepped out onto the street and walked past a saloon. That's what I need—a drink. He found a quiet spot at the end of the bar and signaled the bartender.

"What'll you have?" asked the bald man with a smile.

"Bourbon, if you've got it."

The bartender reached a bottle off the shelf and poured

a shot into a glass.

"First time in El Paso?"

Noah swallowed the shot in one draught and slid the empty glass toward the bartender. "Yes it is."

The warmth in his belly felt good. "Gimme another."

"Staying long or just visiting?" said the bartender as he filled the glass again.

"Is it always this hot here?" Noah wiped the sweat from his forehead.

"It'll cool off in a couple of months. By the way, my name's Oscar."

"Noah," he said, extending his hand.

"What kinda work you do, Noah?"

"I'm a detective with the Southern Pacific."

Oscar seemed unfazed by this and smiled. "Somebody steal a piece of track?"

Noah didn't smile in return, but appreciated the man's sense of humor.

"Nope, but he burned a hundred cars."

Oscar's eyes widened and a whistle escaped his lips.

Noah continued. "I've been looking for him all over, but I think he's headed this way." He locked eyes with Oscar. "His name is J.D. Hooper, and I'm gonna find him." He downed the shot and added, "Yep, I'm gonna find him."

Noah left the bar and returned to the hotel. Before drifting off to sleep, Noah drafted a wire to Harriman summarizing his discoveries in Little Rock and Dallas. He told him about San Antonio and the decision to continue on to El Paso. Then he closed his eyes and slept. When he awoke two hours later, the smelly breeze from the street below had blown the papers onto the floor. Noah gathered them up and took them down to the front desk.

"Please see that this is sent out this evening." He handed the telegraph forms to the clerk and asked him to charge it to his room.

☆ ☆ ☆

Noah spent the next morning diligently canvassing the hotels around the train depot. He called on hotel managers, desk clerks, bell boys, and porters, but none of the establishments had seen or heard of Hooper. By dark he'd headed back to his hotel. Noah wandered along a back corridor and found the employees' lunchroom. A few porters were on a break and a cloud of smoke drifted near the ceiling.

"Gentlemen," he said to the workers, "I'm in need of some information regarding a man who may have stayed in this hotel." He flipped each of them a silver dollar, hoping to loosen their tongues. "His name is J.D. Hooper." Then he showed them the wanted poster and described the arsonist.

Almost on cue, the men slipped the coins into their pockets and nodded their heads. One of them spoke up.

"We don't usually know the names of the folks who stay here, mister. But we do remember those who tip us." The porter smiled, and the others nodded. "There was a fella who looks somethin' like that picture." The other porters chimed their agreement. For the first time, Noah was encouraged that he was on the right track.

"But the man ain't been around for a while. It'd probably be best to check with the night clerk."

Noah nodded. "When does the night clerk get here?"

"He comes on in a couple hours," said one of the other porters. "At eleven."

"What's this night clerk's name?" Noah asked.

The first porter said, "It's Mr. Garrison."

Noah thanked them for their time then went back to the hotel lobby. He picked up a newspaper from the front desk and sat on one of the padded lounges. *If Mr. Garrison is a punctual employee, he'll be at the desk at 11 o'clock.* Noah scanned the paper, looking for hints and clues of Hooper's whereabouts. While waiting, he grew angry at himself for wasting the day on the hot streets of El Paso. *I'll be extremely annoyed at myself if it turns out Hooper stayed in this hotel. Extremely annoyed*, but also relieved that he was still on the man's trail.

At precisely eleven, Garrison showed up at the desk. Noah watched as he relieved the clerk going off duty. His frustration and his need to move on with the case had made him edgy.

"Excuse me, you're Mr. Garrison?"

The man looked up from the registration book. "Yes sir, I am. How may I help you?"

"My name is Jensen. I'm staying in room 402. I'm a detective for the Southern Pacific Railroad and I hope you can provide me with some information on an important case I am working."

"I'll be happy to help, sir, if I can."

Noah pulled out the wanted poster and showed it to Garrison, while describing Hooper. "I have reason to believe that J.D. Hooper came to El Paso and it's possible he stayed here in your hotel."

"Let me look in the book." Garrison opened the leather cover and turned a few pages. "Do you know when the gentleman might have stayed here?"

"He would not have checked in any earlier than five or six weeks ago."

"We get a lot of guests, sir. If you like, I'll look through the last month's pages and let you know in the morning."

"Well, you see Mr. Garrison, this is a criminal case and it is very important for me to apprehend this individual. Is it possible that you could do it for me this evening?"

Garrison paused, wondering how he might turn the request into an opportunity to make a few dollars, then said, "I suppose I could do it now, but that might take me away from my regular duties and ..."

Noah interrupted him and said, "Perhaps a small contribution to your leisure activities will help." He put a twenty-dollar gold piece on the counter.

Garrison quickly pocketed the coin and said, "Let me look." He leafed through eight or ten pages and found Hooper's name, then turned the book toward Noah and pointed to the line.

"It seems that a Mr. Hooper *was* registered here sir. I remember him now, detective."

"Do you know if he's still in El Paso?" Noah's heart started pounding. *Finally*, he thought. *He was here*.

"I wouldn't know that sir. He could be or he could have gone to Juarez."

Noah saw a familiar look, the one an informant uses when he wants more money. "Well, then Mr. Garrison, I thank you for your assistance." Jensen walked across the lobby and up the stairs to his room.

☆ ☆ ☆

After breakfast the next morning, Noah went to the hotel manager's office and spoke to the man's secretary. He was ushered into a compact room with a desk, some shelves, file cabinets and a window looking out onto an alley.

"Good morning, Mr. Jensen. What can I do for you?"

"Good morning to you, sir. I wonder if you can clear something up for me. I understand that in the past month a Mr. J.D. Hooper was a guest of the hotel. I need to find this man and thought that you could help me."

The manager turned away from Noah, opened a file drawer and pulled out several sheets of paper. "Our records show that Mr. Hooper did stay with us. He paid for a month in advance and then, before the month was up, he disappeared. Mr. Hooper hasn't been in the hotel for at least six weeks."

"Do you know where he is?"

"Since Mr. Hooper paid in advance, we were not concerned by his departure."

"Did he take his belongings?"

"No, he left some nice clothes, but we did not save them."

"Did Hooper ever entertain anyone here in the hotel? Did he ever take a guest to his room?" Noah doubted that the hotel would allow prostitutes in the rooms, but he'd learned that unasked questions made for a poor detective.

"Well sir," said the manager, "we don't keep track of our guests in that way, but one of my night managers did mention that Mr. Hooper frequently left the hotel with an old Mexican."

"Did your night manager see where they went?"

"Mexico, I presume."

"What was the date that Mr. Hooper left his room?"

The manager gave the information to Noah then suggested if he had any more questions he should consider talking to the police.

"I know that you are a detective for the Southern Pacific, and we are very grateful for your patronage. Nevertheless, we must protect the privacy of all of our lodgers."

Noah slid a gold double-eagle across the desk, but the manager pushed it back.

"Your company appreciates our discretion," he said. "And so do all of our guests."

Noah left the man's office and walked out into the lobby with a satisfied look on his face.

☆ ☆ ☆

Noah entered the Police Department and the desk sergeant took a cursory glance at his gold badge then pointed to the stairwell. "Better stop at the Deputy Chief's office on the second floor. I'll let him know you're comin'."

Noah walked briskly up the stairs and entered a large

open room, then walked over to the clearly marked door and tapped on the glass. When he heard a muffled "come on in" he opened the door and strode up to the desk.

"Thank you for seeing me, Chief. My name's Noah Jensen. I'm a detective with the Southern Pacific Railroad and if you have the time, I need some assistance." Noah proffered his badge and the portly policeman took it and examined it closely.

"So, you're a Railroad Detective, huh? Did you ever do any real police work?"

"Yes sir I did." Noah ignored the cop's tone. "I spent a couple years walking a beat in San Francisco."

"How'd you end up with the railroad?"

"I saved someone's life, a child important to...a person with the railroad."

The chief handed the badge across the desk and gestured to a chair. "Have a seat and tell me what it is that you need from me."

Noah spent the next ten minutes giving the officer a thorough report on the fire, the destruction, and his investigations in Memphis and Chicago. He described the arsonist and how he ended up in El Paso.

"According to the manager at the hotel, this man Hooper disappeared several weeks ago. He left some nice clothes in the room, but no other clues." Noah waited for the man to speak, but the chief remained silent. "Our company has lost a lot of money because of this man and I need to find him. Have you had any unexplained fires in your city in the past month?"

"We've had a few blazes, but nothing substantial, and nothing we can't explain. Has this fella, Hooper, been known to do anything else?"

"Such as?" asked Noah.

"Such as armed robbery or murder," the chief said.

"I'm not aware of anything that links the man to crimes

like these, but a person who'd burn nearly a hundred rail-cars would likely be capable of other things. Why do you ask?"

"We have an unsolved case from a month or so back and we aren't making much progress on it. A couple of businessmen were found murdered in an alley. They were known to have taken several hundred dollars from the company's safe and it wasn't found on their bodies." The chief paused and then continued. "This may not have anything to do with your Mr. Hooper, because the owner confirmed that the two had no authority to be in possession of the money. I was just wondering if your man was involved, but it doesn't seem to be the case."

"If you do solve your case, Chief, would you let me know? If...no, *when* I catch Hooper I'll find out if he did the killing and I'll let you know. In any case, thanks for your help."

Noah walked out of the chief's office and back down the steps. On the wall next to the sergeant's desk he noticed one of his wanted posters on a crowded bulletin board. Disgusted, he shook his head and left the building. He headed back to the hotel, wondering where J.D. Hooper had gone. *Hooper has some money, otherwise, how'd he disappear so quickly? Where'd he go and why leave without his good clothes. Did he leave in a hurry?* The timing of the El Paso murders and Hooper's disappearance flashed an image into his brain, but it was just out of reach, clouded in a mist. Shaking his head as if to clear it, he thought, *this may be a dead end, but maybe not. Might as well get up to New York and report to Harriman.*

Chapter 23

The harsh croaking of a raven somewhere in the distance dragged J.D. back to consciousness. Gasping and coughing, he awoke with a start. The wind had finally stopped blowing and he was covered with dust and his kerchief was caked with grit. Breathing was very difficult and seeing was impossible. He slowly sat up and tried to open his eyes, but the sand and grit made it painful. J.D. ripped the neckerchief from his throat and wiped the dust from his face, but each needle-sharp grain of sand stabbed into his skin. He tried to swallow, but instead gagged up brown phlegm. He tried again to open his eyes but still couldn't see. Finally opening one eye to a narrow slit, his blurred gaze shifted to the carcass of the horse lying ten yards away and then upward to the clear morning sky. His dust-filled ears still buzzed with the absent sound of the wind, but J.D. could sense that the storm had ended. *But when? Was it yesterday, or the day before?*

Taking a quick breath, he coughed again and felt a sharp pain in his ribs. J.D. tried to spit more dust, but his mouth was dry, and his tongue swollen. He needed water, but it hurt too much to move.

"I ain't dead yet," he growled through spasms of pain and more coughing and cried out again as he rose to his hands and knees. Taking shallow breaths, J.D. crawled over to the dead horse and pulled the canteen from the saddle horn. The raw, vile smell of the dead animal made him wretch, but he fought against the reaction and struggled into a sitting position against the far wall of the arroyo. J.D. unscrewed the cap of the canteen and took a sip of the warm water, swished the liquid around his mouth and spit out the brown sludge. He swallowed the next draught slowly and the one after that actually soothed his dry scratchy throat. "Nope, I ain't dead."

The pain in his side remained a dull ache as long as he didn't move. J.D. began to check himself for other injuries. Moving one hand over his face and head and finding no wounds or bumps, he checked his legs and feet. They, too, seemed unharmed. Taking another sip of the water and half a dozen short breaths, Hooper clenched his jaw, held back a cry, and stood up with his back to the wall.

J.D. knew he couldn't stay in the arroyo and that the water in the half-full canteen wouldn't last long in the desert. *I'll die for sure if I stay here and probably will if I do get out. So, I might as well die tryin' to live.* He moved slowly to the horse and groaned while tugging the saddle bag from under the animal's side, thankful for the loose sand. Opening the bag, he saw that his gun and his money were still there, then he scanned the floor of the canyon until he spotted his derby wedged between two rocks. Picking it up and settling it on his head, J.D. looked around once more and then started slowly walking down what he hoped was the way out.

From the ridge above him, two men watched him struggle.

"Are you alright, friend?"

Hooper looked up and thought he saw the faces of two bearded men wearing broad-brimmed straw hats.

"Are you hurt, sir?" This time J.D. clearly heard the words.

"Yeah," he said, reaching into the saddlebag for his pistol.

"You stay put then. We'll come get you."

One of the men pointed off to his left and said, "The cut runs out about half a mile back that way. We'll send some men to help you get out and see if we can salvage your saddle and bridle." The man looked away from the arroyo for a moment and then back at J.D. "They're on the way now, so just rest there."

Hooper didn't know who these people were and wondered what they might do to him. But he was hurt and tired, so he backed up and rested against the wall of the arroyo, closed his eyes, and held onto his sore side.

☆ ☆ ☆

Two teenage boys helped J.D. mount the burro and shortly after that they led the animal away from the dead horse. Each step the burro took sent a jolt of pain into Hooper's lungs.

Hooper was surprised by what he saw when they came out of the arroyo. At least three dozen people—men, women, and children—stared at him, a dusty man wearing a derby astride a small burro. Some of the children giggled, but the merriment lasted only a moment before a tall, bearded man walked through the crowd and up to J.D.

He called over several of the adult men who helped J.D. down from the burro and led him over to the shade of a wagon.

The old man spoke again. "Had it not been for those buzzards," he said, pointing to the half-dozen carrion eaters circling above the arroyo, "we would not have thought of stopping. It is definitely a miracle that we found you."

J.D. felt strange surrounded by so many people in the middle of the desert. All of the men wore the straw hats and the older ones all sported beards, especially the man in charge. He had more hair on his chin than the few wisps creeping out of his hat. The women and girls wore long dresses and bonnets. Even the children seemed to be wearing miniature versions of their elders' clothing.

"Thank you," J.D. muttered. "I don't know if it's a miracle, but I'm glad you found me."

"Oh, it is definitely a miracle, young man. We are returning from our church headquarters in Juarez and going back to our home at *Colonia Morelos*." He looked at J.D.'s wrinkled brow. "Were you heading west as well?"

"I was. I don't know what happened to the fella I was with, but he told me we were headed west. J.D. stopped, not sure what more to say. "I guess I better ride with you. I sure can't stay here."

"Then you'll come with us. I'm Elder Taylor, and this gathering of souls is my family."

"All of 'em are your family?"

"That's right, they are. My two wives, my five sons and their wives, my daughters—two of them with husbands—and eighteen grandchildren. My first wife, bless her soul, is no longer with us."

J.D. held off asking about the man's *wives* and said, "Sorry."

"Well then, welcome to our family. You'll ride in the back of my wagon. It should be far more comfortable than riding on the back of this creature," he said. gesturing at the burro.

In a short time, J.D. was resting on a layer of quilts in the back of a covered wagon. Knowing that the people were from a church, he relaxed, then closed his eyes and pulled the brim of the derby down over his forehead. The swaying wagon bed soon rocked him to sleep.

☆ ☆ ☆

J.D. woke to the ruckus of playing children and the smell of a juniper wood fire. He carefully sat up and scooted down the wagon bed until his feet and legs hung over the edge. His body was stiff and he felt a little dizzy. One of the children, a young boy slid to a stop in front of J.D. and stared up at his face. The youngster quickly turned and ran off toward the adults gathered around the fire.

"Ah, I see you've finally awakened. Are you hungry?"

"Yes sir, I am."

When he asked J.D. what they should call him, he hesitated about giving them his real name and said, "My name is John Dawson."

"Then let Amos help you down. Come join us, we're about ready to eat." The Elder walked away and his son, a tall muscular man, helped J.D. reach the ground.

"Can you make it to the fire by yourself, Mr. Dawson, or should I help you?"

"Lemme try by myself," said J.D. He took a few tentative steps and then continued slowly to the gathering around the fire. Every step, every breath hurt but he kept moving then sat in a chair offered by one of the ladies and thanked her.

"Mr. Dawson," said Elder Taylor, "we are a praying people, so before we eat, I would like to offer a blessing."

"Sure, go ahead."

"Thank you," said the old man. As hungry as J.D. suddenly felt, he was willing to let the man pray. *After all,* he thought, *if they hadn't stopped I might be dead. And hungry is better than dead.*

After the prayer, a girl of about fifteen brought J.D. a plate of beans, cornbread, and some apple slices. Hooper whispered a thank you and dug into the food. As he scooped up the last of the beans, the girl brought him a cup of water and asked him if he'd like some more to eat.

"If it ain't a problem, I could use another scoop of beans, miss."

When the girl returned, the elder spoke, "When you've finished, I'd like to take a look at your injury. Perhaps we can do something to ease the pain."

"I ain't sure what can be done about broken ribs," said J.D., "but I'm willin' to try."

As J.D. swallowed the last of the beans, Taylor said, "Let me help you with your shirt, Mr. Dawson. I want to see if the ribs are truly broken."

He helped Hooper remove his shirt then asked him to lift his arm. J.D. complied with a grimace but was able to contain the scream he felt building in his throat.

Elder Taylor probed the bruised spot on J.D.'s side.

"I can't determine if any of the ribs are broken, but we should treat the damage as if they were." He picked up a roll of cotton cloth and began to wrap the band around J.D.'s rib cage. "This may be uncomfortable and make it hard to breathe, Mr. Dawson, but the tighter it is the sooner you will heal."

J.D. groaned softly as the old man cinched him up like saddling a horse. The elder had been right. He could only take shallow breaths, but his side felt less vulnerable.

"Thank you, sir."

"You're welcome, Mr. Dawson. You should probably get more rest." He smiled at J.D. "We need to get on the road early if we're going to get to the *colonia* before the end of the week." He helped J.D. back into the wagon bed and pulled a light blanket up just far enough to cover the rib binding.

The pain made it difficult to sleep, but gave J.D. plenty of time to think, even worry about where he was and what these people wanted from him.

☆ ☆ ☆

For the next few days, J.D. rode in the back of Taylor's wagon. He was finally able to sleep and apparently healed some because the pain from his injured ribs began to ebb. Even though the family seemed to have taken a liking to him, it still bothered Hooper that they treated him like he was a nice person. *How would they act if they knew I was a killer? I'm pretty sure that their God would tell 'em to leave me here in the desert so I don't poison their children or bring a plague.*

At sunset the next day, the string of wagons crested a hill and drove into a river valley. On the flats along the river, J.D. saw several brick buildings and a larger number of homes and shops fashioned out of wood. One structure actually looked like a grain mill. When Taylor had mentioned a *colonia*—a colony—J.D. had pictured something like the adobe villages he and Miguel had seen. This was an American town stuck in the Mexican desert. Hooper was clearly surprised.

J.D. crawled out of the wagon and stood for a moment, letting a dizzy spell pass. As he glanced at his surroundings, the young girl who'd brought him food walked up to the wagon and told J.D. that Elder Taylor wanted to see him. He followed the girl down to the path and along the river to the large mill. Taylor and his sons were shaking hands and talking to a gathering of folks who looked and dressed just like the family. At once J.D. felt like a stranger. His derby hat and stained, torn clothing were clearly out of place. *I just need a drink and a bath.*

"My friends, I'd like you to meet Mr. John Dawson, a wounded traveler we happened upon during our journey." He stepped up to J.D. and said, "Mr. Dawson, these are our new neighbors and friends. Welcome to *Colonia Morelos*, the newest Mormon colony in Mexico."

☆ ☆ ☆

For the next several weeks, J.D. spent most of his time in a small cabin belonging to Taylor or sitting under a large cottonwood tree next to the river. One afternoon, the soft-spoken girl walked along the riverbank and J.D. called out to her.

"Excuse me, Miss Taylor."

"Yes, Mister Dawson."

"Could you please ask your father if it would be alright for me to see him tonight before supper?"

"My father?"

"Yes, your father, Elder Taylor."

"Oh, Mister Dawson," she let a tiny smile appear on her lips. "The Elder isn't my *father*, he's my husband."

The girl turned away from J.D. and continued toward the center of the town.

J.D. was stunned, speechless. A dark visceral anger grew quickly in his gut. The thought that the bearded old man would have more than one wife was strange, but that he'd have a wife who was still a child made J.D. sick to his stomach. *I oughta kill that old bastard*, he thought. He began to shake, his heart pounded, and he reached for his knife. But it wasn't on his belt. He'd not worn it since the Mormons had taken him in. Even though the murderous rage didn't go away, the kindness the family had shown him and the freedom they'd allowed him as he healed seemed to quench the fire. He knew, somehow, that he couldn't kill the old man, but he *could* leave. He could steal a horse and sneak away in the dark or he could buy a horse from them and ride away from this sickness. All he needed was an excuse.

"I gotta get outta here," he mumbled to himself. "I need to get on a horse and ride to a real town. And I gotta do it before I do or say somethin' stupid."

☆ ☆ ☆

Before heading to Taylor's house that evening, he packed his gear and took a handful of Mexican silver from the pouch in his saddlebag. Putting on his cleanest shirt and brushing the dust off his derby, J.D. left the room. Arriving at the Elder's house, he knocked on the front door and was greeted by Taylor's young wife.

"Hello, Mr. Dawson, please come in."

"Thank you. Is the Elder in?" J.D. stepped into the room.

"Yes, he is. I'll go get him."

J.D. turned away from the hall that led to the back of the house and gazed out the window. *What'll they think if I just up and leave? The sooner the better. I can't stay in one place too long.*

"Mr. Dawson," said Elder Taylor as he walked up to J.D., "it's good to see you looking so well,"

"I do feel better, and that's why I've wanna see you. I've decided that I need to move on." J.D. struggled to hide his anger.

"Move on, I don't understand. I thought you liked it here."

"I like it here, Mr. Taylor. It's nice and you all've been good to me. You saved my life, but now I need to get movin' along. My friends and business partners will be worrying about me." J.D. lied. He was running out of words and hoped he'd said enough to convince the old man. "I'd like to buy a horse from you or one of your neighbors and pay for all the worries I put on you. I..."

"I understand," Taylor nodded thoughtfully. "I can arrange for you to purchase a horse so you can be on your way as soon as you're ready."

"Thanks so much, Mr. Taylor. I don't know what to say."

"Say nothing more, sir. Just remember us as friends. If you ever head this way again, know that you have a place to stay." He paused and said, "Now, let's go have some supper. I think we're having wild turkey tonight."

Friends, J.D. thought, doing his best to hide his true feelings. *I could never be friends with people who marry children.*

Chapter 24

On the horse he'd purchased, J.D. left the *colonia* an hour before dawn the next day. His saddlebag held enough food for his journey, his canteens were full of fresh water from the river, and he had a crudely drawn map that would guide him north to the states. Elder Taylor had told J.D. to follow the map and keep the mountains on his left side. They run straight north he'd said, and if J.D. followed them he'd get to the border. There was no well-worn road north to the U.S., but even in the dark, J.D. knew where the western mountains were. The black range blotted out stars on the horizon as he rode the horse slowly into the desert. There was no full moon but the thin crescent to the east provided a little illumination.

The Mormon said Naco was a new and fast-growing town, and it provided services and workers for the big mine a dozen miles north in Bisbee, Arizona. Eight miles east of Naco was Agua Prieta, another village which hugged the border just a mile or so from Douglas, Arizona. When J.D. had asked him which was the best place to cross the border, the old man told him it really didn't matter, that the two towns were prosperous because of the mines. The Mexican towns did a lot of business with Bisbee and Douglas, and the citizens of both countries crossed the border frequently. J.D. knew nothing about mining, but at least Douglas and Bisbee were in America, and the people spoke English.

Don't matter which town, he thought, *I can probably find work. Besides, I still have my money.* Just to be sure, J.D.

slipped his hand into the saddle bag which held everything he owned. *I oughta be able to find somethin' to do and still hide out from anyone who might be chasin' me*. He glanced back along the trail.

When the sun cleared the horizon in the east, J.D. thought about El Paso and the two bloody bodies in the alley. He wanted to take Villa's advice and remember that the two men deserved punishment, but part of him had begun to compare the killings with the fires he'd set in Lynnville and Memphis. The time he'd spent in the *colonia* had been good for healing his body and made him feel safe, but now that he was alone in the desert, his head hurt. *Gotta stop thinkin' and worryin'.*

When the sun became too hot to bear, J.D. stopped at a small creek that had been marked on the map. He dismounted to rest and water the horse. While the animal grazed, J.D. wandered along the flowing water, marveling at the Palo Verde trees. Their green bark and bright green leaves were a refreshing contrast to the dirty brown emptiness that stretched toward the mountains. He was about to sit down at the edge of the creek when he spotted a coyote ten yards up stream. The animal stared at J.D. and its hackles stood up on its neck. J.D. didn't move and watched as the coyote took several quick laps of the water and then scurried off into the desert. Rather than risk another encounter with some of the creatures described by the Mormons, he walked back to his hobbled horse and resumed his trip.

☆ ☆ ☆

For the rest of the day, J.D. rode, rested, and rode some more. He was weary of the heat and the saddle and the grit that filled his ears. His eyes were tired from squinting and his headache was relentless. The mountains hadn't moved and despite the hours in the saddle, J.D. wasn't sure he'd made any real progress. He'd found the water holes drawn on the map and at many of them he'd seen mule deer, more coyotes, and the ugly javelinas. By the time the sun finally dipped below the mountain top, he'd been in the saddle for fifteen hours and hoped he was getting close to the border. *How much farther*?

Keeping his eyes on the ground in front of him, J.D. led his horse through a shallow swale and up a short hill. At the top he looked out across the darkness and saw a few sparkling lights in the distance. With a sigh of relief and thankful that the border was close, he mumbled, "Probably not more than an hour to go."

J.D. dismounted and led the horse forward by the reins. While the animal nibbled at some pale desert grass, J.D. stared up at the stars. Needing to make some decisions and wanting to be ready in case the border guards were overly curious, he thought, *if the guards start asking questions, I'll tell 'em I'm an American from Ohio and I've been prospecting down in the middle of Mexico without any luck, and I'm tired of the heat and the work and want to get back to the states to hear English again*.

J.D. walked along for a bit and then re-mounted. *Waitin' ain't gonna make it any easier*. The cool night air felt good on his face as he urged the horse forward.

☆ ☆ ☆

The darker the sky grew as night came on, the brighter the lights of the town became. J.D. had expected that by nightfall the place would be quiet, and the streets deserted. He'd been wrong. Leading the horse along a line of railroad tracks, he came upon dozens of dimly lit adobe houses. But within a few blocks he entered the bright, very busy center of Naco. The unpaved streets were full of people and although there were plenty of Mexicans, there were even more Americans. Some of them were clearly working, even this late at night—a crew was repairing a disassembled train coupler and wagons hauling freight and ore moved through the crowds. But most of the people seemed to be going into or coming out of saloons and cafés.

A bit dazed by the noise and activity, J.D. was unaware he'd stopped in the middle of a road.

"Hey, mister, you wanna move that horse outta the way? We got work to do."

J.D. turned toward the odd-sounding voice and pulled the horse to the side of the road. He watched as the man drove his team through the crowd of people which parted without complaint and immediately filled the empty space behind the wagon. J.D. was tired and hungry, but first he needed to find a place for the horse. He looked around for a livery stable but couldn't see one, then stopped a man staggering by and asked him where he could board his horse.

"Ain't no place around here," the man slurred, "ain't no need for horses anyway." Burping loudly, he smiled at J.D. and continued on his way.

"He's right, you know," said an American standing in the doorway of a saloon not ten feet away. The man was several years older than J.D., and the wrinkles at the edge of his eyes and lips were deep, like arroyos in the desert.

"Right about what?"

"There isn't much need for a horse in these parts. Most of the folks around here don't go anywhere except from home to the mine or smelter and back again. If you're thinkin' of staying around, you might want to sell the beast for what you can get. If your plans are to leave, the closest place is Bisbee and that's about ten miles farther on."

"What's in Bisbee?" J.D. asked, not sure what the man's motives might be.

"Tell you what," he said. "If you wanna tie up your horse onto this post, and step into my bar, I'll sell you a beer and have my cook fix you up some food. Then I'll tell you all you need to know about the booming metropolis of Bisbee,

Arizona."

J.D. didn't move for a moment, but the broad smile of the man and his own growling stomach and dry mouth drew him from the street. He lifted the saddle bag and threw it over his shoulder, tied the reins to the post, and followed the man into the saloon. The place was very busy, and the man led him to a table in the far corner next to the bar. The noise inside the building wasn't nearly as bad as it had been on the street and J.D. welcomed the relief.

The saloonkeeper sat down and signaled a tall, gaunt looking Mexican, to bring two beers to the table. J.D. sat next to the smiling man and put the saddle bag at his feet, then looked around the saloon. He didn't see anyone who looked like a deputy or lawman, so he relaxed. As soon as the beer was set in front of him, Hooper lifted the mug and took a drink. He sighed and finished the rest of the golden liquid without setting down the glass.

"Been a while has it?" The saloonkeeper signaled the bartender again, then said, "Are you hungry?"

"Yeah, I'm hungry," said J.D. "And it has been a spell since I had a beer."

"Chico, send Maria to the table. My friend here is hungry." He looked at J.D. and said, "Maria is a good cook and she can fix most anything."

A short and very curvy Mexican woman walked up to the table. Her round cheeks were flushed, and her eyes sparkled as she looked at her boss.

"Maria, this is my friend..." He gestured toward J.D.

"John Dawson," said J.D., wanting to leave his past and his real name behind.

"This is my friend John Dawson and he is very hungry."

"*Si, Señor*, what would you like to eat?"

J.D. didn't want any of the Mexican food he'd tasted in Juarez and the Mormon's food had been decent but bland, so he said, "I'd like a beef steak and some bread."

"*Si, Señor*, what else would you like?"

"How about some fried eggs and another beer."

Maria left and the bartender brought another beer to the table.

"My name is Edward Harrison, but people call me Lucky Eddie, Mr. Dawson."

"Nice to meet you, Lucky Eddie," said J.D. "You were gonna tell me about this place, uh, Bisbee."

Over the next hour, while J.D. ate his dinner and drank his beer, Lucky Eddie described Bisbee. He told J.D. about the brick buildings and paved streets, about the electric lights and gas heat, and about the saloons and bordellos.

"Everything that goes on in Bisbee is about mining. The railroad carries some passengers, but it was built to move equipment into Bisbee and copper ore out to the smelter in Douglas. The banks are successful because of the mine. The same can be said about the hotels and stores and the whores. Without the mine, there would be no Bisbee." He paused, watching for a response from J.D.

"Twenty years ago it was a wild and dangerous place, but today most of the wildness has disappeared. The rich folks—the mine owners and their type—have worked pretty hard to make the town like those back east. They've put up stores that sell clothes and jewelry. There are bakeries, barbers, and butchers, and a lot of churches."

"How many people live there?" J.D. asked.

"Last I heard there were ten thousand folks in the town. They've even started putting in a streetcar line out to the place where most of the rich families live. But not everyone is rich. The miners come from all over, places like Europe and England. Lots of fellas, some with their families, came from back east. The miners don't get paid much, but they do get paid. Most of them live in shacks."

"So," said J.D., mostly thinking out loud, "a fella could probably find a job doin' most anythin', either workin' for the mine or some place that does business with the mine, right?"

"That's how things work in Bisbee," said Eddie, "and a fella with his own money could probably find a way to make even more of it if he had something that people wanted."

J.D. didn't like where the conversation was headed. He wanted to keep his money secret, so he tried to steer Harrison in another direction. "Are there any towns beyond Bisbee?"

"Of course, if you wanted to you could head on to Tombstone or even west to Tucson, but Bisbee is a town with a future." Harrison looked around his thriving saloon. "There's probably more saloons and bars and whorehouses than you can count, but only a dozen or so here in Naco. I like being here 'cause no one messes with my business."

It was getting late and J.D. was tired. He tried to cover up a yawn, but it didn't work.

"Mr. Dawson, I've got a room upstairs that I rent out and it's vacant tonight. I'll let you stay there for a dollar and I'll put your horse in my back lot for another dollar. Maybe tomorrow you'll want to move along, maybe not, but at least you won't have to decide what to do tonight." He finished what was left of his beer and asked, "What do you say?"

"Well, Mr. Lucky Eddie, if I give you five dollars would you feed my horse and let me sleep as long as I want in the morning?" He smiled and shook Harrison's hand. They stood up from the chairs and Eddie led J.D. up to the room.

"Take care of the man's horse, Chico," the saloonkeeper said over his shoulder.

☆ ☆ ☆

At breakfast J.D. sat with Lucky Eddie at the same table. The saloon was filled to capacity but with a different crowd. Eddie explained that the mines and smelters were twenty-four-hour operations and there were people going on and coming off shift all the time. Even with the sun up, for most of the men in the saloon it was almost time to head home and go to bed. J.D. had slept long and hard the previous night and before sitting down, he'd checked on his horse and found the animal well cared for and munching on oats.

J.D. decided to broach a new topic with Eddie. Sensing that the saloonkeeper was a man willing to take risks and that he knew a lot about his town and Bisbee, J.D. wanted to find out more about Eddie before getting too close to him.

"Can I ask you a question, Eddie?"

"Yep, you can ask and maybe I'll even answer," he replied with a smile.

"Suppose a fella had come into some money—a little bit of money—and this fella wanted to use it to maybe start a new business. What kind of business would you suggest that he get into?"

"Hmmm, would this fella have any experience in saloons, or mining equipment, or whorehouses?"

"Nope."

"How about cobbling, or butchering, or selling dry goods?"

J.D. said no to this list as well, but the image of butchering caught him off guard.

"What kinds of skills would this fella have, Dawson? What has he done in the past that might work in *our* neck of the woods?"

"Lately he's been sorta doin' things for people with money that they don't wanna do themselves." That seemed vague enough to J.D., but he hoped that Eddie would understand.

Eddie stared at J.D. for a moment, wondering if he was on the run from something. He looked into his new acquaintance's eyes, trying to see if the man was being straight with him. Eddie looked down at the table for a moment as if weighing his possible motive. He drummed his fingers on the table and said, "Before I made a suggestion to this fella, I'd have to know him a lot better, Mr. Dawson. I'm familiar with a lot of the things that go on and I'm frequently asked to help folks out because of my standing in the community. I'm sure you understand my caution."

"I do, Eddie, I sure do."

"Maybe we could talk about this fella and his plans some other time."

"That sounds like a good idea." J.D. pushed himself away from the table and said, "What's the best way for me to get to Bisbee? I wanna go up there and look around for a few days. Maybe you could recommend a place for me to stay while I'm there."

Eddie suggested that J.D. leave his horse out back and take the daily train to Bisbee. "The Grand Hotel is on Main Street and is close to most anything in the town. It's just a short walk from there to Brewery Gulch."

"Brewery Gulch?"

"Let me put it this way, Brewery Gulch ain't like any place you've ever seen before. It ain't paved like the other streets and it's narrow and winds all the way up the hill. Last I heard there are lots and lots of saloons and whorehouses on it. The city council has pushed all of the drinking, whoring, and gambling onto that one street. I guess they don't want any trouble in the *good* part of town, so they make sure that the things the miners want, or need are only available in Brewery Gulch."

"I ain't much for whorin', but if the saloons and the saloonkeepers in Bisbee are as good as the one I found here in Naco, then I suppose I'll have a good time."

Eddie laughed at the joke, sent Maria for some more coffee, and started telling J.D. about his time in the army.

J.D. rode in the single passenger car on the freight train that headed north from Naco to Bisbee. He was relaxed because his crossing into the United States was uneventful. The uniformed guard on the American side of the invisible line separating the countries didn't even acknowledge J.D. or any of the Mexicans. Apparently, at least according to Lucky Eddie, any delays in the human traffic could result in lost time on the job and that upset the mine managers. If they got upset, they called the commander and he took out his frustration on the guards.

J.D. looked out the window at the cactus-covered, brown hills as the train made the slow climb into the Mule Mountains and Mule Gulch—and the town of Bisbee.

Chapter 25

On the same afternoon that J.D. re-entered the United States, Noah Jensen waited patiently in E.H. Harriman's outer office in New York.

"Mr. Harriman will see you now, Mr. Jensen."

Noah thanked the secretary and walked into the office of the president of the railroad.

"You wanted to see me, sir?"

"Yes I did, Noah, thanks for getting here so promptly." He set down the stack of papers he'd been perusing and stood up. "Come over to the window for a moment."

Noah joined his boss and they gazed out onto the city.

"I wanted to thank you for your efforts over the past few weeks. As always, your work is effective, prudent, and timely." He paused and turned toward the detective. "I know that you are working hard on the Memphis arson case and I understand how it must trouble you. Despite our significant losses there, I'm not placing any of the blame on you or upon your efforts. Nevertheless, I want you to keep working the case. Get back to El Paso, go to Mexico or wherever it is necessary to find this man Hooper and bring him here to my office."

"Thank you, sir, but..."

"Let me finish, Noah. Your persistence and diligence have never been in doubt and the quality of your work never fades. But I see a change in your spirit and that does concern me. I have long-range plans for this company that include you and if you are to be a part of these plans, then you'll have to regain that spirit. Do you understand me?"

"I think so, sir," said Noah.

Noting the puzzled look on Jensen's face, Harriman said, "Then let me put it to you plainly. Solve this case by the first of September and get back to the Memphis office the same detective I had last spring. If you can do that we'll be together for a long time. If not, then I'll be a very disappointed man and you'll be looking for a job."

Noah hated disappointing Harriman, but even more, he knew the man was right. "Thank you for your trust, sir. I'll leave right away." Noah turned to leave and then stopped. "Mr. Harriman, I *am* going to find Hooper and solve the case." Then he walked out of the office.

☆ ☆ ☆

Noah looked around the small hotel room. His suitcase rested on the unmade bed and the battered wanted poster lay on a side table. Noah slipped his coat on and placed his hat firmly on his head as he stared at the haunting features of Hooper. He'd told Mr. Harriman that he would be back in Memphis by September first, but he'd also made a promise to himself that he would catch Hooper. Finding Hooper was now about more than the destruction of one hundred rail cars. This was about proving himself, showing Mr. Harriman and everybody else that he would not give up. He wasn't going to let J.D. Hooper win.

El Paso was the last place that Noah knew Hooper had been. T*hat's where I lost him and that's where I'll start again to find him,* he thought. *And so help me I will find Mr. J.D. Hooper and I will burn him.*

Noah folded up the wanted poster and placed it into the inside pocket of his coat. He then headed out of the building to Grand Central Station to catch the next train to Texas.

Chapter 26

J.D. realized that Lucky Eddie had been right about Bisbee. Having been in the big cities of Memphis, Dallas, and El Paso, he'd expected that Eddie may have over-described the Arizona mining town, but he was wrong. Bisbee was not a big town, but it *was* busy and crowded. Standing on the station platform, J.D. looked out on paved streets filled with people—shoppers, travelers, and miners. The sun was high and filled the town with light that even the surrounding hills could not block. The buildings in the downtown area were several stories high, and were stacked tightly side by side. Many of them, like the Opera House across the wide-open area in front of the depot, were constructed of brick and stone. The cobble-stoned main street curved along the bottom of a deep canyon and the hills on either side rose over the top of the buildings. Electric lights on poles stood at the corners, ready to light up the night.

J.D. walked to the other end of the platform and looked across the narrow valley to the southeast and the copper mine, the source of the town's wealth and energy. Hooper found the Grand Hotel and took a room on the second floor, overlooking Main Street. The price was reasonable and the view out the window allowed him to watch what was happening on the street. Leaving the hotel, his first stop was a café. A half hour later, filled with a roast beef sandwich, J.D. went in search of a drink.

He turned left out of the cafe and walked along the

curved main street for a few blocks, passing stores and shops. At the end of the block he noticed the post office and library, then turned left at the bank and found Brewery Gulch. J.D. chuckled when the first sign he saw was for the Old Kentucky Home Saloon. "Well, welcome home," he whispered, and walked through the door.

The long, narrow saloon was as crowded as Eddie's place had been. The tables were full, there was little room at the bar, and the buzz of conversations was close to deafening. What J.D. found most interesting was the variety of accents he heard. It seemed that everyone was speaking in English, but not all of them sounded American. A man in overalls stepped away from the bar and J.D. took his place quickly. Behind the long bar, two men wearing aprons and vests scurried between the bar and the taps, keeping their customers' glasses full. J.D. caught the attention of one of the bartenders.

"Yessir, what'll it be?" the bartender said loudly.

"I'll take a beer," J.D. shouted in return.

The man nodded, turned away, and quickly brought J.D. a frothy mug of cold beer.

"Is this place always so busy?" J.D. asked.

"It is and that's just fine with me. As long as fellas like you are drinking, I'm making money and feeding my family." He moved quickly down the bar to fill another glass.

Watching and listening, J.D. drank several more beers. *If Bisbee is like the other places I've been it won't be hard to find work. Or maybe work'll find me if I'm patient.*

When he emerged from the Old Kentucky Home an hour later the sun had slipped behind the hills, but the sky above was still blue. Traffic had slowed down and J.D. fell into the flow of people and headed farther into Brewery Gulch to see if there really were fifty saloons. The buildings at this end of the gulch were all fronted with boardwalks, but the street itself was not paved. The uneven surface was rocky and rutted but that did not seem to affect the scores of men crossing from one saloon to another.

As he followed the curve of the street J.D. noticed that the turn brought another marvel into view. Several big houses and a number of squat, single-story structures lined both sides of the street. Each of them had a glowing red light hanging above the door or hooked to the porch rail. *That damned Eddie was right again*. The whorehouses were doing as brisk a business as the saloons and it wasn't even dark yet. Hooper had no interest in the services offered behind these doors, but he appeared to be just about the only one who didn't.

Hooper turned around and crossed to the other side, stopping to let a young woman and a boy, each carrying a large bundle of laundry, pass by. He watched them for a moment then headed back down the hill. At the end of the street, he went into the Calumet Saloon to have one more beer. He was beginning to feel that the crowds and the noise of the last few days were actually refreshing compared to the quiet openness of the Mexican desert.

J.D. walked slowly up Main Street to the hotel. Before entering the building, he stopped and looked both ways. The electric streetlights were shining, and the glowing lights of the still-open cafés and stores flooded the walks. It reminded him of Memphis. J.D. smiled, entered the hotel, and headed upstairs to his room, relaxed and happy for the first time in a long time. Bisbee was a long way from the dark alley in El Paso. A long way from Memphis. A long way from Lynnville, Kentucky. *Maybe I've finally found a place where I can stop lookin' over my shoulder all the time.*

☆ ☆ ☆

For the next few days J.D. spent his mornings wandering around the town of Bisbee. He'd watched as work crews laid down track for the new streetcar line and other men carved out steps up the mountainside. He'd even spent an hour one morning in the shade of a small building observing several Mexicans build a retaining wall to keep the mountain from pushing a newly built cabin off its rock foundation.

I could do those things. I could go back to workin' hard and gettin' dirty, but I'd never earn the kind of money like I did in Memphis and El Paso. Having come to that conclusion, J.D. began to keep his eyes open for work of a different kind.

In the afternoons, however, Hooper had to get out of the hot sun. The only thing that came close to marring the clear blue sky was the dust and smoke from the mine. Unless he stood in the shade, he couldn't escape the searing glare and the intense heat. J.D. had discovered one of the reasons that the saloons were popular—in addition to selling cold beer, they provided relief from the sun.

On his way back to the hotel, he walked into another bar called the St. Elmo and left the brutal Arizona afternoon outside the door. The darkness of the small saloon made it difficult to see well, but the few scattered gas lamps helped a bit as he made his way to the long, polished wood bar. *This place is different than the others,* he thought.

"What'll you have, mister?"

"I'll take a beer," he said gazing around the room. The St. Elmo was smaller than many of the saloons he'd been in, and it was just as busy, but for some reason, it seemed quieter. The conversations were softer, and the typical harsh chatter and yelling was replaced with a mind-numbing drone.

"It's quiet in here," J.D. said to the bartender as the aproned man brought him another beer. For some reason, Hooper felt comfortable in the St. Elmo.

"Yessir, that's true and we like it that way." He wiped up a ring of moisture from the bar and set down the mug. "We do get noisy on payday, but most of the time it's just like this. Some fellas like all the yellin' and laughin' and such, but lots of 'em know that they can come here when they need a rest from all that." The bartender smiled at J.D., then pulled a lead-filled sap from under the bar and set it down on the plank. "This is the other way we keep the place quiet. It works real good when someone wants to cause trouble."

The sight of the lead-filled sap surprised him. J.D.'s gut clenched, and a foggy image of the El Paso businessman's smashed head invaded his memory. He took a deep draught of the beer, trying to drive the image away.

"You got any whiskey?"

The bartender set a bottle and a shot glass in front of J.D. and walked down the bar to serve a group of miners. J.D. drained his beer and took the whiskey to one of the tables along the wall. He sat down, filled the glass and finished it in one swallow. Quickly pouring another shot, he stared at it for just a moment and drank it quickly as well. Hooper closed his eyes tightly, the bloody image flared in his head again. A third shot of the harsh brown liquor reminded him of the power he'd felt as he confronted the men in the alley and a fourth sent a surge of warmth into his chest.

J.D. rose unsteadily from the chair and returned the bottle to the bar. He left some of his Mexican silver in a pile by the bottle and went out the door. Blinded by the sunlight, J.D. leaned against the wall of the saloon and waited until his head cleared. After a few minutes, feeling steady enough to walk, he made his way up the street, entered the hotel, and closed himself up in his room.

☆ ☆ ☆

The next morning, J.D. walked slowly down the stairs to the lobby. His pounding head and bloodshot eyes were clear evidence he'd drank too much whiskey the night before. Hooper was hungry but knew that anything he managed to get into his stomach was likely to come right back up. As J.D. slowly trudged past the front desk, the clerk called out to him.

"Mr. Dawson," he said quietly, aware that his lodger was dealing with a hangover. "Mr. Dawson, you received a telephone message early this morning."

"I got a what?" said J.D., not sure what the clerk meant.

"Yes sir, a Mr. Lucky Eddie called the hotel this morning and he seemed anxious to speak with you. I knocked on your door but getting no response I decided to wait for you to show up down here." Turning to the key slot behind the counter, the clerk pulled out a small sheet of paper and handed the note to J.D.

"Would you read it to me?" J.D. groaned. "I can't see too well this mornin'."

"Of course, sir." He cleared his throat and read, "Mr. Lucky Eddie would like you to visit his establishment in Naco at your earliest convenience regarding an employment opportunity."

Hooper's head pounded, and his neck felt all wound up like the spring on a pocket watch. Because of his hangover and the nightmares he'd had, he didn't feel like taking the train to Naco. But he also didn't want to miss the chance of finding a job, so he asked the clerk to send someone for a ticket on the afternoon train.

"I'll take care of it for you, Mr. Dawson," the clerk said and turned back to his work.

Shielding his eyes as he exited the hotel, J.D. walked down the street to what was becoming his regular breakfast café. *I feel like hell and I need some coffee.*

☆ ☆ ☆

At the café he'd managed to eat some chicken broth—which made him feel better—and drink lots of coffee, which did not help. Hooper had no clue what type of job Eddie had in mind, but he hoped that it would be something like he'd done in Memphis rather than laying streetcar tracks or building retaining walls.

That afternoon, J.D. was rocked to sleep by the swaying passenger car as it chugged its way south to Naco. When the train rolled to a stop, he was slow to fully awake. His headache hadn't improved, not even a little. Stepping onto the platform, he was immediately surrounded by a less than sonorous din. An incessant steam whistle from the smelter competed with the train's clanging bell and the rush of steam from the boiler. The straight-over-his-head sun was bright and piercing and there was no breeze to cool him. *Welcome to noisy, filthy Naco*, he thought.

J.D. removed his coat and walked down the street to Lucky Eddie's saloon. Hooper was still amazed that neither the time of day nor day of month made a difference. Saloons were always busy and so was Eddie's.

He scanned the crowded room and spotted Eddie at a table in the rear of the building. The proprietor appeared to be discussing something important with two well-dressed Mexicans. Eddie's arms were folded across his chest and even from a distance J.D. could see his furrowed brow and clenched jaw. J.D. went to the bar and debated ordering a drink, finally settling on Eddie's famous *cerveza fria*. Staring intently at the foamy head in the glass, he tipped it to his lips and took a long draught. The icy cold, bitter brew refreshed his dusty throat and the sensation was pleasant. J.D. hoped that his meeting with Eddie would be the same. He'd just ordered another beer when the saloonkeeper tapped him on the shoulder.

"Good to see you, Dawson. I'm glad you came. Let's go back to my office where we can talk." He turned away after reminding J.D. to bring his beer.

The two men walked to the back of the room, dodging the raucous smelter workers and a bartender carrying foaming glasses of beer. Eddie stopped once to speak to the two fancy Mexicans and then continued into his office.

"Close the door, will you."

J.D. pushed the door closed and turned back to Eddie. The man was picking through several stacks of paper, seeming to look for something.

"Ah," he said. "Here it is." Eddie sat in his chair and pulled it up closer to the desk. "Sit down, Dawson, finish your beer."

J.D. eased into the chair across from Eddie and took a sip from his glass. He waited, though, not wanting to say something too quickly. Unless he'd missed a clue of some sort, he was here to listen. Eddie continued to shuffle paper into different piles, and then looked at J.D.

"I've thought a lot about what you said last time, about wanting to work, about making money, and doing jobs for others." He paused for a moment. "I'd have expected to find something for you to try in Tombstone, but things are fairly quiet up there now."

J.D. kept his eyes on Eddie, withholding any reaction until he knew what Eddie had to say.

"There might be a job for you, but I need to ask if you ever hurt anyone?"

J.D. slowly sat back in his chair and considered the question, wondering how much he would tell Eddie.

"Yeah, but only when I had to."

"How badly did you hurt 'em?"

"I busted a fella's arm once when he tried to rob me, and I took care of a couple of others for a friend of mine. Only I didn't just break their arms."

Eddie waited.

"I did things for people with money and people with power. They wanted their problems to go away and I made that happen." J.D. was set on not giving Eddie any details. He wanted the job and hoped that his experience would be enough to get it.

"An acquaintance of mine in Bisbee needs some help with a delicate family situation," Eddie said. "He's a businessman of some influence, a family man and a member of one of the large churches. But we have some history. When my friend first came west he spent a lot of time in one of my saloons and in some other places that he wouldn't want his family or his partners to know about. Over the years we've helped each other—he's loaned me money and I've taken care of some things for him."

Hooper listened, focused not only on the words, but on Eddie's expression.

"This delicate situation concerns his daughter, an attractive young woman of marriageable age. The problem is, according to my friend, that the man who seems to be paying her attention has already been married once and is known as a man of bad character. The daughter is at risk of being caught up in the man's web and her father does not want that to happen." Eddie was quiet for a moment, choosing his words carefully. "My friend would like this man to leave his daughter alone. He would like the man to become convinced that any further pursuit of the young lady would be...undesirable."

J.D. looked intently at Eddie then said, "What kind of deal is your friend offering?" He took a sip of his beer and added, "What does he want done and how much will he pay?"

"There's a lot of detail to go over and it might take some time. Before we cover all that, do you think you might be interested?"

"Yeah, I am," J.D. said.

For the next hour Eddie gave J.D. the details. His friend wanted no connection with any incident that might occur. He hoped that whatever happened might look like an accident as long as the suitor was convinced to leave town. He especially did not want his daughter to know that he'd had a role in driving the man away. Eddie's friend didn't care what happened to the man, he simply wanted him gone.

"Dawson, if you can help my friend by getting rid of the man and making sure that he's not connected in any way to what happens, he's willing to pay one thousand dollars."

J.D. hesitated, thinking about the offer and then said, "I'll do the job, Eddie, if you promise me that your friend will let me handle it my way. I wouldn't want him to go weak on me and get scared because somebody gets hurt. What I don't need is to have him pointin' me out as doin' somethin' on my own. If he's payin' me, he's part of this. I'll keep him clear of it as long as I can do it my way. If you think he'll keep his part of the bargain, then I'll take the job."

"I trust this man. He'll pay up and he'll stay out of the way. I wager that he'll count you as a friend if you make this happen." Eddie stood up, shook J.D.'s hand, and walked him out of the office. "Can you spend the night and take the morning train?" he asked.

"Sure I can. But I think I'll go up to the room now and try to get some sleep if it's okay with you. Besides, I need to do some thinkin' and plannin' if I wanna get this job done soon."

Chapter 27

Alice Carter walked up Brewery Gulch, a heavy bundle of soiled bed sheets slung over her shoulder. She was a slight woman, though the ease at which she carried the bundle implied a great reservoir of strength. The unpaved road rose steeply up the side of the mountain that overlooked the city of Bisbee Arizona. Alice's ten-year-old son, Henry, carried a similar load and barely kept up, frequently stumbling over the ruts and rocks. The hot morning sun bore down on them from a clear sky, and despite the lack of humidity, sweat glistened their faces. Alice wore a light cotton dress and a straw hat that covered her hair and kept the scorching sun off her freckle-sprinkled face.

"Come along now, Henry, I need to get my washing done and you're gonna have to help."

"Alright, Ma," the freckle-faced boy huffed. Henry wanted to drag the bundle, but knew that would not meet with her approval. "Them ladies sure use a lot of sheets."

"You never mind about the ladies and their sheets, son. Just help me get the bundles home."

It took them another ten minutes to reach their cabin up the road. The three-room structure was built on a bedrock slab that had been blasted out of the side of the mountain by Henry's father. Like most of the buildings on the hillside, the Carter home was a wooden structure without any power or plumbing, and folks could stand on their front porch and look down onto the roof of their neighbor below.

"Put the bundle on the steps, Henry, and start filling the tub with water. We should have enough until the water mules make it up the hill. I've saved some for cooking and drinking, but we need to use the rest for the laundry."

The youngster gladly dropped the load of bedding and scurried behind the house for the water bucket. Alice set her bundle down and opened the door to the house. Just the act of touching the doorknob reminded her of her husband and when she touched something he'd built or worked so hard for, she remembered his death and the sad days that followed. She and Albert had moved to Bisbee from Pennsylvania a dozen years before. He'd been a coal miner and had seen too many of his friends and family die of black lung disease, so one day he'd told Alice that they were moving to the southwest where he could still do what he did best—be a miner—but live where the sky was clear and the future was wide open. So, the Carters had left their families behind and moved to the new copper camp of Bisbee. They'd been busy and happy and when Henry was born they were contented, but their plans for the future were shattered on the day Albert died in a tunnel collapse.

The accident had killed four men and injured a dozen others. Most of the families left town afterward, but Alice knew that she and Henry couldn't afford to move back to Pennsylvania. She managed to get by for a while with the help from the church and the rich ladies in town, but eventually even their generosity dried up. To survive, and to give Henry the chance to go to school, Alice ultimately found work from the darkest corner of the town. Half-way down the mountain, between the shacks and homes of the miners and the saloons near Main Street, were the brothels and cribs of the prostitutes. Before Albert's death, whenever Alice walked down Brewery Gulch to the market she'd pass the women who worked the cribs as they sat on their front steps. Even though she didn't approve of what they did, she understood how easily any woman could fall into that work through tragedy or heartbreak. So, she was always cordial to the girls and had even stopped to talk with some of them on occasion.

When the last of the money had run out, Alice was afraid that her future might include a job in a crib, an idea reinforced by a chance encounter with Helen McHenry. Helen ran a brothel with a half-dozen rooms. One afternoon as she worked her way down the gulch, Alice stopped to visit with one of the ladies and Helen stepped out onto her porch and called out.

"Excuse me, Mrs. Carter, do you have a moment?" Even in the heat and dust of the mining town, her clothes and posture appeared elegant.

"Of course, Mrs. McHenry," she said. Excusing herself from the young prostitute, Alice walked across the rock-strewn road and stopped at the bottom of the stairs.

Knowing that it would be unseemly for Alice to come into the whorehouse, Helen stepped down to the road to speak to Alice.

"I know how difficult times must be for you since your husband died. And even though I never met him socially, or for business," she was quick to add, "I know that he truly cared for you and your boy." She looked at Alice and noticed the young woman's confusion. "You see some of the men who visit my girls talk an awful lot. They said that your husband, Albert, spoke so often of you and his son that it made them jealous of him." She paused for a moment and added, "I hope that I haven't upset you with this talk."

"Of course you haven't Mrs. McHenry," Alice whispered. "Thank you."

"I had a particular thing that I wanted to discuss with you and because I know that you are always so kind to all of the girls who work the gulch, I decided I wanted to offer you a job." Seeing the shock on Alice's face, Helen put her gloved hand against her bodice and quickly added, "Not as a prostitute, of course, but I need someone who will launder the bedding we use."

Alice took a deep breath and her expression softened. "I can definitely use work ma'am but aren't there enough laundries downtown to handle your bedding?"

"There are plenty of laundries, but those damned, excuse me, those blasted Chinamen won't work for me. They don't want to upset their society customers by working for madams and prostitutes."

"I'm certain I can do the *work* of washing bed sheets, Mrs. McHenry but I have no idea how much to charge you."

"Well I know how much the Chinamen wanted to charge me before they knew what I did for a living, and I'm willing to pay you that same amount. I'm sure it won't cover what your man used to bring home, but it should be close to that."

"I'll do your laundry, Mrs. McHenry. You can count on it. I'm a hard worker and I'll do anything to take care of my boy."

Helen was comforted by the strength in Alice's voice and her determination. She was also a bit surprised that such power could come from a woman as small as Alice Carter.

"Then we have a deal, Alice. When can you start?"

Alice's arrangement with Helen McHenry had become permanent. She and Henry were not going to get rich doing laundry, but it wasn't likely that her customer would go out of business any time soon.

Following her husband's death, Alice's greatest worry was that Henry would grow up fatherless and end up working and dying in a mine. She didn't want that for him. If washing the soiled sheets from a brothel would give her son a chance for a better life, then Alice Carter would wash sheets. When the church ladies discovered what she was doing they found it difficult to talk to her in public. Their snobbery didn't even bother Alice. She was working for herself and Henry and if that bothered the backbiters, then she would just stop going to services.

Chapter 28

J.D. sat at the small desk in his Bisbee hotel room looking out the window onto Main Street. He tapped his cigar and a shower of ashes drifted toward the floor, a few of them landing on the open letter in his lap. He'd found the message slipped under his door when he woke up this morning and its contents had occupied his thoughts ever since. Two hundred dollars in crisp bank notes lay fanned out on the desk and J.D. was thinking hard, his brain grinding and screeching like the mining equipment across the valley.

The message, written on the Bank of Bisbee letterhead, was brief, containing a name—Jack Walker—an address, and two promises: the balance of the payment would be made when the task was completed and no one—*absolutely no one*—would ever know the message writer's role in the job. The letter wasn't signed, but that meant nothing to J.D. When he'd met with Eddie in Naco, he'd learned all he thought necessary about his client and the problem the man faced.

No deadline for finishing the job had been mentioned by Eddie, nor had any particular urgency been indicated in the letter's wording. Nevertheless, J.D. was intent on developing a plan that would solve the banker's problem quickly. The first thing he had to do was to find Jack Walker, the daughter's suitor, and learn how the man spent his time. Once he knew Walker's routine, he could come up with a plan.

Walker's main route to work took him right past the hotel every morning. All J.D. had to do was sit and wait. Eddie's description of the man was detailed. He was tall—lanky was the word the saloon keeper had used—well-dressed and carried a walking stick. This accessory, said Eddie, was something Walker thought made him look important and successful. The two new friends agreed that it didn't make any sense for a man who had no problem walking to carry a cane.

J.D.'s vigilance at the window paid off near dusk when he saw Walker strolling down the south side of Main Street in the direction of the Copper Queen. Grabbing his coat and derby, J.D. rushed down to the lobby and looked out the door. Off to his left he saw Walker speaking with a short man in front of one of the shops. J.D. slipped on his coat, set his derby snugly on his head, and walked out of the hotel. He lingered in front of the building until Walker shook hands with the short man and then walked on down the street, casually swinging his cane. J.D. followed him.

Walker didn't turn in the direction of the banker's daughter's home. Instead he headed toward Brewery Gulch and entered the Calumet Saloon. Hooper walked up to the door of the saloon, looked in, and saw him standing alone at the bar. *Must be gettin' a shot of courage.* Then J.D. turned from the door and walked across the street, stepping into a narrow, dark alley where he could keep Walker in sight.

The sun had gone down and the few streetlights on Brewery Gulch had come on. J.D. spotted Walker as he staggered out of the Calumet and headed up the gulch. *He ain't goin' to visit the daughter up this way. Wonder where he's headed*? J.D. followed Walker around a curve and watched the thin man take the steps up to a house with a broad porch and a red lantern hanging from a post. *Well,* thought J.D., *it seems the gentleman ain't callin' on the daughter unless she's got a job her pa don't know about.* J.D. passed by the brothel and found a spot next to a dark cabin where he could keep watch.

A short time later, Walker came out of the whorehouse and turned down the gulch toward Main Street. He strutted across the street and walked past the saloons to the corner then turned and headed in the direction of his boarding house. J.D. followed him all the way home and saw a light go on in an upstairs room. Waiting a few minutes until the light went off, he then went back to the hotel. Walker's visit to the brothel added an interesting twist to his job. *Maybe even a way to solve the problem without hurtin' anybody,* he mused disappointedly, *except maybe the daughter's feelin's.*

☆ ☆ ☆

J.D. got up early and walked past Walker's boarding house. The sun was just rising, and the cool air felt good on J.D.'s face as he found a spot to wait and watch. At half-past seven, Walker came out of the house swinging his cane and walked up Main to Subway, then turned left and stepped into a building on the corner. According to J.D.'s notes, the man worked for a mining supply company as a bookkeeper. Hooper expected that he would be in the office for most of the day, so he decided to head back to the boarding house and do a little snooping.

As J.D. stepped up onto the porch, a short middle-aged woman was backing out of the door, lugging a bundle of laundry.

"Can I help you with that heavy load, ma'am?"

Startled, the woman dropped the bag and turned to J.D. "Goodness! You frightened me young man."

He spoke as politely as he could. "Sorry, I didn't mean to. I was just wonderin' if you had any rooms to rent." He reached down for the bundle, picked it up, and said, "Where did you want to take this?" J.D. forced a smile onto his face and waited for her to speak.

"Oh, well, you can just leave it here on the porch. The laundry man will be by in a bit to pick it up." She looked at J.D. and added, "Actually, I do have a room available. Would you like to see it mister...?"

"It's Jones, ma'am." J.D. tipped his hat. "I'm William Jones of Dallas."

"Well, I'm Mrs. Harding. What sort of business are you in, Mr. Jones?"

"I'm in the bankin' business." The lie dripped from J.D.'s lips. "I represent some gentlemen in Texas who are interested in the mining activity in Bisbee."

"Please, come upstairs and I'll show you the room. It's very nice and looks out onto the street." They entered the house and she led him up the staircase and walked past the room where J.D. had seen Walker's lights the night before. She opened a door and J.D. followed her into another room not unlike the one he'd had in Memphis.

"Would you like some coffee or tea, Mr. Jones? You could look around the room while I make some."

"That would be nice, ma'am, I'd certainly like a cup of coffee."

"Well then I'll be back in a few minutes. Feel free to look at the washroom across the hall as well. If you decide to move in here that's one room you'll share with my other border." She walked to the stairway and took her time going down the steep steps.

When J.D. heard her walk across the floor in the direction of the kitchen, he moved quickly toward Walker's room. He found the door unlocked and entered a mirror image of the room he'd just seen. Walker hadn't left anything of interest visible, so J.D. quickly opened a dresser drawer and shuffled through the clothing. Finding nothing in the first drawer, J.D. tried the second. It, too, gave up nothing of value. Stepping back to the open door J.D. heard Mrs. Harding humming in the kitchen. Returning to Walker's dresser, he opened the bottom drawer and underneath a pile of folded shirts found a stack of studio photograph cards.

"Well, well, well, Mr. Walker. What have we here?" J.D. whispered to himself. He slipped the cards into his coat pocket, closed the drawer, and moved quickly back toward the other room. He heard the landlady approaching the stairs, so he opened the door to the bathroom and pretended to look interested.

"Here we are," she said. "I wasn't sure if you took anything in your coffee, so I brought some cream and sugar."

"Actually, I drink my coffee black, but thanks for going to all that trouble."

She set the tray on the dresser in the available room and poured a cup for J.D. "What do you think of the room, Mr. Jones?"

"It's very nice, Mrs. Harding, and so is the coffee." J.D. tried to steady his nerves as he sipped from the cup. Finding the photos of women—most of whom were naked or nearly so—had surprised him at first, but now he needed to leave the boarding house and figure out how to use the pictures and Walker's visit to a brothel to solve the banker's problem.

"Mrs. Harding, ma'am, I need to be moving along. I have to travel to Tucson this afternoon and won't be back in Bisbee for a couple of weeks."

Clearly disappointed she said, "Oh, I was hoping you'd want to move in soon."

"I hope it's still available when I return to Bisbee. If it is I'll become your newest house guest."

"That will be nice Mr. Jones. I do hope you have a safe trip. Please do stop by when you return." J.D. escorted the landlady down the stairs and gently shook her hand and tipped his derby before he walked off the porch and down the street.

Rushing back to the hotel and into his room J.D. began

to think of a plan that might end Mr. Walker's courtship of the banker's daughter. He disliked the man already and felt a strong urge to hurt him and make him disappear.

☆ ☆ ☆

The pictures lay face down on the scarred wooden desk. J.D. hadn't looked at them since he'd left the boarding house and even then he'd only seen the top few of the dozen or so photographs. He knew what they were but had no interest in wasting his time looking at pictures of naked women. There was no profit in that. But for some fellas, men like Walker, women were *all* they thought about besides drinking. As for J.D., women were nothing but a distraction and an annoyance just like his wife, the ugly one who nagged at him, the one who divorced him, the one who sent him to jail in Kentucky. The pictures and the whores would lead to Walker's downfall no doubt. And the banker's daughter would see what Walker does when he's not calling on her.

But how to get that done? wondered J.D. *How do I keep the banker out of the picture*? *How do I get Walker in a place faced with the evidence and witnessed by just the right people so that the girl has no doubt about his bad character*? J.D. always had a second option—he could kill Walker and get rid of his body. That would be quicker, of course, but then the girl would only know he'd gone and not really know how lucky she was to not have married him.

This needs to be ugly and public, J.D. thought.

☆ ☆ ☆

The next day, J.D. walked the few blocks to the banker's address. The house was large and well cared for. Sauntering by, he caught sight of two women gazing at dozens of rose bushes along the side fence. The younger woman was dressed in a long flowered yellow dress and wore a sun bonnet. Hooper could clearly see her delicate, child-like face and blonde hair. When the women turned toward him, he was embarrassed and hurried away down the street.

J.D. stopped when he reached the corner. His heart was pounding like a crushing mill and his eyes grew red in anger. Eddie had said the daughter was ready for marriage. Hooper hadn't seen a woman, but a young, innocent girl. If he had his way, Walker would never marry this child. He'd either get run out of town or J.D. would kill him. *No whore-chasin', woman-cheatin', drunken man is gonna ever touch that little girl.*

☆ ☆ ☆

Hooper had spent a restless night. His brain kept chewing on the ugly bone of Walker's intentions. Needing to use the night jar, he untangled himself from the sweat-stained bedding and grumbled. J.D.'s anger had given him a headache. Hooper walked back across the room and sat on the bed. He wanted to get Walker alone in the desert and beat him to death with his sap, then leave him in an arroyo somewhere out beyond the mountains surrounding the town. He wanted to see the man's bones stripped by the buzzards. Drawing in a deep breath, Hooper's chest was tight. Another breath helped calm the quivering and he focused again on how to get the man alone. He knew that he'd need to save his anger for the killing and use his brain now for the planning, knowing that every day that it took him to get at Walker was another day that the man could harm the girl.

Recalling the banker's note, J.D. decided he had to make a public spectacle of Walker so that he'd disappear, and the girl would know why he was gone. J.D. had to make it clear to her that she'd been saved from making a terrible mistake. His idea involved revealing Walker's nighttime visits to the whorehouses and saloons as well as his possession of the pictures. What Hooper hadn't yet figured out was the when and the where of Walker's destruction and the young girl's redemption. He was anxious to finalize the plan, but patient enough to protect the banker and himself. *I gotta talk to Eddie.*

☆ ☆ ☆

The two men sat in the shade outside Eddie's saloon. The sound of far-off thunder rolled across the valley and the breeze picked up a small, swirling dust devil that drew J.D.'s attention. Heavy white clouds drifted across the sky and occasionally a breeze would swirl around the corner of the building.

"What is it you want, my friend? What brings you to Naco?"

"Do you know any of the newspaper fellas in Bisbee?" J.D. asked the saloonkeeper.

"Two or three of them, why?"

"I'm workin' on a plan for your friend the banker and I got an idea."

"I won't ask you what your plan is," said Eddie, "but how does a reporter fit into it?"

J.D. paused a moment before he answered. "I'm thinkin' that whatever happens to the fella has to be made public, so the girl will know what he's really like."

Eddie interrupted J.D. and asked, "What *is* he really like?"

Hooper looked intently at Eddie and said, "You can read about it in the paper like any other unaware citizen." Then he smiled and added, "Can I buy you a beer?"

A huge grin spread across Eddie's face then he roared out a deep belly laugh.

"Mr. Dawson, you are smart and sneaky. Let's go inside and get a beer."

Although he wasn't used to the hot green chiles that

Maria put on his plate, J.D. was growing fond of the tasty beans wrapped in the flat corn tortillas. Flavored with lard and a bit of salt, the filling burritos and the grilled beef always sat well in his belly. He said as much to Eddie and the barman's response made him laugh.

"Maybe you just like the way my beer makes you relax." Several empty mugs were scattered across the table where they sat in the corner of the saloon.

"Naw," said J.D. "It's the beans."

☆ ☆ ☆

The next morning, back in Bisbee, J.D. walked out of the hotel and turned toward the café. As he rounded the corner he was hit square on by a young boy who seemed to be in a very big hurry. J.D. watched as the boy bounced off and landed on his backside.

"Sorry, mister," the youngster groaned. He stood slowly and brushed the dust off the back of his overalls. "I didn't mean to..."

J.D. looked down at the kid and said softly, "It's alright, but watch where you're goin' next time?"

"I will, I promise."

"You ain't gonna cry, are you?"

"No sir, I'm not, but I'm late for school an' my ma will blister me if I'm late again." He took off running and disappeared around the curve in the street.

J.D. let a faint smile reach his lips, then continued on to the café. He ordered breakfast and pondered his meeting with Eddie. With a plan in mind, all he needed to do was work out the timing and meet with the reporter.

When he left the café, the boy who had run into him was waiting outside the door. J.D. looked at him and said, "I thought you were late for school."

"I was, err, I am, but I needed to apologize for bumping into you, mister."

"You already did, kid."

He looked down at his feet, then up at J.D. "My name's Henry, mister."

"You already did, *Henry*."

"Yeah, but..."

"But what?"

"But I know that my ma would want me to make sure you weren't hurt."

"Well, kid, I ain't the one who fell on his butt." J.D. paused. "Are you hurt?"

"Not yet, but I will be when my ma finds out I didn't go to school."

"Then why ain't you goin'?"

"Bein' late is worse than bein' absent, so I'm just gonna stay down here 'til this afternoon."

J.D. shook his head and said, "Well okay. I gotta go kid. Be sure to keep your head up and watch where you're goin'."

"Okay," said Henry. "I will."

"See you around, Henry."

"Okay, mister," he said, and walked slowly away.

☆ ☆ ☆

J.D. spent the day working on his plan, had a beer at the St. Elmo just before dark, and walked back toward the hotel.

He was surprised to see the faint lightning flashes far off in the darkening sky, but he gave it little thought and walked into the hotel lobby then up the stairs to his room.

Long after dark, the lightning and thunder increased, and the rain started to fall. At first it was sporadic, but soon grew to a continuous shower of ever-larger drops. Before dawn the storm had washed the dust from the buildings and trees of the town and turned the unpaved streets to rivers.

Chapter 29

The rain had mostly stopped by morning, but the steel gray clouds continued to leak a fine mist across Bisbee. Several blocks west of the Elks Club, a group of boys gathered around Henry Carter. He was a bit younger than the others, and because he lived far up Brewery Gulch, he was always the target of their teasing. Sometimes, like today, they laughed at his overalls, other times they called him washer boy. Henry was used to the boys' ribbing and most of the time he simply ignored them. With the night-long storm and the resulting flood spread all around the town there was plenty of opportunity for play.

Henry knew he'd get in trouble for not doing his chores, but the excitement of the flood and being with his friends was too much to miss. The gang of boys was fascinated by the rushing waters that tumbled down Main Street. As light as the rain was, it still soaked their hair and clothes. The muddy water churning between the boardwalks on either side of the street carried logs and branches and trash which pounded against everything in the path of the torrent. The boardwalks were slick with silt, but that didn't quench the boys' excitement.

"Let's have a boat race," one of them yelled.

The others rushed away with a chorus of cheers, scattering into alleys in search of boats. They returned with a variety of buoyant objects—a piece of firewood, a broken barrel stave, and a large, flat cactus leaf.

"That ain't gonna float, Tommy."

"Sure it will," said the boy with the leaf as he pulled tiny spines out of his fingers.

Within minutes, each had added a boat to the flotilla, agreed on a signal for setting them free, and lined up at the edge of the boardwalk. Henry was the last to arrive, and as he leaned over to put his wooden box in the water, one of the boys pushed on his back and laughed. Henry slipped in the gooey silt and fell headfirst into the stream.

Flailing his arms, he tried to grab onto the boardwalk, but he was quickly sucked away by the flood. He opened his mouth to yell for help and swallowed some muddy water.

Henry looked back toward the boys but cried out when a box hit him in the forehead. He reached again for the edge of the walk and missed. His head went under the murky water and he struggled to keep his face above the surface so he could breathe. Bouncing off a sunken wash tub, Henry gurgled and went under again.

☆ ☆ ☆

Enthralled by the flood, J.D. stood on the boardwalk in front of the hotel and watched as the roiling water spilled over the door sills across the street and rushed into the shops. He was about to go back into the hotel when he heard someone shouting up the street and turned in time to see that a boy had fallen into the rushing water. The youngster was being pushed along the edge of the boardwalk and struggled to keep his head above the surface. Without hesitating, J.D. got down on his knees and reached out to grab the boy. Nearly falling in himself, he managed to catch the strap of the kid's overalls and hold on. The current was stronger than he'd expected. Tightening his grip and hanging on to a lamp post with his free arm, J.D. slowly lifted the youngster up onto the walk. Fighting to keep his balance, he awkwardly dragged the boy around the curious bystanders and those who were trying to save their belongings. Out of breath, Hooper carried the boy into the hotel lobby and wiped the mud from his face. He recognized the freckly face of the kid he'd met the day before and noticed that the boy had a bleeding cut above his left eye. He pulled the handkerchief from his coat pocket and gently held it over the wound as he tried to comfort the youngster.

"Are you okay, Henry?" he said, an unfamiliar note of concern in his voice. "You're gonna be alright, I gotcha."

The youngster mumbled something garbled and shook his head.

"Where do you live?"

"Up the gulch," he said, coughing and gagging.

"You live in Brewery Gulch?" J.D. asked, not hiding the surprise in his voice.

The boy nodded and closed his eyes.

"Can you walk?"

"I dunno," he said. Deep, blaring coughs shook his small body.

"Do you think you can point out your house if we get close to it?"

Again, the boy nodded and closed his eyes.

J.D. wiped the rest of the mud from the boy's face then lifted him up against his chest. Outside the flood continued to rush down the street, but the rain had stopped. J.D. headed toward the entrance of the gulch. Slogging along and occasionally slipping in the thick mud, J.D. lugged the near-lifeless boy up the serpentine road, occasionally asking him if they were close to his cabin.

"It's up the hill." The boy pointed and moaned. "We're almost there."

Long since out of breath, J.D. walked onto the flat lot the boy finally indicated. Hooper asked, "Is this the place? Is this where you live?"

The boy threw up what remained of the mud he'd swallowed and nodded. Hearing a shriek, J.D. turned as a slight woman rushed down the hill from the cabin.

"Henry, oh Henry, my boy," she cried.

"Ma," was all the boy could force out.

Alice took Henry from J.D.'s arms and held him close. Touching the wound on his head, she asked, "Are you hurt bad? What happened?"

"The flood on Main Street was huge, Ma. I fell in an' it was too strong."

"He either banged his head when he went into the flood or somethin' in the water hit him, ma'am."

She finally looked up into the face of the man who saved Henry and said, "Oh, thank you, sir, thanks for saving my boy. He's all I have."

Embarrassed, J.D. wanted to leave. He mumbled something to the woman and turned to head back down the hill.

"Please sir, won't you come in and dry off?"

"No, I got some things I gotta do."

"Thank you so much, mister..."

Not looking into her soft eyes, J.D. said, "Dawson, it's Dawson."

"You saved my boy's life, Mr. Dawson. I will always be grateful for that."

"Ma," said the boy, "you're squeezin' me too tight."

"I'm sorry, Henry," she said. "I'm just so happy that you're alright."

She tried once more to get J.D. to stay, but he was determined to go. When he reached the edge of the lot, she said, "Mr. Dawson, my name's Alice Carter and this is my son Henry. You will always be welcome in our home." Then she spun around and carried the boy into the shack.

As he headed down the hill, J.D. felt a longing, a painful emptiness.

☆ ☆ ☆

J.D. was wet, covered with mud, and tired from his

trek up Brewery Gulch. He was also deeply confused. He'd reached into the floodwaters to grab the boy, purely by impulse, and then had gently wiped the kid's face and carried him up the muddy hill to his mother. *Why didn't I just let someone else take him to his ma. And why'd she have to be so nice to me? I didn't do anythin' important.* Making his way down the winding road, J.D. noticed that most of the saloons were still open and he thought about having a drink to dull the thoughts. But he didn't stop and by the time he got back to the hotel he'd pushed the confused thoughts into a far corner of his mind. He wondered when he'd be able to make a connection with the reporter Eddie had recommended to him. Despite the rain and the flood, J.D. wanted to finish his job and get rid of Jack Walker.

☆ ☆ ☆

Inside her warm, dry cabin, Alice bathed her tired son in water that she'd planned to use for laundry. Henry was worn out by his experience and barely able to stay awake. She dried him off, wrapped him in a blanket and sat him in front of their small stove.

"I was scared, Ma," he whispered.

"Yes, I'm sure you were and when you feel better we are going to have a talk about why you were on Main Street instead of doing your chores." Alice was too relieved, too happy to have her son warm and safe to even think about punishment. "You rest now, Henry." She softly brushed his still damp hair away from the puffy eyebrow and pulled the blanket up around his neck. "You just rest."

Alone in her corner of the cabin, Alice wept silently. She had cried so many tears of grief when her husband died, she truly believed she had used them all up. But this time it was relief she felt. She thought about all of the people in Bisbee who care so little for children, especially the poor ones. The snooty businessmen and tired angry miners acted like the children were nothing but a burden. Most of Bisbee's women, except for the prostitutes, looked upon the youngsters simply as nuisances. Yet she'd met a man today, Mr. Dawson, who actually took action to save her boy's life. Then even more interesting, he'd taken the time to carry Henry all the way up the gulch to the cabin. *I owe him so much. How can I ever repay him*?

Alice's salty tears dried on her cheeks and she gently slipped into a dream about the time she and her husband had shared a picnic lunch on the bank of a small creek in Oklahoma before they arrived in Arizona. The rain falling on the tin roof of the cabin became the bubbling stream in the dream and Alice slept soundly.

Chapter 30

On the morning after his return to El Paso, Noah dropped by the police station and met again with the Deputy Chief. Welcoming the railroad detective into his office, the portly uniformed man asked Jensen the purpose of his visit.

"You may recall, chief, that I met with you a number of weeks ago." The policeman nodded slightly but said nothing. "At the time I was looking for a suspect in the destruction last spring of a large number of railroad cars at our yard in Memphis. This suspect, a man named Hooper, had started a fire that totally destroyed the cars and our customers' property. I followed Hooper to El Paso and determined that he'd stayed in one of the city's hotels, although the manager was unwilling to give me much information about him. During our first visit, you had mentioned that you were unaware of Hooper's presence in your community."

"I seem to recall our first visit, Mr. Jensen. Please go on."

"You also told me you were in the midst of investigating the murders of several businessmen but that you had no suspects. Have you made any progress in your case?"

"What does the murder case have to do with your arsonist?"

"The killing of two El Paso men may have nothing to do with my case, but I wonder if the timing of the murders and the disappearance of Hooper are just coincidence or did my suspect have a role in your case."

The chief ran his hand through his thinning hair and smoothed his mustache. "I suppose anything is possible, but the circumstances surrounding the murders and the evidence we've collected suggest that the motive was robbery and the perpetrators were probably Mexicans from Juarez."

"You said 'perpetrators.' Does that mean you think more than one person was involved?"

"That's what my detectives think. Both victims were young and healthy. One had his skull crushed, probably by a club or sap. The other was stabbed repeatedly by a very sharp knife. It is very unlikely that one man could have committed the crime without having been injured himself. We found no evidence of the killer at the scene."

"So, without any evidence and with no suspects, I assume that your investigation is stalled?"

"Mr. Jensen, in your years as a railroad detective have you solved *every* case assigned to you?"

"Of course not, Chief, and I meant no disrespect to you or to your department. It's just that this case was very costly to the Southern Pacific and I owe it to my boss to give my full effort to solving it." By the look on the policeman's face, Noah knew that he'd hit another stone wall. He wasn't going to get any new information or cooperation.

The policeman said, "Well then, since I have no knowledge of your Mr. Hooper, I suppose that our meeting is over."

Noah rose from his chair, thanked the chief, and walked out of the office. He ignored the desk sergeant's disinterested grunt and left the building. On the street, he watched the passing traffic and listened to the sounds of a city going about its business. Noah jumped on a passing streetcar and rode it to his hotel. Looking out the window, Noah realized that not much had changed in El Paso since his earlier visit. The sun was still hot, the streets still dusty, and the sky was still clear and blue.

At the hotel, Noah learned that Hooper had never returned to his room to claim his property and that Garrison, the night clerk, was no longer employed there. The hotel manager's secretary told Noah that everything the hotel could say about a former patron had already been shared with him.

"So your manager won't meet with me?"

"That's correct, Mr. Jensen."

"Then please pass along to him that it will now be the policy of the Southern Pacific Railroad that this hotel will no longer be used by any of the company's employees. Furthermore, we'll make the same request of our customers. Your reluctance to help us will result in this hotel's loss of our business."

Angered by the manager's rejection, Noah checked out of his room and carried his bag across the street to a different hotel. Sitting in the café next door, he contemplated his next moves. Going back over his notes, he concluded that his only clues were that Hooper had left his belongings and had once been visited by an old Mexican. Jensen pondered all of the ramifications of the weak clues. Was Hooper acquainted with the old man? Was the acquaintance, if it was truly that, casual or intimate? Was the Mexican a resident of El Paso or the city across the river? If the old man was living in Juarez, how could Noah find him in a city filled with old Mexicans? If the hotel night clerk saw Hooper with the Mexican, is it possible that others did too? And who, Noah wondered, might these other witnesses be? The longer he sat drinking his coffee, the more questions he generated and his frustration grew when he came up with no answers.

Jensen was disappointed that his first day back in El Paso hadn't led to any progress in the case. Yet he was far from discouraged. Sitting on the edge of the bed in his room he made plans for the next day, plans that included visits to saloons and possibly a trip across the border. *If I truly am the detective Mr. Harriman thinks I am, I need to follow every clue as far as it'll take me. If I don't find answers, then I've got to find new clues.* Noah fell asleep with these thoughts in his head and when he woke up the next morning, he was well-rested and believed that the search for Hooper, which had been a matter of pride, had become a matter of necessity. *I will do whatever it takes to find Hooper.* He dressed and left his room.

Throughout the day, Noah visited dozens of saloons and bars. He asked the bartenders, janitors, and the vast number of drinking patrons if they'd encountered Hooper. He showed them the wanted poster and described the clothes he wore—especially the derby hat. For all his effort, Noah got nothing. Not one person in any of the saloons had heard of or seen Hooper. In the evening, Noah even stopped in a dozen brothels and asked the madams and the whores if they'd met Hooper. That effort, too, came up empty.

Even as Noah dragged his weary body up the stairs to his room, he refused to give up. He closed and locked the door behind him and walked over to the window. Drawing the curtain to the side, and gazing out onto the still busy street, he said, "I'm going to Juarez tomorrow."

☆ ☆ ☆

Despite being well-travelled in the U.S., Noah had never left the country. He'd heard English spoken in dozens of different accents—Italian, Irish, German, and even Polish. But in Juarez, every spoken word he heard was in Spanish or poorly accented English.

The sky and the heat were the same as in El Paso. But the sounds and smells and energy were all different. On the American side of the bridge at this time of day, the streets were full of men in suits and streetcars and freight wagons. In Juarez, freight was hauled on the backs of burros and the dusty streets were crowded with people of all ages.

Noah planned to repeat his efforts of the day before and expected that it would be more difficult since he wasn't fluent in Spanish. He discovered, however, that with patience, he could communicate with most of the bartenders and hotel employees. No one remembered ever seeing Hooper or anyone resembling him. During one of his discussions with a slightly drunk American soldier, he'd learned that the smaller cantinas in the parts of Juarez away from the river were often frequented by Americans who did not want to be noticed.

The next morning, Noah crossed the bridge early and walked away from the Rio Grande and deeper into Juarez. He wandered up and down the streets, stopping in cantinas that had signs and lights and music as well as those that were simply open courtyards with tables and a bar. Noah asked anyone who would listen if they'd seen Hooper. Hour after hour he kept at it, buying but not drinking beer, offering small bribes, and even eating some of the spicy Mexican food. At the end of the day he promised himself to start again as soon as the sun came up.

The mind of Noah the railroad detective was tired and nearly convinced that his prey had never been to Juarez and that the clue regarding the old Mexican was false. His brain was urging him to quit the chase and head back to San Francisco. But Noah's gut, that part of him which had solved impossible cases, that had kept him chasing suspects when others would have given up, wouldn't let him quit. So, he crossed the bridge again the fifth day and wandered to the southwestern edge of the city.

Standing at a small crossroad, wondering which way to turn, Noah shivered as a gentle breeze from the distant river cooled his sweaty neck. He was about to turn up the track to the east when he spotted a middle-aged man watching him from the open entrance of a courtyard a short distance down the road.

Urged by the breeze and his instincts, Noah walked toward the man and greeted him as he approached the arched entrance of the cantina.

"*Buenos dias, Señor.*"

"*Buenos dias*. You are very far from the city, *Señor*. Are you lost?" The man smiled at Noah and set his straw broom against the wall.

Noah returned the smile and glanced up at the face of the arch and noted the faded black sign which read, *Felipé's Cantina*.

"Are you Felipé?" he asked.

"*Si, Señor*. Although it is very early, my cantina is open. Would you like something to eat?"

Noah followed Felipé into the spacious courtyard and led him to a small table against the adobe wall. As he sat in the proffered chair, the Mexican walked through a doorway into the house. He returned in a moment with a steaming cup of dark coffee and a plate of beans and tortillas.

"The tortillas are fresh this morning, *Señor*. Would you like anything else?"

"No, thank you, this will be fine." Noah sipped at the coffee and scooped some of the mashed beans onto a tortilla. While waiting for Felipé to return, Noah took out his small leather casebook and jotted down a few notes. In the week he'd been in El Paso and Juarez he'd filled dozens of pages, but not one of them included a clue about J.D. Hooper's whereabouts. He slipped the pencil into his pocket and folded the casebook just as Felipé returned to the courtyard.

"*Señor* Felipé, I wonder if I could ask you a few questions."

"Of course, *Señor*, what is it you want to know?"

Thinking that his lack of success so far was because the people in Juarez might be reluctant to give information to a detective, Noah had decided to try a different approach. He picked up his coffee and told the Mexican that he was looking for a friend of his, a man whose family needed him.

"Do you think your friend is here in Juarez?"

"He was in El Paso a few months ago, Felipé, but I have not been able to find him."

"Your friend is an American, *si*?"

Before Noah could respond, an old man walked into the courtyard and removed his sombrero. The Mexican glanced at Noah and sat down at a table in the back of the cantina. Felipé excused himself, told Noah he would return momentarily, and joined the old man. The two spoke for a few minutes, then Felipé walked back toward Noah.

"I'm sorry, *Señor*, but Tomás is an old friend and works for my *Patrón*."

"That's alright, Felipé. To answer your question, yes, my friend is an American. He has a family..." Noah paused, thinking quickly, and continued, "In Tennessee and they are very worried about him."

"What is your friend's name? What does he look like?"

"He is about your height, Felipé. He has a mustache, brown hair, and blue eyes, and usually wears a derby hat. He is a very quiet man and keeps to himself." Noah watched the man's eyes closely, looking for a hint of recognition. "My friend's name is J.D. Hooper."

"I have not seen your friend," Felipé said, glancing quickly at the old man in the back of the courtyard. "I am sure that he has not been in my cantina."

Noah had seen the eye contact between the two Mexicans and noticed a change in Felipé's tone.

"Do many Americans come into the cantina?"

"No, not so many. It is a long way from the river and most of the Americans are looking for only two things—tequila and *las putas*. I serve tequila, but I do not sell women." Felipé picked up the empty plate from the table and reached for Noah's cup.

"May I have some more coffee?"

"Of course, *Señor*, I will be right back," said Felipé. He turned and walked into the house. The old man appeared to be sleeping at the corner table, his head rested against the wall.

Noah calmed himself as he waited for Felipé and the coffee. His instincts told him that Felipé wasn't telling the truth and that the old man also knew something. *If Hooper had been in the cantina*, thought Noah, *why would Felipé lie about it*? He glanced again at the old Mexican and wondered if he was the one that the hotel clerk had seen with Hooper.

When the cantina owner returned with his coffee, Noah tried to ask him another question but Felipé's response was abrupt, cold even. The warmth of the man's earlier welcome had faded, and Noah knew then that Hooper *had* been here. *But why would they be protecting him*, he thought. *What possible reason would they have*? Jensen rose from his chair and dropped some Mexican silver on the table. He walked to the back of the courtyard toward the old man.

"Pardon me, *Señor*, I apologize for interrupting your nap, but I wonder if you can help me."

The old man opened his eyes, said a few words in Spanish and pulled his sombrero over his face.

"Excuse me, *Señor*, I just want to know..."

"He does not speak English," interrupted Felipé. "Please do not disturb him." He gestured toward the street and added, "I already told you that your friend has never been in my cantina, so if you have finished your coffee I think you should leave and go back to El Paso."

Well that proves it, Noah thought as he left the courtyard and walked away from the cantina. J.D. Hooper was in Juarez and probably did something *to* these people or *for* these people. Probably the latter. Convinced that he'd get no more information from them, he walked back toward the river for a few blocks. At a small plaza, he sat on a bench near a well and began to write in his leather notebook.

☆ ☆ ☆

Back at the cantina, Tomas stood under the archway and watched until the American was out of sight. He went back to his table and asked Felipé to sit with him.

"You did well, Felipé. If this *gringo* returns, you should tell him nothing about Hooper and answer none of his questions." He was quiet for a moment then added, "Tell everyone that this *gringo* is not welcome here, that if they help him *El Jefe* will be terribly displeased."

"I will do as you ask, Tomás. Please tell *El Jefe* that I am sorry if anything I have said was helpful to the *gringo*."

"You need not worry, Felipé, just make sure that he gets no help from anyone in the *barrio*." Tomas stood and walked to the archway. Setting his sombrero on his head, he drove the wagon toward the *hacienda*.

When the dirt streets cleared for *siesta*, Noah walked back over the bridge and went to his hotel. He spent the rest of the evening in his room making notes. The next morning, while reading the notes, he decided that Hooper most likely left Juarez and headed west. *Hooper could have traveled through Northern Mexico on horseback or by train from El Paso*, he thought. Noah packed his bags, checked out of the hotel, went to the depot, and used his pass to get a ticket without a destination. He planned to search in every stop between El Paso and the coast. The railroad detective was determined to find the arsonist.

Chapter 31

Over the next week J.D. learned that even in the dry desert of the southwest there was a regular rainy season. During July and August, on most every afternoon the sky would open up and dump rain on the dry, thirsty land. Floods like the one he'd experienced were infrequent, but common enough that most of Bisbee's residents simply cleaned up when they were over and went back to work. The mud and destruction had gotten in the way of J.D.'s job, though. Eddie's newspaper contact had been too busy reporting on the flood and the damage it had created. Hooper sent a note to the man's office and asked him to meet at the St. Elmo that night. The note was vague about the purpose, but J.D. had mentioned Eddie's name and he hoped the fella would show up.

Since he'd been in Bisbee, the St. Elmo Bar had become J.D.'s favorite place. He was comfortable there and it seemed to meet his needs. The bartender knew him by sight if not by name and always made him feel welcome. He simply nodded and delivered a full mug of beer in front of J.D. Hooper had learned how to tip during his time in Memphis and the practice seemed to make the same impression at the St. Elmo.

Hooper had arrived early for his appointment with Calvin Langley, the reporter for the Bisbee Daily Review. From Eddie, J.D. had learned that Langley had become civilized in the last ten years or so but in his early days in Arizona he'd had some trouble with the law largely because he was a terrible gambler. Since those days, he'd given up gambling and instead had become a great supporter of the local baseball team. Calvin was, said Eddie, a good man always in need of a few extra dollars and even more interested in a good story. J.D. knew that the information he had on Walker would interest Langley and at the same time be sufficient to ruin the cane-toting clerk's reputation with his employer and, more importantly with the banker's daughter.

A few minutes past seven, Langley walked into the saloon and headed toward the end of the bar. J.D. had only a moment to size-up the reporter. The man was short and wore a derby like Hooper's. His suit was clean, though not pressed, and his tie was crooked, but he was neat enough to present himself well in the businesses and banks in town. J.D. was hopeful.

"Mr. Dawson? I'm Cal Langley."

"I'm John Dawson, Cal. You can call me John if you like." He signaled the bartender for another beer and one for the reporter. "Join me?"

Langley smiled and said, "If you're buying, I'm drinking." He set the leather case he'd carried up on the bar and took the fresh beer from the bartender before the man had a chance to set it down.

"It's been a long day and I'm very thirsty. Thanks, John."

For the next half hour Langley told J.D. about himself. What he revealed matched closely to what Eddie had told him about the reporter. With a growing confidence in his plan, J.D. steered the conversation around to the Walker job.

"Did Eddie tell you why I wanted to meet with you?" J.D. asked.

"He said you had a story that I might find interesting and that you'd be willing to pay me a little if I could get it published quickly. Eddie didn't say what it was about, but he did say I could trust you and that it was important that your name not be connected in any way. He was serious about that last part." Langley dug into his leather case and pulled out a small notebook and a pencil. "Is it okay if I take notes?"

"As long as you don't use any names, particularly Eddie's or mine."

"I've learned in my years as a journalist to keep my sources confidential and I have no intention of breaking my commitment to you. I owe Eddie a lot and if he says to keep you out of this, then you will never be connected with the story."

"That's good, Calvin. I think you'll like the story because it's about a man in town who believes he's got a good reputation, one good enough to connect him with some very wealthy people in Bisbee. But there are some things he does and places he goes that these same wealthy people wouldn't approve of."

Langley wrote down a few words then looked at J.D. "I'm not going to ask what these things and places are, but I assume that you have evidence of the man's habits—where he goes and what he does."

"I do." J.D. waited a moment before he asked another question. "How well are you connected with the Sheriff or any of his deputies?"

"Of course I know the Sheriff, but usually I deal with the deputies. One of them in particular is a close friend of mine. He lets me know when things are happening in the department and I always buy his beer when we go to the baseball games."

J.D. considered the revelation for a moment and then said, "So if I saw somethin' happen that I thought you'd be interested in writin' a story about and it was a situation that required a lawman, the two of you could work together on it?"

"We could do that."

"Then, Calvin, we have a deal."

J.D. spent the next several minutes giving Langley a few details. He told him Walker's name and described the photographs and brothel visits. J.D. reminded Calvin about the secrecy and got the reporter's agreement to be ready right away. Looking for ideas about his story, Langley asked several more questions, made some notes and said, "I guess that's it."

"One more thing," J.D. said, "I'd like to give you some beer money for baseball, enough to share with your friend the deputy. All I ask is that you stay around for the next week or so. When I know that this character is involved in his business, I'll want to find you and be sure that you and the deputy can be where the trouble is gonna happen." J.D. reached into his pocket and pulled out five gold double-eagles. "This should cover your baseball entertainment for a while."

Langley's eyes grew as large as the twenty-dollar gold pieces. He stuttered his thanks and quickly slid the coins into his case. He wrote down the telephone number for the newspaper office, handed it to J.D., and told him that when he called, to be sure to give the operator his name. "That way I'll know that it's time to get ready to write my story."

Hooper leaned back from the bar and extended his hand to Langley. They confirmed the arrangement by shaking hands and Hooper offered the reporter another beer.

"Thanks anyway, John, but one's enough for now. I've got a meeting at the School Board tonight and those fellas aren't partial to drunken reporters." He gathered up his case, tipped his hat to J.D., and hurried out the door.

J.D. paid for the beers and left the St. Elmo. Now he just had to carry out his plan for Walker's downfall.

☆ ☆ ☆

Jack Walker's daily pattern hadn't changed. The man

still left for his office every morning at the same time and returned to the boarding house at the end of the day. Only once during the following week did he venture up to the banker's house. J.D. watched as Walker arrived at the two-story building and knocked on the door. He was not invited in or allowed to talk with the girl. That evening he walked back to Brewery Gulch and had a beer at the Calumet then returned to his room.

A few days later, J.D. followed Walker again when he left his office. This time, however, he turned toward the gulch rather than heading to the boarding house. When the man passed up the Calumet and the other saloons at the lower end of the street, J.D. guessed that he was headed to one of the whorehouses. Making sure that his target couldn't see him, J.D. watched him casually walk up the steps of the same brothel he'd visited before. When Walker didn't immediately come out of the building, J.D. ran down to the newspaper office and found Langley sitting at his desk. J.D. then told him where to go, trusting that he'd bring the deputy with him.

Checking his coat pockets to confirm he still had the small bottle of whiskey, the photographs, and his sap, J.D. rushed back up the hill to the brothel and hid in the dark just off the porch. J.D. looked into the front parlor of the whorehouse through a gap in the drawn curtain and was convinced he'd be able to see Walker come into the room after he finished his business upstairs.

While waiting, J.D. tried to keep his mind clear, focusing on this part of the plan. But his thoughts kept drifting ahead to what he was going to do to Walker. Standing at the side of the whorehouse, J.D.'s thoughts grew darker than the night sky and his heart began to pound. The growing rage distracted him and if he hadn't heard the madam's laughter in the parlor he might have missed the clerk. At the bottom of the staircase, Walker and the woman were finishing up the financial part of their business. J.D. left the shadows and stepped quietly onto the porch, stopping next to the door.

With the heavy sap in his hand, J.D. held his breath and tensed as the door came open. Walker stepped out of the house, pulling the door closed behind him, and turned toward the street. That's when J.D. swung the sap as hard as he could and struck Walker squarely in the nose. The man slumped face-first onto the porch, clearly unconscious. J.D. pulled the bottle from his pocket and emptied it on Walker's head. The whiskey mixed with the growing puddle of blood that streamed from the man's nose. Then Hooper placed the photographs in Walker's hand. The whole process had taken less than a minute. Knowing he needed to get out of sight, J.D. ran back off the porch and headed toward the yard behind the building next door.

From his hiding place he saw Calvin and the deputy arrive at the brothel. A small crowd had begun to gather as some whores and their customers streamed out of the neighboring buildings. Convinced that his accomplices had the situation under control, J.D. worked his way across several of the back yards and then out onto Brewery Gulch.

Not wanting to draw attention to himself, J.D. walked slowly down the hill. The energy from the adrenaline was pumping through his veins and he felt a rush of power and even a sense of satisfaction from smashing the man's face. Hooper liked how that made him feel. As he reached the end of Brewery Gulch and turned toward the hotel, he knew that all he had to do now was wait for the next part—Calvin's story to appear in the newspaper.

☆ ☆ ☆

From the porch of her home on the hill above her own brothel, Helen McHenry had been watching. She recognized Walker when he came out the door across the road.

She was actually pleased to see him knocked out. Walker had given her girls trouble in the past—he roughed them up sometimes and even brought dope into the house. When she saw the stranger slip around toward the back yard, she called for her houseboy.

"Andy, get out here quick."

The young boy ran out onto the porch.

"Get down to the road and follow the man with the derby." She pointed as the man came out onto the road a few doors down. "Can you see him?"

"Yes, ma'am, I can see him."

"Find out where he goes and, if you can, find out his name. Then hurry back up here, understand?"

The boy nodded and took off running. He returned in half an hour and told Helen that he'd followed the man to the Grand Hotel and had overheard someone in the hotel call him Dawson. Helen thanked the boy and smiled.

"Mr. Dawson," she said to herself, "I've got to meet you. We have some business to discuss."

She stepped off the porch and went down the steps to her brothel. She wanted to get a close up look at the damage to Walker and to get her girls back into the house. They weren't making any money watching the excitement.

☆ ☆ ☆

On the front page of the next morning's edition of the *Bisbee Daily Review* under the byline of Calvin Langley, J.D. read the following story:

LOCAL BUSINESSMAN'S PECCADILLOES REVEALED

Last evening, Jack Walker, the senior clerk at Texas Canyon Mining Supply Company, was found unconscious on the porch of Red Jean's

> brothel in Brewery Gulch. The scoundrel, who was seriously intoxicated, had fallen face first onto the establishment's porch. Earning a broken nose in the process, Walker also managed to expose another of his heinous habits. Lying on the porch next to him were a dozen or so photographs of soiled doves and ladies of the street, most of them in various stages of undress. This reporter and Sheriff's Deputy William O'Reilly happened upon the scene and learned from witnesses that Walker was a frequent visitor to the brothels and saloons of our city. Evidently he also traded in illicit materials as his possession of the photographs reveals. Perhaps even more importantly, a small packet of dope was discovered in one of his pockets. His employer confirmed last night that Walker would no longer be an employee of the firm since "men who practice these deplorable acts do not represent my company." Deputy O'Reilly arrested the rogue for disorderly conduct. Walker refused to answer questions when visited in his jail cell but suggested that he would be leaving Bisbee as soon as he paid his fine and cleared up his business with the court.

Langley's story continued on for several more paragraphs, but clearly Walker's reputation was in shambles. J.D. now had to wait to see when Walker left the city and where he went. *I'm not done with you.*

☆ ☆ ☆

On the day after the story appeared in the newspaper, J.D. hid outside the jail and waited. He saw Walker stumble through the steel-clad door and down the long, narrow stairwell and then followed him all the way to the boarding house. Walker's possessions had been unceremoniously piled in the front yard of Mrs. Harding's house and the man was not pleased. Walker gathered up the clothing and other items, clutched them under his arm, and yelled an obscenity at the closed door of the house. J.D. followed Walker back down Main Street all the way to the train station. After Walker bought a ticket he sat on a bench and tried to organize what was left of his life, rolling up the shirts and suits into a bundle and securing it with a belt.

J.D. waited for an hour across from the depot and then casually entered the building and bought a ticket. The local rail line connected with the westbound line at Benson and J.D. believed that he'd have plenty of opportunities to carry out the rest of his plan. All he needed to do was be patient and observant. Walker's face was a mess, his reputation was ruined, and he wanted to get out of Bisbee quickly. Hooper believed that the man would probably be too busy wondering how his life had so quickly crumbled that he wouldn't be watching out for someone behind him.

J.D. was right about Walker's state of mind and didn't have to wait long to finish his own personal plans for the man. When the train made its first stop in Tombstone, Walker left the passenger car and hauled his bundle across the street. He entered the nearest saloon and ordered a bottle of whiskey. From the window, J.D. watched him work his way back to a corner table and sit down where he leaned over the table, quickly pouring and drinking several shots of the liquor. J.D. walked into the building, stood at the end of the bar and kept his eyes on Walker. In less than an hour, the bottle was empty and Walker was slumped over the table as unconscious as he'd been on the porch of the whorehouse. J.D. walked past the man's table and used the outhouse in the alley behind the saloon. When he re-entered the building, J.D. noticed that Walker hadn't stirred.

"I wonder if you'd keep an eye on my friend over there while I get us some transportation home?" J.D. asked the bartender.

The very tall, very thin man said, "It don't look like he's goin' anywhere soon, but make it quick. I don't want the boss to see him."

"You fellas have a livery in town?" asked J.D.

"Just down the street to the right," said the bartender.

J.D. left the saloon, found the livery stable and for a few dollars rented a wagon and a horse. Before half an hour had passed, he pulled the rig up in the alley behind the saloon and walked into the building.

"I thought it'd be better if I took him out the back way," said J.D. "That way your boss won't see him."

"Good idea," said the barman. "Let me give you a hand gettin' him outta here."

Grabbing Walker under his arms, Hooper lifted the man out of the chair while the bartender grabbed the drunk by the feet. They hauled him out the back door and put him down in the bed of the wagon. The bartender retrieved the bundle of clothing and tossed it to J.D.

"Did he owe you anything for the bottle?" asked J.D. Not waiting for the man's response, he tossed a silver dollar at him. The aproned man thanked J.D. and went back to work.

Hooper untied the bundle and spread the loose clothing across Walker's unconscious body. Before he covered his face, J.D. looked both directions in the alley and, seeing no one, he hit Walker in the head with his sap. *Don't need him wakin' up 'til I get him out in the desert,* thought J.D. Assured of Walker's cooperation, J.D. clucked to the horse and drove the wagon out of the alley and quickly out of Tombstone in the direction of the nearby mountains. Before an hour had passed, J.D. found an ideal spot for completing the job.

An arroyo ran away from the wagon road into a side canyon. Although the ground was rough, the horse had little difficulty making its way behind a modest rise and out of sight of the road. J.D. pulled back on the reins and jumped down from the seat. He lifted a heavy wooden bucket of water from the wagon and set it in front of the horse. Then he grabbed Walker by his ankles and pulled him out of the wagon, smiling as the body thumped on the dirt. With quite a bit of effort, J.D. dragged him down into the arroyo leaving a deep trail in the dirt. When he got to the sandy bottom, Hooper left the body face up next to a bed of cactus.

J.D. went back to the wagon, removed the half-filled bucket of water from in front of the horse and returned to Walker's side, placing the bucket by his head. He walked around the area and found a rock about the size of a loaf of bread. Holding the rock in his left hand and satisfied with its weight, J.D. stood next to Walker's supine body and reached down for the bucket. Hooper splashed the water on Walker's face and tossed the bucket aside. Coughing and sputtering, the semi-conscious man shook his head and looked up into J.D.'s angry face.

Hooper lifted the heavy rock above his head, his face a picture of rage and his words as fiery and venomous as a demon's.

"You're goin' to burn in hell you bastard," J.D. yelled. "You won't ever hurt another innocent girl and you'll always remember that it was me who crushed your skull and sent you to hell."

Before Walker could react, J.D. dropped the rock onto his already damaged face, turning the man's head into a flattened mass of bone and brains and blood.

Backing away from Walker's body, J.D. gasped, sucking in air. Still not satisfied with the man's ruin, Hooper kicked sand on the pulpy mess under the rock. J.D.'s howl of rage echoed between the walls of the canyon until its energy finally faded, replaced by the gentle sound of the breeze.

☆ ☆ ☆

Sitting in his seat on the train back to Bisbee, J.D. couldn't recall leaving the arroyo or driving the wagon back to Tombstone, but vividly remembered everything he did to Walker. He'd destroyed an evil man who was ready to hurt an innocent child and felt good and righteous and satisfied with himself. Hooper had finished his job for the banker and had kept his promise to Eddie. He was also very tired and all he wanted to do at the moment was walk down the street to the hotel, go up to his room and sleep, and that's exactly what he did.

Chapter 32

J.D. was amazed at how quickly Main Street had been restored after the monsoon flood. The cobblestones were still stained with mud, and the streetcar tracks needed flushing, but things appeared to be back to normal. His daily visits to the St. Elmo went uninterrupted, and the regular flow of foot and wagon traffic returned.

But things were different just a block south of Main Street. There a massive pile of rubble and silt was still being excavated. The operations manager at the mine had provided mineworkers to assist the building owners in the cleanup effort, but the lower floors of the buildings had been severely damaged and would require repair. J.D. figured that carpenters, plumbers, and fellas who put in glass windows would be busy for another month at least.

Sure glad I'm on the second floor, J.D. thought as he strolled toward the St. Elmo. Just this morning he'd counted up his money and realized he had more than three thousand dollars. Since Hooper had been carrying all of the cash with him, but now that was getting uncomfortable. J.D. had never trusted banks and bankers, but today his plan was to put some of it in the bank managed by the man he'd helped. Perhaps the banker would be encouraged to recommend him to others if he opened an account.

Although he'd only been in Bisbee a short time, Hooper was starting to like the place. He'd said as much to Lucky Eddie in Naco a week earlier. Eddie promised to let him know if any more opportunities came up and told J.D. he was happy that he'd found a home. They'd had a good visit, and when Hooper got back to Bisbee that night, he'd gone straight to the St. Elmo to make a comparison. After two or three foamy mugs of the saloon's beer, he made a decision. Cold beer is just cold beer. Makes no difference where you drink it.

J.D. went to the huge stone building at the end of Main Street and put half of his money in an account. He decided to hang onto the Mexican silver—about two hundred dollars—in case he needed to use it across the border. Hooper spent most of the time with a clerk, but just before the man finished, the banker came over to the counter and invited him into his office. The man shook J.D.'s hand and expressed his gratitude for taking care of the Walker problem and for keeping everything confidential. Then he asked J.D. if it was alright to recommend his services to others.

"Yes, sir," he said, "but I'm only interested in doing work for men of good character," he said.

☆ ☆ ☆

The next afternoon as J.D. was leaving the barber shop, he heard a small voice.

"Hey Mr. Dawson, it's me!"

Recognizing the boy he'd saved, J.D. shook his head and said, "What're you doin' here, Henry?"

"Mr. Dawson I wanna thank you for savin' me from the flood."

"Fine, you did. Now leave me alone, I'm busy."

The boy didn't give up easily. "Please, Mr. Dawson, I promised my Ma I'd find you and thank you and if I don't then she'll be really mad, and I don't want my Ma mad at me." He paused to catch his breath. "She's really not mean, but she don't like me bein' rude or un…un…, ungrateful."

"Listen, Henry, I pulled you outta the water and you're okay, right? So go tell your ma that I'm glad you didn't die."

"I'll tell her, Mr. Dawson, but she ain't gonna like it, 'cause I think she wants you to come to our place for supper."

"Aww, Henry, I ain't gonna..." J.D. paused trying to come up with something that would satisfy the boy. "I did what any man would do, and I'd do it again. But I don't think your ma wants a fella like me to eat at your house."

"But she does, Mr. Dawson, I know she does."

"Henry why are you such a pain in the ass?" he said with a genuine smile.

"My Ma says I'm like my pa was before he died." Henry's smile disappeared. "Maybe it's 'cause of him."

J.D. was quiet for a moment. "You ain't got no pa?"

"Nope, my pa got killed in a mine accident." Henry's eyes turned silver at the edges. "The tunnel he was workin' in collapsed and he died." The boy looked down at the boardwalk.

A distant memory of his own pa flashed across J.D.'s mind. "Did your pa ever beat you?"

"Naw, he'd usually just sit me in a corner and tell me what I did was wrong and that I gotta learn how to be good."

J.D. cleared his throat. "Go tell your ma that I'll think about it, okay?"

Henry quickly darted off down the street. J.D. followed him for a block or so then turned in at the St. Elmo.

He stepped up to the bar and asked for a beer. The conversation with young Henry echoed in his head and J.D. couldn't shake it loose. The kid was like a hangover; annoying, persistent, and a bit painful. But for some reason he found that he liked Henry. What Hooper didn't understand and couldn't quite grasp was the mother, Alice. Why was she so set on meeting with him and why invite him to dinner? Women were an enigma to him—he didn't understand them at all and always felt uncomfortable in their presence. If he did go back to the cabin—and that wasn't yet decided—what would he do? What if she asked about him? What would he say?

"Damn it," he cursed, kicking the spittoon at his feet, spilling some of the slime onto the sawdust. "Why don't she just leave me alone? I don't need this." Hooper ordered another beer, but it didn't numb his thoughts. He considered accepting the invitation just to get her to quit asking. *But what if that don't work.* J.D. turned around and leaned back against the bar, gazing around the smoky room, glad again that the St. Elmo was quiet.

Even though his own pa hadn't died when J.D. was a boy, the man had never been there. His pa spent lots of time away from the family drinking and fighting and when he did come home, J.D. was usually the target of the man's frustration. Nevertheless, Hooper knew the pain of not having a father to turn to for advice or attention. He recalled how often he wished his pa was dead, especially after getting whipped for something he hadn't even done. His ma was no better. She took out her own frustration with his pa on J.D. So Hooper never felt close to his family, never understood why some kids loved their parents. Yet today, a part of him did feel bad for Henry. The compassion nagged at his heart and he wasn't sure why.

He turned back to the bar and thought about ordering another beer but knew he wouldn't enjoy it as long as the face of the shiny-eyed kid kept smiling at him in his thoughts. *Maybe she'll just forget about it.*

☆ ☆ ☆

But she didn't. The next morning as Hooper left the hotel to get something for breakfast, Henry was waiting on the boardwalk.

"G'mornin' Mr. Dawson."

J.D. let out a long sigh. "Have you been waitin' out here for me?"

"I have, but I don't wanna bother you. My Ma said I had to ask you again. Only this time she said I was to tell you that she'd like you to come to supper this Thursday night." Henry smiled and then added, "She said I was supposed to keep askin' you until you said yes."

This time J.D.'s sigh was louder and he started walking away from the boy. Henry tagged along just behind him. "Please Mr. Dawson, can't you just come to supper?"

"I don't know, kid, I ain't really good company. Can't your ma just let me alone?" J.D. looked down at Henry and saw the same silvery look in his eyes he'd seen the day before. He didn't want to hurt the kid, but he also didn't want to sit at a table with the boy's ma. *Maybe if I just do it and get it over with, I can be done with this.*

"Alright, Henry. Your ma wants me to come to supper on Thursday night, right?"

"Yes sir, six o'clock."

"Then you tell her I'll be there, but I can only stay for a little while 'cause I got some business to take care of."

"Thanks, Mr. Dawson, thanks a lot." Henry started to run up the street then stopped and turned around. "Oh boy," he yelled, "see you on Thursday." When the boy disappeared around the corner, J.D. groaned out a sigh, wondering what he'd just done.

☆ ☆ ☆

By Thursday morning, J.D.'s gut was in a knot and his head hurt worse than if he'd had a hangover. For two days he'd kept thinking about Henry's ma and what she was likely to do during supper. She'd ask him questions about himself and his family. She'd get all weepy about her dead husband. She'd start preaching to him about smoking and drinking and gambling and how those things were bad or evil or something. Then she'd put the food on china plates and there would be shiny forks and spoons to use and J.D.

wouldn't know which ones to use. She'd have napkins and would probably serve tea in little dainty cups. J.D. knew—deep in his gut he knew—that he'd spill something or break a dish, or utter some terribly foul word, and that would be the end of the whole meal. *But ain't that what I want, to end supper and get the hell out of the cabin*?

Right after noon, J.D. went to the barber for a shave and a haircut, then picked up his shirts at the laundry. He went into the St. Elmo for a beer, then decided that beer wasn't strong enough and had two shots of bourbon instead. The whiskey seemed to settle him down a little but only for a short time. As soon as he walked into his hotel room J.D. started feeling edgy again. He lay down on his bed, closed his eyes, and quickly fell asleep. His dream was filled with images of Henry poking at him with a spoon, broken dishes, rotten food, and the boy's ma asking him the same question over and over—are you married? Are you married? Are you married?

"No, I ain't," shouted J.D., roaring awake from his nap. "No, I ain't." He looked at the small clock on the desk and saw that it was half past five. He put on a fresh shirt and dusted off his hat and turned toward the mirror. *That's right*, he thought, *I ain't gonna be nice and I ain't gonna answer no silly woman questions. I'll use whatever fork I want and I won't worry about spillin' or swearin'. I won't.* With that, he settled the derby on his head, walked out the door and down the steps to his doom.

☆ ☆ ☆

Even as he walked up the curving slope of Brewery Gulch, passing the saloons and bordellos and the scores of off-shift miners traipsing between the establishments, J.D. began to lose some of the courage he'd shown in his room. His once strong and determined pace slowed to a stroll. At least twice he'd stopped in front of one of the bars and considered going in for a drink, thinking it wouldn't hurt to be relaxed a little. Both times he decided that even a small taste of whiskey in his stomach might weaken his resolve and lead him to say or do too much. Rounding the last curve in the road, J.D. spotted the small cabin and saw Henry standing eagerly at the end of the yard.

"Hi, Mr. Dawson!" Waving his arms like a windmill, the boy ran down the hill and out onto the road and clutched the sleeve of J.D.'s coat. "Ma's still fixin' supper, so she told me to wait for you and keep you on the porch."

He let the boy tug him toward the front of the cabin.

"Are you sure your ma wants me here?"

"I'm sure, Mr. Dawson. She's been fixin' supper ever since she finished workin' on the laundry." Henry's face was split by a large grin when he said, "And she took a long time workin' on her hair and dress." His grin turned into a laugh as he sat down on the porch. J.D. went numb.

Taking a seat next to the boy, J.D. gazed out across the dirt yard, noticing that the lot was clear of trash and rocks. The noise from down the road softened as it drifted up to the top of the hill and the growing quiet did nothing to calm his worries. To break the silence, he asked Henry if he went to school.

"I only go when I have to," he said. "I hate school. Besides, if I'm gonna be a miner like my pa was, I don't need to know what they teach." He bent down and lifted a small pebble from under his shoe and tossed it out into the yard. The smile had left his face for a moment, replaced by a frown. "School don't make much sense, Mr. Dawson. What does readin' and writin' have to do with workin' in a copper mine anyway?"

"So, what *are* you gonna do then when you ain't a kid no more?"

"I dunno, maybe be a sheriff or a cowboy." He started to say something more when the door opened, and Alice stepped out onto the porch.

"Welcome, Mr. Dawson. I'm glad you decided to come." Her voice was soft, but strong. J.D. expected her to be shy maybe even a little afraid, but she spoke with confidence. "It's nice out tonight, isn't it?"

His own confidence slipped away as he stood, searching for something to say.

"Yeah, I mean yes, it is."

"Then why don't we stay out here for a few moments. Supper will be ready soon and I know that Henry needs to wash his hands, don't you Henry?"

The boy nodded and walked into the cabin. Alice stepped out into the yard and looked up at the darkening sky. The full moon was rising in the southeast and in the west, the last of the sun's rays made the few clouds hanging above the mountain turn pink. "Mr. Dawson, I know that you were reluctant to join us tonight, but I'm so glad you decided to come anyway."

J.D. expected that this was when she'd get all weepy about nearly losing Henry or her husband dying, but she didn't. What she said next surprised him.

"I'm a widow, Mr. Dawson, with a young son. I own my own home, earn a good clean living, and take care of my boy." She looked directly at J.D., causing him to glance down at his feet. "So, I hope you don't feel uncomfortable in my home. I invited you here because of what you did for Henry, what you did for me. Saving him from the flood saved my life." She watched as J.D. raised his eyes to her. "So please, come inside and let's have something to eat."

Baffled by the woman and thrown completely off his plan, J.D. followed her into the cabin. She walked around the table toward the wood-burning stove and lifted an iron skillet from the grate. As she busied herself with the food, J.D. had a chance to look around the room. The table, already set with plates and forks, sat under the home's single window, a chair rested on each side. Across the room was a bed—likely Henry's, thought J.D.—and a small sofa sat next to an open door that led to another room. The room was clean and tidy, and the house was nothing like the one he'd lived in as a boy or even after he'd been married. He stood awkwardly, grasping his derby by the rim, and was relieved when Henry walked through the open door and up to him.

"Can I take your hat, Mr. Dawson?"

J.D. reluctantly let him have the derby and watched as he put it on his small head. Not sure what to do next, J.D. shoved his hands into his pockets.

Alice spoke from in front of the stove. "Would you like something to drink, Mr. Dawson?"

Having been tempted during his trek up the hill for a shot of whiskey, his first thought was *yes please*, but he didn't expect that was what she meant. "Yes ma'am, I'll have whatever you're havin'."

"We have water and coffee, of course, but if you'd like a sip of whiskey, I have some left over from before...from last year."

Awkwardly he mumbled, "Sure, I'll have a small glass of whiskey if you will."

She smiled and said, "It has been a long time since I've had a drink, but since I invited you and you're our guest I suppose I'll join you."

"How 'bout me, Ma, can I have some?"

"No, young man, you may not. You will drink water."

"Aww, Ma," Henry groaned but didn't challenge her authority.

"Mr. Dawson, would you please take a seat at the table? Henry, you sit next to Mr. Dawson while I bring supper."

At least the boy will be sittin' between me and her, thought J.D. *But that means I'll hafta look across the table at her*. If he wasn't before, Hooper was nervous now.

Alice set the half-filled bottle of golden liquor on the

table in front of J.D. and asked him to pour some into their glasses. While he complied, she put fried chicken, boiled potatoes, and fresh bread onto the three plates and sat down across from J.D. Sitting between the two adults and facing the window, Henry turned his face from one adult to the other.

Lifting her glass, Alice said, "Mr. Dawson, you are a welcome guest in our home. I'm glad that you've allowed us to thank you for your bravery." She took a healthy sip of the liquor and added, "So let's eat."

☆ ☆ ☆

Over the next hour, Henry did most of the talking. He described his flood experience, and how he'd become a hero among his few friends by surviving. Alice listened to the boy, encouraging him to entertain their guest. She watched J.D. but didn't ask him any of the questions he'd expected. In fact, she never once made him feel awkward. J.D. knew he looked nervous because that's exactly how he felt. But she left him alone with his thoughts by not acknowledging his apparent discomfort, by just eating her dinner and enjoying her glass of whiskey.

When they'd finished the supper and the small pie Alice had prepared, she told Henry that it was time for him to wash up and go to bed. He started to object, but a stern look from his ma ended his resistance and he got up from the table. Henry thanked J.D. for coming to the cabin and left the room.

"Mr. Dawson would you join me on the porch?"

The two adults stood silently, sipping the last of the whiskey. When he'd arrived at the cabin earlier, he'd had plans on how the evening would unfold. But now, well-fed and at least outwardly relaxed, his internal struggle, his anxieties came rushing back.

Without looking at J.D., Alice told him all about her husband and how his death had disrupted their happy life. She described their move from Pennsylvania and the long trip across the country and how she and Albert had built the home and how happy they were to be living in a place like Bisbee. Alice never once got weepy, nor did she dwell on the considerable difficulties her husband's death had led to. She spoke about her love for Henry and her confidence in taking care of him.

"But there is something I can't give Henry, Mr. Dawson." She turned to him. "I can be a good mother, but I cannot be the man my son needs in his life."

J.D. didn't move, couldn't move. *Here it comes,* he thought.

"You have already given me more than I ever needed by saving Henry's life. I only wish that I could find a man who would be willing to spend time with my boy. I don't know if you've noticed, Mr. Dawson, but in this town, most men will have nothing to do with boys like Henry. The men in Bisbee are too busy, or too angry, to help boys become men."

"I haven't been payin' much attention, ma'am."

"Perhaps, but you thought nothing about saving my son from a flood while others watched him float down the street. You did something. You protected my son. That shows me that you care."

"But, I..."

"Let me finish, please." She seemed to gather her thoughts for a moment. "I'm not asking you to be Henry's father, Mr. Dawson. I'm not asking you to change your life for a boy who isn't yours. I only want Henry to know a good man like his father. A man who'll protect him. I just want you to look out for him, protect him if you can."

"I ain't a good man, ma'am," said J.D., his voice soft and wary.

"What do you mean, Mr. Dawson?"

"I mean I ain't the kinda man you want your boy to be

around," he paused and added, "I done a lot of things that, well that you wouldn't approve of."

"It doesn't matter. The only thing I know you've done Mr. Dawson is save Henry's life and that's what matters to me. I don't care if you drink or gamble. It seems like all men do those things."

"I done other things, mean things, ugly things so bad that if you knew 'em you'd kick me outta your place." J.D. didn't know why he said this and was suddenly afraid that she'd ask what he meant.

But she didn't. "Would you like a cup of coffee, Mr. Dawson?"

Now J.D. was really confused. Why wouldn't she want to know the bad things he'd done? Why, even if she didn't know the details, would she want a man like him to be a friend for her son? His head was spinning, and it wasn't the whiskey. For the first time in his life J.D. was talking to a woman who wasn't afraid of him and who didn't care about his past. It was too much for him to handle. His chest tightened. *I gotta get outta here*, he thought.

He waited a few moments and said, "The food was good, and I thank you for invitin' me here tonight, but I need to go."

"I understand," she said. "But I hope you will come again. Henry likes you and I'm grateful for...for..." She stopped but didn't start crying like he'd expected her to. "I'm just glad you came to supper. If you see Henry on the street, would you be kind enough to say hello to him, maybe at least be friendly to him?"

J.D. wanted her to leave him alone, but instead he just nodded. "I'll try," he said softly, and walked across the yard and down the hill.

☆ ☆ ☆

On his way back to the hotel, J.D. saw the light on in

Calvin's office and thought about Henry. He headed to the building and walked in, finding Cal hunched over a desk.

"You got a minute Cal?"

"Yeah, I do," he said, "if you can make it quick. I've still got a lot of work to do on my latest story."

"There's a kid who lives up the gulch who ain't got a pa." Hooper felt awkward making his request but continued anyway. "I wonder if you and the deputy would take him along the next time you two go to a baseball game. I think it would mean a lot to him and I'm pretty sure his ma would be okay with it."

"How old is he?"

"I dunno, ten I guess. But he's a good kid. He just needs to have some fun."

Calvin thought about it for just a moment and then said, "Tell you what, Dawson, before the next game I'll go talk to the woman first. If she's okay with it, I'll take him along."

"Thanks, Cal."

Chapter 33

The next day, J.D. rested in his room at the hotel. He'd gone out early for breakfast, wanting to avoid running into Henry. He thought about the strangeness of Alice Carter as he lay back on his bed. Hooper didn't want to be comfortable with her or Henry. He didn't want to be a positive influence on the boy. He just wanted to be left alone. He tried to push them out of his mind, but they kept creeping back in. He had just about nodded off when someone tapped at the door.

"Who is it?"

"It's the desk clerk, Mr. Dawson. I have a message for you."

J.D. opened the door and the young man handed him an envelope.

"Who's it from?"

"I don't know, sir. It was brought by a messenger boy."

Without another word, J.D. shut the door and walked over to the small desk. He turned the envelope over in his hands and smelled a faint scent. He opened the flap and slid out the folded paper. He feared at first that it was a note of some kind from Alice Carter, but while slowly reading the fine script he discovered that she hadn't sent it.

Mr. Dawson,

All of Bisbee was shocked by the unbecoming actions of Mr. Walker, though to be fair he deserved what he got. I would like to thank you personally for your assistance in ridding Bisbee of this man and for making our town a much safer place. Please rest assured that my intentions are honorable, and that your secret is safe with me.

Would you do me the honor of meeting with me at my business at your earliest convenience regarding a business opportunity that I believe will suit your unique talent. Please come to my establishment, directly across the road from where Mr. Walker so justly met his downfall, so we may discuss this opportunity in detail.

Cordially,

Mrs. Helen McHenry

P.S. Please reply to my invitation confirming that you will meet me this evening. The hotel clerk will know where to send your response.

Someone saw me? A warm flash of panic rushed up his spine. *This woman knows something or guessed something about the business with Walker. And she was able to learn my name and where I'm staying. I should just get outta Bisbee and go back to Mexico.*

Hooper figured that she must have been in the crowd on the street that night, or watching out a window. *But how could she have seen me? The porch was dark, and I left pretty quick.* He put the message on the desk and stared out the window. *And that don't explain how she knew my name or where I live. This don't sound like trouble, but it sure feels like it.* As J.D. thought more about it, he realized that Mrs. McHenry could have gone to the sheriff or even the paper with this information. She knew his name, and what he'd done. *But she hasn't gone to 'em. So what's this about a business opportunity*? J.D. knew he had to meet with the woman to find out exactly what she knew, and what she really wanted. *Just when I was startin' to like this town.*

He put on his coat and hat and walked down to the front

desk. "The message says you know how to get in touch with the sender."

"Yes, Mr. Dawson, the boy who brought the message is out front. Shall I get him, or do you just want to write a response?"

J.D. hesitated for a moment. "Bring him in. I wanna talk to him."

Hooper walked away from the desk and stood at the foot of the staircase. He watched as the clerk went out the door and returned quickly, a young boy followed close behind. The boy walked slowly toward J.D. while the clerk went back to work.

"You know who sent the message?"

"Yes sir, I do."

"I'm not gonna write anythin' down. I want you to tell her that I'll meet with her tonight. Can you do that?"

"Yes sir, I can."

"Go on, then, tell her I'll see her tonight." The boy told J.D. where to meet the woman, then J.D. watched him cross the lobby and leave the hotel. J.D. glanced at the clerk who was busily working in a ledger, paying no attention to the boy, then he walked back upstairs, trying to decide how to handle this latest complication in his life.

☆ ☆ ☆

At dark, J.D. knocked on the door of Helen McHenry's brothel, fully aware that the place he'd clobbered Walker was just across the dirt road. J.D. purposely looked away from the red lamp over the door as he waited for a response. He felt exposed standing on the porch of a whorehouse and was relieved when the door opened and the boy who'd carried the message invited him into the house.

"Evenin', sir. Mrs. McHenry will be right with you. Can I take your hat?"

"No, I'll hang on to it."

J.D. glanced around the small parlor, making note of the soft furniture, the heavy curtains, and the rugs on the wooden floor. The paintings on the wall reminded him of Walker's photographs and the sounds coming from the back rooms and from upstairs, although muted, made it pretty clear to him that he was in a whorehouse for the first time in his life.

He heard footsteps coming down the stairs and turned to see a woman a bit older than himself, dressed in a long silk gown.

"Mr. Dawson?"

"That's right."

"Thank you for coming. Rather than talk here in a public room, let's go to my office in the back." She turned away and J.D. followed, removing his hat as they made their way down the hall.

"Please take a seat, Mr. Dawson. Would you have a drink with me?"

Hooper sat down on the striped cushion of the sofa and nodded. "Sure, I'll take one." He was surprised again. Since when do women drink liquor? First Alice Carter and now Helen McHenry.

Helen sat at the other end of the sofa and turned toward J.D. She poured whiskey into his glass and then filled hers. After setting the bottle on an end table, she lifted the glass and said, "Cheers."

J.D. nodded again and finished his glass in one draught.

"Mr. Dawson, I'm a businesswoman and I like to get to the point. I suspect that you were surprised to get my message."

"I was."

"I also imagine that you may have figured out how I could have seen you that night, so going over it again would just be a waste of time. But I did see you and wanted you to know how happy your actions made me feel. Mr. Walker has been a source of trouble ever since he came to Bisbee. You did our community a great service getting him run out of town. I won't ask why you smashed his nose, that's none of my business. I'm just glad he's gone."

J.D. thought that the woman would be even more pleased that he was dead, but he decided not to tell her that part of the story.

"Walker was rough with my girls and those of the other houses on the Reservation."

"The Reservation?"

That's what they call this part of the gulch," she clarified. "Walker was also bringing dope into my house and he'd driven away some of my girls."

"That's interestin', but what does it have to do with me?"

"I have a proposition for you, Mr. Dawson. I need someone like you working in my house on the weekends. That's when the mine pays the workers and when things get wild. I need someone who can handle rough men, someone who can protect my girls and keep them from getting hurt."

"Why do you think I can help you?"

"I know you can help. I saw how you took care of a man larger than you without any help. I'd be willing to pay you in cash or trade for working just two days a week."

"Whatta you mean trade?"

"Well, I mean if you'd rather receive payment by spending time with the girl of your choice, of course."

"I ain't interested in spendin' time with any girls."

A bit surprised at his response, she said, "Then, Mr. Dawson, I'd be willing to pay you one hundred dollars a month for your services two nights every week." She watched J.D. mull over the offer. "Of course I would include a meal each night as well."

J.D. looked at the woman while he thought about the offer. Two nights every week, plus supper and all he had to do was what he liked doing most—being tough.

"As long as what I'm doin' won't get me in trouble with the Sheriff or the bosses at the mine, I guess I can start whenever you want."

"Well," she said, "it's Friday night, and payday's tomorrow, so how about right now?"

They stood and shook hands and Helen took J.D. back into the parlor. Over the next few hours Hooper was introduced to each of the ladies. They were cordial to J.D. while he simply nodded and ignored them. His first night on the new job went by without a single incident and he returned to his room at the hotel before dawn, slept until noon, then got dressed and headed to the St. Elmo.

☆ ☆ ☆

The first few hours on Saturday night were fairly quiet. J.D. had to escort a couple of drunks out of the house. But a little after midnight, Andy came running downstairs and told J.D. that there was trouble in Hazel's room.

"Which one is that?" asked J.D. as he started up the stairs, feeling the weight of the sap in his coat pocket.

"All the way down on the left, Mr. Dawson."

J.D. really didn't need the directions; he could hear the noise from the top of the stairs. He pushed the door open and walked in to find the young woman, Hazel, trying to get away from her customer.

The miner was taller than J.D. and clearly outweighed him. He let go of the frightened woman's throat and reached for his gun on the dresser.

Stepping in front of Hazel, J.D. growled, "You don't wanna do that."

"How're you gonna stop me? I paid to use her and I'll use her like I want to."

J.D. didn't flinch. "Your money's no good here. You need to leave...now!"

As soon as the man touched the gun butt, J.D. slammed the sap on top of the man's wrist, crushing it against the dresser. The sound of broken bones was quickly joined by the man's howling rage. J.D. watched as the miner turned in anger and pain, leaving his hand on the dresser.

"How'd that feel?"

"I'm gonna kill you," he screamed.

J.D. moved quickly, driving his boot into the miner's thigh, and pushing the point of his knife against the big man's throat. The cries of pain ceased abruptly, and the man's eyes opened wide.

"You ain't killin' nobody mister and you ain't gonna ever beat up no young girl," J.D. said. "You got two choices. You can put your pants on one-handed and get outta here or you can let me finish what I started."

The wounded miner's already large eyes opened even wider as Hooper moved the razor-sharp blade away from his throat and rested the fine edge on top of the man's wrist. J.D. slipped the sap into his pocket and placed his now empty hand on the back of the blade. The miner's eyes flicked between J.D.'s face and the knife.

"What's it gonna be, mister?"

The man turned slightly toward his clothes on the floor.

"Leave 'em," said J.D. "You get out now or you go without your hand."

The man's eyes quickly filled with glistening moisture. Sliding his hand slowly between the blade's edge and the scarred wooden dresser top, he limped quickly out of the room and stumbled down the stairs.

J.D. slipped the knife back into its sheath and looked at the naked woman. Then he turned quickly and headed toward the door.

"Wait, Mr. Dawson." Suddenly modest, Hazel covered herself with the bed sheet and raised her free hand to her face. Her eyes filled with tears as she pushed a lock of soft hair away from the bloody lip.

"What," said J.D., turning to look at her.

"I…well, thank you."

J.D. handed her the handkerchief from his coat pocket.

He went downstairs and out the back door. For a while he stood quietly thinking. Long as I'm workin' here ain't nobody gonna hurt them girls.

There was no more trouble that night and for a few days business slowed at Helen's brothel. Helen wasn't worried because other than Hazel's busted lip and bruised throat, there'd been no more trouble. J.D. was unconcerned as well—he had the week off and money in his pocket.

☆ ☆ ☆

J.D. showed up at the brothel early the next Friday evening. He ate supper in the kitchen and watched Andy go about his chores. Helen had stopped by to get a cup of coffee and thanked him again for taking the job. J.D. acknowledged her words with a brief nod but didn't speak. He didn't relax until she left the kitchen.

The early part of the evening was busy, but J.D. didn't have much to do. The customers seemed content to spend time drinking in the parlor and then head upstairs with the ladies. Hooper was smoking a cigar outside on the back step a little after midnight when Andy opened the door.

"Mr. Dawson, I need your help."

"What's up, kid?"

"Two men drinkin' in the parlor are arguin' about which one of 'em gets to go upstairs with Miss Cora."

J.D. threw the cigar stub into the yard and rushed into the brothel. He heard the loud voices before he got to the parlor at the front of the house and entered the room just as the smaller of the two men drew his knife. The room was crowded, and J.D. didn't want any of the girls to get hurt so he stepped quickly between the men. The few women in the room had backed away to the walls.

"Put that knife away," he said, his voice deep and strong. "Ain't no fightin' allowed in here." J.D. grabbed the fella's wrist. "Put it away. Now!"

The man tried to pull away from him without success. Hooper strengthened his grip and let the knife fall to the floor.

"Now," J.D. said. "What's goin' on here?"

"I'm takin' Cora to her room," said the disarmed man.

"No you ain't," yelled the heavy man. His accented words slurred. "I vill take Cora. You must choose anudder girl."

"Both of you shut up," said J.D. "Neither one of you is takin' Cora or any other girl upstairs. Unless you wanna get carried out of here, you'll stop yellin' and walk with me out to the front porch." Neither of the two spoke. "Alright, then, let's go out front and talk."

J.D. let go of the short man and pushed him toward the door. The man with the accent grinned, likely thinking he'd won the fight. "You too," said J.D., grabbing the man by the front of his shirt. "Let's go."

As J.D. talked to the two drunks, Andy watched from the porch and Helen gazed through the front window.

"Listen, you two. If you ever wanna come back here again, you're gonna have to do your fightin' some other place. Try it again and you'll both wake up somewhere dark and cold and you'll be missin' some very important body parts." He paused to see if he had their attention. "You understand what I'm tellin' you?"

"I understan'," said the short one.

The drunk foreigner nodded and asked if they could go back inside.

"Not tonight, you can't. Get on outta here and come back some other time when you're sober."

Each of them was clearly unhappy, but also unwilling

to get into a fight with J.D. They frowned at him and then headed across the road together. J.D. watched until they were out of sight then reentered the house.

Andy met him in the hallway just past the parlor and handed him the knife.

"What you want me to do with this, Mr. Dawson?"

"Get rid of it. Put it in a box or somethin'."

J.D. glanced into the parlor and saw that things were back to normal. Helen was talking to Cora while the other ladies spread out to chat with the few men who remained.

☆ ☆ ☆

A few days later, Helen was going through some papers at her desk when Andy tapped on the door.

"Come in."

"Mrs. McHenry, can I tell you somethin'?"

"What is it, Andy?"

"I heard the ladies upstairs talkin' about somethin'."

"Well, what were they talking about? Speak up boy."

"They was sayin' that they ain't makin' any money, or not much money since Mr. Dawson was here the other night." He was quiet for a moment then added, "Mostly they was sayin' that it's his fault that there ain't been many gentlemen comin' to the house this week."

"Could you tell who was talking, Andy?"

"No ma'am. I think most of the ladies 'cept Miss Hazel was in the room, but I ain't sure."

"Thank you, Andy. You go on about your chores and don't say anything about this to anyone."

Helen thought about what Andy had told her and decided to have a chat with her employees.

She waited until the next morning and gathered them all together in the parlor. "Look, ladies," said Helen. "If you want to keep on getting hit and cut and squeezed, I'll fire Mr. Dawson." She looked around the room, staring at each of the women. "But we haven't had any trouble with the customers since he started here. None of you have been hurt." She paused, letting her words sink in before continuing. "So, make up your minds. What's worth more, money or your health?"

By the end of that week, Helen had lost one girl—she'd been the least bothered by the customers' habits and had decided that she'd rather make more money. As it turned out, had she stuck around, she'd have enjoyed the opportunity to make even more. On the next payday, when J.D. reported to work, the place was full. Word had spread that Helen's place was quieter and safer and most of the patrons that night were men with lots of money—visiting salesmen and even local authorities and businessmen. Everyone was well behaved and nobody caused any problems. Business was good for Mrs. McHenry, but J.D. didn't get back to his room until well after sunrise.

Chapter 34

The sun was just peeking over the mountain top to the east, but in the Carter cabin near the end of Brewery Gulch, Alice was busy fixing a pot of oatmeal for breakfast. Even though it was Sunday morning, she wasn't going to church. She still believed in God, and she still read her Bible on occasion, but she saw no value in getting dressed up and sitting in a building with women who thought she was a sinner for washing the bedding from a brothel. So, for Alice and her son Henry, Sunday was just another workday and usually the busiest day of her week. Alice expected that the sun would set in the western sky before she finished.

"Henry! Get up, son, we've got to get down the gulch and pick up the laundry."

She continued stirring the mush in the pot on the wood stove. Although the process of building the fire and boiling the water, scrubbing the sheets, rinsing them, and hanging them on the line was tedious, it was good work. *Good hard work that I get paid for*, she thought.

"Henry, get out of bed now. It's time to eat and we need to get busy."

When Henry walked into the room, he was trying to button the strap on his overalls. His thick hair stuck out at odd angles from his head and he was still barefoot. Finally succeeding in fastening the strap, Henry yawned and rubbed the grit out of his eyes. He didn't speak until he'd sat in his chair at the table.

"What's for breakfast?"

"Oats, just like yesterday, son." She watched as he squeezed his face into a frown. "I'll get something better after we get paid." Alice filled his bowl with the cooked grain and set it on the table next to a cup of milk.

"Eat up and meet me down at Mrs. McHenry's. I'm going down to get started, so don't fiddle around, hear me?"

"Yes, Ma."

Alice wiped her hands on a towel and rolled down her sleeves. Draping a light shawl over her shoulders and placing a small straw hat on her head she stepped out into the cool morning air. The road was dusty as usual and clouds of it followed her as she made her way down the gulch. When she turned the curve toward Helen's place, she saw John Dawson come out onto Helen's porch and cross the short yard to the road. She quickly stepped back behind the rocky ledge at the side of the hill and watched as he walked slowly down the hill and out of sight. She brought her hands to her mouth and stifled a cry of disappointment. *Why is he there*? she asked herself. No matter how much she tried to reason, to understand, she knew the answer. *There was only one reason a man would be at a place like Mrs. McHenry's*. Alice was angry and disappointed at herself for trusting him.

When Alice was sure Dawson was really gone, she trudged down to Helen's house and walked through the side yard to the back door. Andy was making a pile of the dirty sheets on the porch and didn't notice her right away.

"Good morning, Andy," she said softly.

"Oh, good mornin' Mrs. Carter. I'm about finished here. I only got one more load to get from upstairs." He left quickly, and Alice sat down on the step, put her face in her hands and wondered how she could have been so wrong about Mr. Dawson. She heard footsteps coming from the hallway and stood up expecting Andy and the last of the laundry. It was Helen McHenry who walked out onto the steps.

"Good morning to you, Alice. You're here quite early. I didn't expect you 'til later." When she didn't respond, Helen could tell that something was wrong. "Alice, what's the matter dear? You look like you've had a shock. Is Henry alright?" Alice rose from the steps and fiddled with the laundry.

"Yes ma'am, he's fine. He'll be along shortly to help."

"I'm glad he's okay, but how are you? Has Andy said anything to upset you?"

"Oh, no, Mrs. McHenry, I'm just not feeling well, that's all. Andy is always a gentleman. He said he'd be right back with the last load."

Helen wasn't convinced that Alice was telling her everything, but she knew better than to pry. She waited quietly until Andy arrived with the sheets.

"I tied up this last bundle for Mr. Henry, ma'am. Let me fix up this big load next." He looked at Helen then added, "If it's okay with you, Miss Helen, I'll carry these up the hill for Mrs. Carter."

Alice started to object, but when Helen said, "What a wonderful idea, Andy. You go on ahead, I need to talk to Mrs. Carter."

"Yes, ma'am," he said as Henry ran into the yard.

"I'm here, Ma." He caught his breath and addressed Helen. "Mornin' Mrs. McHenry."

"Good morning young man. Andy's going to carry the large bundle. Can you carry the other one home for your mother?"

"Sure I can," he said, lifting the wadded sheets onto his back and trotting after the older boy.

"Before you go, Alice, I just wanted to tell you how much I appreciate you and your boy. I admire you for your strength and how you've managed to raise such a nice young man." She looked at Alice. "I can tell something is wrong, but I won't pry. I want you to know that if you ever need to talk about anything or if you just need a friendly ear you can count on me."

"Thank you, Mrs. McHenry. I truly appreciate your offer, but right now I just need to think through some things." Alice turned to walk away. She started to ask the madam something and then changed her mind. "I'll bring the laundry back tomorrow afternoon."

Through all her years of business, Helen McHenry had become a student of women's moods and signals. She could tell that Alice had something on her mind and that it was fresh and painful. But Helen had also learned patience when dealing with troubled women. *I'll give her some time to think about this,* she thought, *but I won't let it stew so long that it kills her spirit.*

✯ ✯ ✯

For the rest of the day, Alice and Henry boiled water, soaked sheets, rinsed wet laundry, and hung it out to dry. Load after load throughout the long Sunday Henry did his job. He may not have had the experience that Helen McHenry had in understanding women, but he did know his Ma and was convinced that she was upset. He just hoped it wasn't something he had done.

"We're almost done, Ma."

She placed the last clothespin on the line and glanced over her shoulder at Henry. The boy's shirt was wet, and his hair was mussed, but his face glowed with one of his warmest smiles.

"We did a good job today, Ma. We got it all done and it ain't even dark yet." The smile never left his face. "Anything else I can do for you?" he asked.

Alice felt awful. When she realized that even her son could see that she wasn't happy and that he was trying so hard to cheer her up, she wanted to grab him up into her arms and never let him go. Instead, she swallowed hard and said, "Yes we did Henry. You and I did all of this and because you worked so hard, I'm going to make you a special supper tonight."

Late into the night, while Henry slept, and the laundry dried in the dry desert air, Alice lay awake thinking about John Dawson. She'd believed that he was different. She'd been willing to make allowances for his past—even though she knew nothing about the things he had done. She'd asked him to watch out for her boy and now she had seen him walk out of a whorehouse at dawn. *How could I have been so foolish*, she thought. *How could I ever trust a man like that to protect my son*?

☆ ☆ ☆

On Monday morning, Alice was standing on the front porch gazing out into her yard when Henry came out of the house. Her son walked to her side and she put her arm on his shoulder, pulling him close. He looked up at her, still searching without success for what bothered her.

"Henry, I need to ask you something."

"What, Ma?'

"Have you seen Mr. Dawson, lately?"

"No, Ma, I ain't...I mean I haven't."

Alice struggled with what to say next. "Henry, I want you to stay away from Mr. Dawson. I don't want you to talk to him at all."

"But why, Ma? I thought you liked Mr. Dawson."

"Maybe I did, but now I don't want you anywhere near him. I don't want any argument from you, I just don't want you to talk to him or be with him."

"But..."

"I said no arguments and I mean it. Now get ready for school, you're going today whether you like it or not."

Henry grumbled softly as he walked back into the cabin, confused. Yesterday his ma was sad, this morning she still wasn't happy and now he had to go to school. *I'll go to school, but that don't mean I have to like it.*

Alice was convinced that keeping Henry away from Dawson was the right thing to do, nevertheless she felt bad for the boy. She knew he'd been growing closer to Dawson. She understood somehow that boys need men to show them how to grow up. *But I won't have Henry learn that it's alright to use prostitutes. Damn that man, why was I so foolish to invite him here? Why couldn't I just leave him alone like he asked?*

Later that morning, she bought a load of firewood and paid in advance for two deliveries of water. She tried to stay focused on her business, but her thoughts kept going to the sight of Dawson walking out of the brothel. Faint images of what he probably did in the house with the women kept interrupting her concentration. Trying to keep busy, she walked around the cabin's main room rearranging the table, making Henry's bed, washing their few dishes from breakfast. She made a pot of coffee and sat down at the table. When she lifted the cup to her lips, she spilled some of the hot liquid on her shirtwaist and yelped.

"Damn that man! He makes me so mad at myself I could scream." Alice got up and began to clean up the mess around the stove. She chided herself for her foolishness—for letting Dawson get to her, for trusting him with Henry, for letting his actions drive her to becoming someone she didn't want to be. She decided that she was right to keep Henry away from Dawson and that was that.

"Good," she said as she walked out into the yard. "That's it. I'm done being a fool."

☆ ☆ ☆

The next morning Alice knocked on the back door of Helen's brothel. When Andy opened the door, she asked to speak to Mrs. McHenry.

"She's here Mrs. Carter, but she's speakin' to someone

right now."

"Oh, then I'll come back later."

"I don't think she'll be long, ma'am. She's just talkin' business and I think she'd like to talk to you."

Alice wasn't sure she should stay but decided it wouldn't hurt to wait on the back porch.

"Alright, Andy, I'll just stay out here."

The boy nodded. "I'll let her know you're here." Then he closed the door. Alice turned around and gazed at the small yard and noticed that a stairway had been built up on the bluff. She wondered whose home was on the lot looking down on the brothel.

Andy opened the door once more and offered Alice a cup.

"I thought you might like some tea, Mrs. Carter."

"Thank you, Andy."

She accepted the cup from the boy and asked, "Who lives up those stairs?"

"Them steps go up to Mrs. McHenry's home, ma'am."

"I thought she lived here in the…in the house."

"Oh no, she don't live where she works. She told me once that she needs to get away from this place sometimes."

"I suppose that's true." Alice sipped from her cup. "I don't want to keep you from your chores, Andy. Thank you for the tea."

"You're welcome, ma'am. Let me go see if Mrs. McHenry is finished up."

What am I going to say to her, Alice thought. She was about to leave when the door opened, and Helen emerged from the brothel.

"Good morning, Alice, how nice to see you. If you've come for the laundry, you're too early."

"Oh no," Alice said, "This is sort of a social call. I wanted to apologize for my behavior the other day. I had something on my mind, and I let it get the better of me. I'm sure I was rude to you and I wanted to apologize."

"Of course, my dear, I accept your apology. But you should know that it is not necessary to do so. I, too, often get distracted. So please forget about it." Helen smiled at her laundress and invited her in.

"Oh, no, I can't do that, Mrs. McHenry, I've got to get back up to the house."

"Please come in, Alice. I need your advice on something. We can talk in my office. It's just inside."

Helen extended her hand. Alice took it reluctantly and stepped inside the back door and followed her into a small office. She could hear voices down the hall. Feeling a little uncomfortable surrounded by the nice furnishings and being inside a brothel, she sat on the edge of a small settee.

"I was hoping," Helen said, "that you could help me with something. It's business of course but I needed the insight of a woman like you—a businesswoman, a strong woman, a person who has worked herself out of tragedy."

"I'm not sure that I am all of those things, Helen."

"Oh, but you are." Helen sat on the cushion next to Alice. "My dear, I never married, and have little knowledge of men outside of my business dealings with them. I have a new employee, a man who takes care of things around here. I just had a meeting with him and trying to get him to talk was like, oh, how do people say it sometimes? It was like pulling hen's teeth, that's it. He just doesn't talk much. I couldn't tell if he didn't want to answer my questions or if he simply couldn't form the words."

Alice listened politely.

"This man, Mr. Dawson, is quiet, almost too quiet. He's nice looking and respectful and does his work well."

"I know Mr. Dawson," she said. "He's the man who saved Henry from the flood."

Surprised, Helen said, "I heard about that, but never imagined that Mr. Dawson was the hero."

"When he brought Henry to our place, I was so grateful, but he seemed uneasy and wanted to leave. He would hardly let me thank him."

Helen listened closely as Alice described her experience with Dawson, and then replied, "That's how he is around here. I never know what he's thinking. I was wondering how you dealt with your late husband in this type of situation. Did he ever stay quiet, unresponsive?"

"My husband was a kind and gentle man." Alice began to relax. "We talked often and seldom had words. But, at times, he would seem sullen, as if he was upset. In time, I learned to let him work himself out of whatever was on his mind."

"I suppose that's what he needs. You know, Alice," she said, "Mr. Dawson is one of the few men I've met who's like your late husband. He has absolutely no interest in my girls. He's quiet, seldom smiles, and is good at what he does."

"And what is that Mrs. McHenry? What does Mr. Dawson do for you?"

"He makes certain that none of my customers hurt the ladies." Helen paused a moment, considering how much to share with Alice.

"I have noticed," whispered Alice, "that the linens have not been bloody of late."

"How sweet you are, Alice. It's alright to call them sheets. They certainly aren't made of linen." She chuckled, holding her gloved hand to her lips. "In the past, not just here in Bisbee, but nearly everywhere I've worked...Kansas City, Omaha, and even Dallas...the men want to get what they pay for and it often includes violence. Their rough ways make it very difficult to keep healthy ladies."

"I imagine so," said Alice. "Are your..." she paused a moment, "ladies hurt often?"

"Not since I hired Mr. Dawson. With respect to you and the valuable and efficient service you provide, Mr. Dawson is my most reliable and trustworthy employee."

"How nice," she replied, but her focus was now on the things she'd just learned about Dawson.

"My girls are by practice involved in enticing men to do certain things, but they have repeatedly failed in their efforts to entice Mr. Dawson. Now go on home and see that wonderful son of yours."

As she walked back up the hill, Alice reflected on the conversation. But it wasn't the words that were spoken or the information she gained about Dawson that filled her thoughts. She realized that it had been a long time since she'd had a woman to talk to, someone who felt like a friend. By the time she reached her cabin, Alice's mood had changed.

☆ ☆ ☆

On his way home from school that afternoon, Henry saw J.D. sitting on a bench by the St. Elmo. The boy wanted to obey his ma, but he also thought that Mr. Dawson needed to know about it.

"Mr. Dawson," he said, tapping J.D. on the shoulder, "I need to tell you something."

"Been to school, have you Henry? You're carryin' a lot of books for a kid who don't wanna go to school," he teased.

"Yeah, I still hate it, but that isn't why I wanted to talk."

"What do you wanna tell me?"

"My Ma says I gotta stop talking to you."

J.D. studied Henry's face, unsure about what he'd just heard. "Did she say why?"

"No, sir, she didn't. She'd be mad at me if she knew I was talking to you now, but I thought I should tell you since you saved my life and all."

"Then I guess you better do what your ma said. So long, Henry."

Henry watched as J.D. walked into the saloon. *It ain't*

fair, he thought. *Mr. Dawson's the only real friend I have*. He wiped a tear from his cheek with the sleeve of his shirt and headed up the gulch toward home.

Henry walked into the cabin and threw his bundle of books onto the floor. He sat on the edge of his bed and rested his chin in his hands.

"What's wrong, son?"

"Nothing's wrong, Ma." Henry looked up at her and sighed.

"Alright, then, go wash up and I'll fix supper." Alice had noticed his bloodshot eyes and had heard the sadness in his words. She suspected that his mood was related to what she'd told him the day before. Yesterday she was convinced that keeping the man and the boy apart was the best for all involved. But that was yesterday and today she wasn't quite as sure as she'd been then. Throughout the evening, while they ate supper, and while she helped Henry with his reading, she wondered what she ought to do with the new information from Helen.

After Henry went to bed, she walked out onto her small porch. The night sounds from the hill above and the noise from down the gulch were about what they always were. Yet, she still found peace in the dark yard. Sitting on the wooden crate by the door, Alice had a long conversation with herself about her son and his future. She struggled with her decision about Mr. Dawson and even more with her notion to change her mind. For an hour or more, without ever speaking aloud, she grappled with how to resolve her dilemma. Not knowing what else to do, she walked into the cabin and watched as Henry snored lightly in his bed. She knelt by his side and brushed the unruly hair off his forehead, the small scar on his forehead reminding her of Dawson's efforts. Saying a silent prayer, she rose and walked into her room, ready for another sleepless night.

☆ ☆ ☆

Henry didn't say anything to his ma when she walked out of her room the next morning. He got dressed, went out to the water tub to wash his face, and came back into the cabin.

"Henry, I want to talk to you about what I said the other day."

He looked up for a moment, then continued eating his mush.

"Henry, please look at me. This is important. I've thought a lot about what I told you to do. At the time I really meant what I said, that I didn't want you to be with Mr. Dawson or even talk to him, and I believed that I had good reasons for making that decision."

Alice sat in the chair across from her son. "Henry, I think I made a mistake."

"Whatta you mean, Ma?"

"I learned that I've got to be sure about something or someone before making a decision. I should not make a decision without having all of the facts. Do you understand?"

"I guess so, Ma."

"Then, I want you to forget what I said about Mr. Dawson. I don't want you to get in his way, of course. But if you see him again, it's alright to talk to him."

"Really, Ma?"

"Yes, really, son."

"Thanks, Ma." Henry ran to his mother and hugged her tightly, then rushed out the door with his bundle of books.

"I truly hope I've done the right thing," she said as she gathered the dishes from the table.

☆ ☆ ☆

On Friday afternoon, Henry saw J.D. walking ahead of him up Brewery Gulch.

"Mr. Dawson!"

J.D. looked over his shoulder and saw Henry running

after him. *What am I gonna do with this kid*, he thought, chuckling a little.

"I thought you weren't supposed to talk to me."

"I wasn't then, but I can now. Ma told me that she'd made a mistake and that it was okay for me to be around you."

J.D. had just gotten used to the idea of living without the boy and his ma, and now it seemed that nothing had changed.

"What?" He smiled this time. "Did she say why she changed her mind?"

"She said a lot of things I didn't understand. She just said she changed her mind."

J.D. shook his head and said, "Women don't know what they're thinkin'."

☆ ☆ ☆

The next morning, holding a basket of fresh biscuits, Alice stood on the porch of an empty building just down the road from the brothel waiting for Mr. Dawson. When J.D. left Helen's and drew near, she called out to him.

"Mr. Dawson, could I talk to you for a moment?"

J.D. stopped abruptly. "Mrs. Carter, I..."

"Mr. Dawson, you need to know that I acted hastily when I told Henry to avoid you. I'd seen you leaving Helen's and thought that you were a customer of hers. But when I learned from Mrs. McHenry that you worked for her and that you protected the ladies just as you protected my son, I was ashamed of myself. I realized that you and I are the same. We work for a whorehouse madam and get paid with the money earned by prostitutes."

"Go on," said J.D., wondering what else she wanted to say.

"So, if you'll please forgive me, I'd like to give you these biscuits and I hope that you'll still be willing to be kind to my son."

J.D. waited.

"Mr. Dawson. Despite what you have said about yourself, I believe that you are a good man, one of the few who protects women and children."

"Mrs. Carter," his voice faltered, "I'm sorry, but I gotta go. Be good to your son and be happy he loves you." With his hands full of biscuits, J.D. slowly worked his way down the hill. He felt like they'd come to an agreement. She would leave him alone, and he would be polite to Henry if he saw him. Reaching the bottom of Brewery Gulch, Hooper stepped into the St. Elmo, had a beer, and shared the biscuits with the bartender.

Chapter 35

Noah Jensen stood on the platform at the depot in Benson, Arizona. He'd left the train at every stop since El Paso and travelled to the larger towns north and south of the rail line. Noah had searched for Hooper in Las Cruces and Deming in New Mexico, and even as far north as Silver City. Once the train crossed into Arizona, he repeated the pattern. In all of the towns, he spoke to as many people as he could, describing Hooper, showing them the wanted poster, asking questions, and just watching the flow of people, looking for someone, anyone who might be the arsonist. But in those long weeks he got nowhere. Noah was tired and not sleeping well. He felt he should take a few days off and rest. But he was getting closer to Harriman's deadline and he was determined to not stop. Failure was not an option. He either had to find his suspect soon or go back to Memphis and forget about the case and his job with it.

Even though he hadn't found a trace of Hooper in New Mexico, he was certain that he'd find some evidence of him here. Benson was a small town, but Noah knew that the rail lines from here ran south forty or fifty miles to the mining communities near the Mexican border. He'd been tracking Hooper so long that he was starting to feel that he really knew the man. Even if Hooper had left El Paso and gone to Mexico, he was sure he wouldn't stay long in that country. Hooper would have come back to the United States. And he was sure he'd have done it here, instead of farther west. Noah wasn't sure why he felt this way, and he couldn't have explained it if he'd wanted to. But he knew that a side trip down to Tombstone, Bisbee, and even Douglas would be fruitful. *One day at a time and one town at a time.*

☆ ☆ ☆

When he got off the train in Tombstone, Noah picked up his bag from the platform and trudged across the street to the hotel. He noticed a number of saloons up and down the street and decided to visit them after he found a room and something to eat.

Jensen started his search just after sundown and he walked into the first saloon on the street. All of them were beginning to look the same to him—mirrors on the wall, sawdust on the floor, drunks and smelly cowboys—and the Silver Dollar or whatever the sign hanging over the boardwalk had said, met all of the criteria. Even though he'd never been in this town, Noah felt as if he'd been in this saloon before.

He found a place at the bar, put a gold Eagle in front of the bartender and asked for a beer.

"You can get a lot of beer for all that gold, mister."

Noah smiled. "I suppose I could. What I'm looking for though is a beer and some information."

"Information about what or whom?"

"I'll get to that in a bit. When you bring my beer, pour one for yourself."

The bartender walked toward the mirror, filled two mugs from the tap, and returned.

"Thanks, mister. It's been a quiet day around here and not many of the regulars tip the bartender." He wiped a cloth across the polished wood, although Noah saw no dust or moisture on the surface.

"So, if you had to describe most of the folks you see in here, would they be locals or visitors?"

"Hmmm, that's interesting." He twisted the towel in his

hands and looked at the high ceiling. "I'd guess that most of those I see are locals or at least regular visitors to town."

"Okay," said Noah. "And the locals are shopkeepers and farmers, miners and, what? Cowboys I suppose."

"Well mostly town folks, but we do have miners."

"What about the people you've *never* seen before? What about them?"

"Oh, they're mostly traveling salesmen either going to the mines south of here or headed back to St. Louis or Boston or someplace else back east."

Noah sipped at his beer again then rubbed his weary eyes. "Would some of these visitors be familiar to you?"

"Some are familiar, I guess, but lots of 'em are just strangers. They all look the same, dress the same, and usually talk the same. It's easy to tell they aren't from around here." The bartender turned serious. "What are you askin' mister?"

"I'm looking for a man, one specific man." Noah pulled the now folded and tattered wanted poster from his coat pocket. He showed it to the bartender as he had hundreds of times over the last months and added that the man might appear cautious. "This fella I'm looking for set fire to eighty rail cars in Memphis and I need to find him. His name is J.D. Hooper. He's hiding out somewhere in these parts."

"What's your interest in him?" asked the bartender.

Noah gave him one of his few remaining calling cards. "I'm a detective for the Southern Pacific Railroad. It was our cars he burned, and I aim to find Hooper and put him in prison."

"As much as I'd like a piece of that Eagle, I can't help you. The fella on your paper could be any of a hundred men who have come through here in the past six months."

Disappointed again, Noah decided to move on. There were still a dozen or more saloons to hit and an equal number of brothels. "Tell you what," he said. "You keep the coin.

I've never met a man in a saloon so honest he'd give up the chance for free money. If you do run into Hooper, send a wire to my office in Memphis."

"Thanks, mister." He looked at the card. "I'll do that."

By midnight, Jensen had stopped in ten more saloons, bought ten more beers and ended up with the same answers. No one, not one barkeeper in Tombstone had seen anyone resembling Hooper. By the time he made it into the last bar on the main street, he was worn out.

Noah was tired of going to bed and not sleeping well. "Am I turning into a drunk?" he asked himself and mumbled, "One more saloon and I'll go back to the hotel."

When he walked into the Orient Saloon, the crowd had thinned out. The room smelled of stale beer, cigar smoke, vomit, and sweat. The few customers who remained were either slumped over their mugs of beer or playing poker at one of the round tables in the back of the saloon. Noah walked up to the bar.

"Help you sir?" asked the tall, thin man with a towel in his hand.

"Kinda slow tonight?"

"It's late, but some nights are worse than others. What can I get you?"

"Actually, I'll pay for a beer just to sit here, but you don't have to pour it except for yourself if you like."

"Okay, thanks, mister."

"You're welcome."

Noah was tired, and getting bored with his own words. He'd asked the same questions so many times he was never sure that he wasn't repeating himself. He actually had considered just going back to the hotel. But having already entered one more saloon, Noah asked one more question.

"I wonder if you can help me." With an audible sigh, Noah placed his last calling card in front of the bartender. Next to it he set a five-dollar gold piece. Looking into the man's eyes, he said, "I need some help. I'm a railroad detective and I'm trying to locate a man who destroyed a great deal of my company's property." Noah pulled the poster from his pocket and set it face up on the bar. The sketch was partially covered by a beer stain and the frequent folding and creasing he'd done this night had finally torn the sheet. He pushed the two halves together and said, "It seems that this man always wore a brown derby hat."

"Mr. Jensen," said the bartender, looking at the card, "lots of fellas wear derbies, although most of them are from somewhere else, back east usually."

"I understand that, but perhaps you remember one of them. I'm only talking about the past four weeks or so. Does any event, no matter how peculiar, stand out involving a man wearing a derby in your saloon in the past month?"

The bartender picked up the gold piece and slipped it into his vest pocket. "It's been a long day, Mr. Jensen, and I'm kinda beat. But I'll do this. I'll think about it tonight and maybe I can come up with something for you. But right now, I can't. The boss will be around soon and I gotta get these drunks outta here before I close. I can't promise I'll remember, but I'll try."

"I'm planning on taking the train tomorrow to Bisbee. Can we meet before that, perhaps here in the saloon or even at the hotel?"

"I don't usually get outta bed by that time, but you're payin' me to think, so how 'bout I meet you at your hotel around seven."

"Alright, let's do that." Noah told the man where he was staying, and they shook hands. "See you in the morning at seven, okay?"

"Okay, Mr. Jensen."

Noah was disappointed in the results of his long night of detective work. The search in Tombstone was representative of those in all the other towns and the entire trek across the west. But the last bartender hadn't come out right away to say that he'd never seen Hooper. That gave Noah a small glimmer of hope as he headed back to the hotel. *So, what's one more night*, he thought. A*t least the man said he'd think about it.*

☆ ☆ ☆

When Noah walked into the lobby at seven, the bartender was chatting with the desk clerk. Seeing Noah, he walked over to him and shook his hand.

"Thanks to you and the five dollars, I didn't get a wink of sleep all night. I tried to remember all of the strangers wearing derbies I've seen in the last month and for a while, not many of them stood out, you know what I mean? Anyway, there were two or three that did, but only one was peculiar—that's the word you used."

"What was it about this one that stood out?"

"Three or four weeks back, right after the train from Bisbee got in, two fellas came into the saloon at about the same time. One of 'em, the one not wearin' a derby, bought a bottle of whiskey and sat at a table in the back. He drank the whole thing in an hour or so. The man in the derby stayed at the bar, watchin' the other fella in the mirror. When the man drinkin' the whiskey finally passed out, the derby fella walked out back to use the outhouse and then came back in."

"Then what happened?"

"The derby fella asked me where he could rent a wagon."

"Rent a wagon? Did he say what he wanted it for?"

"I don't recall. I told him how to get to the livery stable and he left, but he came back in fifteen or twenty minutes and paid me to help load his friend in the wagon he'd tied up out back of the saloon." The bartender scratched his head and continued. "That's what was peculiar. Why wasn't he drinkin' at the table with his friend instead of standing at the bar and watching him? But it wasn't none of my business. I just didn't want the boss to find a passed-out drunk in the place, so I helped him put the first fella in the wagon." He paused for a short time, as if trying to clear his thoughts. "Then he just left."

"Do you know where he went?"

"Nope, but I bet you could find out more if you talk to Edgar down at the livery stable."

With directions to the stable, Noah thanked the bartender and headed toward the edge of town. When he walked into the huge barn, he found a man fixing the damaged wheel of a large wagon. Noah cleared his throat and the man looked up at him.

"Help you mister?"

"I hope so. I was just talking to the bartender from the Oriental and he said that about a month ago he sent a man in your direction to rent a wagon."

"Billy was up at this hour?

"Who's Billy?"

"The Oriental's bartender. He don't usually get up 'til dark."

"I'm not familiar with his nocturnal activities, but he did remember this man and that he sent him to you to rent a wagon."

"When did you say this was?"

"Early one afternoon a month ago."

"Well soon as I get this wheel put back on, I'll take a look in my ledger."

"If I give you ten dollars will you do it now?"

"It must be pretty important for you to find this fella to pay me for what I'd give you for free."

"It is important and it's worth it if he turns out to be the man I'm trying to find."

Edgar got up from this stool and wiped the dirt from

his hands with a rag. He limped toward the small office at the front of the stable. From behind the counter he pulled out a large cloth-bound ledger. The green cover was stained with grease and dirt and once opened displayed equally dirty pages.

"Four weeks ago, huh?"

"About. Maybe if you checked back as far as six I could be sure."

The livery stable must not be too busy, thought Noah, since Edgar got to the spot in the ledger which represented the period in question in only a few pages.

"I rent two or three wagons a week. What'd this fella look like?"

Jensen showed him the torn poster and made sure to mention the derby.

"The only one I rented during the time you're talkin' about that took place in the afternoon was to a fella who needed a rig for just a few hours. I didn't get his name, just marked it in the ledger. I'm not sure he was wearin' a derby, but he mighta been. It ain't often someone can do whatever they need to do with a wagon in just an hour or so." He checked the notes he'd penciled in the book and added, "But this fella paid up front in Mexican silver and brought the rig back just as he promised."

"Mexican silver, huh," said Noah, his thoughts going back to his visit to Juarez.

"Yessir. I don't usually take it, but since he gave me twice what I usually charge I didn't complain. I can't say for sure he was wearin' a derby, though." Edgar paused, almost grasping at a lost memory. "I ain't sure, but I think I remember that he had some dried blood on his shirt when he got back. Wasn't none of my business."

This caught Noah's attention.

"Do you know where he took the wagon? Do you remember where he went when he left the stable?"

"I don't know where he went with the rig, but after he brought it back, he hurried off to the depot, said he didn't want to miss the train."

"Which train would that be?"

"We only got one that leaves in the afternoon—the train to Bisbee."

"Thank you for your help."

Noah gave the man the promised ten dollars and hurried back to the hotel. He picked up his bags and headed over to the train station. The clerk told him he'd missed the morning train, but when Jensen showed his Southern Pacific badge the man handed him a ticket for the afternoon train to Bisbee.

Noah walked to the nearest café, took a seat at a small table and ordered coffee and breakfast. He pulled out his casebook and wrote down everything he could remember from the two conversations. When the food arrived, Noah shoved the food into his mouth, chewing and grinning at the same time.

A single, clear thought flared in his mind—Hooper, I know you're in Bisbee, and I'm coming to get you, so help me God.

Chapter 36

J.D. entered the St. Elmo, went to his usual spot at the end of the bar and ordered a cup of coffee. When the bartender brought him the cup, he pointed to J.D.'s derby.

"Have you met him yet?"

"Met who?"

"The word on the street is that there's a detective from Tennessee in town a couple of days now who's been lookin' for a fella wearin' a derby."

"Forget the coffee, bring me a whiskey instead."

J.D. sat silently as the fear built up inside him. The words Tennessee, detective, and derby were so loud in his brain he could barely think about where he was and what was happening. He took a few deep breaths to relieve the tightness in his chest, needing to calm himself so he could find out more. He had many questions he wanted to ask but didn't want to appear too interested in the information he had just learned.

He drank the whiskey slowly, and he said, "So, who is this detective?"

"He called himself Noah Jensen, said he worked for the Southern Pacific Railroad."

"A railroad detective? What the hell is he doing in Bisbee? Ain't nobody done anything to the railroad here that I know of."

The bartender laughed. "That's the truth. He said he was searching for a man who set fire to a hundred railroad cars in Memphis."

J.D. sipped his whiskey again to hide his nervousness. This Noah Jensen was definitely looking for him. He needed to get out of town, but he wanted to find out more. Maybe he could do to Mr. Jenson what he'd done to Walker and them fellas in El Paso. That would solve all of J.D.'s problems.

"A hundred rail cars? And why does this detective think the fellas who did it are here in Bisbee?"

"He didn't say, just that he believed the man he was searching for was here."

"So, who is this man?" J.D. asked as the bartender turned to pull a beer for another patron.

"He called him J.D. Hooper." J.D. was glad the barman was turned away as he knew his face had just gone pale. *If this Jensen fellow knows I'm here, then his bosses with the railroad know it too. I can't run, they'll keep houndin' me. I gotta end this my way.*

"So, who's this J.D. Hooper then?" asked J.D.

"I don't know. The detective described him, but he could fit the description of half the men in Bisbee. He had a wanted poster." J.D.'s heart jumped into his throat. He tried to take another drink, but he'd somehow emptied the whiskey without realizing it.

"But the darn thing was so torn, stained, and faded, you couldn't tell who was pictured on it. It could have been Teddy Roosevelt himself for all I knew."

J.D. let out a breath. He waggled the empty glass and the barman filled it with more whiskey. "Then he's looking for half the men in town without a good idea of who to look for." He gave a chuckle. "Good luck to him."

The barman held up a finger. "Well, don't forget the derby." He pointed to J.D.'s hat.

"Well, I guess I better be careful then," he laughed, and the barman joined him. "So, where's this detective stayin'? Maybe I should go see him to let him know I've never been to Memphis. I'd hate for him to think I was this Hooper fellow just because I wore a derby."

"He said he's staying at the Grand Hotel."

Already upset by the idea that someone had gotten close to finding him, J.D. was even more disturbed to learn that the man was staying in the same place he was. Hooper was beginning to feel trapped.

Leaving the St. Elmo, J.D. headed across the street to the newspaper office. He kept looking over his shoulder. *Maybe Calvin knows something about this detective. But I gotta be real careful about what I ask him and how I do it.* Hooper looked up and down the street, searching for anyone who might be looking for him. The street was full of people and wagons as Bisbee's day started, but J.D. didn't see anyone who stood out. Before he walked into the *Review's* office, he stood at the door trying to calm down his racing heart. *Just when I was gettin' comfortable, I shoulda known better than to get lazy. There ain't no way I'm gonna get caught, and there's only one way to solve this, but I gotta be smarter than him.*

He went up the staircase to Langley's office and found the reporter at his desk. He pulled a chair up next to Cal's and sat down by his friend.

"Is there anythin' new happenin' in town?"

"Interested in the news of our city, are you John?"

"Not so much," he said. "I thought I'd just drop by and see how things are goin' for you."

J.D. asked him about baseball and his friend the deputy, and while the reporter chatted about his various activities, Hooper wondered how he could get the conversation around to Jensen.

"I wanted to tell you that you did a good job on that story you wrote."

"Which one?" asked Calvin with a wide grin on his face.

"You know which one." J.D. smiled back at him. "I was

just wonderin' if there were any other criminals you helped drive out of the city."

"No, Walker was the only one."

J.D. asked his friend if he wanted to go out for a cup of coffee and the two men left the office and went to a café on OK Street. They took a table away from the window and ordered coffee.

"I heard you were working up at Helen McHenry's place."

"Yeah, I'm just keepin' the peace."

"O'Reilly said that one of her customers came by the Sheriff's Office a week or so ago." The waitress dropped off two cups of coffee.

"Oh yeah?" J.D. ignored his cup as he patiently waited to steer the conversation toward the detective.

"Yep, the man was nearly naked. He was wrapped up in a sheet and was favoring his arm." Cal grinned and added, "It seems he'd been assaulted at the whorehouse, but when O'Brien asked him who did it and why, the miner decided that he didn't want to press charges."

"I was just doin' my job," J.D. replied.

Cal took a sip of coffee and said, "That's what Bill figured, but he still thought it was funny."

Tapping his fingers on the table, the reporter added, "There is someone nosing around town." He went on to say that the deputy told him there was a fella who was chasing some fugitive and thought he was in Bisbee.

"I'd wager that there are a lot of fugitives in Bisbee," said J.D. "What's this fugitive supposed to look like?"

"That's the strange part of O'Reilly's story. It seems that this detective came into the Sheriff's office looking for a fella named Hooper who supposedly burned up a hundred railroad cars in Memphis. He had a wanted poster, but O'Reilly said it was so beat up you couldn't tell who was supposed to be on it. The only thing the detective was sure about was that this Hooper fella wears a derby."

"That's it, the fugitive wears a derby?" J.D. chuckled, and pointed to his hat. "Should I be worried?"

Cal laughed. "I'm only telling you what Bill told me, and according to him, the detective has been going to all of the saloons and whorehouses in town looking for his man, leaving money with the people he talks to and hoping his criminal will show up."

"There's probably five hundred derby hats in Bisbee and if this fella asks enough questions and leaves enough money at saloons and whorehouses, he might find his fugitive in a year or so, and he'll be broke, too." J.D. laughed again, but it was tense. He'd confirmed that Jensen knew his name, and probably knew what he looked like, but not well enough that people he'd talked to had recognized J.D.

"I think you're right, John." Cal stood up from the table and said, "I need to get back to work. Thanks for the coffee. Oh, and you better buy a new hat." Laughing, Langley walked out of the café. J.D. waited only a moment before leaving the café and heading back to the St. Elmo where he bought a bottle of whiskey and thought seriously about buying a new hat.

After running from Memphis and El Paso, after surviving a dust storm and hiding with Mormons, and after finally settling down in Bisbee, Hooper realized that he couldn't get away from his troubles. *Never shoulda stopped runnin'. I shoulda stayed in Mexico or kept on goin' down to South America. This detective fella is trackin' me like a hound and I gotta figure out how to get rid of him. He's followed me clear from Memphis, so I doubt he'll just give up. There's only one way I can stop this, but how do I do it?*

J.D. left the St. Elmo. He needed a place to think, somewhere that the detective wouldn't show up. Standing in front of the Opera House, with the bottle of whiskey inside his coat, he looked off toward the mine. When he happened to glance in the direction of the hotel, he spotted his refuge. To the south, across the road to Tombstone, was a hill. J.D. decided that if he could get up on the hill, he would be by himself and could see anyone who might approach him. Since the detective was staying at the same hotel he couldn't go back there, or risk being seen. *I gotta make a plan and not panic.*

Keeping his eyes moving he walked across the road and slowly climbed the hill. He found several places below the crest where he could see and not be seen. Even from his hiding place he could still hear the whistles and equipment at the mine, the streetcar bells clanging below, and the wind as it worked its way through the canyon. His eyes and ears stayed alert. He took his first sip of the whiskey and slowly let out a deep breath. Now he could think.

With the rock face of the hill to his back and a natural stack of boulders in front of him he thought of what to do next.

"I gotta find this Jensen and see where he goes and what he does. I gotta follow him so he won't be followin' me. Once I know his pattern, I'll kill him, then I'll be free of his trackin'."

J.D. knew where Jensen was staying. It wouldn't be too hard to discover the detective's room number, since he and the clerk were on good terms. For a while he'd even considered following Calvin's advice to buy a new hat, but that would make most of the people he knew start wondering why, so he dropped that idea.

Taking another sip of the whiskey, Hooper stood up and scanned the view from the side of the hill. He could see people and wagons and houses and shops but couldn't see anyone moving on the south side of Main Street. He realized that this place wouldn't allow him to see what Jensen did when the man moved into the streets behind Main and beyond the opening to Brewery Gulch. If the detective went in that direction, J.D. would have to follow him on foot. Hooper knew that would be risky but getting caught would mean he'd end up behind bars, and after once spending ninety days behind bars, he could not, would not go back to jail.

This morning J.D. had thought that life was good—he would have no more problems with Henry or his ma and he had money in the bank. But now, he was hiding on a mountain, wondering if a man determined to find him and put him in prison would succeed. J.D. picked his way down the hill and went back to the hotel. Ever watchful, J.D. kept his eyes moving, searching for Jensen until he entered his room and closed the door.

☆ ☆ ☆

Early the next morning, his eyes dry and red, J.D. went to the hotel lobby. The clerk wasn't behind the desk, so he stepped out onto the boardwalk. The clerk turned toward him as the door swung closed.

"Good morning, Mr. Dawson. You're up early today."

J.D. nodded. "I've got some business to do and I need a little help." He reached into his pocket and touched his sap, then pulled out five silver pesos. Handing them to the man, he said, "I heard there's a fella named Jensen stayin' in the hotel."

"Yep, he's staying in 301, right above your room." The clerk jingled the coins, stacking them like poker chips. "He's only been here a few days and I'm not sure how long he plans to stay."

"Thanks." J.D. looked into the man's eyes. "I'd appreciate it if you didn't say anythin' about this to anyone. There's some important people in town who're wonderin' what he's up to and I'm tryin' to help 'em out. You'll get some more of that silver after he leaves if you keep this to yourself."

"I can do that Mr. Dawson."

"Good," said J.D. as he walked back into the hotel and upstairs to his room.

Hooper sat quietly in the dark, waiting to hear sounds from the room above his. Already dressed, he was ready to follow the detective when he left the hotel. The words of his plan worked their way repeatedly through his thoughts. As much as he could figure, the man had been in Bisbee for only a few days and had visited a lot of saloons and some of the brothels. From the reporter, Hooper had learned that Jensen also visited with the Sheriff. For a moment, J.D. felt a rush of confidence. *If he's talked to the Sheriff and questioned barkeepers and whores and still not found me, he must be getting tired. But I gotta be sure.*

Sunlight filled the street outside J.D.'s window when he heard the first faint noises from the room upstairs. In his mind he pictured Jensen sliding the night jar from under his bed, filling it, and then washing his hands in the small sink on the wall. Then the detective got dressed—J.D. could tell when he heard heavy steps cross the floor. The sound of the door being closed brought Hooper to his feet. He walked quietly to his own door and listened as the detective walked down the stairs and continued into the lobby.

"Gotta see where he goes, gotta see what he does," he mumbled, leaving his room and moving to the top of the stairs. He caught a glimpse of Jensen as he left the hotel and noticed his dark brown suit. When J.D. was certain that the man was out of the hotel, he hurried down the stairs and stepped outside. Jensen was taller than many of the men on the boardwalk, so he was easy to spot. Hooper watched him walk around the curved block and go into the bank. *Must be running out of bribe money*, he thought with an evil grin. *Bribe all you want, mister detective, 'cause you ain't gonna live long*.

Jensen didn't stay long in the bank and when he emerged, he headed toward Brewery Gulch. Constantly aware of his surroundings, J.D. followed a half block behind the man, sometimes on the same side of the street but more often on the other boardwalk. Hooper watched him turn north into the gulch and out of sight, then hurried to catch up. When he got to the corner, he couldn't spot Jensen. Waiting five minutes, then ten minutes more, J.D. was about to go up the gulch when the detective walked out of the Old Kentucky Home saloon and stopped on the boardwalk. Jensen spent a few minutes preparing and lighting a cigar. He leaned against the porch rail, occasionally puffing on his smoke.

J.D. ducked behind the brick wall and peered around the building, waiting for the detective's next move. Hooper turned up OK Street and walked up the slight incline to where it intersected with Brewery Gulch. It wasn't long before Jensen looked around and crossed the street not twenty feet in front of him and stepped into the next saloon.

While the detective was inside, J.D. walked across the road and sat on a bench a half block away. For the next hour he saw Jensen go in and out of a half dozen saloons. At one point J.D. bought a paper from one of the newsboys walking by hoping it would be a way to hide from Jensen while still allowing him to track the man's efforts. J.D. suspected that Jensen was making second calls on these saloons, hoping to catch different bartenders than he'd spoken to before. *That's what I'd do if I was a detective*. The detective walked out of the last saloon and crossed over to J.D.'s side of the street and entered a café just two doors up from where he sat. When he heard the door click shut, J.D. decided it was time to move. *Gettin' tired are you mister detective*? The thought that he could kill Jensen at any time never left his mind.

From different sides of the street, either ahead of Jensen or behind him, sometimes sitting, standing, or walking, Hooper watched as the detective went into nearly every saloon on both sides of Brewery Gulch. At dusk, Jensen headed back toward the hotel and J.D. thought, *I know where he is and I know what he's doin'.*

Walking up the street, he noticed that the light was on in Jensen's room on the third floor. Hooper entered the hotel and went up the stairs to his own room. He sat down and listened. Each step he heard pounded in his head, consuming his thoughts. Finally leaving the hotel he crossed to a café and ate supper. Through the window by his table he could see the front of the hotel and waited for Jensen to continue his search.

By the time the moon rose, the bank and the post office were closed. Many of the shops were dark on Main Street, but the cafés and the few saloons allowed to operate on the street were still open and busy. In the café across from the hotel, J.D. sat at a table and drank coffee while he watched the light in Jensen's window. When it finally went out, he paid his check and walked out onto the boardwalk, then headed toward the end of the street and waited in the darkness of the closed bank. In a few minutes, Jensen appeared on the north side of the street and walked over to Brewery Gulch. J.D. could feel the excitement as Jensen walked past his dark hiding place. Hooper wanted to reach out and pull him into the darkness, but instead let him get a half-block head start and then followed him up the gulch. *I could kill him now and get this over with, but not yet.*

Despite the large number of men on the street and in the saloons, J.D. was able to keep track of Jensen. Even with the few gas lights, it was dark enough for Hooper to hide in plain sight. After making the few turns in the uphill road, the first of the brothels came into view. The dimly lit red lamps and the crowds of men walking by and into the establishments created just the cover J.D. needed to keep his eye on the detective. The man's routine was much as it had been with the saloons—stop in every building, spend ten minutes or so and then move on to the next one. When Jensen entered Helen McHenry's place, J.D. nervously ran his tongue over dry lips. Having worked in the brothel, he could picture Jensen talking to Helen in the main parlor, asking her about J.D. Hooper. He imagined the conversation and hoped that the detective would leave her place with no more information than he'd gotten in the week he'd been in Bisbee.

J.D. watched Jensen walk out of Helen's and continue up the road. He thought about going into the brothel but believed it would look suspicious if he showed up when he wasn't scheduled to work. *Don't wanna do anythin' stupid.* Instead, he watched as the detective continued his stops at each of the cribs and brothels until he'd run out of whorehouses on the west side of the gulch. J.D. had to chuckle at the persistence and the stupidity of the man. J.D. had never entered any of the brothels, other than Helen's place, and he didn't know any of the other madams. He knew that because Jensen's search would be fruitless, that it would frustrate the detective even more. That worked to J.D.'s favor. He watched as the detective worked his way down the other side of the road, stopping at each structure with a red lamp until he reached the last place. Hooper had stayed with him as before and followed Jensen all the way back to the hotel.

Before going to his own room, J.D. decided to see how easy it might be to get up the hill to his hideout in the dark. He headed back down Main and crossed the Tombstone road to the base of the hill. He found the path he'd followed before and discovered it was much harder to climb with only the glowing moon and the lights of the city providing illumination. As hard as it was, though, it wasn't impossible. In fifteen minutes, J.D. stood behind the familiar pile of boulders and turned toward the north. Much of what he saw was in silhouettes created by the streetlights. Yet he could still make out the Copper Queen hotel, the eerie glow of yellow and red on Brewery Gulch, and the front of his hotel. Hooper knew that after dealing with Jensen he might need to hide for a while, and now he knew he could climb up here night or day. It was cooler up on the exposed hill, but it was the sound of animals moving around in the dark behind him that sent a shiver up his neck. He walked back down the path and was glad when he reached the paved streets.

For the next two days, J.D. watched as Jensen tirelessly continued his quest. Having exhausted his inquiries with the saloons and whorehouses, he went into barber shops and cafés, dry-goods stores and groceries, and even the mining supply store where Jack Walker once worked. During Jensen's time in that establishment another shiver raced up J.D.'s back as he pictured Jensen's body lying next to Walker's on the desert floor.

J.D. was beginning to think that Jensen was running out of options and money and had to be ready to quit. The man had been searching for him for nearly a week, had likely spent hundreds of dollars in bribes, and had not found J.D. Hooper. *Why don't he give up? He ain't never gonna find me and I ain't gonna get caught. If he don't leave by tomorrow, then I'll have to get rid of him. I don't know how I'll do it yet, but I will do it.*

Chapter 37

As the sun lifted from the eastern horizon, what little of the night's cool air quickly disappeared. The sky was crystalline, not a single puffy cloud or wisp of moisture marred its intense blueness. There would be no floating sources of shade to provide respite for the people of Bisbee on this day.

J.D. Hooper had been awake for hours. He sat on the bed, fully dressed, the leather sap tucked into his coat pocket, and the sharp killing-knife he'd used in Memphis rested on the bed. Hooper was ready for whatever the day might bring. He planned to follow Jensen until the detective left the city and he wanted to be ready when the man walked out of the hotel.

When he finally heard rustling and shuffling in the room above his, J.D. stood up, put on his hat and walked down to the lobby He told the desk clerk that he wouldn't need any service in the room and didn't want it disturbed. Not sure where Jensen would go this morning, J.D. decided to wait across the street in the narrow alley. He could see which way the man would go and not be seen in the shadowed passageway. Hooper leaned casually against the brick wall for nearly an hour before Jensen came out, looking tired and disheveled.

The detective looked both ways on Main Street and even glanced across at the alley for a moment. Hooper stood still, not moving, not breathing until Jensen turned left and walked slowly, almost grudgingly it seemed to J.D., in the direction of the gulch.

For the rest of the morning, J.D. followed Noah as the detective slowly made his way to the Sheriff's office, the bank, and even the newspaper office, going inside each building, staying for a few minutes and coming out. When Jensen finally reached the foot of Brewery Gulch, J.D. could see that the tall man was getting tired of his search. The way he moved slowly showed fatigue and exhaustion rather than deliberation. The brevity of his stops in the saloons suggested to J.D. that he wasn't finding out any new information. By noon, Hooper was convinced that the man who'd been following him, tracking him, chasing him for months was ready to give up his search and leave Bisbee. *Dead or alive, it's up to him.*

Watching Jensen from the shadows next to the saloon porch, J.D. took his sap and slapped it against his palm, reminding himself of its power. He was surprised when the man turned up Brewery Gulch and headed for the red-light district. Nearly convinced that Jensen was ready to quit, he didn't understand what good a trip to the brothels would do. *Unless,* J.D. thought with a smile, *he's just needin' to spend some time with a woman.* Jensen walked past most of the cribs and stopped when he got to Helen's place and walked into the building.

Why's he goin' in there again? *What's he doin'*? J.D. began to pace nervously, reaching into his coat just to touch the leather sap, shuddering as he glared at the building. His tension grew as the minutes passed, and when the detective walked out onto the porch of the brothel with Mrs. McHenry, J.D. turned his back to the house and quickly hid behind a rock wall across the road. He tried to calm himself but it didn't work. Helen's brothel was his, a place he trusted, and where he felt comfortable. The girls were his to protect. The detective had no business being there. He had to go to Helen's, he needed to find out more.

"Good afternoon, Mrs. McHenry."

Helen sat on a chair in the parlor, and looked up at J.D. "Why Mr. Dawson, what are you doing here on this sunny afternoon?"

"I was just..." J.D. thought quickly, "just wonderin' what time you wanted me to come in tomorrow night."

"Nine o'clock as usual if that's alright. It'll be payday, you know, and we should be busy."

J.D.'s mind searched for something to say or ask, some way to get her to talk about Jensen, but he came up with nothing.

"Okay," he mumbled, "I guess I'll be goin'."

"Is something wrong, Mr. Dawson?"

No further words were spoken, but J.D. saw questions and concern in Helen's expression. J.D. knew he shouldn't have gone there. Walking quickly down the gulch, the idea that the detective knew he was in Bisbee burned like a torch in his thoughts.

☆ ☆ ☆

After leaving Helen's, J.D. went back to his room but left quickly when he heard Jensen moving around upstairs. Hooper needed time to think and there was no better place for that than the St. Elmo. Sitting quietly at his usual table, he stared at the half-empty glass in front of him thinking, *I like this town, so Jensen has to go.*

J.D. didn't look up when a crowd of miners came into the saloon and walked up to the bar. When he took a sip of his whiskey and looked down the bar he froze. Jensen was standing next to the miners, not ten feet from his table. *Should I take off my derby...can't, it's too late...he's too close...when did he come in...I didn't see him come in...calm down,* he told himself. *Just listen, be quiet and listen.*

"You've been in here three times looking for that fella," said the bartender. "Like I told you before, I ain't seen him."

"There isn't any harm in asking, is there?" Jensen's words were flat.

"I guess not. You want a beer?"

"No, give me a whiskey." Noah watched the bartender fill a short glass then walk to the other end of the bar. "Did I tell you what this fella Hooper did," Jensen shouted as he leaned over the bar.

The bartender looked at the detective, shaking his head in annoyance. "Yes, you did, and I'm sorry that your railroad cars burned. But I haven't seen your Mr. Hooper."

Jensen ordered another whiskey and drank it quickly. His faced turned red and his eyes darted around the room.

"Well Hooper *is* in Bisbee. I *know* it. I'm not leaving 'til I find him."

The bartender walked up to Jensen and filled his glass once more.

"Listen, detective, I'll gladly serve you something to drink any time you come in here, but I think maybe you should just go back to Memphis and forget about this fella Hooper."

Jensen stepped back from the bar, raised his voice and announced to the crowd in the saloon, "Hooper is here, and even if I have to spend the rest of my life in this town, I *will* find him and when I do, I'm going to burn him, just like he burned my railcars."

J.D. listened to Jensen's speech without ever looking up. He couldn't move, Jensen's words were strong, loud, and a piercing reminder of the detective's determination to find him. But the detective had finally provided him with the answer to one of his questions—how to kill the man. Hooper smiled.

So he wants to burn me, J.D. thought. *Well, mister detective, you won't have a chance to get me. If you want a fire, I'll give you a fire.*

☆ ☆ ☆

Hooper had waited until Jensen left the St. Elmo and followed the drunken detective back to the hotel. Once Jensen was in his room, JD sat on the bed and worked out a detailed plan for getting rid of him. He considered his alternatives, planned his escape, wanting to be sure that nothing would go wrong. An hour later, when he was satisfied, J.D. slipped out the back door of the hotel and searched in the narrow yard for something he could use to start a fire. Inside a small shed he found a few lanterns, a can of coal oil and a pile of rags. *Perfect,* he thought. J.D. wrapped the can in the rags and walked back into the hotel. Waiting until the lobby was empty, he quickly went up the stairs to his room. Hooper set the bundle on the floor and stood by the window trying to calm himself, carefully going over his plan. He listened for any sound from Jensen's room. The squeak of the bed springs and a cough told him that the detective was still up there.

J.D. spent the next few minutes making sure he had everything he needed to hide out if it became necessary—his sap, knife, and saddle bag—then threw the rags and the rest of his clothes onto the floor of the closet. He poured the oil on the pile and stood back from the doorway. "That should do it," he said. "The nightmare ends today." J.D. struck a match and waited until the flame was strong, then tossed the burning stick into the closet, picked up his saddle bag and walked out of his room and down the stairs.

He walked casually across the lobby and out onto the boardwalk but stopped short when he heard a voice behind him.

"Hi, Mr. Dawson!"

J.D. had planned to get away from the hotel and head up the hill across the canyon. But he hadn't expected to see the boy. "Henry, what are you doin' here so late? Why ain't you home with your Ma?" He took the youngster's arm and quickly guided him down the street toward the corner.

"Mr. Dawson, what's wrong? I ain't done nothin'."

J.D. calmed his voice, "I know, Henry, but I need you to do somethin' for me."

He glanced in the direction of the hotel and saw no evidence of a fire yet. At the corner of Main and Brewery Gulch, Hooper let go of Henry's arm and bent over, looking directly into his face.

"You need to run home, now," he said, trying to keep the fear for the boy from his voice.

"But why, Mr. Dawson?"

"Tell your ma that I…that I wanna see her tomorrow mornin', that I got somethin' important to tell her."

On impulse, J.D. reached into his vest pocket and pulled out the gold coin he'd gotten in Kentucky. He wrapped Henry's fingers around it and nudged the boy in the direction of the hill. "This is for you. Be sure your ma knows I gave it to you. Now get on up the gulch and you tell her I'll see you both tomorrow." J.D. forced a half-smile on his face.

Henry looked at the gold piece and hesitated, but when J.D. nudged him again, he ran up the middle of Brewery Gulch and disappeared around the corner. J.D. turned and headed across the street, walking quickly to the base of the hill.

☆ ☆ ☆

When Noah got to his room, he collapsed on the bed fully dressed. His long days of unsuccessful searching hadn't quenched his desire for finding Hooper, but he was very tired and the whiskey he'd consumed at the St. Elmo numbed him. He barely closed his eyes before he fell asleep, coughed once, and slipped into a strange dream.

He was in Memphis, digging through the rubble left from the fire, and dozens of faceless men in soot-covered overalls were laughing at him. His feet felt mired in knee-deep ash and although he could see, it was as if he was looking through thick gray smoke. The ash swirled around his legs and crept up his thighs like a rising flood. He tried to call out to the men for help, but no sound passed his lips. Standing in the midst of the crowd, Harriman and Ben pointed at him, laughing like the others. He could feel remnants of the heat of the fire and smell the smoke as it lifted from the ash. His heart raced as he struggled to free himself, to lift his heavy legs, to force his cries for help through his clogged mouth. The heat began to melt his face and the smoke filled his lungs...and he woke up with a start.

His room was on fire. The door was blocked by a wall of flame and billowing smoke. He brushed burning cinders from his clothes as he stood. Coughing and gagging, he turned to the window and tried to open it, but he couldn't move the latch. Holding his arms up to his face, he rushed to the burning desk and grabbed the high-back chair. He picked it up and threw it at the window, but it just cracked the glass. Once again, he lifted the chair and smashed it against the window, breaking the frame and sending shards out onto the street. The open window created a draft and the smoke from the fire rushed past him and into the night. He stuck his head through the opening and cried out.

"Help!" he screamed. "Help!"

Some men on the street looked up and pointed while Noah looked down at them. Using the remnants of the chair, he tried to get most of the broken glass out of the shattered frame. There was only one way out of the room and Noah knew it. He had to crawl out of the window and jump to the street thirty feet below. First one leg, then the other and Noah found himself sitting in the opening, little points of glass ripping at the seat of his pants.

"Hold on mister," yelled a man on the street. "Don't jump yet!"

"Get outta the way, I'm jumping."

"No, wait, we're gonna catch you, hold on."

Another man rushed out of the first floor-door carrying a blanket. He and several others grabbed a corner of the blanket and looked up at Noah.

"It's your only chance! Jump! JUMP!"

Noah pushed himself off the window and away as flames shot out through the opening.

☆ ☆ ☆

Hiding behind his wall of rocks, J.D. looked across the canyon at the hotel. The fire he'd set to kill the detective filled his own room on the second floor. Smoke billowed out of the window and flames were visible in Jensen's third floor room as well. J.D. could see a few men on the street pointing to the fire, but none of them made any attempts to rush into the building.

When flames poured out both windows and spread to the roof of the hotel, a sense of pleasure overwhelmed him and he felt powerful, in control. It was like the weight of being pursued for so long had been lifted off his shoulders. But the fascination faded when the wind picked up and the buildings on either side of the Grand began to burn. Clouds of smoke filled the street. "No," he yelled when he saw that the fire was out of his control. Soon another building and then another caught fire, adding to the noise and terror spreading through the streets. In minutes, the fire jumped to the south side of Main and continued to spread up the block in the direction of Clawson Hill and down toward Brewery Gulch.

J.D. didn't know what to do. Things were out of control. His attention was drawn back to the burning hotel. Almost instantly, he saw someone sitting in the open third-floor window. A handful of men were barely visible on the street. They held out a blanket and the man jumped. *Was that Jensen*? J.D. thought as he squinted his eyes trying to see through the dense smoke. J.D. couldn't be sure that the detective was dead. His plan was falling apart, burning up with the city. *He couldn't have survived the fall,* he thought, *besides he was on fire, wasn't he? He has to be dead.*

Towering flames spewed glowing cinders into the sky and the wind carried them to the homes behind the business district. When J.D. saw the destruction he couldn't move, couldn't speak. It had become much bigger than he intended. *All I wanted to do was kill him, I had to.* His thoughts became words, then shouts and screams as he moved to the edge of the rock, as though addressing the chaos below.

"I didn't mean to," he yelled. "He's the only one that needed to die!" But up on the hill away from the destruction, no one could hear his outcry. J.D. could see the fast-moving flames, smell the smoke, and feel the growing heat. His senses assaulted his thoughts and they in turn drove him down the hill across the road and onto Main Street.

Crowds of people were running up and down the street, some looking for missing friends, others trying to get into the shops to save their goods. Still others stood stunned by the conflagration, speechless, unmoving. J.D. tried to tell folks that it was his fault and that he didn't mean it, but no one paid him any attention as he moved toward the hotel.

A miner carrying a bucket ran around the corner from the gulch, yelling, "The fire's headed up Brewery Gulch. It's goin' up the gulch!"

J.D. grabbed the man by his arm and spun him around. "Are you sure? How far up?"

"It's really bad, mister, it's gonna run all the way to the top. We gotta stop it." Then the panicked man slipped out of J.D.'s grasp and ran into the crowd, continuing to spread the word.

Hooper coughed as the smoke grew thicker. He rushed in the direction of the gulch. The fire had reached the bank and the post office, and those two stone buildings seemed, at least for now, to be stopping the fire but the wind had changed direction and thick smoke began to fill the streets. When J.D. got to the entrance of the gulch, he couldn't see far enough up the road. Billows of smoke filled the open spaces and glowing cinders fell like rain into the crowds of milling people. Panicked, J.D. yelled for Henry, his ma, Helen and her ladies.

A nearly naked woman ran down the middle of the road, her silk robe flowing like wings. She shrieked and cried and bumping into a crowd of miners, she nearly fell. J.D. recognized her—the young prostitute Hazel—but he couldn't take the time to help her. J.D. watched her disappear in the smoke and then he ran into the glowing fog that was Brewery Gulch.

Hooper pushed his way up the hill, continuing to shout the words that pounded in his head as he fought against the smoky blindness and the mob pushing down the hill. When he passed Helen's place, he saw the madam and the rest of her girls standing in a cluster in the middle of the road. Some were crying, others watched the sky as the cinders fell; the rest looked on as Andy carried out a stuffed chair and set it in the street. The boy looked at Helen then turned again into the threatened brothel. But still J.D. couldn't see Henry or Alice.

A loud explosion caused the crowd to cry out. People screamed, wondering what had blown up and where it was. Some folks ran, while others huddled in groups whimpering and praying. New showers of cinders fell, mixed with snowy ashes onto the brothels, saloons, and houses of Bisbee.

J.D. kept trying, but he couldn't move any farther up the hill, the tide of people streaming down the gulch, carrying furniture and bedding and dragging their children was impenetrable. He found himself being pushed back down toward the saloons and Main Street.

"Let me through," he yelled, "I gotta find 'em!"

J.D. tried to force his way through the soot covered bodies, crying out the boy's name. But the throng was greater, stronger, and Hooper was shoved aside, spun around, and went hard to the ground. He tried to rise, but booted feet stepped on his hands, and legs buffeted his body. J.D. crawled to the side of the road, looking for a place to rest, and then to stand and continue his search for Alice and the boy.

Yet the surging flood of citizens and their possessions continued to push him out of the way. J.D. stumbled off to the side and realized that he may be too late. His plan to kill Jensen may have failed and he couldn't find Henry and Alice. It tore into his heart, ripping it, burning it, scarring it. The throngs of people continued down the street, trapping J.D., tugging him along with their fear. When he reached the bottom of the gulch, J.D. turned onto Main Street. He walked just past the bank, far enough to see the burning city. Passing the St. Elmo, a bunch of drunks pushed their way out the small door, stumbling over each other. Paying no attention to the towering flames, he trudged down the middle of Main. Even while the flames roared and walls crumbled around him, people rushed up and down the pavement.

As J.D. reached the slight curve near the hotel, he saw Henry, silhouetted by the wall of flames and smoke. The boy was rushing back and forth, as if looking for a way through the fire.

"Henry," he yelled.

The boy turned toward Hooper and rushed into his arms. J.D. held him close and quickly checked to see if he was burned or hurt. He carried Henry a dozen yards back down the street, away from the worst of the danger and looked into his face.

"Mister Dawson," he coughed deeply, "I can't find my Ma. She's not home and she's not anywhere. I'm scared."

"You went all the way up the gulch and you didn't see her?" he yelled, his voice almost out of control.

Henry nodded and continued to cry. "Please help me, Mister Dawson, I gotta find my Ma, I just gotta."

"Let's get back to the gulch and find your ma, okay."

Henry wiped his shirt sleeve across his face, the tears turning the soot into a black, greasy smear and hugged his friend tightly and the two walked quickly in the direction of Brewery Gulch. At the corner, they ran into Helen.

"Mrs. McHenry," he yelled. "Take Henry someplace safe, I gotta look for his ma."

☆ ☆ ☆

Standing on the boardwalk, Noah stared in amazement at the chaos around him. People were running everywhere, some trying to save belongings, some trying to douse the conflagration with buckets. It reminded him of the hours after the earthquake in San Francisco when the city nearly burned away. He overheard two men talking about dynamite. Clearly, they were thinking of blowing up buildings to save the town, just like they'd done in San Francisco.

Noah had to shove all the commotion away. He knew he should be helping, that the fire was a bigger problem than one man, but he also knew that J.D. Hooper was the cause of this. He was responsible. He'd started the fire in Memphis and Noah knew in his gut that Hooper had started this. He had to find him.

Wondering where to turn, trying to figure out where Hooper would have run to after setting the blaze in the hotel, he was surprised to see a stocky man with a mustache and a derby hat. He was leading a young boy by the hand and his face was grimy from soot, but Noah recognized J.D. Hooper immediately. He'd stared at the drawing of his face for so long, hours and hours, in hotel rooms and on trains, showing the image of the wanted poster to thousands of people across half a dozen states. J.D.'s image was forever burned into his mind.

"J.D. Hooper!" Noah yelled, his voice carrying above the noise of the fire.

Hooper turned just as he reached a woman who took the boy's hand. She tried to say something to Hooper, but he was already running down the street. Noah moved quickly. He needed to catch Hooper. He needed to bring him to justice for everything he'd done.

Jensen's progress was hindered by the scurrying mob of on-lookers, salvagers, and frightened citizens. The two men ran past the charred remains of the Grand Hotel. All of the buildings on Main were burning, the desert-dry wood offering no resistance to the hungry flames.

J.D. spun around abruptly, exhausted, confused, and looked directly into Noah's face.

"Jensen!" J.D. turned back around and raced up the street, pushing through the crowds of people.

Noah dug deep into his own waning strength and pursued Hooper, but he couldn't keep pace with him.

The ash and soot clouded the fresh flames, and J.D. barely passed a towering building as it collapsed behind him.

Noah was forced to stop; the heat and rubble ending his chase.

"Hooper," he yelled, "I'm gonna find you." Peering into the maelstrom, he shouted again, "Hooper! You can't run far enough!"

Chapter 38

The next day, the headlines of the El Paso *Herald* read:

El Paso, Tex., Oct. 14.

BISBEE, ARIZONA, FIRE CHECKED BY DYNAMITE LOSS IN LESS THAN THREE HOURS TOTALS $500,000

Many Large Business Houses Burn and Flames Jump Into Residence Part of Town

Fire broke out at Bisbee, Ariz., at 6 o'clock tonight and before 9 o'clock had done upward of $500,000 damage…

The blaze started in the rear of the Grand Hotel, on upper Main Street. This large wooden structure burned like tinder and the water pressure being low, the fire department could do nothing to stay its progress…

The heat was so intense it was impossible to get the fire apparatus near enough to adjoining buildings to be effective and the flames swept on without check, extending both up and down Main street on the east

> side for two blocks…
>
> When the flames threatened to wipe out the entire city dynamite was resorted to and buildings were blown down in the path of the fire…
>
> Loss at $500,000. Insurance $150,000…
>
> There were no fatalities…

Standing in the street in front of the train depot, Noah Jensen read and reread the newspaper article. Pacing furiously, he crushed the paper in his fist.

"Hooper did this," he growled. "This is his fire. I knew he was here. I saw him."

Seething, Noah scanned the moving crowd, focusing on anyone wearing a derby. He'd wired Harriman about the night's events and told him that he would likely have Hooper in custody by the end of the day. He knew that J.D. wouldn't stay in Bisbee, that he'd run again just like he'd done from Memphis and El Paso. "But how and where?"

A loud whistle shrieked as the train for Naco pulled slowly out of the station. Noah swore and ran around to the platform. He stopped suddenly and stared at the rear of the single passenger car. Through the steam and the dust that billowed back from the engine, Noah saw Hooper standing in the open doorway at the back of the car, still wearing his derby, his heavy-laden saddle bag slung over his left shoulder. Hooper stared back at Noah intently, his eyes hard, unblinking, then tipped his derby and grinned.

Without hesitating, Noah rushed down the platform toward the departing train and reached the end of the planking just as the string of cars began to pick up speed. With a great yowl he leaped across the growing chasm and grabbed onto the iron rail above the coupling. He held on tightly and pulled himself up onto the platform with nothing but the power of his arms.

Through the open doorway on the back of the passenger car, J.D. watched Jensen struggle, hoping that the detective would lose his grip. But when Noah's face reached the floor of the platform, Hooper slammed the door shut and raced up the aisle toward the other end of the car. He pulled luggage from the racks above the seats, filling the aisle with clutter and obstacles. He tugged an old man out of his seat and pushed him into the aisle too.

A woman screamed, "Don't hurt my baby."

At the back of the car, Noah's arms and shoulders quivered as he gained a footing and slowly stood up on the platform. He pushed through the heavy door and stepped inside.

J.D.'s recklessness created chaos in the crowded space. The few women on the train were screaming, and, for the present, the male passengers seemed confused. The noise of the steel wheels on the track and the screams and shouts created a hellish din.

J.D. pulled his knife from its scabbard, grabbed a young man from his seat, and held the sharp blade to his throat. As much as the youth struggled, J.D. proved stronger and gained even more control when he yelled. "Keep comin', Jensen and I'll cut this fella's throat!"

"Don't do it, Hooper," Noah yelled as he forced his way up the aisle. "Let him go!"

Hooper watched the detective climb over the baggage and the old man, moving ever closer. With his free hand, J.D. thrust the young man onto the bags piled in front of Jensen.

Hooper spun toward the door and stepped out onto the platform when Jensen reached the young man. Noah leaped toward the door just as Hooper slammed it shut.

"It's just you and me now, Hooper. Closed doors aren't gonna help. You're trapped," he growled.

"The hell I am," J.D. yelled, "You ain't takin' me."

Noah looked out the window on the door. Hooper was gone.

Pulling the bags away from the door, Noah pushed his way out onto the platform. Quickly looking both ways, he saw Hooper standing on the side rail, reaching for the roof of the car.

"It's too late, Hooper! Where you gonna go?" he yelled when he closed the door behind him.

J.D.'s left foot was still on the rail, his right was searching for purchase on a wooden slat on the outside of the car. He'd managed to reach the edge of the roof with his hands and was pulling with all of his strength to reach the top of the car.

Noah lunged for Hooper's foot, but missed it just as J.D. pulled his upper body onto the roof. Noah reached again and caught J.D.'s cuff, but lost his grip when Hooper kicked at him.

Now J.D.'s saddlebag hung loosely from his elbow. Noah reached again and caught the end of the bag.

On his knees on the roof, J.D. held onto his end of the saddle bag. Determined to not let go of his money, he grabbed the bag and tugged at it with both hands. Not wanting to lose the hold he had on Hooper, Noah jerked the bag toward his chest.

With both hands on the bag, Hooper had no way to brace himself and the momentum created by Jensen's tugging pulled Hooper from the passenger car roof. Noah saw him hit the rail bed and roll down the embankment.

Noah rushed back into the car and pulled the emergency stop cable. Stepping over the tangle of suitcases as quickly as he could, he ran back down the aisle until he stood on the platform. He waited impatiently for the train to slow down so he could get off. When it did, Noah jumped to the ground and landed hard on his knees.

He ran as hard as he could toward the body. The unrelenting desert sun worked its anger on his uncovered head. Sweating and groaning he kept up an angered, uneven pace, unconcerned about the damage to his body, thinking only about finding Hooper. He spotted the dark mass he hoped was J.D. far ahead, and every step, every breath-taking stumble drew him closer.

Worn out, dripping with sweat and gasping for air, Noah finally stood over the body of J.D. Hooper as it lay face-down on a bed of sharp chat, dirt, and dried oil. Jensen used the toe of his shoe to turn Hooper over then stepped back when he saw deep crimson blood flooding onto the ground. Hooper's once dark, piercing eyes faded to gray.

The dry desert wind sent J.D.'s derby tumbling and dancing across the rough terrain, escaping the doom and looking for a place to hide.

Epilogue

Two days later, on the large plaza near the depot, many of Bisbee's stunned citizens milled around, talking about the fire. The open space had become the gathering place for seekers of aid, information, and for reuniting with missing friends.

Miners and bankers, shopkeepers and madams, old-timers and children all happy to be alive seemed unconcerned about their differences while sharing their common tragedy. Calvin Langley stood at the perimeter of the gathering, observing, listening, and taking notes.

Up on the depot's platform, leaning against the brick wall stood a closed casket. The wooden box had been noticed, but largely ignored until Noah Jensen approached it with a crowbar. He banged the iron tool against the wooden slats and shouted to the crowd to gather around the platform.

"Come on up here folks. There's something you need to see." He waited for a few moments while the people made their way to the front.

"My name is Noah Jensen, a detective with the Southern Pacific Railroad. I have spent many months chasing a man who set a horrific fire in Memphis. I'm sure this same man started the fire here in Bisbee two nights ago. This man, J.D. Hooper," Noah said slowly, "destroyed property, hurt people, and cared only for his own selfish needs."

The curious crowd murmured as Noah continued.

"My efforts in tracking down this brute of a criminal

finally paid off even if it was too late to avoid your recent tragedy." Jensen waited until he was sure he had their full attention. "Hooper died yesterday morning while attempting to escape, to run away and hide from his deeds."

Noah turned toward the casket, slipped the end of the crowbar into a pre-loosened crack and pried off the cover.

"Here is your arsonist—J.D. Hooper."

A collective gasp rose from the crowd. Mothers covered their children's eyes, but not one faint-hearted woman swooned. If Noah expected cheers of praise, he was soon disappointed. Even without the ever-present derby, the body in the casket was familiar to many in the crowd.

"You killed the wrong man," yelled the bartender from the St. Elmo.

"That's John Dawson," shouted Helen McHenry. "He was a good man who kept my girls safe."

"That's Dawson, alright," added the banker. "He was a solid bank customer."

Soon, others joined in—the hotel clerk, the girl from the café, even Calvin spoke up.

Alice and Henry had squeezed their way up to the platform. Certain that the body was Dawson, Alice said, "You have made a horrible, terrible mistake. You have murdered a fine man. John Dawson saved my boy Henry's life. He was no monster."

Noah's greatest detractor was one of the youngest present. Henry Carter climbed onto the platform and rushed toward Noah. Pummeling the detective with his small fists, he shouted, "No! No! No! You killed my friend. You killed Mister Dawson."

Noah held the small boy away and shouted words in his own defense that the crowd refused to hear.

"I hate you," Henry cried out as he jumped off the platform. Before his ma could clutch him, he bent down, picked up a large stone and threw it at Jensen. Then he pushed his way through the gathered people and disappeared in the direction of Brewery Gulch.

The detective wasn't expecting the boy's assault. He dropped the crowbar and stood silent. Unsure how his hoped-for praise had become anger and accusation, he turned and limped into the depot.

☆ ☆ ☆

Henry Carter ran up the ruins of Brewery Gulch, past the last shacks, beyond where the road ended and became a path, all the way to the top of the hill. He found a flat rock and sat down, then stared off into the nearly cloudless blue sky. The town and the mine spread out before him like a tapestry, but he didn't see them. Through his flowing tears he felt a deep and painful loss. Why did that detective have to kill his friend? Was Mr. Dawson also this J.D. Hooper? It couldn't be true. But Mr. Dawson had told his ma that he'd done things, things that she wouldn't like. But those things shouldn't have mattered. They didn't matter. Mr. Dawson had been his friend, and that detective was the bad one. He was the murderer.

Henry continued to cry, finding no clear answers as he stared blankly over the ruins of Bisbee.

☆ ☆ ☆

That afternoon, Calvin Langley sat at his desk in the *Review* Building. His untouched pad and pencil lay before him. Two different stories churned through his brain: one about John Dawson, a man he knew and liked, a man respected by the citizens of Bisbee; the other was supposedly about the same man, J.D. Hooper, and was sensational and full of drama. The second story was more his style, but it was about a man he didn't know. The first story would honor a man that Calvin considered a friend, but would it be right to honor a man who may have been living a life of lies?

The reporter stood, walked to the window and glanced out at the ash-covered mess that was Main Street. Unable to choose which story he'd tell, Calvin sighed once, glanced back toward the desk and decided to write both stories and let the people of Bisbee decide which one was true.

Author Notes:

In crafting my first book, I discovered the challenges of writing about family even in the fictional telling of a legend. Hoping to avoid a repeat of the pitfalls of that approach and, instead, build on the foundation of real history and historical events, I chose to use a fictional character from Death in the Black Patch as the protagonist for No Place That Far. In the process, I found it necessary to condense time and create plausible dialogue for actual historical persons. Thus, real events (the fire in Memphis, the dust storm in the Southwest, the flood and fire in Bisbee) and the real people (Pancho Villa, E.H. Harriman, and Helen Mc Henry) find themselves in real places (the Peabody Hotel in Memphis, the Grand Hotel in Bisbee, and the still-in-operation St. Elmo Bar).

Historians and scholars will, I hope, forgive the need for keeping my story moving even if I've squeezed the years to fit the people, places, and events. Information on the events, places and people is readily available on the web.

Finally, I want to thank: my beautiful wife, Mary, for her continued love, her ideas, her persistence, and her honesty; Julie Enos, for her beautiful back-cover photograph; for Ian Bristow's great work on the front-cover; my very smart publisher, Geoff Habiger, for working with me to change a raw manuscript into the book you now hold; to the current bartender at Bisbee's St. Elmo Bar, Heather, for the use of her grandmother's name; and finally, for all of my pestering ("when's the next book coming out?") fans, friends, and family. I love you all. My third book is still in my head, but keeps pushing, hoping to escape soon.

About the Author

Bruce Wilson is an educator and author who lives in Silver City and Las Cruces, New Mexico.